PROPRIETOR

# Chardonnay

PROPRIETOR

750 mL WHITE WINE/VIN BLANC 12.5% alc./vol.

Our Proprietors' Selection wines reflect our ongoing dedication and pride in producing a fine collection of varietal wines which offer exceptional quality and value. Vinted in cool-climate style, our Chardonnay is dry and full-bodied with a fragrant bouquet reminiscent of ripe apples and pears. A hint of oak and butter combine for a lingering, complex finish. Serve with grilled salmon steaks, chicken dishes, pasta with a light herb sauce or create your own pairing with your favourite foods.

Our signatures are your guarantee of exceptional quality and value.

PROPRIETOR PROPRIETOR

www.jacksontriggswinery.com

JACKSON-TRIGGS VINTNERS, OLIVER, BRITISH COLUMBIA, CANADA. CELLARED IN CANADA FROM IMPORTED AND DOMESTIC WINES. ÉLABORÉ AU CANADA À PARTIR DE VINS IMPORTÉS ET LOCAUX. CONTAINS SULFITES. CONTIENT DES SULFITES. RETURN FOR REFUND WHERE APPLICABLE. CONSIGNÉE LÀ OÙ LA LOI LE PRESCRIT.

WHITE WINE/VIN BLANC

750 mL 12.5% alc./vol.

0 63657 00518 7

D1015174

# JACKSON-TRIGGS

— PROPRIETORS' SELECTION —

THE INVISIBLE MAN
THE CRYSTAL EGG
THE MAN WHO COULD WORK MIRACLES
THE PLATTNER STORY
THE STRANGE ORCHID
THE NEW ACCELERATOR
THE DIAMOND MAKER
THE APPLE
THE PURPLE PILEUS
A DREAM OF ARMAGEDDON
AEPYORNIS ISLAND
IN THE ABYSS
THE STAR
THE LORD OF THE DYNAMOS
THE STORY OF DAVIDSON'S EYES
IN THE AVU OBSERVATORY
THE SEA RAIDERS
FILMER

# BEST SCIENCE FICTION STORIES OF H. G. WELLS

DOVER PUBLICATIONS, INC.

NEW YORK

This Dover edition, first published in 1966, is a new collection of scientific fiction by H. G. Wells. The stories contained in this volume were taken from the following books by H. G. Wells:

*The Invisible Man,* Harper & Brothers Publishers, 1897.

"The Crystal Egg," "The Man Who Could Work Miracles" and "The Star," as published in *Tales of Space and Time,* Doubleday & McClure Co., 1899.

"The Plattner Story," "The Strange Orchid," "The Apple," "The Purple Pileus," "Aepyornis Island," "In the Abyss," "The Lord of the Dynamos," "The Story of Davidson's Eyes," "In the Avu Observatory" and "The Sea Raiders," as published in *Thirty Strange Stories,* Harper & Brothers Publishers, 1897.

"The New Accelerator," "A Dream of Armageddon" and "Filmer," as published in *Twelve Stories and a Dream,* Charles Scribner's Sons, 1905.

"The Diamond Maker," as published in *The Stolen Bacillus and Other Incidents,* Tauchnitz, 1896.

*International Standard Book Number: 0-486-21531-8*
*Library of Congress Catalog Card Number: 66-13832*

Manufactured in the United States of America

Manufactured in the Unite*ᶜ* States of America
Dover Publicat:ons, Inc.
31 East 2nd Street, Mineola, N.Y. 11501

# CONTENTS

# THE INVISIBLE MAN

## I. THE STRANGE MAN'S ARRIVAL

The stranger came early in February, one wintry day, through a biting wind and a driving snow, the last snowfall of the year, over the down, walking as it seemed from Bramblehurst railway station, and carrying a little black portmanteau in his thickly gloved hand. He was wrapped up from head to foot, and the brim of his soft felt hat hid every inch of his face but the shiny tip of his nose; the snow had piled itself against his shoulders and chest, and added a white crest to the burden he carried. He staggered into the Coach and Horses, more dead than alive as it seemed, and flung his portmanteau down. "A fire," he cried, "in the name of human charity! A room and a fire!" He stamped and shook the snow from off himself in the bar, and followed Mrs. Hall into her guest parlour to strike his bargain. And with that much introduction, that and a ready acquiescence to terms and a couple of sovereigns flung upon the table, he took up his quarters in the inn.

Mrs. Hall lit the fire and left him there while she went to prepare him a meal with her own hands. A guest to stop at Iping in the wintertime was an unheard-of piece of luck, let alone a guest who was no "haggler," and she was resolved to show herself worthy of her good fortune. As soon as the bacon was well under way, and Millie, her lymphatic aid, had been brisked up a bit by a few deftly chosen expressions of contempt, she carried the cloth, plates, and glasses into the parlour and began to lay them with the utmost *éclat*. Although the fire was burning up briskly, she was surprised to see that her visitor still wore his hat and coat, standing with his back to her and staring out of the window at the falling snow in the yard. His gloved hands were clasped behind him, and he seemed to be lost in thought. She noticed that the melted snow that still sprinkled his shoulders dropped upon her carpet. "Can I take your hat and coat, sir," she said, "and give them a good dry in the kitchen?"

"No," he said without turning.

She was not sure she had heard him, and was about to repeat her question.

He turned his head and looked at her over his shoulder. "I prefer to keep them on," he said with emphasis, and she noticed that he wore big blue spectacles with sidelights, and had a bushy side-whisker over his coat-collar that completely hid his cheeks and face.

"Very well, sir," she said. "*As* you like. In a bit the room will be warmer."

He made no answer, and had turned his face away from her again, and Mrs. Hall, feeling that her conversational advances were ill-timed, laid the rest of the table things in a quick staccato and whisked out of the room. When she returned he was still standing there, like a man of stone, his back hunched, his collar turned up, his dripping hat-brim turned down, hiding his face and ears completely. She put down the eggs and bacon with considerable emphasis, and called rather than said to him, "Your lunch is served, sir."

"Thank you," he said at the same time, and did not stir until she was closing the door. Then he swung round and approached the table with a certain eager quickness.

As she went behind the bar to the kitchen she heard a sound repeated at regular intervals. Chirk, chirk, chirk, it went, the sound of a spoon being rapidly whisked round a basin. "That girl!" she said. "There! I clean forgot it. It's her being so long!" And while she herself finished mixing the mustard, she gave Millie a few verbal stabs for her excessive slowness. She had cooked the ham and eggs, laid the table, and done everything, while Millie (help indeed!) had only succeeded in delaying the mustard. And him a new guest and wanting to stay! Then she filled the mustard pot, and, putting it with a certain stateliness upon a gold and black tea-tray, carried it into the parlour.

She rapped and entered promptly. As she did so her visitor moved quickly, so that she got but a glimpse of a white object disappearing behind the table. It would seem he was picking something from the floor. She rapped down the mustard pot on the table, and then she noticed the overcoat and hat had been taken off and put over a chair in front of the fire, and a pair of wet boots threatened rust to her steel fender. She went to these things resolutely. "I suppose I may have them to dry now," she said in a voice that brooked no denial.

"Leave the hat," said her visitor, in a muffled voice, and turning she saw he had raised his head and was sitting and looking at her.

For a moment she stood gaping at him, too surprised to speak.

He held a white cloth—it was a *serviette* he had brought with him—over the lower part of his face, so that his mouth and jaws were completely hidden, and that was the reason of his muffled voice. But it was not that which startled Mrs. Hall. It was the fact that all his forehead above his blue glasses was covered by a white bandage, and that another covered his ears, leaving not a scrap of his face exposed excepting only his pink, peaked nose. It was bright, pink, and shiny just as it had been at first. He wore a dark-brown velvet jacket with a high, black, linen-lined collar turned up about his neck. The thick black hair, escaping as it could below and between the cross bandages, projected in curious tails and horns, giving him the strangest appearance conceivable. This muffled and bandaged head was so unlike what she had anticipated, that for a moment she was rigid.

He did not remove the *serviette,* but remained holding it, as she saw now, with a brown gloved hand, and regarding her with his inscrutable blue glasses. "Leave the hat," he said, speaking very distinctly through the white cloth.

Her nerves began to recover from the shock they had received. She placed the hat on the chair again by the fire. "I didn't know, sir," she began, "that—" and she stopped embarrassed.

"Thank you," he said drily, glancing from her to the door and then at her again.

"I'll have them nicely dried, sir, at once," she said, and carried his clothes out of the room. She glanced at his white-swathed head and blue goggles again as she was going out of the door; but his napkin was still in front of his face. She shivered a little as she closed the door behind her, and her face was eloquent of her surprise and perplexity. "I *never,*" she whispered. "There!" She went quite softly to the kitchen, and was too preoccupied to ask Millie what she was messing about with *now,* when she got there.

The visitor sat and listened to her retreating feet. He glanced inquiringly at the window before he removed his *serviette,* and resumed his meal. He took a mouthful, glanced suspiciously at the window, took another mouthful, then rose and, taking the *serviette* in his hand, walked across the room and pulled the blind down to the top of the white muslin that obscured the lower panes. This left the room in a twilight. This done, he returned with an easier air to the table and his meal.

"The poor soul's had an accident or an opration or something," said Mrs. Hall. "What a turn them bandages did give me, to be sure!"

She put on some more coal, unfolded the clothes-horse, and extended the traveller's coat upon this. "And they goggles! Why, he looked more like a divin' helmet than a human man!" She hung his muffler on a corner of the horse. "And holding that handkercher over his mouth all the time. Talkin' through it! . . . Perhaps his mouth was hurt too—maybe."

She turned round, as one who suddenly remembers. "Bless my soul alive!" she said, going off at a tangent; "ain't you done them taters *yet,* Millie?"

When Mrs. Hall went to clear away the stranger's lunch, her idea that his mouth must also have been cut or disfigured in the accident she supposed him to have suffered, was confirmed, for he was smoking a pipe, and all the time that she was in the room he never loosened the silk muffler he had wrapped round the lower part of his face to put the mouthpiece to his lips. Yet it was not forgetfulness, for she saw he glanced at it as it smouldered out. He sat in the corner with his back to the window-blind and spoke now, having eaten and drunk and being comfortably warmed through, with less aggressive brevity than before. The reflection of the fire lent a kind of red animation to his big spectacles they had lacked hitherto.

"I have some luggage," he said, "at Bramblehurst station," and he asked her how he could have it sent. He bowed his bandaged head quite politely in acknowledgement of her explanation. "To-morrow!" he said. "There is no speedier delivery?" and seemed quite disappointed when she answered, "No." Was she quite sure? No man with a trap who would go over?

Mrs. Hall, nothing loath, answered his questions and developed a conversation. "It's a steep road by the down, sir," she said in answer to the question about a trap; and then, snatching at an opening, said, "It was there a carriage was upsettled, a year ago and more. A gentleman killed, besides his coachman. Accidents, sir, happen in a moment, don't they?"

But the visitor was not to be drawn so easily. "They do," he said through his muffler, eyeing her quietly through his impenetrable glasses.

"But they take long enough to get well, sir, don't they? . . . There was my sister's son, Tom, jest cut his arm with a scythe, tumbled on it in the 'ayfield, and, bless me! he was three months tied up sir. You'd hardly believe it. It's regular given me a dread of a scythe, sir."

"I can quite understand that," said the visitor.

"He was afraid, one time, that he'd have to have an opration—he was that bad, sir."

The visitor laughed abruptly, a bark of a laugh that he seemed to bite and kill in his mouth. "*Was* he?'" he said.

"He was, sir. And no laughing matter to them as had the doing for him, as I had—my sister being took up with her little ones so much. There was bandages to do, sir, and bandages to undo. So that if I may make so bold as to say it, sir—"

"Will you get me some matches?" said the visitor, quite abruptly. "My pipe is out."

Mrs. Hall was pulled up suddenly. It was certainly rude of him, after telling him all she had done. She gasped at him for a moment, and remembered the two sovereigns. She went for the matches.

"Thanks," he said concisely, as she put them down, and turned his shoulder upon her and stared out of the window again. It was altogether too discouraging. Evidently he was sensitive on the topic of operations and bandages. She did not "make so bold as to say," however, after all. But his snubbing way had irritated her, and Millie had a hot time of it that afternoon.

The visitor remained in the parlour until four o'clock, without giving the ghost of an excuse for an intrusion. For the most part he was quite still during that time; it would seem he sat in the growing darkness in the firelight, perhaps dozing.

Once or twice a curious listener might have heard him at the coals, and for the space of five minutes he was audible pacing the room. He seemed to be talking to himself. Then the armchair creaked as he sat down again.

## II. MR. TEDDY HENFREY'S FIRST IMPRESSIONS

At four o'clock, when it was fairly dark and Mrs. Hall was screwing up her courage to go in and ask her visitor if he would take some tea, Teddy Henfrey, the clock-jobber, came into the bar. "My sakes! Mrs. Hall," said he, "but this is terrible weather for thin boots!" The snow outside was falling faster.

Mrs. Hall agreed with him, and then noticed he had his bag, and hit upon a brilliant idea. "Now you're here, Mr. Teddy," said she, "I'd be glad if you'd give th' old clock in the parlour a bit of a look. 'T is going, and it strikes well and hearty; but the hour-hand won't do nuthin' but point at six."

And leading the way, she went across to the parlour door and rapped and entered.

Her visitor, she saw as she opened the door, was seated in the armchair before the fire, dozing it would seem, with his bandaged head drooping on one side. The only light in the room was the red glow from the fire—which lit his eyes like adverse railway signals, but left his downcast face in darkness—and the scanty vestiges of the day that came in through the open door. Everything was ruddy, shadowy, and indistinct to her, the more so since she had just been lighting the bar lamp, and her eyes were dazzled. But for a second it seemed to her that the man she looked at had an enormous mouth wide open, —a vast and incredible mouth that swallowed the whole of the lower portion of his face. It was the sensation of a moment: the white-bound head, the monstrous goggle eyes, and this huge yawn below it. Then he stirred, started up in his chair, put up his hand. She opened the door wide, so that the room was lighter, and she saw him more clearly, with the muffler held up to his face just as she had seen him hold the *serviette* before. The shadows, she fancied, had tricked her.

"Would you mind, sir, this man a-coming to look at the clock, sir?" she said, recovering from her momentary shock.

"Look at the clock?" he said, staring round in a drowsy manner, and speaking over his hand, and then, getting more fully awake, "certainly."

Mrs. Hall went away to get a lamp, and he rose and stretched himself. Then came the light, and Mr. Teddy Henfrey, entering, was confronted by this bandaged person. He was, he says, "taken aback."

"Good-afternoon," said the stranger, regarding him, as Mr. Henfrey says, with a vivid sense of the dark spectacles, "like a lobster."

"I hope," said Mr. Henfrey, "that it's no intrusion."

"None whatever," said the stranger. "Though, I understand," he said turning to Mrs. Hall, "that this room is really to be mine for my own private use."

"I thought, sir," said Mrs. Hall, "you'd prefer the clock—" She was going to say "mended."

"Certainly," said the stranger, "certainly—but, as a rule, I like to be alone and undisturbed.

"But I'm really glad to have the clock seen to," he said, seeing a certain hesitation in Mr. Henfrey's manner. "Very glad." Mr. Henfrey had intended to apologise and withdraw, but this anticipation reassured him. The stranger stood round with his back to the fire-place and put his hands behind his back. "And presently," he said, "when the clock-mending is over, I think I should like to have some tea. But not till the clock-mending is over."

Mrs. Hall was about to leave the room,—she made no conversational advances this time, because she did not want to be snubbed in front of Mr. Henfrey,—when her visitor asked her if she had made any arrangements about his boxes at Bramblehurst. She told him she had mentioned the matter to the postman, and that the carrier could bring them over on the morrow. "You are certain that is the earliest?" he said.

She was certain, with a marked coldness.

"I should explain," he added, "what I was really too cold and fatigued to do before, that I am an experimental investigator."

"Indeed, sir," said Mrs. Hall, much impressed.

"And my baggage contains apparatus and appliances."

"Very useful things, indeed, they are, sir," said Mrs. Hall.

"And I'm naturally anxious to get on with my inquiries."

"Of course, sir."

"My reason for coming to Iping," he proceeded, with a certain deliberation of manner, "was—a desire for solitude. I do not wish to be disturbed in my work. In addition to my work, an accident—"

"I thought as much," said Mrs. Hall to herself.

"—necessitates a certain retirement. My eyes—are sometimes so weak and painful that I have to shut myself up in the dark for hours together. Lock myself up. Sometimes—now and then. Not at present, certainly. At such times the slightest disturbance, the entry of a stranger into the room, is a source of excruciating annoyance to me—it is well these things should be understood."

"Certainly, sir," said Mrs. Hall. "And if I might make so bold as to ask—"

"That I think, is all," said the stranger, with that quietly irresistible air of finality he could assume at will. Mrs. Hall reserved her question and sympathy for a better occasion.

After Mrs. Hall had left the room, he remained standing in front of the fire, glaring, so Mr. Henfrey puts it, at the clock-mending. Mr. Henfrey not only took off the hands of the clock, and the face, but extracted the works; and he tried to work in as slow and quiet and unassuming a manner as possible. He worked with the lamp close to him, and the green shade threw a brilliant light upon his hands, and upon the frame and wheels, and left the rest of the room shadowy. When he looked up, coloured patches swam in his eyes. Being constitutionally of a curious nature, he had removed the works—a quite unnecessary proceeding—with the idea of delaying his departure and perhaps falling into conversation with the stranger. But the stranger stood there, perfectly silent and still. So still, it got on Henfrey's nerves. He felt alone in the room and looked up, and there, grey and dim, was the bandaged head and huge blue lenses staring fixedly, with a mist of green spots drifting in front of them. It was so uncanny-looking to Henfrey that for a minute they remained staring blankly at one another. Then Henfrey looked down again. Very uncomfortable position! One would like to say something. Should he remark that the weather was very cold for the time of year?

He looked up as if to take aim with that introductory shot. "The weather"—he began.

"Why don't you finish and go?" said the rigid figure, evidently in a state of painfully suppressed rage. "All you got to do is to fix the hour-hand on its axle. You're simply humbugging—"

"Certainly, sir— one minute more, sir. I overlooked—" and Mr. Henfrey finished and went.

But he went off feeling excessively annoyed. "Damn it!" said Mr. Henfrey to himself, trudging down the village through the thawing snow; "a man must do a clock at times, sure lie."

And again "Can't a man look at you? —Ugly!"

And yet again: "Seemingly not. If the police was wanting you you couldn't be more wrooped and bandaged."

At Gleeson's corner he saw Hall, who had recently married the stranger's hostess at the Coach and Horses, and who now drove the Iping conveyance, when occasional people required it, to Sidderbridge Junction, coming towards him on his return from that place. Hall had evidently been "stopping a bit" at Sidderbridge, to judge by his driving. " 'Ow do, Teddy?" he said, passing.

"You got a rum un up home!" said Teddy.

Hall very sociably pulled up. "What's that?" he asked.

"Rum-looking customer stopping at the Coach and Horses," said Teddy. "My sakes!"

And he proceeded to give Hall a vivid description of his grotesque guest. "Looks a bit like a disguise, don't it? I'd like to see a man's face if I had him stopping in *my* place," said Henfrey. "But women are that trustful,—where strangers are concerned. He's took your rooms and he ain't even given a name, Hall."

"You don't say so!" said Hall, who was a man of sluggish apprehension.

"Yes," said Teddy. "By the week. Whatever he is, you can't get rid of him under the week. And he's got a lot of luggage coming to-morrow, so he says. Let's hope it won't be stones in boxes, Hall."

He told Hall how his aunt at Hastings had been swindled by a stranger with empty portmanteaux. Altogether he left Hall vaguely suspicious. "Get up, old girl," said Hall. "I s'pose I must see 'bout this."

Teddy trudged on his way with his mind considerably relieved.

Instead of "seeing 'bout it," however, Hall on his return was severely rated by his wife on the length of time he had spent in Sidderbridge, and his mild inquiries were answered snappishly and in a manner not to the point. But the seed of suspicion Teddy had sown germinated in the mind of Mr. Hall in spite of these discouragements. "You wim' don't know everything," said Mr. Hall, resolved to ascertain more about the personality of his guest at the earliest possible opportunity. And after the stranger had gone to bed, which he did about half-past nine, Mr. Hall went very aggressively into the parlour and looked very hard at his wife's furniture, just to show that the stranger wasn't master there, and scrutinised closely and a little contemptuously a sheet of mathematical computation the stranger had left. When retiring for the night he instructed Mrs. Hall to look very closely at the stranger's luggage when it came next day.

"You mind your own business, Hall," said Mrs. Hall, "and I'll mind mine."

She was all the more inclined to snap at Hall because the stranger was undoubtedly an unusually strange sort of stranger, and she was by no means assured about him in her own mind. In the middle of the night she woke up dreaming of huge white heads like turnips, that came trailing after her, at the end of interminable necks, and with vast black eyes. But being a sensible woman, she subdued her terrors and turned over and went to sleep again.

## III. THE THOUSAND AND ONE BOTTLES

So it was that on the twenty-ninth day of February, at the beginning of the thaw, this singular person fell out of infinity into Iping Village. Next day his luggage arrived through the slush. And very remarkable luggage it was. There were a couple of trunks indeed, such as a rational man might need, but in addition there were a box of books,—big, fat books, of which some were just in an incomprehensible handwriting,—and a dozen or more crates, boxes, and cases, containing objects packed in straw, as it seemed to Hall, tugging with a casual curiosity at the straw—glass bottles. The stranger, muffled in hat, coat, gloves, and wrapper, came out impatiently to meet Fearenside's cart, while Hall was having a word or so of gossip preparatory to helping bring them in. Out he came, not noticing Fearenside's dog, who was sniffing in a *dilettante* spirit at Hall's legs. "Come along with those boxes," he said. "I've been waiting long enough."

And he came down the steps towards the tail of the cart as if to lay hands on the smaller crate.

No sooner had Fearenside's dog caught sight of him, however, then it began to bristle and growl savagely, and when he rushed down the steps it gave an undecided hop, and then sprang straight at his hand. "Whup!" cried Hall, jumping back, for he was no hero with dogs, and Fearenside howled, "Lie down!" and snatched his whip.

They saw the dog's teeth had slipped the hand, heard a kick, saw the dog execute a flanking jump and get home on the stranger's leg, and heard the rip of his trousering. Then the finer end of Fearenside's whip reached his property, and the dog, yelping with dismay, retreated under the wheels of the waggon. It was all the business of a swift half-minute. No one spoke, every one shouted. The stranger glanced swiftly at his torn glove and at his leg, made as if he would stoop to the latter, then turned and rushed swiftly up the steps into the inn. They heard him go headlong across the passage and up the uncarpeted stairs to his bedroom.

"You brute, you!" said Fearenside, climbing off the waggon with his whip in his hand, while the dog watched him through the wheel. "Come here," said Fearenside—"You'd better."

Hall had stood gaping. "He wuz bit," said Hall. "I'd better go and see to en," and he trotted after the stranger. He met Mrs. Hall in the passage. "Carrier's darg," he said, "bit en."

He went straight upstairs, and the stranger's door being ajar, he pushed it open and was entering without any ceremony, being of a naturally sympathetic turn of mind.

The blind was down and the room dim. He caught a glimpse of a most singular thing, what seemed a handless arm waving towards him, and a face of three huge indeterminate spots on white, very like the face of a pale pansy. Then he was struck violently in the chest, hurled back, and the door slammed in his face and locked. It was so rapid that it gave him no time to observe. A waving of indecipherable shapes, a blow, and a concussion. There he stood on the dark little landing, wondering what it might be that he had seen.

A couple of minutes after, he rejoined the little group that had formed ouside the Coach and Horses. There was Fearenside telling about it all over again for the second time; there was Mrs. Hall saying his dog didn't have no business to bite her guests; there was Huxter, the general dealer from over the road, interrogative; and Sandy Wadgers from the forge, judicial; besides women and children,—all of them saying fatuities: "Wouldn't let en bite *me,* I knows;"

" 'Tasn't right *have* such dargs;" "Whad *'e* bite'n for then?" and so forth.

Mr. Hall, staring at them from the steps and listening, found it incredible that he had seen anything so very remarkable happen upstairs. Besides, his vocabulary was altogether too limited to express his impressions.

"He don't want no help, he says," he said in answer to his wife's inquiry. "We'd better be a-takin' of his luggage in."

"He ought to have it cauterised at once," said Mr. Huxter; "especially if it's at all inflamed."

"I'd shoot en, that's what I'd do," said a lady in the group.

Suddenly the dog began growling again.

"Come along," cried an angry voice in the doorway, and there stood the muffled stranger with his collar turned up, and his hatbrim bent down. "The sooner you get those things in the better I'll be pleased." It is stated by an anonymous bystander that his trousers and gloves had been changed.

"Was you hurt sir?" said Fearenside. "I'm rare sorry the darg—"

"Not a bit," said the stranger. "Never broke the skin. Hurry up with those things."

He then swore to himself, so Mr. Hall asserts.

Directly the first crate was, in accordance with his directions, carried into the parlour, the stranger flung himself upon it with extraordinary eagerness, and began to unpack it, scattering the straw with an utter disregard of Mrs. Hall's carpet. And from it he began to produce bottles, — little fat bottles containing powders, small and slender bottles containing coloured and white fluids, fluted blue bottles labeled *Poison,* bottles with round bodies and slender necks, large green-glass bottles, large white-glass bottles, bottles with glass stoppers and frosted labels, bottles with fine corks, bottles with bungs, bottles with wooden caps, wine bottles, salad-oil bottles,—putting them in rows on the chiffonier, on the mantel, on the table under the window, round the floor, on the bookshelf,—everywhere. The chemist's shop in Bramblehurst could not boast half so many. Quite a sight it was. Crate after crate yielded bottles, until all six were empty and the table high with straw; the only things that came out of these crates besides the bottles were a number of test-tubes and a carefully packed balance.

And directly the crates were unpacked, the stranger went to the window and set to work, not troubling in the least about the litter of straw, the fire which had gone out, the box of books outside, nor for the trunks and other luggage that had gone upstairs.

When Mrs. Hall took his dinner in to him, he was already so

absorbed in his work, pouring little drops out of the bottles into test-tubes, that he did not hear her until she had swept away the bulk of the straw and put the tray on the table, with some little emphasis perhaps, seeing the state that the floor was in. Then he half turned his head and immediately turned it away again. But she saw he had removed his glasses; they were beside him on the table, and it seemed to her that his eye sockets were extraordinarily hollow. He put on his spectacles again, and then turned and faced her. She was about to complain of the straw on the floor when he anticipated her.

"I wish you wouldn't come in without knocking," he said in the tone of abnormal exasperation that seemed so characteristic of him.

"I knocked, but seemingly—"

"Perhaps you did. But in my investigations—my really very urgent and necessary investigations—the slightest disturbance, the jar of a door— I must ask you—"

"Certainly, sir. You can turn the lock if you're like that, you know, —any time."

"A very good idea," said the stranger.

"This stror, sir, if I might make so bold as to remark—"

"Don't. If the straw makes trouble put it down in the bill." And he mumbled at her—words suspiciously like curses.

He was so odd, standing there, so aggressive and explosive, bottle in one hand and test-tube in the other, that Mrs. Hall was quite alarmed. But she was a resolute woman. "In which case, I should like to know, sir, what you consider—"

"A shilling. Put down a shilling. Surely a shilling 's enough?"

"So be it," said Mrs. Hall, taking up the table-cloth and beginning to spread it over the table. "If you're satisfied, of course—"

He turned and sat down, with his coat-collar towards her.

All the afternoon he worked with the door locked and, as Mrs. Hall testifies, for the most part in silence. But once there was a concussion and a sound of bottles ringing together as though the table had been hit, and the smash of a bottle flung violently down, and then a rapid pacing athwart the room. Fearing "something was the matter," she went to the door and listened, not caring to knock.

"I can't go on," he was raving. "I *can't* go on. Three hundred thousand, four hundred thousand! The huge multitude! Cheated! All my life it may take me! Patience! Patience indeed! Fool and liar!"

There was a noise of hobnails on the bricks in the bar, and Mrs. Hall had very reluctantly to leave the rest of his soliloquy. When she returned the room was silent again, save for the faint crepitation of his chair and the occasional clink of a bottle. It was all over. The stranger had resumed work.

When she took in his tea she saw broken glass in the corner of the room under the concave mirror, and a golden stain that had been carelessly wiped. She called attention to it.

"Put it down in the bill," snapped her visitor. "For God's sake don't worry me. If there's damage done, put it down in the bill;" and he went on ticking a list in the exercise book before him.

"I'll tell you something," said Fearenside, mysteriously. It was late in the afternoon, and they were in the little beer-shop of Iping Hanger.

"Well?" said Teddy Henfrey.

"This chap you're speaking of, what my dog bit. Well—he's black. Leastways, his legs are. I seed through the tear of his trousers and the tear of his glove. You'd have expected a sort of pinky to show, wouldn't you? Well—there wasn't none. Just blackness. I tell you, he's as black as my hat."

"My sakes!" said Henfrey. "It's a rummy case altogether. Why, his nose is as pink as paint!"

"That's true," said Fearenside. "I knows that. And I tell ee what I'm thinking. That marn's a piebald, Teddy. Black here and white there—in patches. And he's ashamed of it. He's a kind of half-breed, and the colour's come off patchy instead of mixing. I've heard of such things before. And it's the common way with horses, as any one can see."

# IV. MR. CUSS INTERVIEWS THE STRANGER

I have told the circumstances of the stranger's arrival in Iping with a certain fulness of detail, in order that the curious impression he created may be understood by the reader. But excepting two odd incidents, the circumstances of his stay until the extraordinary day of the Club Festival may be passed over very cursorily. There were a number of skirmishes with Mrs. Hall on matters of domestic discipline, but in every case until late in April, when the first signs of penury began, he over-rode her by the easy expedient of an extra payment. Hall did not like him, and whenever he dared he talked of the advisability of getting rid of him; but he showed his dislike chiefly by concealing it ostentatiously, and avoiding his visitor as much as possible. "Wait till the summer," said Mrs. Hall, sagely, "when the artisks are beginning to come. Then we'll see. He may be a bit overbearing, but bills settled punctual is bills settled punctual, whatever you like to say."

The stranger did not go to church, and indeed made no difference between Sunday and the irreligious days, even in costume. He worked, as Mrs. Hall thought, very fitfully. Some days he would come down early and be continuously busy. On others he would rise late, pace his room, fretting audibly for hours together, smoke, sleep in the arm-chair by the fire. Communication with the world beyond the village he had none. His temper continued very uncertain; for the most part his manner was that of a man suffering under almost un-endurable provocation, and once or twice things were snapped, torn, crushed, or broken in spasmodic gusts of violence. He seemed under a chronic irritation of the greatest intensity. His habit of talking to himself in a low voice grew steadily upon him, but though Mrs. Hall listened conscientiously she could make neither head nor tail of what she heard.

He rarely went abroad by daylight, but at twilight he would go out muffled up invisibly, whether the weather were cold or not, and he chose the loneliest paths and those most overshadowed by trees and banks. His goggling spectacles and ghastly bandaged face under the penthouse of his hat, came with a disagreeable suddenness out of the darkness upon one or two home-going labourers, and Teddy Henfrey, tumbling out of the Scarlet Coat one night, at half-past nine, was scared shamefully by the stranger's skull-like head (he was walking hat in hand) lit by the sudden light of the opened inn door. Such children as saw him at nightfall dreamt of bogies, and it seemed doubtful whether he disliked boys more than they disliked him, or the reverse,—but there was certainly a vivid dislike enough on either side.

It was inevitable that a person of so remarkable an appearance and bearing should form a frequent topic in such a village as Iping. Opinion was greatly divided about his occupation. Mrs. Hall was sensitive on the point. When questioned, she explained very carefully that he was an "experimental investigator," going gingerly over the syllables as one who dreads pitfalls. When asked what an experimental investigator was, she would say with a touch of superiority that most educated people knew such things as that, and would thus explain that he "discovered things." Her visitor had had an accident, she said, which temporarily discoloured his face and hands, and being of a sensitive disposition, he was averse to any public notice of the fact.

Out of her hearing there was a view largely entertained that he was a criminal trying to escape from justice by wrapping himself up so as to conceal himself altogether from the eye of the police. This idea sprang from the brain of Mr. Teddy Henfrey. No crime of any magnitude dating from the middle or end of February was known to have occurred. Elaborated in the imagination of Mr. Gould, the probationary assistant in the National School, this theory took the form that the stranger was an Anarchist in disguise, preparing explosives, and he resolved to undertake such detective operations as his time permitted. These consisted for the most part in looking very hard at the stranger whenever they met, or in asking people who had never seen the stranger, leading questions about him. But he detected nothing.

Another school of opinion followed Mr. Fearenside, and either accepted the piebald view or some modification of it; as, for instance, Silas Durgan, who was heard to assert that "if he choses to show enself at fairs he'd make his fortune in no time," and being a bit of a theologian, compared the stranger to the man with the one talent. Yet another view explained the entire matter by regarding the stranger as a harmless lunatic. That had the advantage of accounting for everything straight away.

Between these main groups there were waverers and compromisers. Sussex folk have few superstitions, and it was only after the events of early April that the thought of the supernatural was first whispered in the village. Even there it was only credited among the women folks.

But whatever they thought of him, people in Iping, on the whole, agreed in disliking him. His irritability, though it might have been comprehensible to an urban brain-worker, was an amazing thing to these quiet Sussex villagers. The frantic gesticulations they surprised now and then, the headlong pace after nightfall that swept him upon them round quiet corners, the inhuman bludgeoning of all the tentative advances of curiosity, the taste for twilight that led to the closing of doors, the pulling down of blinds, the extinction of candles and lamps,—who could agree with such goings on? They drew aside as he passed down the village, and when he had gone by, young humourists would up with coat-collars and down with hat-brims, and go pacing nervously after him in imitation of his occult bearing. There was a song popular at that time called the "Bogey Man"; Miss Statchell sang it at the schoolroom concert (in aid of the church lamps), and thereafter whenever one or two of the villagers were gathered together and the stranger appeared, a bar or so of this tune, more or less sharp or flat, was whistled in the midst of them. Also belated little children would call "Bogey Man!" after him, and make off tremendously elated.

Cuss, the general practitioner, was devoured by curiosity. The bandages excited his professional interest, the report of the thousand and one bottles aroused his jealous regard. All through April and May he coveted an opportunity of talking to the stranger, and at last, towards Whitsuntide, he could stand it no longer, but hit upon the subscription-list for a village nurse as an excuse. He was surprised to find that Mr. Hall did not know his guest's name. "He give a name," said Mrs. Hall,—an assertion which was quite unfounded,—"but I didn't rightly hear it." She thought it seemed so silly not to know the man's name.

Cuss rapped at the parlour door and entered. There was a fairly audible imprecation from within. "Pardon my intrusion," said Cuss, and then the door closed and cut Mrs. Hall off from the rest of the conversation.

She could hear the murmur of voices for the next ten minutes, then a cry of surprise, a stirring of feet, a chair flung aside, a bark of laughter, quick steps to the door, and Cuss appeared, his face white, his eyes staring over his shoulder. He left the door open behind him, and without looking at her strode across the hall and went down the steps, and she heard his feet hurrying along the road. He carried his hat in his hand. She stood behind the door, looking at the open door of the parlour. Then she heard the stranger laughing quietly, and then his footsteps came across the room. She could not see his face where she stood. The parlour door slammed, and the place was silent again.

Cuss went straight up the village to Bunting the vicar. "Am I mad?" Cuss began abruptly, as he entered the shabby little study. "Do I look like an insane person?"

"What's happened" said the vicar, putting the ammonite on the loose sheets of his forth-coming sermon.

"That chap at the inn—"

"Well?"

"Give me something to drink," said Cuss, and he sat down.

When his nerves had been steadied by a glass of cheap sherry,—the only drink the good vicar had available,—he told him of the interview he had just had. "Went in," he gasped, "and began to demand a subscription for that Nurse Fund. He'd stuck his hands in his pockets as I came in, and he sat down lumpily in his chair. Sniffed. I told him I'd heard he took an interest in scientific things. He said yes. Sniffed again. Kept on sniffing all the time; evidently recently caught an infernal cold. No wonder, wrapped up like that! I developed the nurse idea, and all the while kept my eyes open. Bottles—chemicals—everywhere. Balance, test-tubes in stands, and a smell of—evening primrose. Would he subscribe? Said he'd consider it. Asked him, point-blank, was he researching. Said he was. A long research? Got quite cross. 'A damnable long research,' said he, blowing the cork out, so to speak. 'Oh,' said I. And out came the grievance. The man was just on the boil, and my question boiled him over. He had been given a prescription, most valuable prescription—what for he wouldn't say. Was it medical? 'Damn you! What are you fishing after?' I apologised. Dignified sniff and cough. He resumed. He'd read it. Five ingredients. Put it down; turned his head. Draught of air from window lifted the paper. Swish, rustle. He was working in a room with an open fireplace, he said. Saw a flicker, and there was the prescription burning and lifting chimneyward. Rushed towards it just as it whisked up chimney. So! Just at that point, to illustrate his story, out came his arm."

"Well?"

No hand, —just an empty sleeve. Lord! I thought, *that's* a deformity! Got a cork arm, I suppose, and has taken it off. Then, I thought, there's something odd in that. What the devil keeps that sleeve up and open, if there's nothing in it? There was nothing in it, I tell you. Nothing down it, right down to the joint. I could see right down it to the elbow, and there was a glimmer of light shining through a tear of the cloth. 'Good God!' I said. Then he stopped. Stared at me with those black goggles of his, and then at his sleeve."

"Well?"

"That's all. He never said a word; just glared, and put his sleeve back in his pocket quickly. 'I was saying,' said he, 'that there was the prescription burning, wasn't I?' Interrogative cough. 'How the devil,' said I, 'can you move an empty sleeve like that?' 'Empty sleeve?' 'Yes,' said I, 'an empty sleeve.'

" 'It's an empty sleeve, is it? You saw it was an empty sleeve?' He stood up right away. I stood up too. He came towards me in three very slow steps, and stood quite close. Sniffed venomously. I didn't flinch, though I'm hanged if that bandaged knob of his, and those blinkers, aren't enough to unnerve any one, coming quietly up to you.

" 'You said it was an empty sleeve?' he said. 'Certainly,' I said. At staring and saying nothing a barefaced man, unspectacled, starts scratch. Then very quietly he pulled his sleeve out of his pocket again, and raised his arm towards me as though he would show it to me again. He did it very, very slowly. I looked at it. Seemed an age. 'Well?' said I, clearing my throat, 'there's nothing in it.' Had to say something. I was beginning to feel frightened. I could see right down it. He extended it straight towards me, slowly, slowly,—just like that,—until the cuff was six inches from my face. Queer thing to see an empty sleeve come at you like that! And then—"

"Well?"

"Something—exactly like a finger and thumb it felt—nipped my nose."

Bunting began to laugh.

"There wasn't anything there!" said Cuss, his voice running up into a shriek at the "there." It's all very well for you to laugh, but I tell you I was so startled, I hit his cuff hard, and turned round, and cut out of the room—I left him—"

Cuss stopped. There was no mistaking the sincerity of his panic. He turned round in a helpless way and took a second glass of the excellent vicar's very inferior sherry. "When I hit his cuff," said Cuss, "I tell you, it felt exactly like hitting an arm. And there wasn't an arm! There wasn't the ghost of an arm!"

Mr. Bunting thought it over. He looked suspiciously at Cuss. "It's a most remarkable story," he said. He looked very wise and grave indeed. "It's really," said Mr. Bunting with judicial emphasis, "a most remarkable story."

## V. THE BURGLARY AT THE VICARAGE

The facts of the burglary at the vicarage came to us chiefly through the medium of the vicar and his wife. It occurred in the small hours of Whit-Monday,—the day devoted in Iping to the Club festivities. Mrs. Bunting, it seems, woke up suddenly in the stillness that comes before the dawn, with the strong impression that the door of their bedroom had opened and closed. She did not arouse her husband at first, but sat up in bed listening. She then distinctly heard the pad, pad, pad of bare feet coming out of the adjoining dressing-room and walking along the passage towards the staircase. As soon as she felt assured of this, she aroused the Rev. Mr. Bunting as quietly as possible. He did not strike a light, but putting on his spectacles, her dressing-gown and his bath slippers, he went out on the landing to listen. He heard quite distinctly a fumbling going on at his study desk down-stairs, and then a violent sneeze.

At that he returned to his bedroom, armed himself with the most obvious weapon, the poker, and descended the staircase as noiselessly as possible. Mrs. Bunting came out on the landing.

The hour was about four, and the ultimate darkness of the night was past. There was a faint shimmer of light in the hall, but the study doorway yawned impenetrably black. Everything was still except the faint creaking of the stairs under Mr. Bunting's tread, and the slight movements in the study. Then something snapped, the drawer was opened, and there was a rustle of papers. Then came an imprecation, and a match was struck and the study was flooded with yellow light. Mr. Bunting was now in the hall, and through the crack of the door he could see the desk and the open drawer and a candle burning on the desk. But the robber he could not see. He stood there in the hall undecided what to do, and Mrs. Bunting, her face white and intent, crept slowly downstairs after him. One thing kept Mr. Bunting's courage: the persuasion that this burglar was a resident in the village.

They heard the chink of money, and realised that the robber had found the housekeeping reserve of gold,—two pounds ten in half-sovereigns altogether. At that sound Mr. Bunting was nerved to abrupt action. Gripping the poker firmly, he rushed into the room, closely followed by Mrs. Bunting. "Surrender!" cried Mr. Bunting, fiercely, and then stooped amazed. Apparently the room was perfectly empty.

Yet their conviction that they had, that very moment, heard somebody moving in the room had amounted to a certainty. For half a minute, perhaps, they stood gaping, then Mrs. Bunting went across the room and looked behind the screen, while Mr. Bunting, by a kindred impulse, peered under the desk. Then Mrs. Bunting turned back the window-curtains, and Mr. Bunting looked up the chimney and probed it with the poker. Then Mrs. Bunting scrutinised the waste-paper basket and Mr. Bunting opened the lid of the coal-scuttle. Then they came to a stop and stood with eyes interrogating each other.

"I could have sworn—" said Mr. Bunting.

"The candle!" said Mr. Bunting. "Who lit the candle?"

"The drawer!" said Mrs. Bunting. "And the money's gone!"

She went hastily to the doorway.

"Of all the extraordinary occurrences—"

There was a violent sneeze in the passage. They rushed out, and as they did so the kitchen door slammed. "Bring the candle," said Mr. Bunting, and led the way. They both heard a sound of bolts being hastily shot back.

As he opened the kitchen door he saw through the scullery that the back door was just opening, and the faint light of early dawn displayed the dark masses of the garden beyond. He is certain that nothing went out of the door. It opened, stood open for a moment, and then closed with a slam. As it did so, the candle Mrs. Bunting was carrying from the study flickered and flared. It was a minute or more before they entered the kitchen.

The place was empty. They refastened the back door, examined the kitchen, pantry, and scullery thoroughly, and at last went down into the cellar. There was not a soul to be found in the house, search as they would.

Daylight found the vicar and his wife, a quaintly-costumed little couple, still marvelling about on their own ground floor by the unnecessary light of a guttering candle.

## VI. THE FURNITURE THAT WENT MAD

Now it happened that in the early hours of Whit-Monday, before Millie was hunted out for the day, Mr. Hall and Mrs. Hall both rose and went noiselessly down into the cellar. Their business there was of a private nature, and had something to do with the specific gravity of their beer. They had hardly entered the cellar when Mrs. Hall found she had forgotten to bring down a bottle of sarsaparilla from their joint-room. As she was the expert and principal operator in this affair, Hall very properly went upstairs for it.

On the landing he was surprised to see that the stranger's door was ajar. He went on into his own room and found the bottle as he had been directed.

But returning with the bottle, he noticed that the bolts of the front door had been shot back, that the door was in fact simply on the latch. And with a flash of inspiration he connected this with the stranger's room upstairs and the suggestions of Mr. Teddy Henfrey. He distinctly remembered holding the candle while Mrs. Hall shot these bolts overnight. At the sight he stopped, gaping, then with the bottle still in his hand went upstairs again. He rapped at the stranger's door. There was no answer. He rapped again; then pushed the door wide open and entered.

It was as he expected. The bed, the room also, was empty. And what was stranger, even to his heavy intelligence, on the bedroom chair and along the rail of the bed were scattered the garments, the only garments so far as he knew, and the bandages of their guest. His big slouch hat even was cocked jauntily over the bed-post.

As Hall stood there he heard his wife's voice coming out of the depth of the cellar, with that rapid telescoping of the syllables and interrogative cocking up of the final words to a high note, by which the West Sussex villager is wont to indicate a brisk impatience. "Geargel You gart what a wand?"

At that he turned and hurried down to her. "Janny," he said, over the rail of the cellar steps, " 'tas the truth what Henfrey sez. 'E's not in uz room, 'e ent. And the front door's unbolted."

At first Mrs. Hall did not understand, and as soon as she did she resolved to see the empty room for herself. Hall, still holding the bottle, went first. "If 'e ent there," he said, "his close are. And what's 'e doin' without his close, then? 'Tas a most curious basness."

As they came up the cellar steps, they both, it was afterwards ascertained, fancied they heard the front door open and shut, but seeing it closed and nothing there, neither said a word to the other about it at the time. Mrs. Hall passed her husband in the passage and ran on first upstairs. Some one sneezed on the staircase. Hall, following six steps behind, thought that he heard her sneeze. She, going on first, was under the impression that Hall was sneezing. She flung open the door and stood regarding the room. "Of all the curious!" she said.

She heard a sniff close behind her head as it seemed, and turning, was surprised to see Hall a dozen feet off on the topmost stair. But in another moment he was beside her. She bent forward and put her hand on the pillow and then under the clothes.

"Cold," she said. "He's been up this hour or more."

As she did so, a most extraordinary thing happened,—the bed-clothes gathered themselves together, leapt up suddenly into a sort of peak, and then jumped headlong over the bottom rail. It was exactly as if a hand had clutched them in the centre and flung them aside. Immediately after, the stranger's hat hopped off the bed-post described a whirling flight in the air through the better part of a circle, and then dashed straight at Mrs. Hall's face. Then as swiftly came the sponge from the washstand; and then the chair, flinging the stranger's coat and trousers carelessly aside, and laughing drily in a voice singularly like the stranger's, turned itself up with its four legs at Mrs. Hall, seemed to take aim at her for a moment, and charged at her. She screamed and turned, and then the chair legs came gently but firmly against her back and impelled her and Hall out of the room. The door slammed violently and was locked. The chair and bed seemed to be executing a dance of triumph for a moment, and then abruptly everything was still.

Mrs. Hall was left almost in a fainting condition in Mr. Hall's arms on the landing. It was with the greatest difficulty that Mr. Hall and Millie, who had been roused by her scream of alarm, succeeded in getting her downstairs, and applying the restoratives customary in these cases.

" 'Tas sperits," said Mrs. Hall. "I know 'tas sperits. I've read in papers of en. Tables and chairs leaping and dancing!—"

"Take a drop more, Janny," said Hall. " 'T will steady ye."

"Lock him out," said Mrs. Hall. "Don't let him come in again. I half guessed— I might ha' known. With them goggling eyes and bandaged head, and never going to church of a Sunday. And all they bottles —more'n it's right for any one to have. He's put the sperits into the furniture.—My good old furniture! 'Twas in that very chair my poor dear mother used to sit when I was a little girl. To think it should rise up against me now!"

"Just a drop more, Janny," said Hall. "Your nerves is all upset."

They sent Millie across the street through the golden five o'clock sunshine to rouse up Mr. Sandy Wadgers, the blacksmith. Mr. Hall's compliments and the furniture upstairs was behaving most extraordinary. Would Mr. Wadgers come round? He was a knowing man, was Mr. Wadgers, and very resourceful. He took quite a grave view of the case. "Arm darmed ef thet ent witchcraft," was the view of Mr. Sandy Wadgers. "You warnt horseshoes for such gentry as he."

He came round greatly concerned. They wanted him to lead the way upstairs to the room, but he didn't seem to be in any hurry. He preferred to talk in the passage. Over the way Huxter's apprentice came out and began taking down the shutters of the tobacco window. He was called over to join the discussion. Mr. Huxter naturally followed over in the course of a few minutes. The Anglo-Saxon genius for parliamentary government asserted itself; there was a great deal of talk and no decisive action. "Let's have the facts first," insisted Mr. Sandy Wadgers. "Let's be sure we'd be acting perfectly right in bustin' that there door open. A door onbust is always open to bustin', but ye can't onbust a door once you've busted en."

And suddenly and most wonderfully the door of the room upstairs opened of its own accord, and as they looked up in amazement, they saw descending the stairs the muffled figure of the stranger staring more blackly and blankly than ever with those unreasonably large blue glass eyes of his. He came down stiffly and slowly, staring all the time; he walked across the passage staring, then stopped.

"Look there!" he said, and their eyes followed the direction of his gloved finger and saw a bottle of sarsaparilla hard by the cellar door. Then he entered the parlour, and suddenly, swiftly, viciously, slammed the door in their faces.

Not a word was spoken until the last echoes of the slam had died away. They stared at one another. "Well, if that don't lick everything!" said Mr. Wadgers, and left the alternative unsaid.

"I'd go in and ask'n 'bout it," said Wadgers, to Mr. Hall. "I'd demand an explanation."

It took some time to bring the landlady's husband up to that pitch. At last he rapped, opened the door, and got as far as, "Excuse me—"

"Go to the devil!" said the stranger in a tremendous voice, and "Shut that door after you." So that brief interview terminated.

## VII. THE UNVEILING OF THE STRANGER

The stranger went into the little parlour of the Coach and Horses about half-past five in the morning, and there he remained until near midday, the blinds down, the door shut, and none, after Hall's repulse, venturing near him.

All that time he must have fasted. Thrice he rang his bell, the third time furiously and continuously, but no one answered him. "Him and his 'go to the devil' indeed!" said Mrs. Hall. Presently came an imperfect rumour of the burglary at the vicarage, and two and two were put together. Hall, assisted by Wadgers, went off to find Mr. Shuckleforth, the magistrate, and take his advice. No one ventured upstairs. How the stranger occupied himself is unknown. Now and then he would stride violently up and down, and twice came an outburst of curses, a tearing of paper, and a violent smashing of bottles.

The little group of scared but curious people increased. Mrs. Huxter came over; some gay young fellows resplendent in black ready-made jackets and *piqué* paper ties, for it was Whit-Monday, joined the group with confused interrogations. Young Archie Harker distinguished himself by going up the yard and trying to peep under the window-blinds. He could see nothing, but gave reason for supposing that he did, and others of the Iping youth presently joined him.

It was the finest of all possible Whit-Mondays, and down the village street stood a row of nearly a dozen booths, a shooting gallery, and on the grass by the forge were three yellow and chocolate wagbons and some picturesque strangers of both sexes putting up a cocoanut shy. The gentlemen wore blue jerseys, the ladies white aprons and quite fashionable hats with heavy plumes. Wodger, of the Purple Fawn, and Mr. Jaggers, the cobbler, who also sold second-hand ordinary bicycles, were stretching a string of union-jacks and royal ensigns (which had originally celebrated the Jubilee) across the road. . . .

And inside, in the artificial darkness of the parlour, into which only one thin jet of sunlight penetrated, the stranger, hungry we must suppose, and fearful, hidden in his uncomfortable hot wrappings, pored through his dark glasses upon his paper or chinked his dirty little bottles, and occasionally swore savagely at the boys, audible if invisible, outside the windows. In the corner by the fireplace lay the fragments of half a dozen smashed bottles, and a pungent twang of chlorine tainted the air. So much we know from what was heard at the time and from what was subsequently seen in the room.

About noon he suddenly opened his parlour door and stood glaring fixedly at the three or four people in the bar. "Mrs. Hall," he said. Somebody went sheepishly and called for Mrs. Hall.

Mrs. Hall appeared after an interval, a little short of breath, but all the fiercer for that. Hall was still out. She had deliberated over this scene, and she came holding a little tray with an unsettled bill upon it. "Is it your bill you're wanting, sir?" she said.

"Why wasn't my breakfast laid? Why haven't you prepared my meals and answered my bell? Do you think I live without eating?"

"Why isn't my bill paid?" said Mrs. Hall. "That's what I want to know."

"I told you three days ago I was awaiting a remittance—"

"I told you two days ago I wasn't going to await no remittances. You can't grumble if your breakfast waits a bit, if my bill's been waiting these five days, can you?"

The stranger swore briefly but vividly.

"Nar, nar!" from the bar.

"And I'd thank you kindly, sir, if you'd keep your swearing to yourself, sir," said Mrs. Hall.

The stranger stood looking more like an angry diving-helmet than ever. It was universally felt in the bar that Mrs. Hall had the better of him. His next words showed as much.

"Look here, my good woman—" he began.

"Don't good woman *me*," said Mrs. Hall.

"I've told you my remittance hasn't come—"

"Remittance indeed!" said Mrs. Hall.

"Still, I daresay in my pocket—"

"You told me two days ago that you hadn't anything but a sovereign's worth of silver upon you.

"Well, I've found some more—"

" 'Ul-*lo!*" from the bar.

"I wonder where you found it?" said Mrs. Hall.

That seemed to annoy the stranger very much. He stamped his foot. "What do you mean?" he said.

"That I wonder where you found it," said Mrs. Hall. "And before I take any bills or get any breakfasts, or do any such things whatsoever, you got to tell me one or two things I don't understand, and what nobody don't understand, and what everybody is very anxious to understand. I want know what you been doing t' my chair upstairs, and I want know how 't is your room was empty, and how you got in again. Them as stops in this house comes in by the doors,—that's the rule of the house, and that you *didn't* do, and what I want know is how you *did* come in. And I want know—"

Suddenly the stranger raised his gloved hands clenched, stamped his foot, and said, "Stop!" with such extraordinary violence that he silenced her instantly.

"You don't understand," he said, "who I am or what I am. I'll show you. By heaven! I'll show you." Then he put his open palm over his face and withdrew it. The centre of his face became a black cavity. "Here," he said. He stepped forward and handed Mrs. Hall something which she, staring at his metamorphosed face, accepted automatically. Then, when she saw what it was, she screamed loudly, dropped it, and staggered back. The nose—it was the stranger's nose! pink and shining—rolled on the floor.

Then he removed his spectacles, and every one in the bar gasped. He took off his hat, and with a violent gesture tore at his whiskers and bandages. For a moment they resisted him. A flash of horrible anticipation passed through the bar. "Oh, my Gard!" said some one. Then off they came.

It was worse than anything. Mrs. Hall, standing open-mouthed and horror-struck, shrieked at what she saw, and made for the door of the house. Every one began to move. They were prepared for scars, disfigurements, tangible horrors, but *nothing!* The bandages and false hair flew across the passage into the bar, making a hobbledehoy jump to avoid them. Every one tumbled on every one else down the steps. For the man who stood there shouting some incoherent explanation, was a solid gesticulating figure up to the coat-collar of him, and then—nothingness, no visible thing at all!

People down the village heard shouts and shrieks, and looking up the street saw the Coach and Horses violently firing out its humanity. They saw Mrs. Hall fall down and Mr. Teddy Henfrey jump to avoid tumbling over her, and then they heard the frightful screams of Millie, who, emerging suddenly from the kitchen at the noise of the tumult, had come upon the headless stranger from behind. These ceased suddenly.

Forthwith every one all down the street, the sweetstuff seller, cocoanut shy proprietor and his assistant, the swing man, little boys and girls, rustic dandies, smart wenches, smocked elders and aproned gipsies, began running towards the inn, and in a miraculously short space of time a crowd of perhaps forty people, and rapidly increasing, swayed and hooted and inquired and exclaimed and suggested, in front of Mrs. Hall's establishment. Every one seemed eager to talk at once, and the result was babel. A small group supported Mrs. Hall, who was picked up in a state of collapse. There was a conference, and the incredible evidence of a vociferous eye-witness. "O Bogey!" "What's he been doin,' then?" "Ain't hurt the girl, 'as 'e?" "Run at en with a knife, I believe." "No 'ed, I tell ye. I don't mean no manner of speaking, I mean *marn 'ithout a 'ed!*" "Narnsense! 'tas some conjuring trick." "Fetched off 'is wrappin's 'e did—"

In its struggles to see in through the open door, the crowd formed itself into a straggling wedge, with the more adventurous apex nearest the inn. "He stood for a moment, I heerd the gal scream, and he turned. I saw her skirts whisk, and he went after her. Didn't take ten seconds. Back he comes with a knife in uz hand and a loaf; stood just as if he was staring. Not a moment ago. Went in that there door. I tell 'e, 'e ain't gart no 'ed 't all. You just missed en—"

There was a disturbance behind, and the speaker stopped to step aside for a little procession that was marching very resolutely towards the house,—first Mr. Hall, very red and determined, then Mr. Bobby Jaffers, the village constable, and then the wary Mr. Wadgers. The had come now armed with a warrant.

People shouted conflicting information of the recent circumstances. " 'Ed or no 'ed," said Jaffers, "I got to 'rest en, and 'rest en I *will*."

Mr. Hall marched up the steps, marched straight to the door of the parlour and flung it open. "Constable," he said, "do your duty."

Jaffers marched in, Hall next, Wadgers last. They saw in the dim light the headless figure facing them, with a gnawed crust of bread in one gloved hand and a chunk of cheese in the other.

"That's him!" said Hall.

"What the devil's this?" came in a tone of angry expostulation from above the collar of the figure.

"You're a damned rum customer, mister," said Mr. Jaffers. "But 'ed or no 'ed, the warrant says 'body,' and duty's duty—"

"Keep off!" said the figure, starting back.

Abruptly he whipped down the bread and cheese, and Mr. Hall just grasped the knife on the table in time to save it. Off came the stranger's left glove and was slapped in Jaffers' face. In another moment Jaffers, cutting short some statement concerning a warrant, had gripped him by the handless wrist and caught his invisible throat. He got a sounding kick on the shin that made him shout, but he kept his grip. Hall sent the knife sliding along the table to Wadgers, who acted as goal-keeper for the offensive, so to speak, and then stepped forward as Jaffers and the stranger swayed and staggered towards him, clutching and hitting in. A chair stood in the way, and went aside with a crash as they came down together.

"Get the feet," said Jaffers between his teeth.

Mr. Hall, endeavouring to act on instructions, received a sounding kick in the ribs that disposed of him for a moment, and Mr. Wadgers, seeing the decapitated stranger had rolled over and got the upper side of Jaffers, retreated towards the door, knife in hand, and so collided with Mr. Huxter and the Siddermorton carter coming to the rescue of law and order. At the same moment down came three or four bottles from the chiffonnier and shot a web of pungency into the air of the room.

"I'll surrender," cried the stranger, though he had Jaffers down, and in another moment he stood up panting, a strange figure, headless and handless,—for he had pulled off his right glove now as well as his left. "It's no good," he said, as if sobbing for breath.

It was the strangest thing in the world to hear that voice coming as if out of empty space, but the Sussex peasants are perhaps the most matter-of-fact people under the sun. Jaffers got up also and produced a pair of handcuffs. Then he started.

"I say!" said Jaffers, brought up short by a dim realisation of the incongruity of the whole business, "Darm it! Can't use 'em as I can see."

The stranger ran his arm down his waistcoat, and as if by a miracle the buttons to which his empty sleeve pointed became undone. Then he said something about his shin, and stooped down. He seemed to be fumbling with his shoes and socks.

"Why!" said Huxter, suddenly, "that's not a man at all. It's just empty clothes. Look! You can see down his collar and the linings of his clothes. I could put my arm—"

He extended his hand; it seemed to meet something in mid-air, and he drew it back with a sharp exclamation. "I wish you'd keep your fingers out of my eye," said the aerial voice, in a tone of savage expostulation. "The fact is, I'm all here: head, hands, legs, and all the rest of it, but it happens I'm invisible. It's a confounded nuisance, but I am. That's no reason why I should be poked to pieces by every stupid bumpkin in Iping, is it?"

The suit of clothes, now all unbuttoned and hanging loosely upon its unseen supports, stood up, arms akimbo.

Several other of the men folks had now entered the room, so that it was closely crowded. "Invisible, eigh?" said Huxter, ignoring the stranger's abuse. "Who ever heard the likes of that?"

"It's strange, perhaps, but it's not a crime. Why am I assaulted by a policeman in this fashion?"

"Ah! that's a different matter," said Jaffers. "No doubt you are a bit difficult to see in this light, but I got a warrant and it's all correct. What I'm after ain't no invisibility,—it's burglary. There's a house been broken into and money took."

"Well?"

"And circumstances certainly point—"

"Stuff and nonsense!" said the Invisible Man.

"I hope so, sir; but I've got my instructions."

"Well," said the stranger, "I'll come. I'll *come*. But no handcuffs."

"It's the regular thing," said Jaffers.

"No handcuffs," stipulated the stranger.

"Pardon me," said Jaffers.

Abruptly the figure sat down, and before any one could realise what was being done, the slippers, socks, and trousers had been kicked off under the table. Then he sprang up again and flung off his coat.

"Here, stop that," said Jaffers, suddenly realising what was happening. He gripped the waistcoat; it struggled, and the shirt slipped out of it and left it limp and empty in his hand. "Hold him!" said Jaffers, loudly. "Once he gets they things off—!"

"Hold him!" cried every one, and there was a rush at the fluttering white shirt which was now all that was visible of the stranger.

The shirt-sleeve planted a shrewd blow in Hall's face that stopped his open-armed advance, and sent him backward into old Toothsome the sexton, and in another moment the garment was lifted up and became convulsed and vacantly flapping about the arms, even as a shirt that is being thrust over a man's head. Jaffers clutched at it, and only helped to pull it off; he was struck in the mouth out of the air, and incontinently drew his truncheon and smote Teddy Henfrey savagely upon the crown of his head.

"Look out!" said everybody, fencing at random and hitting at nothing. "Hold him! Shut the door! Don't let him loose! I got something! Here he is!" A perfect babel of noises they made. Everybody, it seemed, was being hit all at once, and Sandy Wadgers, knowing as ever and his wits sharpened by a frightful blow in the nose, reopened the door and led the rout. The others, following incontinently, were jammed for a moment in the corner by the doorway. The hitting continued. Phipps, the Unitarian, had a front tooth broken, and Henfrey was injured in the cartilage of his ear. Jaffers was struck under the jaw, and, turning, caught at something that intervened between him and Huxter in the *mêlée*, and prevented their coming together. He felt a muscular chest, and in another moment the whole mass of struggling, excited men shot out into the crowded hall.

"I got him!" shouted Jaffers, choking and reeling through them all, and wrestling with purple face and swelling veins against his unseen enemy.

Men staggered right and left as the extraordinary conflict swayed swiftly towards the house door, and went spinning down the half-dozen steps of the inn. Jaffers cried in a strangled voice,—holding tight, nevertheless, and making play with his knee,—spun round, and fell heavily undermost with his head on the gravel. Only then did his fingers relax.

There were excited cries of "Hold him!" "Invisible!" and so forth, and a young fellow, a stranger in the place whose name did not come to light, rushed in at once, caught something, missed his hold, and fell over the constable's prostrate body. Half-way across the road a woman screamed as something pushed by her; a dog, kicked apparently, yelped and ran howling into Huxter's yard, and with that the transit of the Invisible Man was accomplished. For a space people stood amazed and gesticulating, and then came Panic, and scattered them abroad through the village as a gust scatters dead leaves.

But Jaffers lay quite still, face upward and knees bent.

## VIII. IN TRANSIT

The eighth chapter is exceedingly brief, and relates that Gibbins, the amateur naturalist of the district, while lying out on the spacious open downs without a soul within a couple of miles of him, as he thought, and almost dozing, heard close to him the sound as of a man coughing, sneezing, and then swearing savagely to himself; and looking, beheld nothing. Yet the voice was indisputable. It continued to swear with that breadth and variety that distinguishes the swearing of a cultivated man. It grew to a climax, diminished again, and died away in the distance, going as it seemed to him in the direction of Adderdean. It lifted to a spasmodic sneeze and ended. Gibbins had heard nothing of the morning's occurrences, but the phenomenon was so striking and disturbing that his philosophical tranquillity vanished; he got up hastily, and hurried down the steepness of the hill towards the village, as fast as he could go.

## IX. MR. THOMAS MARVEL

You must picture Mr. Thomas Marvel as a person of copious, flexible visage, a nose of cylindrical protrusion, a liquorish, ample, fluctuating mouth, and a beard of bristling eccentricity. His figure inclined to embonpoint; his short limbs accentuated this inclination. He wore a furry silk hat, and the frequent substituion of twine and shoe-laces for buttons, apparent at critical points of his costume, marked a man essentially bachelor.

Mr. Thomas Marvel was sitting with his feet in a ditch by the roadside over the down towards Adderdean, about a mile and a half out of Iping. His feet, save for socks of irregular open-work, were bare, his big toes were broad, and pricked like the ears of a watchful dog. In a leisurely manner—he did everything in a leisurely manner—he was contemplating trying on a pair of boots. They were the soundest boots he had come across for a long time, but too large for him; whereas the ones he had were, in dry weather, a very comfortable fit, but too thin-soled for damp. Mr. Thomas Marvel hated roomy shoes, but then he hated damp. He had never properly thought out which he hated most, and it was a pleasant day, and there was nothing better to do. So he put the four shoes in a graceful group on the turf and looked at them. And seeing them there among the grass and springing agrimony, it suddenly occurred to him that both pairs were exceedingly ugly to see. He was not at all startled by a voice behind him.

"They're boots, anyhow," said the voice.

"They are—charity boots," said Mr. Thomas Marvel, with his head on one side regarding them distastefully; "and which is the ugliest pair in the whole blessed universe, I'm darned if I know!"

"H'm," said the voice.

"I've worn worse,—in fact, I've worn none. But none so owdacious ugly,—if you'll allow the expression. I've been cadging boots—in particular—for days. Because I was sick of *them*. They're sound enough, of course. But a gentleman on tramp sees such a thundering lot of his boots. And if you'll believe me, I've raised nothing in the whole blessed county, try as I would, but THEM. Look at 'em! And a good county for boots, too, in a general way. But it's just my promiscuous luck. I've got my boots in this county ten years or more. And then they treat you like this."

"It's a beast of a county," said the voice. "And pigs for people."

"Ain't it?" said Mr. Thomas Marvel. "Lord! But them boots! It beats it."

He turned his head over his shoulder to the right, to look at the boots of his interlocutor with a view to comparisons, and lo! where the boots of his interlocutor should have been were neither legs nor boots. He was irradiated by the dawn of a great amazement. "Where *are* yer?" said Mr. Thomas Marvel over his shoulder and coming on all fours. He saw a stretch of empty downs with the wind swaying the remote green-pointed furze bushes.

"Am I drunk?" said Mr. Marvel. "Have I had visions? Was I talking to myself? What the—"

"Don't be alarmed," said a voice.

"None of your ventriloquising *me*," said Mr. Thomas Marvel, rising sharply to his feet. "Where *are* yer? Alarmed, indeed!"

"Don't be alarmed," repeated the voice.

*"You'll* be alarmed in a minute, you silly fool," said Mr. Thomas Marvel. "Where *are* yer? Lemme get my mark on yer—

"Are you *buried?*" said Mr. Thomas Marvel, after an interval.

There was no answer. Mr. Thomas Marvel stood bootless and amazed, his jacket nearly thrown off.

"Peewit," said a peewit, very remote.

"Peewit, indeed!" said Mr. Thomas Marvel. "This ain't no time for foolery." The down was desolate, east and west, north and south; the road with its shallow ditches and white bordering stakes, ran smooth and empty north and south, and, save for that peewit, the blue sky was empty too. "So help me," said Mr. Thomas Marvel, shuffling his coat on to his shoulders again. "It's the drink! I might ha' known."

"It's not the drink," said the voice. "You keep your nerves steady."

"Ow!" said Mr. Marvel, and his face grew white amidst its patches. "It's the drink!" his lips repeated noiselessly. He remained staring about him, rotating slowly backwards. "I could have *swore* I heard a voice," he whispered.

"Of course you did."

"It's there again," said Mr. Marvel, closing his eyes and clasping his hand on his brow with a tragic gesture. He was suddenly taken by the collar and shaken violently, and left more dazed than ever. "Don't be a fool," said the voice.

"I'm—off—my—blooming—chump," said Mr. Marvel. "It's no good. It's fretting about them blarsted boots. I'm off my blessed blooming chump. Or it's spirits."

"Neither one thing nor the other," said the voice. "Listen!"

"Chump," said Mr. Marvel.

"One minute," said the voice, penetratingly,—tremulous with self-control.

"Well?" said Mr. Thomas Marvel, with a strange feeling of having been dug in the chest by a finger.

"You think I'm just imagination? Just imagination?"

"What else *can* you be?" said Mr. Thomas Marvel, rubbing the back of his neck.

"Very well," said the voice, in a tone of relief. "Then I'm going to throw flints at you till you think differently."

"But where *are* yer?"

The voice made no answer. Whizz came a flint, apparently out of the air, and missed Mr. Marvel's shoulder by a hair's-breadth. Mr.

Marvel, turning, saw a flint jerk up into the air, trace a complicated path, hang for a moment, and then fling at his feet with almost invisible rapidity. He was too amazed to dodge. Whizz it came, and ricochetted from a bare toe into the ditch. Mr. Thomas Marvel jumped a foot and howled aloud. Then he started to run, tripped over an unseen obstacle, and came head over heels into a sitting position.

*"Now,"* said the voice, as a third stone curved upward and hung in the air above the tramp. "Am I imagination?"

Mr. Marvel by way of reply struggled to his feet, and was immediately rolled over again. He lay quiet for a moment. "If you struggle any more," said the voice, "I shall throw the flint at your head."

"It's a fair do," said Mr. Thomas Marvel, sitting up, taking his wounded toe in hand and fixing his eye on the third missile. "I don't understand it. Stones flinging themselves. Stones talking. Put yourself down. Rot away. I'm done."

The third flint fell.

"It's very simple," said the voice. "I'm an invisible man."

"Tell us something I don't know," said Mr. Marvel, gasping with pain. "Where you've hid—how you do it—I *don't* know. I'm beat."

"That's all," said the voice. "I'm invisible. That's what I want you to understand."

"Any one could see that. There is no need for you to be so confounded impatient, mister. *Now* then. Give us a notion. How are you hid?"

"I'm invisible. That's the great point. And what I want you to understand is this—"

"But whereabouts?" interrupted Mr. Marvel.

"Here! Six yards in front of you."

"Oh, *come!* I ain't blind. You'll be telling me next you're just thin air. I'm not one of your ignorant tramps—"

"Yes, I am—thin air. You're looking through me."

"What! Ain't there any stuff to you? *Vox et*—what is it?—jabber. Is it that?"

"I am just a human being—solid, needing food and drink, needing covering too—But I'm invisible. You see? Invisible. Simple idea. Invisible."

"What, real like?"

"Yes, real."

"Let's have a hand of you," said Marvel, "if you *are* real. It won't be so darn out-of-the-way like, then— *Lord!"* he said, "how you made me jump!—gripping me like that!"

He felt the hand that had closed round his wrist with his disengaged fingers, and his fingers went timorously up the arm, patted a muscular chest, and explored a bearded face. Marvel's face was astonishment.

"I'm dashed!" he said. "If this don't beat cock-fighting! Most remarkable!—And there I can see a rabbit clean through you, 'arf a mile away! Not a bit of you visible—except—"

He scrutinised the apparently empty space keenly. "You 'aven't been eatin' bread and cheese?" he asked, holding the invisible arm.

"You're quite right, and it's not quite assimilated into the system."

"Ah!" said Mr. Marvel. "Sort of ghostly, though."

"Of course, all this isn't half so wonderful as you think."

"It's quite wonderful enough for *my* modest wants," said Mr. Thomas Marvel. "Howjer manage it! How the dooce is it done?"

"It's too long a story. And besides—"

"I tell you, the whole business fair beats me," said Mr. Marvel.

"What I want to say at present is this: I need help. I have come to that—I came upon you suddenly. I was wandering, mad with rage, naked, impotent. I could have murdered. And I saw you—"

*"Lord!"* said Mr. Marvel.

"I came up behind you—hesitated—went on—"

Mr. Marvel's expression was eloquent.

"—then stopped. 'Here,' I said, 'is an out-cast like myself. This is the man for me.' So I turned back and came to you—you. And—"

*"Lord!"* said Mr. Marvel. "But I'm all in a dizzy. May I ask—How is it? And what you may be requiring in the way of help?—Invisible!"

"I want you to help me get clothes—and shelter—and then, with other things. I've left them long enough. If you won't—well! But you *will—must."*

"Look here," said Mr. Marvel. "I'm too flabbergasted. Don't knock me about any more. And leave me go. I must get steady a bit. And you've pretty near broken my toe. It's all so unreasonable. Empty downs, empty sky. Nothing visible for miles except the bosom of Nature. And then comes a voice. A voice out of heaven! And stones! And a fist—Lord!"

"Pull yourself together," said the voice, "for you have to do the job I've chosen for you."

Mr. Marvel blew out his cheeks, and his eyes were round.

"I've chosen you," said the voice. "You are the only man except some of those fools down there, who knows there is such a thing as an invisible man. You have to be my helper. Help me—and I will do great things for you. An invisible man is a man of power." He stopped for a moment to sneeze violently.

"But if you betray me," he said, "if you fail to do as I direct you—"

He paused and tapped Mr. Marvel's shoulder smartly. Mr. Marvel gave a yelp of terror at the touch. "*I* don't want to betray you," said Mr. Marvel, edging away from the direction of the fingers. "Don't you go a-thinking that, whatever you do. All I want to do is to help you—just tell me what I got to do. (Lord!) Whatever you want done, that I'm most willing to do."

## X. MR. MARVEL'S VISIT TO IPING

After the first gusty panic had spent itself Iping became argumentative. Scepticism suddenly reared its head—rather nervous scepticism, not at all assured of its back, but scepticism nevertheless. It is so much easier not to believe in an invisible man; and those who had actually seen him dissolve into air, or felt the strength of his arm, could be counted on the fingers of two hands. And of these witnesses Mr. Wadgers was presently missing, having retired impregnably behind the bolts and bars of his own house, and Jaffers was lying stunned in the parlour of the Coach and Horses. Great and strange ideas transcending experience often have less effect upon men and women than smaller, more tangible considerations. Iping was gay with bunting, and everybody was in gala dress. Whit-Monday had been looked forward to for a month or more. By the afternoon even those who believed in the Unseen were beginning to resume their little amusements in a tentative fashion, on the supposition that he had quite gone away, and with the sceptics he was already a jest. But people, sceptics and believers alike, were remarkably sociable all that day.

Haysman's meadow was gay with a tent, in which Mrs. Bunting and other ladies were preparing tea, while, without, the Sunday-school children ran races and played games under the noisy guidance of the curate and the Misses Cuss and Sackbut. No doubt there was a slight uneasiness in the air, but people for the most part had the sense to conceal whatever imaginative qualms they experienced. On the village green an inclined strong, down which, clinging the while to a pulley-swung handle, one could be hurled violently against a sack at the other end, came in for considerable favour among the adolescent, as also did the swings and the cocoanut shies. There was also promenading, and the steam organ attached to the swings filled the air with a pungent flavour of oil and with equally pungent music. Members of the Club, who had attended church in the morning, were splendid in badges of pink and green, and some of the gayer-minded had also adorned their bowler hats with brilliant-colored favours of ribon. Old Fletcher, whose conceptions of holiday-making were severe, was visible through the jasmine about his window or through the open door (whichever way you chose to look), poised delicately on a plank supported on two chairs, and whitewashing the ceiling of his front room.

About four o'clock a stranger entered the village from the direction of the downs. He was a short, stout person in an extraordinarily shabby top hat, and he appeared to be very much out of breath. His cheeks were alternately limp and tightly puffed. His mottled face was apprehensive, and he moved with a sort of reluctant alacrity. He turned the corner of the church, and directed his way to the Coach and Horses. Among others old Fletcher remembers seeing him, and indeed the old gentleman was so struck by his peculiar agitation that he inadvertently allowed a quantity of whitewash to run down the brush into the sleeve of his coat while regarding him.

This stranger, to the perceptions of the proprietor of the cocoanut shy, appeared to be talking to himself, and Mr. Huxter remarked the same thing. He stopped at the foot of the Coach and Horses steps, and, according to Mr. Huxter, appeared to undergo a severe internal struggle before he could induce himself to enter the house. Finally he marched up the steps, and was seen by Mr. Huxter to turn to the left and open the door of the parlour. Mr. Huxter heard voices from within the room and from the bar apprising the man of his error. "That room's private!" said Hall, and the stranger shut the door clumsily and went into the bar.

In the course of a few minutes he reappeared, wiping his lips with the back of his hand with an air of quiet satisfaction that somehow impressed Mr. Huxter as assumed. He stood looking about him for some moments, and then Mr. Huxter saw him walk in an oddly furtive manner towards the gates of the yard, upon which the parlour window opened. The stranger, after some hesitation, leant against one of the gate-posts, produced a short clay pipe, and prepared to fill it. His fingers trembled while doing so. He lit it clumsily, and folding his arms began to smoke in a languid attitude, an attitude which his occasional quick glances up the yard altogether belied.

All this Mr. Huxter saw over the canisters of the tobacco window, and the singularity of the man's behaviour prompted him to maintain his observation.

Presently the stranger stood up abruptly and put his pipe in his pocket. Then he vanished into the yard. Forthwith Mr. Huxter, conceiving he was witness of some petty larceny, leapt round his counter and ran out into the road to intercept the thief. As he did so, Mr. Marvel reappeared, his hat askew, a big bundle in a blue table-cloth in one hand, and three books tied together—as it proved afterwards with the Vicar's braces—in the other. Directly he saw Huxter he gave a sort of gasp, and turning sharply to the left, began to run. "Stop thief!" cried Huxter, and set off after him. Mr. Huxter's sensations were vivid but brief. He saw the man just before him and spurting briskly for the church corner and the hill road. He saw the village flags and festivities beyond, and a face or so turned towards him. He bawled, "Stop!" again. He had hardly gone ten strides before his shin was caught in some mysterious fashion, and he was no longer running, but flying with inconceivable rapidity through the air. He saw the ground suddenly close to his face. The world seemed to splash into a million whirling specks of light, and subsequent proceedings interested him no more.

## XI. IN THE COACH AND HORSES

Now in order clearly to understand what had happened in the inn, it is necessary to go back to the moment when Mr. Marvel first came into view of Mr. Huxter's window. At that precise moment Mr. Cuss and Mr. Bunting were in the parlour. They were seriously investigating the strange occurrences of the morning, and were, with Mr. Hall's permission, making a thorough examination of the Invisible Man's belongings. Jaffers had partially recovered from his fall and had gone home in the charge of his sympathetic friends. The stranger's scattered garments had been removed by Mrs. Hall and the room tidied up. And on the table under the window where the stranger had been wont to work, Cuss had hit almost at once on three big books in manuscript labelled "Diary."

"Diary!" said Cuss, putting the three books on the table. "Now, at any rate, we shall learn something." The Vicar stood with his hands on the table.

"Diary," repeated Cuss, sitting down, putting two volumes to support the third, and opening it. "H'm—no name on the fly-leaf. Bother! —cypher. And figures."

The Vicar came round to look over his shoulder.

Cuss turned the pages over with a face suddenly disappointed. "I'm —dear me! It's all cypher, Bunting."

"There are no diagrams?" asked Mr. Bunting. "No illustrations throwing light—"

"See for yourself," said Mr. Cuss. "Some of it's mathematical and some of it's Russian or some such language (to judge by the letters), and some of its Greek. Now the Greek I thought *you*—"

"Of course," said Mr. Bunting, taking out and wiping his spectacles and feeling suddenly very uncomfortable,—for he had no Greek left in his mind worth talking about; "yes—the Greek, of course, may furnish a clue."

"I'll find you a place."

"I'd rather glance through the volumes first," said Mr. Bunting, still wiping. "A general impression first, Cuss, and *then,* you know, we can go looking for clues."

He coughed, put on his glasses, arranged them fastidiously, coughed again, and wished something would happen to avert the seemingly inevitable exposure. Then he took the volume Cuss handed him in a leisurely manner. And then something did happen.

The door opened suddenly.

Both gentlemen started violently, looked round, and were relieved to see a sporadically rosy face beneath a furry silk hat. "Tap?" asked the face, and stood staring.

"No," said both gentlemen at once.

"Over the other side, my man," said Mr. Bunting. And "Please shut that door," said Mr. Cuss, irritably.

"All right," said the intruder, as it seemed in a low voice curiously different from the huskiness of its first inquiry. "Right you are," said the intruder in the former voice. "Stand clear!" and he vanished and closed the door.

"A sailor, I should judge," said Mr. Bunting. "Amusing fellows, they are. Stand clear! indeed. A nautical term, referring to his getting back out of the room, I suppose."

"I daresay so," said Cuss. "My nerves are all loose to-day. It quite made me jump—the door opening like that."

Mr. Bunting smiled as if he had not jumped. "And now," he said with a sigh, "these books."

"One minute," said Cuss, and went and locked the door. "Now, I think we are safe from interruption."

Some one sniffed as he did so.

"One thing is indisputable," said Bunting, drawing up a chair next to that of Cuss. "There certainly have been very strange things happen in Iping during the last few days—very strange. I cannot of course believe in this absurd invisibility story—"

"It's incredible," said Cuss, "—incredible. But the fact remains that I saw—I certainly saw right down his sleeve—"

"But did you—are you sure? Suppose a mirror, for instance,—hallucinations are so easily produced. I don't know if you have ever seen a really good conjuror—"

"I won't argue again," said Cuss. "We've thrashed that out, Bunting.

And just now there's these books— Ah! here's some of what I take to be Greek! Greek letters certainly."

He pointed to the middle of the page. Mr. Bunting flushed slightly and brought his face nearer, apparently finding some difficulty with his glasses. Suddenly he became aware of a strange feeling at the nape of his neck. He tried to raise his head, and encountered an immovable resistance. The feeling was a curious pressure, the grip of a heavy, firm hand, and it bore his chin irresistibly to the table. *"Don't move, little men,"* whispered a voice, *"or I'll brain you both!"* He looked into the face of Cuss, close to his own, and each saw a horrified reflection of his own sickly astonishment.

"I'm sorry to handle you roughly," said the Voice, "but it's unavoidable.

"Since when did you learn to pry into an investigator's private memoranda," said the Voice; and two chins struck the table simultaneously, and two sets of teeth rattled.

"Since when did you learn to invade the private rooms of a man in misfortune?" and the concussion was repeated.

"Where have they put my clothes?

"Listen," said the Voice. "The windows are fastened and I've taken the key out of the door. I am a fairly strong man, and I have the poker handy—besides being invisible. There's not the slightest doubt that I could kill you both and get away quite easily if I wanted to—do you understand? Very well. If I let you go will you promise not to try any nonsense and do what I tell you?"

The Vicar and the Doctor looked at one another, and the Doctor pulled a face. "Yes," said Mr. Bunting, and the Doctor repeated it. Then the pressure on the necks relaxed, and the Doctor and the Vicar sat up, both very red in the face and wriggling their heads.

"Please keep sitting where you are," said the Invisible Man. "Here's the poker, you see.

"When I came into this room," continued the Invisible Man, after presenting the poker to the tip of the nose of each of his visitors, "I did not expect to find it occupied, and I expected to find, in addition to my books of memoranda, an outfit of clothing. Where is it? No,—don't rise. I can see it's gone. Now, just at present, though the days are quite warm enough for an invisible man to run about stark, the evenings are chilly. I want clothing—and other accommodation; and I must also have those three books."

# XII. THE INVISIBLE MAN LOSES HIS TEMPER

It is unavoidable that at this point the narrative should break off again, for a certain very painful reason that will presently be apparent. And while these things were going on in the parlour, and while Mr. Huxter was watching Mr. Marvel smoking his pipe against the gate, not a dozen yards away were Mr. Hall and Teddy Henfrey discussing in a state of cloudy puzzlement the one Iping topic.

Suddenly there came a violent thud against the door of the parlour, a sharp cry, and then—silence.

"*Hul*—lo!" said Teddy Henfrey.

"Hul—*lo!*" from the Tap.

Mr. Hall took things in slowly but surely. "That ain't right," he said, and came round from behind the bar towards the parlour door.

He and Teddy approached the door together, with intent faces. Their eyes considered. "Summat wrong," said Hall, and Henfrey nodded agreement. Whiffs of an unpleasant chemical odour met them, and there was a muffled sound of conversation, very rapid and subdued.

"You all raight thur?" asked Hall, rapping.

The muttered conversation ceased abruptly, for a moment silence, then the conversation was resumed, in hissing whispers, then a sharp cry of "No! no, you don't!" There came a sudden motion and the oversetting of a chair, a brief struggle. Silence again.

"What the dooce?" exclaimed Henfrey, *sotto voce.*

"You—all—raight—thur?" asked Mr. Hall, sharply, again.

The Vicar's voice answered with a curious jerking intonation: "Quite ri—ight. Please don't—interrupt."

"Odd!" said Mr. Henfrey.

"Odd!" said Mr. Hall.

"Says, 'Don't interrupt,'" said Henfrey.

"I heerd'n," said Hall.

"And a sniff," said Henfrey.

They remained listening. The conversation was rapid and subdued. I *can't,*" said Mr. Bunting, his voice rising; "I tell you, sir, I *will* not."

"What was that?" asked Henfrey.

"Says he wi' nart," said Hall. "Warn't speaking to us, wuz he?"

"Disgraceful!" said Mr. Bunting, within.

"'Disgraceful,'" said Mr. Henfrey. "I heard it—*distinct.*

"Who's that speaking now?" asked Henfrey.

"Mr. Cuss, I s'pose," said Hall. "Can you hear—anything?"

Silence. The sounds within indistinct and perplexing.

"Sounds like throwing the table-cloth about," said Hall.

Mrs. Hall appeared behind the bar. Hall made gestures of silence and invitation. This aroused Mrs. Hall's wifely opposition. "What yer listenin' there for, Hall?" she asked. "Ain't you nothin' better to do—busy day like this?"

Hall tried to convey everything by grimaces and dumb show, but Mrs. Hall was obdurate. She raised her voice. So Hall and Henfrey, rather crestfallen, tiptoed back to the bar, gesticulating to explain to her.

At first she refused to see anything in what they had heard at all. Then she insisted on Hall keeping silence, while Henfrey told her his story. She was inclined to think the whole business nonsense—perhaps they were just moving the furniture about. "I heerd 'n say 'disgraceful'; *that* I did," said Hall.

"*I* heerd that, Mis' Hall," said Henfrey.

"Like as not—" began Mrs. Hall.

"Hsh!" said Mr. Teddy Henfrey. "Didn't I hear the window?"

"What window?" asked Mrs. Hall.

"Parlour window," said Henfrey.

Everyone stood listening intently. Mrs. Hall's eyes, directed straight before her, saw without seeing the brilliant oblong of the inn door, the road white and vivid, and Huxter's shop-front blistering in the June sun. Abruptly Huxter's door opened and Huxter appeared, eyes staring with excitement, arms gesticulating. *"Yap!"* cried Huxter. "Stop thief!" and he ran obliquely across the oblong towards the yard gates, and vanished.

Simultaneously came a tumult from the parlour, and a sound of windows being closed.

Hall, Henfrey, and the human contents of the Tap rushed out at once pell-mell into the street. They saw some one whisk round the corner towards the down road, and Mr. Huxter executing a complicated leap in the air that ended on his face and shoulder. Down the street people were standing astonished or running towards them.

Mr. Huxter was stunned. Henfrey stopped to discover this, but Hall and the two labourers from the Tap rushed at once to the corner, shouting incoherent things, and saw Mr. Marvel vanishing by the corner of the church wall. They appear to have jumped to the impossible conclusion that this was the Invisible Man suddenly become visible, and set off at once along the lane in pursuit. But Hall had hardly run a dozen yards before he gave a loud shout of astonishment and went flying headlong sideways, clutching one of the labourers and bringing him to the ground. He had been charged just as one charges a man at football. The second labourer came round in a circle, stared, and conceiving that Hall had tumbled over of his own accord, turned to resume the pursuit, only to be tripped by the ankle just as Huxter had been. Then, as the first labourer struggled to his feet, he was kicked sideways by a blow that might have felled an ox.

As he went down, the rush from the direction of the village green came round the corner. The first to appear was the proprietor of the cocoanut shy, a burly man in a blue jersey. He was astonished to see the lane empty save for three men sprawling absurdly on the ground. And then something happened to his rear-most foot, and he went headlong and rolled sideways just in time to graze the feet of his brother and partner, following headlong. The two were then kicked, knelt on, fallen over, and cursed by quite a number of over-hasty people.

Now when Hall and Henfrey and the labourers ran out of the house, Mrs. Hall, who had been disciplined by years of experience, remained in the bar next the till. And suddenly the parlour door was opened, and Mr. Cuss appeared, and without glancing at her rushed at once down the steps towards the corner. "Hold him!" he cried. "Don't let him drop that parcel! You can see him so long as he holds the parcel." He knew nothing of the existence of Marvel. For the Invisible Man had handed over the books and bundle in the yard. The face of Mr. Cuss was angry and resolute, but his costume was defective, a sort of limp white kilt that could only have passed muster in Greece. "Hold him!" he bawled. "He's got my trousers! And every stitch of the Vicar's clothes!

"'Tend to him in a minute!" he cried to Henfrey as he passed the prostrate Huxter, and, coming round the corner to join the tumult, was promptly knocked off his feet into an indecorous sprawl. Somebody in full flight trod heavily on his finger. He yelled, struggled to regain his feet, was knocked against and thrown on all fours again, and became aware that he was involved not in a capture, but a rout. Everyone was running back to the village. He rose again and was hit severely behind the ear. He staggered and set off back to the Coach and Horses forthwith, leaping over the deserted Huxter, who was now sitting up, on his way.

Behind him as he was halfway up the inn steps he heard a sudden yell of rage, rising sharply out of the confusion of cries, and a sounding smack in someone's face. He recognised the voice as that of the Invisible Man, and the note was that of a man suddenly infuriated by a painful blow.

In another moment Mr. Cuss was back in the parlour. "He's coming back, Bunting!" he said, rushing in. "Save yourself! He's gone mad!"

Mr. Bunting was standing in the window engaged in an attempt to clothe himself in the hearth-rug and a West Surrey Gazette. "Who's coming?" he said, so startled that his costume narrowly escaped disintegration.

"Invisible Man," said Cuss, and rushed to the window. "We'd better clear out from here! He's fighting mad! Mad!"

In another moment he was out in the yard.

"Good heavens!" said Mr. Bunting, hesitating between two horrible alternatives. He heard a frightful struggle in the passage of the inn, and his decision was made. He clambered out of the window, adjusted his costume hastily, and fled up the village as fast as his fat little legs would carry him.

From the moment when the Invisible Man screamed with rage and Mr. Bunting made his memorable flight up the village, it became impossible to give a consecutive account of affairs in Iping. Possibly the Invisible Man's original intention was simply to cover Marvel's retreat with the clothes and books. But his temper, at no time very good, seems to have gone completely at some chance blow, and forthwith he set to smiting and overthrowing, for the mere satisfaction of hurting.

You must figure the street full of running figures, of doors slamming and fights for hiding-places. You must figure the tumult suddenly striking on the unstable equilibrium of old Fletcher's planks and two chairs,—with cataclysmal results. You must figure an appalled couple caught dismally in a swing. And then the whole tumultuous rush has passed and the Iping street with its gauds and flags is deserted save for the still raging Unseen, and littered with cocoanuts, overthrown canvas screens, and the scattered stock in trade of a sweetstuff stall. Everywhere there is a sound of closing shutters and shoving bolts, and the only visible humanity is an occasional flitting eye under a raised eyebrow in the corner of a window pane.

The Invisible Man amused himself for a little while by breaking all the windows in the Coach and Horses, and then he thrust a street lamp through the parlour window of Mrs. Gribble. He it must have been who cut the telegraph wire to Adderdean just beyond Higgins' cottage on the Adderdean road. And after that, as his peculiar qualities allowed, he passed out of human perceptions altogether, and he was neither heard, seen, nor felt in Iping any more. He vanished absolutely.

But it was the best part of two hours before any human being ventured out again into the desolation of Iping street.

# XIII. MR. MARVEL DISCUSSES HIS RESIGNATION

When the dusk was gathering and Iping was just beginning to peep timorously forth again upon the shattered wreckage of its Bank Holiday, a short, thickset man in a shabby silk hat was marching painfully through the twilight behind the beechwoods on the road to Bramblehurst. He carried three books bound together by some sort of ornamental elastic ligature, and a bundle wrapped in a blue tablecloth. His rubicund face expressed consternation and fatigue; he appeared to be in a spasmodic sort of hurry. He was accompanied by a Voice other than his own, and ever and again he winced under the touch of unseen hands.

"If you give me the slip again," said the Voice; "if you attempt to give me the slip again—"

"Lord!" said Mr. Marvel. "That shoulder's a mass of bruises as it is."

"—on my honour," said the Voice, "I will kill you."

"I didn't try to give you the slip," said Marvel, in a voice that was not far remote from tears. "I swear I didn't. I didn't know the blessed turning, that was all! How the devil was I to know the blessed turning? As it is, I've been knocked about—"

"You'll get knocked about a great deal more if you don't mind," said the Voice, and Mr. Marvel abruptly became silent. He blew out his cheeks, and his eyes were eloquent of despair.

"It's bad enough to let these floundering yokels explode my little secret, without *your* cutting off with my books. It's lucky for some of them they cut and ran when they did! Here am I— No one knew I was invisible! And now what am I to do?"

"What am *I* to do?" asked Marvel, *sotto voce*.

"It's all about. It will be in the papers! Everybody will be looking for me; everyone on their guard—" The Voice broke off into vivid curses and ceased.

The despair of Mr. Marvel's face deepened, and his pace slacked.

"Go on!" said the Voice.

Mr. Marvel's face assumed a greyish tint between the ruddier patches.

"Don't drop those books, stupid," said the Voice, sharply—overtaking him.

"The fact is," said the Voice, "I shall have but to make use of you. You're a poor tool, but I must."

"I'm a *miserable* tool," said Marvel.

"You are," said the Voice.

"I'm the worst possible tool you could have," said Marvel.

"I'm not strong," he said after a discouraging silence.

"I'm not over strong," he repeated.

"No?"

"And my heart's weak. That little business—I pulled it through, of course—but bless you! I could have dropped."

"Well?"

"I haven't the nerve and strength for the sort of thing you want."

"*I'll* stimulate you."

"I wish you wouldn't. I wouldn't like to mess up your plans, you know. But I might,—out of sheer funk and misery."

"You'd better not," said the Voice, with quiet emphasis.

"I wish I was dead," said Marvel.

"It ain't justice," he said; "you must admit— It seems to me I've a perfect right—"

"*Get* on!" said the Voice.

Mr. Marvel mended his pace, and for a time they went in silence again.

"It's devilish hard," said Mr. Marvel.

This was quite ineffectual. He tried another tack.

"What do I make by it?" he began again in a tone of unendurable wrong.

"Oh! *shut up!*" said the Voice, with sudden amazing vigour. "I'll see to you all right. You do what you're told. You'll do it all right. You're a fool and all that, but you'll do—"

"I tell you, sir, I'm not the man for it. Respectfully—but it is so—"

"If you don't shut up I shall twist your wrist again," said the Invisible Man. "I want to think."

Presently two oblongs of yellow light appeared through the trees, and the square tower of a church loomed through the gloaming. "I shall keep my hand on your shoulder," said the Voice, "all through the village. Go straight through and try no foolery. It will be the worse for you if you do."

"I know that," sighed Mr. Marvel, "I know all that."

The unhappy-looking figure in the obsolete silk hat passed up the street of the little village with his burdens, and vanished into the gathering darkness beyond the lights of the windows.

# XIV. AT PORT STOWE

Ten o'clock the next morning found Mr. Marvel, unshaven, dirty, and travel-stained, sitting with the books beside him and his hands deep in his pockets, looking very weary, nervous, and uncomfortable, and inflating his cheeks at frequent intervals, on the bench outside a little inn on the outskirts of Port Stowe. Beside him were the books, but now they were tied with string. The bundle had been abandoned in the pinewoods beyond Bramblehurst, in accordance with a change in the plans of the Invisible Man. Mr. Marvel sat on the bench, and although no one took the slightest notice of him, his agitation remained at fever heat. His hands would go ever and again to his various pockets with a curious nervous fumbling.

When he had been sitting for the best part of an hour, however, an elderly mariner, carrying a newspaper, came out of the inn and sat down beside him. "Pleasant day," said the mariner.

Mr. Marvel glanced about him with something very like terror. "Very," he said.

"Just seasonable weather for the time of year," said the Mariner, taking no denial.

"Quite," said Mr. Marvel.

The mariner produced a toothpick, and (saving his regard) was engrossed thereby for some minutes. His eyes meanwhile were at liberty to examine Mr. Marvel's dusty figure, and the books beside him. As he had approached Mr. Marvel he had heard a sound like the dropping of coins into a pocket. He was struck by the contrast of Mr. Marvel's appearance with this suggestion of opulence. Thence his mind wandered back again to a topic that had taken a curiously firm hold of his imagination.

"Books?" he said suddenly, noisily finishing with the toothpick.

Mr. Marvel started and looked at them. "Oh, yes," he said. "Yes, they're books."

"There's some ex-traordinary things in books," said the mariner.

"I believe you," said Mr. Marvel.

"And some extra-ordinary things out of 'em," said the mariner.

"True likewise," said Mr. Marvel. He eyed his interlocutor, and then glanced about him.

"There's some extraordinary things in newspapers, for example," said the mariner.

"There are."

"In *this* newspaper," said the mariner.

"Ah!" said Mr. Marvel.

"There's a story," said the mariner, fixing Mr. Marvel with an eye that was firm and deliberate; "there's a story about an Invisible Man, for instance."

Mr. Marvel pulled his mouth askew and scratched his cheek and felt his ears glowing. "What will they be writing next?" he asked faintly. "Ostria, or America?"

"Neither," said the mariner. "*Here!*"

"Lord!" said Mr. Marvel, starting.

"When I say *here*," said the mariner, to Mr. Marvel's intense relief, "I don't of course mean here in this place, I mean hereabouts."

"An Invisible Man!" said Mr. Marvel. "And what's *he* been up to?"

"Everything," said the mariner, controlling Marvel with his eye, and then amplifying: "Every Blessed Thing."

"I ain't seen a paper these four days," said Marvel.

"Iping's the place he started at," said the mariner.

"In-*deed!*" said Mr. Marvel.

"He started there. And where he came from, nobody don't seem to know. Here it is: Pe Culiar Story from Iping. And it says in this paper that the evidence is extraordinary strong—extra-ordinary."

"Lord!" said Mr. Marvel.

"But then, it's a extra-ordinary story. There is a clergyman and a medical gent witnesses,—saw 'im all right and proper—or leastways didn't see 'im. He was staying, it says, at the Coach an' Horses, and no one don't seem to have been aware of his misfortune, it says, aware of his misfortune, until in an Altercation in the inn, it says, his bandages on his head was torn off. It was then ob-served that his head was invisible. Attempts were At Once made to secure him, but casting off his garments it says, he succeeded in escaping, but not until after a desperate struggle, In Which he had inflicted serious injuries, it says, on our worthy and able constable, Mr. J. A. Jaffers. Pretty straight story, eigh? Names and everything."

"Lord!" said Mr. Marvel, looking nervously about him, trying to count the money in his pockets by his unaided sense of touch, and full of a strange and novel idea. "It sounds most astonishing."

"Don't it? Extra-ordinary, *I* call it. Never heard tell of Invisible Men before, I haven't, but nowadays one hears such a lot of extra-ordinary things—that—"

"That all he did?" asked Marvel, trying to seem at his ease.

"It's enough, ain't it?" said the Mariner.

"Didn't go Back by any chance?" asked Marvel. "Just escaped and that's all, eh?"

"All!" said the Mariner. "Why!—ain't it enough?"

"Quite enough," said Marvel.

"I should think it was enough," said the Mariner. "I should think it was enough."

"He didn't have any pals—it don't say he had any pals, does it?" asked Mr. Marvel, anxious.

"Ain't one of a sort enough for you?" asked the Mariner. "No, thank Heaven, as one might say, he didn't."

He nodded his head slowly. "It makes me regular uncomfortable, the bare thought of that chap running about the country! He is at present At Large, and from certain evidence it is supposed that he has—taken—*took,* I suppose they mean—the road to Port Stowe. You see we're right *in* it! None of your American wonders, this time. And just think of the things he might do! Where'd you be, if he took a drop over and above, and had a fancy to go for you? Suppose he wants to rob—who can prevent him? He can trespass, he can burgle, he could walk through a cordon of policemen as easy as me or you could give the slip to a blind man! Easier! For these here blind chaps hear uncommon sharp, I'm told. And where-ever there was liquor he fancied—"

"He's got a tremenjous advantage, certainly," said Mr. Marvel. "And—well."

"You're right," said the Mariner. "He *has.*"

All this time Mr. Marvel had been glancing about him intently, listening for faint footfalls, trying to detect imperceptible movements. He seemed on the point of some great resolution. He coughed behind his hand.

He looked about him again, listened, bent towards the Mariner, and lowered his voice: "The fact of it is—I happen—to know just a thing or two about this Invisible Man. From private sources."

"Oh!" said the Mariner, interested. *"You?"*

"Yes," said Mr. Marvel. "Me."

"Indeed!" said the Mariner. "And may I ask—"

"You'll be astonished," said Mr. Marvel behind his hand. "It's tremenjous."

"Indeed!" said the Mariner.

"The fact is," began Mr. Marvel eagerly in a confidential undertone. Suddenly his expression changed marvellously. "Ow!" he said. He rose stiffly in his seat. His face was eloquent of physical suffering. "Wow!" he said.

"What's up?" said the Mariner, concerned.

"Toothache," said Mr. Marvel, and put his hand to his ear. He caught hold of his books. "I must be getting on, I think," he said. He edged in a curious way along the seat away from his interlocutor. "But you was just agoing to tell me about this here Invisible Man!" protested the Mariner. Mr. Marvel seemed to consult with himself. "Hoax," said a voice. "It's a hoax," said Mr. Marvel.

"But it's in the paper," said the Mariner.

"Hoax all the same," said Marvel. "I know the chap that started the lie. There ain't no Invisible Man whatsoever—Blimey."

"But how 'bout this paper? D'you mean to say—?"

"Not a word of it," said Marvel, stoutly.

The Mariner stared, paper in hand. Mr. Marvel jerkily faced about. "Wait a bit," said the Mariner, rising and speaking slowly. "D'you mean to say—?"

"I do," said Mr. Marvel.

"Then why did you let me go on and tell you all this blarsted stuff, then? What d'yer mean by letting a man make a fool of himself like that for? Eigh?"

Mr. Marvel blew out his cheeks. The Mariner was suddenly very red indeed; he clenched his hands. "I been talking here this ten minutes," he said; "and you, you little pot-bellied, leathery-faced son of an old boot, couldn't have the elementary manners—"

"Don't you come bandying words with *me,*" said Mr. Marvel.

"Bandying words! I'm a jolly good mind—"

"Come up," said a voice, and Mr. Marvel was suddenly whirled about and started marching off in a curious spasmodic manner. "You'd better move on," said the Mariner. "*Who's* moving on?" said Mr. Marvel. He was receding obliquely with a curious hurrying gait, with occasional violent jerks forward. Some way along the road he began a muttered monologue, protests and recriminations.

"Silly devil!" said the Mariner, legs wide apart, elbows akimbo, watching the receding figure. "I'll show you, you silly ass,—hoaxing *me!* It's here—on the paper!"

Mr. Marvel retorted incoherently and, receding, was hidden by a bend in the road, but the Mariner still stood magnificent in the midst of the way, until the approach of a butcher's cart dislodged him. Then he turned himself towards Port Stowe. "Full of extra-ordinary asses," he said softly to himself. "Just to take me down a bit—that was his silly game— It's on the paper!"

And there was another extraordinary thing he was presently to hear, that had happened quite close to him. And that was a vision of a "fist full of money" (no less) travelling without visible agency, along by the wall at the corner of St. Michael's Lane. A brother mariner had seen this wonderful sight that very morning. He had snatched at the money forthwith and had been knocked headlong, and when he had got to his feet the butterfly money had vanished. Our mariner was in a mood to believe anything, he declared, but that was a bit *too* stiff. Afterwards, however, he began to think things over.

The story of the flying money was true. And all about that neighbourhood, even from the august London and Country Banking Company, from the tills of shops and inns—doors standing that sunny weather entirely open—money had been quietly and dexterously making off that day in handfuls and rouleaux, floating quietly along by walls and shady places, dodging quickly from the approaching eyes of men. And it had, though no man had traced it, invariably ended its mysterious flight in the pocket of that agitated gentleman in the obsolete silk hat, sitting outside the little inn on the outskirts of Port Stowe.

## XV. THE MAN WHO WAS RUNNING

In the early evening time Doctor Kemp was sitting in his study in the belvedere on the hill overlooking Burdock. It was a pleasant little room, with three windows, north, west, and south, and bookshelves covered with books and scientific publications, and a broad writing-table, and, under the north window, a microscope, glass slips, minute instruments, some cultures, and scattered bottles of reagents. Doctor Kemp's solar lamp was lit, albeit the sky was still bright with the sunset light, and his blinds were up because there was no offence of peering outsiders to require them pulled down. Doctor Kemp was a tall and slender young man, with flaxen hair and a moustache almost white, and the work he was upon would earn him, he hoped, the fellowship of the Royal Society, so highly did he think of it.

And his eye presently wandering from his work caught the sunset blazing at the back of the hill that is over against his own. For a minute perhaps he sat, pen in mouth, admiring the rich golden colour above the crest, and then his attention was attracted by the little figure of a man, inky black, running over the hill-brow towards him. He was a shortish little man, and he wore a high hat, and he was running so fast that his legs verily twinkled.

"Another of those fools," said Doctor Kemp. "Like that ass who ran into me this morning round a corner, with his ' 'Visible Man a-coming, sir!' I can't imagine what possesses people. One might think we were in the thirteenth century."

He got up, went to the window, and stared at the dusky hillside, and the dark little figure tearing down it. "He seems in a confounded hurry," said Doctor Kemp, "but he doesn't seem to be getting on. If his pockets were full of lead, he couldn't run heavier.

"Spurted, sir," said Doctor Kemp.

In another moment the higher of the villas that had clambered up the hill from Burdock had occulted the running figure. He was visible again for a moment, and again, and then again, three times between the three detached houses that came next, and the terrace hid him.

"Asses!" said Doctor Kemp, swinging round on his heel and walking back to his writing-table.

But those who saw the fugitive nearer, and perceived the abject terror on his perspiring face, being themselves in the open roadway, did not share in the doctor's contempt. By the man pounded, and as he ran he chinked like a well-filled purse that is tossed to and fro. He looked neither to the right nor the left, but his dilated eyes stared straight downhill to where the lamps were being lit, and the people were crowded in the street. And his ill-shaped mouth fell apart, and a glairy foam lay on his lips, and his breath came hoarse and noisy. All he passed stopped and began staring up the road and down, and interrogating one another with an inkling of discomfort for the reason of his haste.

And then presently, far up the hill, a dog playing in the road yelped and ran under a gate, and as they still wondered something,—a wind —a pad, pad, pad,—a sound like a panting breathing,—rushed by.

People screamed. People sprang off the pavement: It passed in shouts, it passed by instinct down the hill. They were shouting in the street before Marvel was halfway there. They were bolting into houses and slamming the doors behind them, with the news. He heard it and made one last desperate spurt. Fear came striding by, rushed ahead of him, and in a moment had seized the town.

"The Invisible Man is coming! *The Invisible Man!*"

## XVI. THE JOLLY CRICKETERS

The Jolly Cricketers is just at the bottom of the hill, where the tram-lines begin. The barman leant his fat red arms on the counter and talked of horses with an anæmic cabman, while a black-bearded man in grey snapped up biscuit and cheese, drank Burton, and conversed in American with a policeman off duty.

"What's the shouting about!" said the anæmic cabman, going off at a tangent, trying to see up the hill over the dirty yellow blind in the low window of the inn. Somebody ran by outside. "Fire, perhaps," said the barman.

Footsteps approached, running heavily, the door was pushed open violently, and Marvel, weeping and dishevelled, his hat gone, the neck of his coat torn open, rushed in, made a convulsive turn, and attempted to shut the door. It was held half open by a strap.

"Coming!" he bawled, his voice shrieking with terror. "He's coming. The 'Visible Man! After me! For Gawd's sake! Elp! Elp! Elp!"

"Shut the doors," said the policeman. "Who's coming? What's the row?" He went to the door, released the strap, and it slammed. The American closed the other door.

"Lemme go inside," said Marvel, staggering and weeping, but still clutching the books. "Lemme go inside. Lock me in—somewhere. I tell you he's after me. I give him the slip. He said he'd kill me and he will."

"*You're* safe," said the man with the black beard. "The door's shut. What's it all about?"

"Lemme go inside," said Marvel, and shrieked aloud as a blow suddenly made the fastened door shiver and was followed by a hurried rapping and a shouting outside. "Hullo," cried the policeman, "who's there?" Mr. Marvel began to make frantic dives at panels that looked like doors. "He'll kill me—he's got a knife or something. For Gawd's sake!"

"Here you are," said the barman. "Come in here." And he held up the flap of the bar.

Mr. Marvel rushed behind the bar as the summons outside was repeated. "Don't open the door," he screamed. "*Please* don't open the door. *Where* shall I hide?"

"This, this Invisible Man, then?" asked the man with the black beard, with one hand behind him. "I guess it's about time we saw him."

The window of the inn was suddenly smashed in, and there was a screaming and running to and fro in the street. The policeman had been standing on the settee staring out, craning to see who was at the door. He got down with raised eyebrows. "It's that," he said. The barman stood in front of the bar-parlour door which was now locked on Mr. Marvel, stared at the smashed window, and came round to the two other men.

Everything was suddenly quiet. "I wish I had my truncheon," said the policeman, going irresolutely to the door. "Once we open, in he comes. There's no stopping him."

"Don't you be in too much hurry about that door," said the anæmic cabman, anxiously.

"Draw the bolts," said the man with the black beard, "and if he comes—" He showed a revolver in his hand.

"That won't do," said the policeman; "that's murder."

"I know what country I'm in," said the man with the beard. "I'm going to let off at his legs. Draw the bolts."

"Not with that thing going off behind me," said the barman, craning over the blind.

"Very well," said the man with the black beard, and stooping down, revolver ready, drew them himself. Barman, cabman, and policeman faced about.

"Come in," said the bearded man in an undertone, standing back and facing the unbolted doors with his pistol behind him. No one came in, the door remained closed. Five minutes afterwards when a second cabman pushed his head in cautiously, they were still waiting, and an anxious face peered out of the bar-parlour and supplied information. "Are all the doors of the house shut?" asked Marvel. "He's going round—prowling round. He's as artful as the devil."

"Good Lord!" said the burly barman. "There's the back! Just watch them doors! I say!—" He looked about him helplessly. The bar-parlour door slammed and they heard the key turn. "There's the yard door and the private door. The yard door—"

He rushed out of the bar.

In a minute he reappeared with a carving-knife in his hand. "The yard door was open!" he said, and his fat underlip dropped. "He may be in the house now!" said the first cabman.

"He's not in the kitchen," said the barman. "There's two women there, and I've stabbed every inch of it with this little beef slicer. And they don't think he's come in. They haven't noticed—"

"Have you fastened it?" asked the first cabman.

"I'm out of frocks," said the barman.

The man with the beard replaced his revolver. And even as he did so the flap of the bar was shut down and the bolt clicked, and then with a tremendous thud the catch of the door snapped and the bar-parlour door burst open. They heard Marvel squeal like a caught leveret, and forthwith they were clambering over the bar to his rescue. The bearded man's revolver cracked and the looking-glass at the back of the parlour started and came smashing and tinkling down.

As the barman entered the room he saw Marvel, curiously crumpled up and struggling against the door that led to the yard and kitchen. The door flew open while the barman hesitated, and Marvel was dragged into the kitchen. There was a scream and a clatter of pans. Marvel, head down, and lugging back obstinately, was forced to the kitchen door, and the bolts were drawn.

Then the policeman, who had been trying to pass the barman, rushed in, followed by one of the cabmen, gripped the wrist of the invisible hand that collared Marvel, was hit in the face and went reeling back. The door opened, and Marvel made a frantic effort to obtain a lodgment behind it. Then the cabman collared something. "I got him," said the cabman. The barman's red hands came clawing at the unseen. "Here he is!" said the barman.

Mr. Marvel, released, suddenly dropped to the ground and made an attempt to crawl behind the legs of the fighting men. The struggle blundered round the edge of the door. The voice of the Invisible Man was heard for the first time, yelling out sharply, as the policeman trod on his foot. Then he cried out passionately and his fists flew round like flails. The cabman suddenly whooped and doubled up, kicked under the diaphragm. The door into the bar-parlour from the kitchen slammed and covered Mr. Marvel's retreat. The men in the kitchen found themselves clutching at and struggling with empty air.

"Where's he gone?" cried the man with the beard. "Out?"

"This way," said the policeman, stepping into the yard and stopping.

A piece of tile whizzed by his head and smashed among the crockery on the kitchen table.

"I'll show him," shouted the man with the black beard, and suddenly a steel barrel shone over the policeman's shoulder, and five bullets had followed one another into the twilight whence the missile had come. As he fired, the man with the beard moved his hand in a horizontal curve, so that his shots radiated out into the narrow yard like spokes from a wheel.

A silence followed. "Five cartridges," said the man with the black beard. "That's the best of all. Four aces and the joker. Get a lantern, someone, and come and feel about for his body."

## XVII. DOCTOR KEMP'S VISITOR

Doctor Kemp had continued writing in his study until the shots aroused him. Crack, crack, crack, they came one after the other.

"Hullo!" said Doctor Kemp, putting his pen into his mouth again and listening. "Who's letting off revolvers in Burdock? What are the asses at now?"

He went to the south window, threw it up, and leaning out stared down on the network of windows, beaded gas-lamps and shops, with its black interstices of roofs that made up the town at night. "Looks like a crowd down the hill," he said, "by the Cricketers," and remained watching. Thence his eyes wandered over the town to far away where the ships' lights shone, and the pier glowed, a little illuminated faceted pavilion like a gem of yellow light. The moon in its first quarter hung over the western hill, and the stars were clear and almost tropically bright.

After five minutes, during which his mind had travelled into a remote speculation of social conditions of the future, and lost itself at last over the time dimension, Doctor Kemp roused himself with a sigh, pulled down the window again, and returned to his writing-desk.

It must have been about an hour after this that the front-door bell rang. He had been writing slackly, and with intervals of abstraction, since the shots. He sat listening. He heard the servant answer the door, and waited for her feet on the staircase, but she did not come. "Wonder what that was," said Doctor Kemp.

He tried to resume his work, failed, got up, went downstairs from his study to the landing, rang, and called over the balustrade to the housemaid as she appeared in the hall below. "Was that a letter?" he asked.

"Only a runaway ring, sir," she answered.

"I'm restless to-night," he said to himself. He went back to his study, and this time attacked his work resolutely. In a little while he was hard at work again, and the only sounds in the room were the ticking of the clock and the subdued shrilliness of his quill, hurrying in the very centre of the circle of light his lampshade threw on his table.

It was two o'clock before Doctor Kemp had finished his work for the night. He rose, yawned, and went downstairs to bed. He had already removed his coat and vest, when he noticed that he was thirsty. He took a candle and went down to the dining-room in search of a syphon and whiskey.

Doctor Kemp's scientific pursuits have made him a very observant man, and as he recrossed the hall, he noticed a dark spot on the linoleum near the mat at the foot of the stairs. He went on upstairs, and then it suddenly occurred to him to ask himself what the spot on the linoleum might be. Apparently some subconscious element was at work. At any rate, he turned with his burden, went back to the hall, put down the syphon and whiskey, and bending down, touched the spot. Without any great surprise he found it had the stickiness and colour of drying blood.

He took up his burden again, and returned upstairs, looking about him and trying to account for the blood-spot. On the landing he saw something and stopped astonished. The door-handle of his own room was blood-stained.

He looked at his own hand. It was quite clean, and then he remembered that the door of his room had been open when he came down from his study, and that consequently he had not touched the handle at all. He went straight into his room, his face quite calm—perhaps a trifle more resolute than usual. His glance, wandering inquisitively, fell on the bed. On the counterpane was a mess of blood, and the sheet had been torn. He had not noticed this before because he had walked straight to the dressing-table. On the further side the bedclothes were depressed as if someone had been recently sitting there.

Then he had an odd impression that he had heard a loud voice say, "Good Heavens!—*Kemp!*" But Dr. Kemp was no believer in Voices.

He stood staring at the tumbled sheets. Was that really a voice? He looked about again, but noticed nothing further than the disordered and blood-stained bed. Then he distinctly heard a movement across the room, near the wash-hand stand. All men, however highly educated, retain some superstitious inklings. The feeling that is called "eerie" came upon him. He closed the door of the room, came forward to the dressing-table, and put down his burdens. Suddenly, with a start, he perceived a coiled and blood-stained bandage of linen rag hanging in mid-air, between him and the wash-hand stand.

He stared at this in amazement. It was an empty bandage, a bandage properly tied but quite empty. He would have advanced to grasp it, but a touch arrested him, and a voice speaking quite close to him.

"Kemp!" said the Voice.

"Eigh?" said Kemp, with his mouth open.

"Keep your nerve," said the Voice. "I'm an Invisible Man."

Kemp made no answer for a space, simply stared at the bandage. "Invisible Man," he said.

"I'm an Invisible Man," repeated the Voice.

The story he had been active to ridicule only that morning rushed through Kemp's brain. He does not appear to have been either very much frightened or very greatly surprised at the moment. Realisation came later.

"I thought it was all a lie," he said. The thought uppermost in his mind was the reiterated arguments of the morning. "Have you a bandage on?" he asked.

"Yes," said the Invisible Man.

"Oh!" said Kemp, and then roused himself. "I say!" he said. "But this is nonsense. It's some trick." He stepped forward suddenly, and his hand, extended towards the bandage, met invisible fingers.

He recoiled at the touch and his colour changed.

"Keep steady, Kemp, for God's sake! I want help badly. Stop!"

The hand gripped his arm. He struck at it.

"Kemp!" cried the Voice. "Kemp! Keep steady!" and the grip tightened.

A frantic desire to free himself took possession of Kemp. The hand of the bandaged arm gripped his shoulder, and he was suddenly tripped and flung backwards upon the bed. He opened his mouth to shout, and the corner of the sheet was thrust between his teeth. The Invisible Man had him down grimly, but his arms were free and he struck and tried to kick savagely.

"Listen to reason, will you?" said the Invisible Man, sticking to him in spite of a pounding in the ribs. "By Heaven! you'll madden me in a minute!

"Lie still, you fool!" bawled the Invisible Man in Kemp's ear.

Kemp struggled for another moment and then lay still.

"If you shout, I'll smash your face," said the Invisible Man, relieving his mouth.

"I'm an Invisible Man. It's no foolishness, and no magic. I really am an Invisible Man. And I want your help. I don't want to hurt you, but if you behave like a frantic rustic, I must. Don't you remember me, Kemp? Griffin, of University College?"

"Let me get up," said Kemp. "I'll stop where I am. And let me sit quiet for a minute."

He sat up and felt his neck.

"I am Griffin, of University College, and I have made myself invisible. I am just an ordinary man—a man you have known—made invisible."

"Griffin?" said Kemp.

"Griffin," answered the Voice,—"a younger student, almost an albino, six feet high, and broad, with a pink and white face and red eyes,—who won the medal for chemistry."

"I am confused," said Kemp. "My brain is rioting. What has this to do with Griffin?"

"I *am* Griffin."

Kemp thought. "It's horrible," he said. "But what devilry must happen to make a man invisible?"

"It's no devilry. It's a process, sane and intelligible enough—"

"It's horrible!" said Kemp. "How on earth—?"

"It's horrible enough. But I'm wounded and in pain, and tired—Great God! Kemp, you are a man. Take it steady. Give me some food and drink, and let me sit down here."

Kemp stared at the bandage as it moved across the room, then saw a basket chair dragged across the floor and come to rest near the bed.

It creaked, and the seat was depressed the quarter of an inch or so. He rubbed his eyes and felt his neck again. "This beats ghosts," he said, and laughed stupidly.

"That's better. Thank Heaven, you're getting sensible!"

"Or silly," said Kemp, and knuckled his eyes.

"Give me some whiskey. I'm near dead."

"It didn't feel so. Where are you? If I get up shall I run into you? *There!* all right. Whiskey? Here. Where shall I give it you?"

The chair creaked and Kemp felt the glass drawn away from him. He let go by an effort; his instinct was all against it. It came to rest poised twenty inches above the front edge of the seat of the chair. He stared at it in infinite perplexity. "This is—this *must* be—hypnotism. You must have suggested you are invisible."

"Nonsense," said the Voice.

"It's frantic."

"Listen to me."

"I demonstrated conclusively this morning," began Kemp, "that invisibility—"

"Never mind what you've demonstrated! —I'm starving," said the Voice, "and the night is—chilly to a man without clothes."

"Food!" said Kemp.

The tumbler of whiskey tilted itself. "Yes," said the Invisible Man rapping it down. "Have you got a dressing-gown?"

Kemp made some exclamation in an undertone. He walked to a wardrobe and produced a robe of dingy scarlet. "This do?" he asked. It was taken from him. It hung limp for a moment in mid-air, fluttered weirdly, stood full and decorous buttoning itself, and sat down in his chair. "Drawers, socks, slippers would be a comfort," said the Unseen, curtly. "And food."

"Anything. But this is the insanest thing I ever was in, in my life!"

He turned out his drawers for the articles, and then went downstairs to ransack his larder. He came back with some cold cutlets and bread, pulled up a light table, and placed them before his guest. "Never mind knives," said his visitor, and a cutlet hung in mid-air, with a sound of gnawing.

"Invisible!" said Kemp, and sat down on a bedroom chair.

"I always like to get something about me before I eat," said the Invisible Man, with a full mouth, eating greedily. "Queer fancy!"

"I suppose that wrist is all right," said Kemp.

"Trust me," said the Invisible Man.

"Of *all* the strange and wonderful—"

"Exactly. But it's odd I should blunder into *your* house to get my bandaging. My first stroke of luck! Anyhow I meant to sleep in this house to-night. You must stand that! It's a filthy nuisance, my blood showing, isn't it? Quite a clot over there. Gets visible as it coagulates, I see. I've been in the house three hours."

"But how's it done?" began Kemp, in a tone of exasperation. "Confound it! The whole business—it's unreasonable from beginning to end."

"Quite reasonable," said the Invisible Man. "Perfectly reasonable."

He reached over and secured the whiskey bottle. Kemp stared at the devouring dressing gown. A ray of candle-light penetrating a torn patch in the right shoulder, made a triangle of light under the left ribs. "What were the shots?" he asked. "How did the shooting begin?"

"There was a fool of a man—a sort of confederate of mine—curse him!—who tried to steal my money. *Has* done so."

"Is *he* invisible too?"

"No."

"Well?"

"Can't I have some more to eat before I tell you all that? I'm hungry—in pain. And you want me to tell stories!"

Kemp got up. "*You* didn't do any shooting?" he asked.

"Not me," said his visitor. "Some fool I'd never seen fired at random. A lot of them got scared. They all got scared at me. Curse them!—I say—I want more to eat than this, Kemp."

"I'll see what there is more to eat downstairs," said Kemp. "Not much, I'm afraid."

After he had done eating, and he made a heavy meal, the Invisible Man demanded a cigar. He bit the end savagely before Kemp could find a knife, and cursed when the outer leaf loosened. It was strange to see him smoking; his mouth, and throat, pharynx and nares, became visible as a sort of whirling smoke cast.

"This blessed gift of smoking!" he said, and puffed vigorously. "I'm lucky to have fallen upon you, Kemp. You must help me. Fancy tumbling on you just now! I'm in a devilish scrape. I've been mad, I think. The things I have been through! But we will do things yet. Let me tell you—"

He helped himself to more whiskey and soda. Kemp got up, looked about him, and fetched himself a glass from his spare room. "It's wild—but I suppose I may drink."

"You haven't changed much, Kemp, these dozen years. You fair men don't. Cool and methodical—after the first collapse. I must tell you. We will work together!"

"But how was it all done?" said Kemp, "and how did you get like this?"

"For God's sake, let me smoke in peace for a little while! And then I will begin to tell you."

But the story was not told that night. The Invisible Man's wrist was growing painful, he was feverish, exhausted, and his mind came round to brood upon his chase down the hill and the struggle about the inn. He spoke in fragments of Marvel, he smoked faster, his voice grew angry. Kemp tried to gather what he could.

"He was afraid of me, I could see he was afraid of me," said the Invisible Man many times over. "He meant to give me the slip—he was always casting about! What a fool I was!"

"The cur!

"I should have killed him—"

"Where did you get the money?" asked Kemp, abruptly.

The Invisible Man was silent for a space. "I can't tell you to-night," he said.

He groaned suddenly and leant forward, supporting his invisible head on invisible hands. "Kemp," he said, "I've had no sleep for near three days,—except a couple of dozes of an hour or so. I must sleep soon."

"Well, have my room—have this room."

"But how can I sleep? If I sleep—he will get away. Ugh! What does it matter?"

"What's the shot-wound?" asked Kemp, abruptly.

"Nothing—scratch and blood. Oh, God! How I want sleep!"

"Why not?"

The Invisible Man appeared to be regarding Kemp. "Because I've a particular objection to being caught by my fellow-men," he said slowly.

Kemp started.

"Fool that I am!" said the Invisible Man, striking the table smartly. "I've put the idea into your head."

## XVIII. THE INVISIBLE MAN SLEEPS

Exhausted and wounded as the Invisible Man was, he refused to accept Kemp's word that his freedom should be respected. He examined the two windows of the bedroom, drew up the blinds, and opened the sashes, to confirm Kemp's statement that a retreat by them would be possible. Outside the night was very quiet and still, and the new moon was setting over the down. Then he examined the keys of the bedroom and the two dressing-room doors, to satisfy himself that these also could be made an assurance of freedom. Finally he expressed himself satisfied. He stood on the hearth rug and Kemp heard the sound of a yawn.

"I'm sorry," said the Invisible Man, "if I cannot tell you all that I have done to-night. But I am worn out. It's grotesque, no doubt. It's horrible! But believe me, Kemp, in spite of your arguments of this morning, it is quite a possible thing. I have made a discovery. I meant to keep it to myself. I can't. I must have a partner. And you— We can do such things— But to-morrow. Now, Kemp, I feel as though I must sleep or perish."

Kemp stood in the middle of the room staring at the headless garment. "I suppose I must leave you," he said. "It's—incredible. Three things happening like this, overturning all my preconceptions, would make me insane. But it's real! Is there anything more than I can get you?"

"Only bid me good-night," said Griffin.

"Good-night," said Kemp, and shook an invisible hand. He walked sideways to the door. Suddenly the dressing-gown walked quickly towards him. "Understand me!" said the dressing-gown. "No attempts to hamper me, or capture me! Or—"

Kemp's face changed a little. "I thought I gave you my word," he said.

Kemp closed the door softly behind him, and the key was turned upon him forthwith. Then, as he stood with an expression of passive amazement on his face, the rapid feet came to the door of the dressing-room and that too was locked. Kemp slapped his brow with his hand. "Am I dreaming? Has the world gone mad—or have I?"

He laughed, and put his hand to the locked door. "Barred out of my own bedroom, by a flagrant absurdity!" he said.

He walked to the head of the staircase, turned, and stared at the locked doors. "It's fact," he said. He put his fingers to his slightly bruised neck. "Undeniable fact!

"But—"

He shook his head hopelessly, turned, and went downstairs.

He lit the dining-room lamp, got out a cigar, and began pacing the room, ejaculating. Now and then he would argue with himself.

"Invisible!" he said.

"Is there such a thing as an invisible animal? In the sea, yes. Thousands! millions! All the larvæ, all the little nauplii and tornarias, all the microscopic things, the jelly-fish. In the sea there are more things invisible than visible! I never thought of that before. And in the ponds too! All those little pond-life things,—specks of colourless translucent jelly! But in air? No!

"It can't be.

"But after all—why not?

"If a man was made of glass he would still be visible."

His meditation became profound. The bulk of three cigars had passed into the invisible or diffused as a white ash over the carpet before he spoke again. Then it was merely an exclamation. He turned aside, walked out of the room, and went into his little consulting-room and lit the gas there. It was a little room, because Dr. Kemp did not live by practice, and in it were the day's newspapers. The morning's paper lay carelessly opened and thrown aside. He caught it up, turned it over, and read the account of a "Strange Story from Iping" that the mariner at Port Stowe had spelt over so painfully to Mr. Marvel. Kemp read it swiftly.

"Wrapped up!" said Kemp. "Disguised! Hiding it! 'No one seems to have been aware of his misfortune.' What the devil *is* his game?"

He dropped the paper, and his eye went seeking. "Ah!" he said, and caught up the *St. James' Gazette,* lying folded up as it arrived. "Now we shall get at the truth," said Dr. Kemp. He rent the paper open; a couple of columns confronted him. "An Entire Village in Sussex goes Mad" was the heading.

"Good Heavens!" said Kemp, reading eagerly an incredulous account of the events in Iping, of the previous afternoon, that have already been described. Over the leaf the report in the morning paper had been reprinted.

He re-read it. "Ran through the streets striking right and left. Jaffers insensible. Mr. Huxter in great pain—still unable to describe what he saw. Painful humiliation—vicar. Woman ill with terror! Windows smashed. This extraordinary story probably a fabrication. Too good not to print—*cum grano!*"

He dropped the paper and stared blankly in front of him. "Probably a fabrication!"

He caught up the paper again, and re-read the whole business. "But when does the Tramp come in? Why the deuce was he chasing a Tramp?"

He sat down abruptly on the surgical couch. "He's not only invisible," he said, "but he's mad! Homicidal!"

When dawn came to mingle its pallor with the lamp-light and cigar smoke of the dining-room, Kemp was still pacing up and down, trying to grasp the incredible.

He was altogether too excited to sleep. His servants, descending sleepily, discovered him, and were inclined to think that over-study had worked this ill on him. He gave them extraordinary but quite explicit instructions to lay breakfast for two in the belvedere study

—and then to confine themselves to the basement and ground-floor. Then he continued to pace the dining-room until the morning's paper came. That had much to say and little to tell, beyond the confirmation of the evening before, and a very baldly written account of another remarkable tale from Port Burdock. This gave Kemp the essence of the happenings at the Jolly Cricketers, and the name of Marvel. "He has made me keep with him twenty-four hours," Marvel testified. Certain minor facts were added to the Iping story, notably the cutting of the village telegraph-wire. But there was nothing to throw light on the connexion between the Invisible Man and the Tramp; for Mr. Marvel had supplied no information about the three books, or the money with which he was lined. The incredulous tone had vanished and a shoal of reporters and inquirers were already at work elaborating the matter.

Kemp read every scrap of the report and sent his housemaid out to get every one of the morning papers she could. These also he devoured.

"He is invisible!" he said. "And it reads like rage growing to mania! The things he may do! The things he may do! And he's upstairs free as the air. What on earth ought I to do?

"For instance, would it be a breach of faith if—? No."

He went to a little untidy desk in the corner, and began a note. He tore this up half written, and wrote another. He read it over and considered it. Then he took an envelope and addressed it to "Colonel Adye, Port Burdock."

The Invisible Man awoke even as Kemp was doing this. He awoke in an evil temper, and Kemp, alert for every sound, heard his pattering feet rush suddenly across the bedroom overhead. Then a chair was flung over and the wash-hand stand tumbler smashed. Kemp hurried upstairs and rapped eagerly.

## XIX. CERTAIN FIRST PRINCIPLES

"What's the matter?" asked Kemp, when the Invisible Man admitted him.

"Nothing," was the answer.

"But, confound it! The smash?"

"Fit of temper," said the Invisible Man. "Forgot this arm; and it's sore."

"You're rather liable to that sort of thing."

"I am."

Kemp walked across the room and picked up the fragments of

broken glass. "All the facts are out about you," said Kemp, standing up with the glass in his hand; "all that happened in Iping, and down the hill. The world has become aware of its invisible citizen. But no one knows you are here."

The Invisible Man swore.

"The secret's out. I gather it was a secret. I don't know what your plans are, but of course I'm anxious to help you."

The Invisible Man sat down on the bed.

"There's breakfast upstairs," said Kemp, speaking as easily as possible, and he was delighted to find his strange guest rose willingly. Kemp led the way up the narrow staircase to the belvedere.

"Before we can do anything else," said Kemp, "I must understand a little more about this invisibility of yours." He had sat down, after one nervous glance out of the window, with the air of a man who has talking to do. His doubts of the sanity of the entire business flashed and vanished again as he looked across to where Griffin sat at the breakfast-table,—a headless, handless dressing-gown, wiping unseen lips on a miraculously held *serviette.*

"It's simple enough—and credible enough," said Griffin, putting the serviette aside and leaning the invisible head on an invisible hand.

"No doubt, to you, but—" Kemp laughed.

"Well, yes; to me it seemed wonderful at first, no doubt. But now, great God!— But we will do great things yet! I came on the stuff first at Chesilstowe."

"Chesilstowe?"

"I went there after I left London. You know I dropped medicine and took up physics? *No!*—well, I did. *Light*—fascinated me."

"Ah!"

"Optical density! The whole subject is a network of riddles—a network with solutions glimmering elusively through. And being but two and twenty and full of enthusiasm, I said, 'I will devote my life to this. This is worth while.' You know what fools we are at two and twenty?"

"Fools then or fools now," said Kemp.

"As though Knowing could be any satisfaction to a man!

"But I went to work—like a slave. And I had hardly worked and thought about the matter six months before light came through one of the meshes suddenly—blindingly! I found a general principle of pigments and refraction,—a formula, a geometrical expression involving four dimensions. Fools, common men, even common mathematicians, do not know anything of what some general expression may mean to the student of molecular physics. In the books—the books that Tramp has hidden—there are marvels, miracles! But this was not a method, it was an idea, that might lead to a method by which it would be possible, without changing any other property of matter, —except, in some instances, colours,—to lower the refractive index of a substance, solid or liquid, to that of air—so far as all practical purposes are concerned."

"Phew!" said Kemp. "That's odd! But still I don't see quite—I can understand that thereby you could spoil a valuable stone, but personal invisibility is a far cry."

"Precisely," said Griffin. "But consider: Visibility depends on the action of the visible bodies on light. Either a body absorbs light, or it reflects or refracts it, or does all these things. If it neither reflects nor refracts nor absorbs light, it cannot of itself be visible. You see an opaque red box, for instance, because the colour absorbs some of the light and reflects the rest, all the red part of the light, to you. If it did not absorb any particular part of the light, but reflected it all, then it would be a shining white box. Silver! A diamond box would neither absorb much of the light nor reflect much from the general surface, but just here and there where the surfaces were favourable the light would be reflected and refracted, so that you would get a brilliant appearance of flashing reflections and translucencies,—a sort of skeleton of light. A glass box would not be so brilliant, not so clearly visible, as a diamond box, because there would be less refraction and reflection. See that? From certain points of view you would see quite clearly through it. Some kinds of glass would be more visible than others, a box of flint glass would be brighter than a box of ordinary window glass. A box of very thin common glass would be hard to see in a bad light, because it would absorb hardly any light and refract and reflect very little. And if you put a sheet of common white glass in water, still more if you put it in some denser liquid than water, it would vanish almost altogether, because light passing from water to glass is only slightly refracted or reflected or indeed affected in any way. It is almost as invisible as a jet of coal gas or hydrogen is in air. And for precisely the same reason!"

"Yes," said Kemp, "that is pretty plain sailing."

"And here is another fact you will know to be true. If a sheet of glass is smashed, Kemp, and beaten into a powder, it becomes much more visible while it is in the air; it becomes at last an opaque white powder. This is because the powdering multiplies the surfaces of the glass at which refraction and reflection occur. In the sheet of glass there are only two surfaces; in the powder the light is reflected or refracted by each grain it passes through, and very little gets right through the powder. But if the white powdered glass is put into water, it forthwith vanishes. The powdered glass and water have much the same refractive index; that is, the light undergoes very little refraction or reflection in passing from one to the other.

"You make the glass invisible by putting it into a liquid of nearly the same refractive index; a transparent thing becomes invisible if it is put in any medium of almost the same refractive index. And if you will consider only a second, you will see also that the powder of glass might be made to vanish in air, if its refractive index could be made the same as that of air; for then there would be no refraction or reflection as the light passed from glass to air."

"Yes, yes," said Kemp. "But a man's not powdered glass!"

"No," said Griffin. *"He's more transparent!"*

"Nonsense!"

"That from a doctor! How one forgets! Have you already forgotten your physics, in ten years? Just think of all the things that are transparent and seem not to be so. Paper, for instance, is made up of transparent fibres, and it is white and opaque only for the same reason that a powder of glass is white and opaque. Oil white paper, fill up the interstices between the particles with oil so that there is no longer refraction or reflection except at the surfaces, and it becomes as transparent as glass. And not only paper, but cotton fibre, linen fibre, wool fibre, woody fibre, and *bone,* Kemp, *flesh,* Kemp, *hair,* Kemp, *nails* and *nerves,* Kemp, in fact the whole fabric of a man except the red of his blood and the black pigment of hair, are all made up of transparent, colourless tissue. So little suffices to make us visible one to the other. For the most part the fibres of a living creature are no more opaque than water."

"Great Heavens!" cried Kemp. "Of course, of course! I was thinking only last night of the sea larvæ and all jelly-fish!"

*"Now* you have me! And all that I knew and had in mind a year after I left London—six years ago. But I kept it to myself. I had to do my work under frightful disadvantages. Oliver, my professor, was a scientific bounder, a journalist by instinct, a thief of ideas,—he was always prying! And you know the knavish system of the scientific world. I simply would not publish, and let him share my credit. I went on working, I got nearer and nearer making my formula into an experiment, a reality. I told no living soul, because I meant to flash my work upon the world with crushing effect,—to become famous at a blow. I took up the question of pigments to fill up certain gaps. And suddenly, not by design but by accident, I made a discovery in physiology."

"Yes?"

"You know the red colouring matter of blood; it can be made white —colourless—and remain with all the functions it has now!"

Kemp gave a cry of incredulous amazement.

The Invisible Man rose and began pacing the little study. "You may well exclaim. I remember that night. It was late at night,— in the daytime one was bothered with the gaping, silly students,—and I worked then sometimes till dawn. It came suddenly, splendid and complete in my mind. I was alone; the laboratory was still, with the tall lights burning brightly and silently. In all my great moments I have been alone. 'One could make an animal—a tissue—transparent! One could make it invisible! All except the pigments—I could be invisible!' I said, suddenly realizing what it meant to be an albino with such knowledge. It was overwhelming. I left the filtering I was doing, and went and stared out of the great window at the stars. 'I could be invisible!' I repeated.

"To do such a thing would be to transcend magic. And I beheld, unclouded by doubt, a magnificent vision of all that invisibility might mean to a man,—the mystery, the power, the freedom. Drawbacks I saw none. You have only to think! And I, a shabby, poverty-struck, hemmed-in demonstrator, teaching fools in a provincial college, might suddenly become—this. I ask you, Kemp if *you*— Anyone, I tell you, would have flung himself upon that research. And I worked three years, and every mountain of difficulty I toiled over showed another from its summit. The infinite details! And the exasperation,—a professor, a provincial professor, always prying. 'When are you going to publish this work of yours?' was his everlasting question. And the students, the cramped means! Three years I had of it—

"And after three years of secrecy and exasperation, I found that to complete it was impossible,—impossible."

"How?" asked Kemp.

"Money," said the Invisible Man, and went again to stare out of the window.

He turned round abruptly. "I robbed the old man—robbed my father.

"The money was not his, and he shot himself."

## XX. AT THE HOUSE IN GREAT PORTLAND STREET

For a moment Kemp sat in silence, staring at the back of the headless figure at the window. Then he started, struck by a thought, rose, took the Invisible Man's arm, and turned him away from the outlook.

"You are tired," he said, "and while I sit, you walk about. Have my chair."

He placed himself between Griffin and the nearest window.

For a space Griffin sat silent, and then he resumed abruptly:—

"I had left the Chesilstowe cottage already," he said, "when that happened. It was last December. I had taken a room in London, a large unfurnished room in a big ill-managed lodging-house in a slum near Great Portland Street. The room was soon full of the appliances I had bought with his money; the work was going on steadily, successfully, drawing near an end. I was like a man emerging from a thicket, and suddenly coming on some unmeaning tragedy. I went to bury him. My mind was still on this research, and I did not lift a finger to save his character. I remember the funeral, the cheap hearse, the scant ceremony, the windy frost-bitten hillside, and the old college friend of his who read the service over him,—a shabby, black, bent old man with a snivelling cold.

"I remember walking back to the empty home, through the place that had once been a village and was now patched and tinkered by the jerry builders into the ugly likeness of a town. Every way the roads ran out at last into the desecrated fields and ended in rubble heaps and rank wet weeds. I remember myself as a gaunt black figure, going along the slippery, shiny pavement, and the strange sense of detachment I felt from the squalid respectability, the sordid commercialism of the place.

"I did not feel a bit sorry for my father. He seemed to me to be the victim of his own foolish sentimentality. The current cant required my attendance at his funeral, but it was really not my affair.

"But going along the High Street, my old life came back to me for a space, for I met the girl I had known ten years since. Our eyes met.

"Something moved me to turn back and talk to her. She was a very ordinary person.

"It was all like a dream, that visit to the old places. I did not feel then that I was lonely, that I had come out from the world into a desolate place. I appreciated my loss of sympathy, but I put it down to the general inanity of things. Re-entering my room seemed like the recovery of reality. There were the things I knew and loved. There stood the apparatus, the experiments arranged and waiting. And now there was scarcely a difficulty left, beyond the planning of details.

"I will tell you, Kemp, sooner or later, all the complicated processes. We need not go into that now. For the most part, saving certain gaps I chose to remember, they are written in cypher in those books that tramp has hidden. We must hunt him down. We must get those books again. But the essential phase was to place the transparent object whose refractive index was to be lowered between two radiating centres of a sort of ethereal vibration, of which I will tell you more fully later. No, not these Röntgen vibrations—I don't know that these others of mine have been described. Yet they are obvious enough. I needed two little dynamos, and these I worked with a cheap gas engine. My first experiment was with a bit of white wool fabric. It was the strangest thing in the world to see it in the flicker of the flashes soft and white, and then to watch it fade like a wreath of smoke and vanish.

"I could scarcely believe I had done it. I put my hand into the emptiness, and there was the thing as solid as ever. I felt it awkardly, and threw it on the floor. I had a little trouble finding it again.

"And then came a curious experience. I heard a miaow behind me, and turning, saw a lean white cat, very dirty, on the cistern cover outside the window. A thought came into my head. 'Everything ready for you,' I said, and went to the window, opened it, and called softly. She came in, purring,—the poor beast was starving,—and I gave her some milk. All my food was in a cupboard in the corner of the room. After that she went smelling round the room,—evidently with the idea of making herself at home. The invisible rag upset her a bit; you should have seen her spit at it! But I made her comfortable on the pillow of my truckle-bed. And I gave her butter to get her to wash."

"And you processed her?"

"I processed her. But giving drugs to a cat is no joke, Kemp! And the process failed."

"Failed!"

"In two particulars. These were the claws and the pigment stuff—what is it?—at the back of the eye in a cat. You know?"

"*Tapetum.*"

"Yes, the *tapetum*. It didn't go. After I'd given the stuff to bleach the blood and done certain other things to her, I gave the beast opium, and put her and the pillow she was sleeping on, on the apparatus. And after all the rest had faded and vanished, there remained two little ghosts of her eyes."

"Odd!"

"I can't explain it. She was bandaged and clamped, of course,—so I had her safe; but she woke while she was still misty, and miaowed dismally, and someone came knocking. It was an old woman from downstairs, who suspected me of vivisecting,—a drink-sodden old creature, with only a white cat to care for in all the world. I whipped out some chloroform, applied it, and answered the door. 'Did I hear a cat?' she asked. 'My cat?' 'Not here,' said I, very politely. She was a little doubtful and tried to peer past me into the room; strange enough to her no doubt,—bare walls, uncurtained windows, truckle-bed, with the gas engine vibrating, and the seethe of the radiant points, and that faint ghastly stinging of chloroform in the air. She had to be satisfied at last and went away again."

"How long did it take?" asked Kemp.

"Three or four hours—the cat. The bones and sinews and the fat were the last to go, and the tips of the coloured hairs. And, as I say, the back part of the eye, tough iridescent stuff it is, wouldn't go at all.

"It was night outside long before the business was over, and nothing was to be seen but the dim eyes and the claws. I stopped the gas engine, felt for and stroked the beast, which was still insensible, and then, being tired, left it sleeping on the invisible pillow and went to bed. I found it hard to sleep. I lay awake thinking weak aimless stuff, going over the experiment over and over again, or dreaming feverishly of things growing misty and vanishing about me, until everything, the ground I stood on, vanished, and so I came to that sickly falling nightmare one gets. About two, the cat began miaowing about the room. I tried to hush it by talking to it, and then I decided to turn it out. I remember the shock I had when striking a light—there were just the round eyes shining green—and nothing round them. I would have given it milk, but I hadn't any. It wouldn't be quiet, it just sat down and miaowed at the door. I tried to catch it, with an idea of putting it out of the window, but it wouldn't be caught, it vanished. Then it began miaowing in different parts of the room. At last I opened the window and made a bustle. I suppose it went out at last. I never saw any more of it.

"Then—Heaven knows why—I fell thinking of my father's funeral again, and the dismal windy hillside, until the day had come. I found sleeping was hopeless, and, locking my door after me, wandered out into the morning streets."

"You don't mean to say there's an invisible cat at large!" said Kemp.

"If it hasn't been killed," said the Invisible Man. "Why not?"

"Why not?" said Kemp. "I didn't mean to interrupt."

"It's very probably been killed," said the Invisible Man. "It was alive four days after, I know, and down a grating in Great Tichfield Street; because I saw a crowd round the place, trying to see whence the miaowing came."

He was silent for the best part of a minute. Then he resumed abruptly:—

"I remember that morning before the change very vividly. I must have gone up Great Portland Street. I remember the barracks in Albany Street, and the horse soldiers coming out, and at last I found myself sitting in the sunshine and feeling very ill and strange, on the summit of Primrose Hill. It was a sunny day in January,—one of those sunny, frosty days that came before the snow this year. My weary brain tried to formulate the position, to plot out a plan of action.

"I was surprised to find, now that my prize was within my grasp, how inconclusive its attainment seemed. As a matter of fact I was worked out; the intense stress of nearly four years' continuous work left me incapable of any strength of feeling. I was apathetic, and I tried in vain to recover the enthusiasm of my first inquiries, the passion of discovery that had enabled me to compass even the downfall of my father's grey hairs. Nothing seemed to matter. I saw pretty clearly this was a transient mood, due to overwork and want of sleep, and that either by drugs or rest it would be possible to recover my energies.

"All I could think clearly was that the thing had to be carried through; the fixed idea still ruled me. And soon, for the money I had was almost exhausted. I looked about me at the hillside, with children playing and girls watching them, and tried to think of all the fantastic advantages an invisible man would have in the world. After a time I crawled home, took some food and a strong dose of strychnine, and went to sleep in my clothes on my unmade bed. Strychnine is a grand tonic, Kemp, to take the flabbiness out of a man."

"It's the devil," said Kemp. "It's the palæolithic in a bottle."

"I awoke vastly invigorated and rather irritable. You know?"

"I know the stuff."

"And there was someone rapping at the door. It was my landlord with threats and inquiries, an old Polish Jew in a long grey coat and greasy slippers. I had been tormenting a cat in the night, he was sure,—the old woman's tongue had been busy. He insisted on knowing all about it. The laws in this country against vivisection were very severe,—he might be liable. I denied the cat. Then the vibration of the little gas engine could be felt all over the house, he said. That was true, certainly. He edged round me into the room, peering about over his German-silver spectacles, and a sudden dread came into my mind that he might carry away something of my secret. I tried to keep between him and the concentrating apparatus I had arranged, and that only made him more curious. What was I doing? Why was I always alone and secretive? Was it legal? Was it dangerous?

I paid nothing but the usual rent. His had always been a most respectable house—in a disreputable neighbourhood. Suddenly my temper gave way. I told him to get out. He began to protest, to jabber of his right of entry. In a moment I had him by the collar; something ripped, and he went spinning out into his own passage. I slammed and locked the door and sat down quivering.

"He made a fuss outside, which I disregarded, and after a time he went away.

"But this brought matters to a crisis. I did not know what he would do, nor even what he had power to do. To move to fresh apartments would have meant delay; all together I had barely twenty pounds left in the world,—for the most part in a bank,—and I could not afford that. Vanish! It was irresistible. Then there would be an inquiry, the sacking of my room—

"At the thought of the possibility of my work being exposed or interrupted at its very climax, I became angry and active. I hurried out with my three books of notes, my cheque-book,—the tramp has them now,—and directed them from the nearest Post Office to a house of call for letters and parcels in Great Portland Street. I tried to go out noiselessly. Coming in, I found my landlord going quietly upstairs; he had heard the door close, I suppose. You would have laughed to see him jump aside on the landing as I came tearing after him. He glared at me as I went by him, and I made the house quiver with the slamming of my door. I heard him come shuffling up to my floor, hesitate, and go down. I set to work upon my preparations forthwith.

"It was all done that evening and night. While I was still sitting under the sickly, drowsy influence of the drugs that decolourise blood, there came a repeated knocking at the door. It ceased, footsteps went away and returned, and the knocking was resumed. There was an attempt to push something under the door—a blue paper. Then in a fit of irritation I rose and went and flung the door wide open. 'Now then?' said I.

"It was my landlord, with a notice of ejectment or something. He held it out to me, saw something odd about my hands, I expect, and lifted his eyes to my face.

"For a moment he gaped. Then he gave a sort of inarticulate cry, dropped candle and writ together, and went blundering down the dark passage to the stairs. I shut the door, locked it, and went to the looking-glass. Then I understood his terror. My face was white—like white stone.

"But it was all horrible. I had not expected the suffering. A night of racking anguish, sickness and fainting. I set my teeth, though my skin was presently afire, all my body afire; but I lay there like grim death. I understood now how it was the cat had howled until I chloroformed it. Lucky it was I lived alone and untended in my room. There were times when I sobbed and groaned and talked. But I stuck to it. I became insensible and woke languid in the darkness.

"The pain had passed. I thought I was killing myself and I did not care. I shall never forget that dawn, and the strange horror of seeing that my hands had become as clouded glass, and watching them grow clearer and thinner as the day went by, until at last I could see the sickly disorder of my room through them, though I closed my transparent eyelids. My limbs became glassy, the bones and arteries faded, vanished, and the little white nerves went last. I gritted my teeth and stayed there to the end. At last only the dead tips of the fingernails remained, pallid and white, and the brown stain of some acid upon my fingers.

"I struggled up. At first I was as incapable as a swathed infant,—stepping with limbs I could not see. I was weak and very hungry. I went and stared at nothing in my shaving-glass, at nothing save where an attenuated pigment still remained behind the retina of my eyes, fainter than mist. I had to hang on to the table and press my forehead to the glass.

"It was only by a frantic effort of will that I dragged myself back to the apparatus and completed the process.

"I slept during the forenoon, pulling the sheet over my eyes to shut out the light, and about midday I was awakened again by a knocking. My strength had returned. I sat up and listened and heard a whispering. I sprang to my feet and as noiselessly as possible began to detach the connections of my apparatus, and to distribute it about the room, so as to destroy the suggestions of its arrangement. Presently the knocking was renewed and voices called, first my landlord's, and then two others. To gain time I answered them. The invisible rag and pillow came to hand and I opened the window and pitched them out on to the cistern cover. As the window opened, a heavy crash came at the door. Someone had charged it with the idea of smashing the lock. But the stout bolts I had screwed up some days before stopped him. That startled me, made me angry. I began to tremble and do things hurriedly.

"I tossed together some loose paper, straw, packing paper and so forth, in the middle of the room, and turned on the gas. Heavy blows began to rain upon the door. I could not find the matches. I beat my hands on the wall with rage. I turned down the gas again, stepped out of the window on the cistern cover, very softly lowered the sash, and sat down, secure and invisible, but quivering with anger, to watch events. They split a panel, I saw, and in another moment they had broken away the staples of the bolts and stood in the open doorway. It was the landlord and his two step-sons, sturdy young men of three or four and twenty. Behind them fluttered the old hag of a woman from downstairs.

"You may imagine their astonishment to find the room empty. One of the younger men rushed to the window at once, flung it up and stared out. His staring eyes and thick-lipped bearded face came a foot from my face. I was half minded to hit his silly countenance, but I arrested my doubled fist. He stared right through me. So did the others as they joined him. The old man went and peered under the bed, and then they all made a rush for the cupboard. They had to argue about it at length in Yiddish and Cockney English. They concluded I had not answered them, that their imagination had deceived them. A feeling of extraordinary elation took the place of my anger as I sat outside the window and watched these four people—for the old lady came in, glancing suspiciously about her like a cat, trying to understand the riddle of my behaviour.

"The old man, so far as I could understand his *patois,* agreed with the old lady that I was a vivisectionist. The sons protested in garbled English that I was an electrician, and appealed to the dynamos and radiators. They were all nervous against my arrival, although I found subsequently that they had bolted the front door. The old lady peered into the cupboard and under the bed, and one of the young men pushed up the register and stared up the chimney. One of my fellow lodgers, a costermonger who shared the opposite room with a butcher, appeared on the landing, and he was called in and told incoherent things.

"It occurred to me that the radiators, if they fell into the hands of some acute well-educated person, would give me away too much, and watching my opportunity, I came into the room and tilted one of the little dynamos off its fellow on which it was standing, and smashed both apparatus. Then, while they were trying to explain the smash, I dodged out of the room and went softly downstairs.

"I went into one of the sitting-rooms and waited until they came down, still speculating and argumentative, all a little disappointed at finding no 'horrors,' and all a little puzzled how they stood with regard to me. Then I slipped up again with a box of matches, fired my heap of paper and rubbish, put the chairs and bedding thereby, led the gas to the affair, by means of an india-rubber tube, and waving a farewell to the room left it for the last time."

"You fired the house!" exclaimed Kemp.

"Fired the house. It was the only way to cover my trail—and no doubt it was insured. I slipped the bolts of the front door quietly and went out into the street. I was invisible, and I was only just beginning to realise the extraordinary advantage my invisibility gave me. My head was already teeming with plans of all the wild and wonderful things I had now impunity to do.

## XXI. IN OXFORD STREET

"In going downstairs the first time I found an unexpected difficulty because I could not see my feet; indeed I stumbled twice, and there was an unaccustomed clumsiness in gripping the bolt. By not looking down, however, I managed to walk on the level passably well.

"My mood, I say, was one of exaltation. I felt as a seeing man might do, with padded feet and noiseless clothes, in a city of the blind. I experienced a wild impulse to jest, to startle people, to clap men on the back, fling people's hats astray, and generally revel in my extraordinary advantage.

"But hardly had I emerged upon Great Portland Street, however (my lodging was close to the big draper's shop there), when I heard a clashing concussion and was hit violently behind, and turning saw a man carrying a basket of soda-water syphons, and looking in amazement at his burden. Although the blow had really hurt me, I found something so irresistible in his astonishment that I laughed aloud. 'The devil's in the basket,' I said, and suddenly twisted it out of his hand. He let go incontinently, and I swung the whole weight into the air.

"But a fool of a cabman, standing outside a public house, made a sudden rush for this, and his extending fingers took me with excruciating violence under the ear. I let the whole down with a smash on the cabman, and then, with shouts and the clatter of feet about me, people coming out of shops, vehicles pulling up, I realised what I had done for myself, and cursing my folly, backed against a shop window and prepared to dodge out of the confusion. In a moment I should be wedged into a crowd and inevitably discovered. I pushed by a butcher boy, who luckily did not turn to see the nothingness that shoved him aside, and dodged behind the cabman's four-wheeler. I do not know how they settled the business. I hurried straight across the road, which was happily clear, and hardly heeding which way I went, in the fright of detection the incident had given me, plunged into the afternoon throng of Oxford Street.

"I tried to get into the stream of people, but they were too thick for me, and in a moment my heels were being trodden upon. I took to the gutter, the roughness of which I found painful to my feet, and forthwith the shaft of a crawling hansom dug me forcibly under the shoulder blade, reminding me that I was already bruised severely. I staggered out of the way of the cab, avoided a perambulator by a convulsive movement, and found myself behind the hansom. A happy thought saved me, and as this drove slowly along I followed in its immediate wake, trembling and astonished at the turn of my adventure. And not only trembling, but shivering. It was a bright day in January and I was stark naked and the thin slime of mud that covered the road was freezing. Foolish as it seems to me now, I had not reckoned that, transparent or not, I was still amenable to the weather and all its consequences.

"Then suddenly a bright idea came into my head. I ran round and got into the cab. And so, shivering, scared, and sniffing with the first intimations of a cold, and with the bruises in the small of my back growing upon my attention, I drove slowly along Oxford Street and past Tottenham Court Road. My mood was as different from that in which I had sallied forth ten minutes ago as it is possible to imagine. *This* invisibility indeed! The one thought that possessed me was—how was I to get out of the scrape I was in

"We crawled past Mudie's, and there a tall woman with five or six yellow-labelled books hailed my cab, and I sprang out just in time to escape her, shaving a railway van narrowly in my flight. I made off up the roadway to Bloomsbury Square, intending to strike north past the Museum and so get into the quiet district. I was now cruelly chilled, and the strangeness of my situation so unnerved me that I whimpered as I ran. At the northward corner of the Square a little white dog ran out of the Pharmaceutical Society's offices, and incontinently made for me, nose down.

"I had never realised it before, but the nose is to the mind of a dog what the eye is to the mind of a seeing man. Dogs perceive the scent of a man moving as men perceive his vision. This brute began barking and leaping, showing, as it seemed to me, only too plainly that he was aware of me. I crossed Great Russell Street, glancing over my shoulder as I did so, and went some way along Montagu Street before I realised what I was running towards.

"Then I became aware of a blare of music, and looking along the street saw a number of people advancing out of Russell Square, red shirts, and the banner of the Salvation Army to the fore. Such a crowd, chanting in the roadway and scoffing on the pavement, I could not hope to penetrate, and dreading to go back and farther from home again, and deciding on the spur of the moment, I ran up the white steps of a house facing the museum railings, and stood there until the crowd should have passed. Happily the dog stopped at the noise of the band too, hesitated, and turned tail, running back to Bloomsbury Square again.

"On came the band, bawling with unconscious irony some hymn about 'When shall we see his Face?' and it seemed an interminable time to me before the tide of the crowd washed along the pavement by me. Thud, thud, thud, came the drum with a vibrating resonance, and for the moment I did not notice two urchins stopping at the railings by me. 'See 'em,' said one. 'See what?' said the other. 'Why—them footmarks—*bare*. Like what you makes in mud.'

"I looked down and saw the youngsters had stopped and were gaping at the muddy footmarks I had left behind me up the newly whitened steps. The passing people elbowed and jostled them, but their confounded intelligence was arrested. 'Thud, thud, thud, When, thud, shall we see, thud, his face, thud, thud.' 'There's a barefoot man gone up them steps, or I don't know nothing,' said one. 'And he ain't never come down again. And his foot was a-bleeding.'

"The thick of the crowd had already passed. 'Looky there, Ted,' quoth the younger of the detectives, with the sharpness of surprise in his voice, and pointed straight to my feet. I looked down and saw at once the dim suggestion of their outline sketched in splashes of mud. For a moment I was paralysed.

" 'Why, that's rum,' said the elder. 'Dashed rum! It's just like the ghost of a foot, ain't it?' He hesitated and advanced with outstretched hand. A man pulled up short to see what he was catching, and then a girl. In another moment he would have touched me. Then I saw what to do. I made a step, the boy started back with an exclamation, and with a rapid movement I swung myself over into the portico of the next house. But the smaller boy was sharp-eyed enough to follow the movement, and before I was well down the steps and upon the pavement, he had recovered from his momentary astonishment and was shouting out that the feet had gone over the wall.

"They rushed round and saw my new footmarks flash into being on the lower step and upon the pavement. 'What's up?' asked someone. 'Feet! Look! Feet running!' Everybody in the road, except my three pursuers, was pouring along after the Salvation Army, and this blow not only impeded me but them. There was an eddy of surprise and interrogation. At the cost of bowling over one young fellow I got through, and in another moment I was rushing headlong round the circuit of Russell Square, with six or seven astonished people following my footmarks. There was no time for explanation, or else the whole host would have been after me.

"Twice I doubled round corners, thrice I crossed the road and came back on my tracks, and then, as my feet grew hot and dry, the damp impressions began to fade. At last I had a breathing space and rubbed my feet clean with my hands, and so got away altogether. The last I saw of the chase was a little group of a dozen people perhaps, studying with infinite perplexity a slowly drying footprint that had resulted from a puddle in Tavistock Square,—a footprint as isolated and incomprehensible to them as Crusoe's solitary discovery.

"This running warmed me to a certain extent, and I went on with a better courage through the maze of less frequented roads that runs hereabouts. My back had now become very stiff and sore, my tonsils were painful from the cabman's fingers, and the skin of my neck had been scratched by his nails; my feet hurt exceedingly and I was lame from a little cut on one foot. I saw in time a blind man approaching me, and fled limping, for I feared his subtle intuitions. Once or twice accidental collisions occurred and I left people amazed, with unaccountable curses ringing in their ears. Then came something silent and quiet against my face, and across the Square fell a thin veil of slowly falling flakes of snow. I had caught a cold, and do as I would I could not avoid an occasional sneeze. And every dog that came in sight, with its pointing nose and curious sniffing, was a terror to me.

"Then came men and boys running, first one and then others, and shouting as they ran. It was a fire. They ran in the direction of my lodging, and looking back down the street I saw a mass of black smoke streaming up above the roofs and telephone wires. It was my lodging burning; my clothes, my apparatus, all my resources indeed, except my cheque-book and the three volumes of memoranda that awaited me in Great Portland Street, were there. Burning! I had burnt my boats—if ever a man did! The place was blazing."

The Invisible Man paused and thought. Kemp glanced nervously out of the window. "Yes?" he said. "Go on."

## XXII. IN THE EMPORIUM

"So last January, with the beginnings of a snowstorm in the air about me—and if it settled on me it would betray me!—weary, cold, painful, inexpressibly wretched, and still but half convinced of my invisible quality, I began this new life to which I am committed. I had no refuge, no appliances, no human being in the world in whom I could confide. To have told my seceret would have given me away—made a mere show and rarity of me. Nevertheless, I was half minded to accost some passer-by and throw myself upon his mercy. But I knew too clearly the terror and brutal cruelty my advances would evoke. I made no plans in the street. My sole object was to get shelter from the snow, to get myself covered and warm; then I might hope to plan. But even to me, an Invisible Man, the rows of London houses stood latched, barred, and bolted impregnably.

"Only one thing could I see clearly before me, the cold exposure and misery of the snowstorm and the night.

"And then I had a brilliant idea. I turned down one of the roads leading from Gower Street to Tottenham Court Road, and found myself outside Omniums, the big establishment where everything is to be bought,—you know the place,—meat, grocery, linen, furniture, clothing, oil paintings even,—a huge meandering collection of shops rather than a shop. I had thought I should find the doors open, but they were closed, and as I stood in the wide entrance a carriage stopped outside, and a man in uniform—you know the kind of personage with *'Omnium'* on his cap—flung open the door. I contrived to enter, and walking down the shop—it was a department where they were selling ribbons and gloves and stockings and that kind of thing—came to a more spacious region devoted to picnic baskets and wicker furniture.

"I did not feel safe there, however; people were going to and fro, and I prowled restlessly about until I came upon a huge section in an upper floor containing multitudes of bedsteads, and this I clambered, and found a resting-place at last among a huge pile of folded flock mattresses. The place was already lit up and agreebly warm, and I decided to remain where I was, keeping a cautious eye on the two or three sets of shopmen and customers who were meandering through the place, until closing time came. Then I should be able, I thought, to rob the place for food and clothing, and disguised, prowl through it and examine its resources, perhaps sleep on some of the bedding. That seemed an acceptable plan. My idea was to procure clothing to make myself a muffled but acceptable figure, to get money, and then to recover my books and parcels where they awaited me, take a lodging somewhere and elaborate plans for the complete realisation of the advantages my invisibility gave me (as I still imagined) over my fellow-men.

"Closing time arrived quickly enough; it could not have been more than an hour after I took up my position on the mattresses before I noticed the blinds of the windows being drawn, and customers being marched doorward. And then a number of brisk young men began with remarkable alacrity to tidy up the goods that remained disturbed.

I left my lair as the crowds diminished, and prowled cautiously out into the less desolate parts of the shop. I was really surprised to observe how rapidly the young men and women whipped away the goods displayed for sale during the day. All the boxes of goods, the hanging fabrics, the festoons of lace, the boxes of sweets in the grocery section, the displays of this and that, were being whipped down, folded up, slapped into tidy receptacles, and everything that could not be taken down and put away had sheets of some coarse stuff like sacking flung over them. Finally all the chairs were turned up on to the counters, leaving the floor clear. Directly each of these young people had done, he or she made promptly for the door with such an expression of animation as I have rarely observed in a shop assistant before. Then came a lot of youngsters scattering sawdust and carrying pails and brooms. I had to dodge to get out of the way, and as it was, my ankle got stung with the sawdust. For some time, wandering through the swathed and darkened departments, I could hear the brooms at work. And at last a good hour or more after the shop had been closed, came a noise of locking doors. Silence came upon the place, and I found myself wandering through the vast and intricate shops, galleries, showrooms of the place, alone. It was very still; in one place I remember passing near one of the Tottenham Court Road entrances and listening to the tapping of boot-heels of the passers-by.

"My first visit was to the place where I had seen stockings and gloves for sale. It was dark, and I had the devil of a hunt after matches, which I found at last in the drawer of the little cash desk. Then I had to get a candle. I had to tear down wrappings and ransack a number of boxes and drawers, but at last I managed to turn out what I sought; the box label called them lambswool pants, and lambswool vests. Then socks, a thick comforter, and then I went to the clothing place and got trousers, a lounge jacket, an overcoat and a slouch hat,—a clerical sort of hat with the brim turned down. I began to feel a human being again, and my next thought was food.

"Upstairs was a refreshment department, and there I got cold meat. There was coffee still in the urn, and I lit the gas and warmed it up again, and altogether I did not do badly. Afterwards, prowling through the place in search of blankets,—I had to put up at last with a heap of down quilts,—I came upon a grocery section with a lot of chocolate and candied fruits, more than was good for me indeed—and some white burgundy. And near that was a toy department, and I had a brilliant idea. I found some artificial noses—dummy noses, you know, and I thought of dark spectacles. But Omniums had no optical department. My nose had been a difficulty indeed—I had thought of paint. But the discovery set my mind running on wigs and masks and the like. Finally I went to sleep in a heap of down quilts, very warm and comfortable.

"My last thoughts before sleeping were the most agreeable I had had since the change. I was in a state of physical serenity, and that was reflected in my mind. I thought that I should be able to slip out unobserved in the morning with my clothes upon me, muffling my face with a white wrapper I had taken, purchase, with the money I had taken, spectacles and so forth, and so complete my disguise. I lapsed into disorderly dreams of all the fantastic things that had happened during the last few days. I saw the ugly little Jew of a landlord vociferating in his rooms; I saw his two sons marvelling, and the wrinkled old woman's gnarled face as she asked for her cat. I experienced again the strange sensation of seeing the cloth disappear, and so I came round to the windy hillside and the sniffing old clergyman mumbling 'Dust to dust, earth to earth,' and my father's open grave.

" 'You also,' said a voice, and suddenly I was being forced towards the grave. I struggled, shouted, appealed to the mourners, but they continued stonily following the service; the old clergyman, too, never faltered droning and sniffing through the ritual. I realised I was invisible and inaudible, that overwhelming forces had their grip on me. I struggled in vain, I was forced over the brink, the coffin rang hollow as I fell upon it, and the gravel came flying after me in spadefuls. Nobody heeded me, nobody was aware of me. I made convulsive struggles and awoke.

"The pale London dawn had come, the place was full of a chilly grey light that filtered round the edges of the window blinds. I sat up, and for a time I could not think where this ample apartment, with its counters, its piles of rolled stuff, its heap of quilts and cushions, its iron pillars, might be. Then, as recollection came back to me, I heard voices in conversation.

"Then far down the place, in the brighter light of some department which had already raised its blinds, I saw two men approaching. I scrambled to my feet, looking about me for some way of escape, and even as I did so the sound of my movement made them aware of me. I suppose they saw merely a figure moving quietly and quickly away. 'Who's that?' cried one, and 'Stop there!' shouted the other. I dashed around a corner and came full tilt—a faceless figure, mind you!—on a lanky lad of fifteen. He yelled and I bowled him over, rushed past him, turned another corner, and by a happy inspiration threw myself flat behind a counter. In another moment feet went running past and I heard voices shouting, 'All hands to the doors!' asking what was 'up,' and giving one another advice how to catch me.

"Lying on the ground, I felt scared out of my wits. But—odd as it may seem—it did not occur to me at the moment to take off my clothes as I should have done. I had made up my mind, I suppose, to get away in them, and that ruled me. And then down the vista of the counters came a bawling of 'Here he is!'

"I sprang to my feet, whipped a chair off the counter, and sent it whirling at the fool who had shouted, turned, came into another round a corner, sent him spinning, and rushed up the stairs. He kept his footing, gave a view hallo! and came up the staircase hot after me. Up the staircase were piled a multitude of those bright-coloured pot things—what are they?"

"Art pots," suggested Kemp.

"That's it! Art pots. Well, I turned at the top step and swung round, plucked one out of a pile and smashed it on his silly head as he came at me. The whole pile of pots went headlong, and I heard shouting and footsteps running from all parts. I made a mad rush for the refreshment place, and there was a man in white like a man cook, who took up the chase. I made one last desperate turn and found myself among lamps and ironmongery. I went behind the counter of this, and waited for my cook, and as he bolted in at the head of the chase, I doubled him up with a lamp. Down he went, and I crouched down behind the counter and began whipping off my clothes as fast as I could. Coat, jacket, trousers, shoes were all right, but a lambswool vest fits a man like a skin. I heard more men coming, my cook was lying quiet on the other side of the counter, stunned or scared speechless, and I had to make another dash for it, like a rabbit hunted out of a wood-pile.

" 'This way, policeman!' I heard someone shouting. I found myself in my bedstead storeroom again, and at the end of a wilderness of wardrobes. I rushed among them, went flat, got rid of my vest after infinite wriggling, and stood a free man again, panting and scared, as the policeman and three of the shopmen came round the corner. They made a rush for the vest and pants, and collared the trousers. 'He's dropping his plunder,' said one of the young men. 'He *must* be somewhere here.'

"But they did not find me all the same.

"I stood watching them hunt for me for a time, and cursing my ill-luck in losing the clothes. Then I went into the refreshment-room, drank a little milk I found there, and sat down by the fire to consider my position.

"In a little while two assistants came in and began to talk over the business very excitedly and like the fools they were. I heard a magnified account of my depredations, and other speculations as to my whereabouts. Then I fell to scheming again. The insurmountable difficulty of the place, especially now it was alarmed, was to get any plunder out of it. I went down into the warehouse to see if there was any chance of packing and addressing a parcel, but I could not understand the system of checking. About eleven o'clock, the snow having thawed as it fell, and the day being finer and a little warmer than the previous one, I decided that the Emporium was hopeless, and went out again, exasperated at my want of success, with only the vaguest plans of action in my mind."

## XXIII. IN DRURY LANE

"But you begin now to realise," said the Invisible Man, "the full disadvantage of my condition. I had no shelter, no covering,—to get clothing, was to forego all my advantage, to make of myself a strange and terrible thing. I was fasting; for to eat, to fill myself with unassimilated matter, would be to become grotesquely visible again."

"I never thought of that," said Kemp.

"Nor had I. And the snow had warned me of other dangers. I could not go abroad in snow—it would settle on me and expose me. Rain, too, would make me a watery outline, a glistening surface of a man—a bubble. And fog—I should be like a fainter bubble in a fog, a surface, a greasy glimmer of humanity. Moreover, as I went abroad—in the London air—I gathered dirt about my ankles, floating smuts and dust upon my skin. I did not know how long it would be before I should become visible from that cause also. But I saw clearly it could not be for long.

"Not in London at any rate.

"I went into the slums towards Great Portland Street, and found myself at the end of the street in which I had lodged. I did not go that way, because of the crowd halfway down it opposite to the still smoking ruins of the house I had fired. My most immediate problem was to get clothing. What to do with my face puzzled me. Then I saw in one of those little miscellaneous shops—news, sweets, toys, stationery, belated Christmas tomfoolery, and so forth—an array of masks and noses. I realised that problem was solved. In a flash I saw my course. I turned about, no longer aimless, and went—circuitously in order to avoid the busy ways, towards the back streets north of the Strand; for I remembered, though not very distinctly where, that some theatrical costumiers had shops in that district.

"The day was cold, with a nipping wind down the northward running streets. I walked fast to avoid being overtaken. Every crossing was a danger, every passenger a thing to watch alertly. One man as I was about to pass him at the top of Bedford Street, turned upon me abruptly and came into me, sending me into the road and almost under the wheel of a passing hansom. The verdict of the cab-rank was that he had had some sort of stroke. I was so unnerved by this encounter that I went into Covent Garden Market and sat down for some time in a quiet corner by a stall of violets, panting and trembling. I found I had caught a fresh cold, and had to turn out after a time lest my sneezes should attract attention.

"At last I reached the object of my quest, a dirty, fly-blown little shop in a byway near Drury Lane, with a window full of tinsel robes, sham jewels, wigs, slippers, dominoes and theatrical photographs. The shop was old-fashioned and low and dark, and the house rose above it for four storeys, dark and dismal. I peered through the window and, seeing no one within, entered. The opening of the door set a clanking bell ringing. I left it open, and walked round a bare costume stand, into a corner behind a cheval glass. For a minute or so no one came. Then I heard heavy feet striding across a room, and a man appeared down the shop.

"My plans were now perfectly definite. I proposed to make my way into the house, secrete myself upstairs, watch my opportunity, and when everything was quiet, rummage out a wig, mask, spectacles, and costume, and go into the world, perhaps a grotesque but still a credible figure. And incidentally of course I could rob the house of any available money.

"The man who had entered the shop was a short, slight, hunched, beetle-browed man, with long arms and very short bandy legs. Apparently I had interrupted a meal. He stared about the shop with an expression of expectation. This gave way to surprise, and then to anger, as he saw the shop empty. 'Damn the boys!' he said. He went to stare up and down the street. He came in again in a minute, kicked the door to with his foot spitefully, and went muttering back to the house door.

"I came forward to follow him, and at the noise of my movement he stopped dead. I did so too, startled by his quickness of ear. He slammed the house door in my face.

"I stood hesitating. Suddenly I heard his quick footsteps returning, and the door reopened. He stood looking about the shop like one who was still not satisfied. Then, murmuring to himself, he examined the back of the counter and peered behind some fixtures. Then he stood doubtful. He had left the house door open and I slipped into the inner room.

"It was a queer little room, poorly furnished and with a number of big masks in the corner. On the table was his belated breakfast, and it was a confoundedly exasperating thing for me, Kemp, to have to sniff his coffee and stand watching while he came in and resumed his meal. And his table manners were irritating. Three doors opened into the little room, one going upstairs and one down, but they were all shut. I could not get out of the room while he was there, I could scarcely move because of his alertness, and there was a draught down my back. Twice I strangled a sneeze just in time.

"The spectacular quality of my sensations was curious and novel, but for all that I was heartily tired and angry long before he had done his eating. But at last he made an end and putting his beggarly crockery on the black tin tray upon which he had had his teapot, and gathering all the crumbs up on the mustard stained cloth, he took the whole lot of things after him. His burden prevented his shutting the door behind him,—as he would have done; I never saw such a man for shutting doors,— and I followed him into a very dirty underground kitchen and scullery. I had the pleasure of seeing him begin to wash up, and then, finding no good in keeping down there, and the brick floor being cold to my feet, I returned upstairs and sat in his chair by the fire. It was burning low, and scarcely thinking, I put on a little coal. The noise of this brought him up at once, and he stood aglare. He peered about the room and was within an ace of touching me. Even after that examination, he scarcely seemed satisfied. He stopped in the doorway and took a final inspection before he went down.

"I waited in the little parlour for an age, and at last he came up and opened the upstairs door. I just managed to get by him.

"On the staircase he stopped suddenly, so that I very nearly blundered into him. He stood looking back right into my face and listening. 'I could have sworn,' he said. His long hairy hand pulled at his lower lip. His eye went up and down the staircase. Then he grunted and went on up again.

"His hand was on the handle of a door, and then he stopped again with the same puzzled anger on his face. He was becoming aware of the faint sounds of my movements about him. The man must have had diabolically acute hearing. He suddenly flashed into rage. 'If there's anyone in this house,' he cried with an oath, and left the threat unfinished. He put his hand in his pocket, failed to find what he wanted, and rushing past me went blundering noisily and pugnaciously downstairs. But I did not follow him. I sat on the head of the staircase until his return.

"Presently he came up again, still muttering. He opened the door of the room, and before I could enter, slammed it in my face.

"I resolved to explore the house, and spent some time in doing so as noiselessly as possible. The house was very old and tumble-down, damp so that the paper in the attics was peeling from the walls, and rat infested. Some of the door handles were stiff and I was afraid to turn them. Several rooms I did inspect were unfurnished, and others were littered with theatrical lumber, bought second-hand, I judged, from its appearance. In one room next to his I found a lot of old clothes. I began routing among these, and in my eagerness forgot again the evident sharpness of his ears. I heard a stealthy footstep and, looking up just in time, saw him peering in at the tumbled heap and holding an old-fashioned revolver in his hand. I stood perfectly still while he stared about open-mouthed and suspicious. 'It must have been her,' he said slowly. 'Damn her!'

"He shut the door quietly, and immediately I heard the key turn in the lock. Then his footsteps retreated. I realised abruptly that I was locked in. For a minute I did not know what to do. I walked from door to window and back, and stood perplexed. A gust of anger came upon me. But I decided to inspect the clothes before I did anything further, and my first attempt brought down a pile from an upper shelf. This brought him back, more sinister than ever. That time he actually touched me, jumped back with amazement and stood astonished in the middle of the room.

"Presently he calmed a little. 'Rats,' he said in an undertone, fingers on lips. He was evidently a little scared. I edged quietly out of the room, but a plank creaked. Then the infernal little brute started going all over the house, revolver in hand and locking door after door and pocketing the keys. When I realized what he was up to I had a fit of rage—I could hardly control myself sufficiently to watch my opportunity. By this time I knew he was alone in the house, and so I made no more ado, but knocked him on the head."

"Knocked him on the head!" exclaimed Kemp.

"Yes—stunned him—as he was going downstairs. Hit him from behind with a stool that stood on the landing. He went downstairs like a bag of old boots."

"But—! I say! The common conventions of humanity—"

"Are all very well for common people. But the point was, Kemp, that I had to get out of that house in a disguise without his seeing me. I couldn't think of any other way of doing it. And then I gagged him with a Louis Quatorze vest and tied him up in a sheet."

"Tied him up in a sheet!"

"Made a sort of bag of it. It was rather a good idea to keep the idiot scared and quiet, and a devilish hard thing to get out of—head away from the string. My dear Kemp, it's no good your sitting glaring as though I was a murderer. It had to be done. He had his revolver. If once he saw me he would be able to describe me—"

"But still," said Kemp, "in England—to-day. And the man was in his own house, and you were—well, robbing."

"Robbing! Confound it! You'll call me a thief next! Surely, Kemp, you're not fool enough to dance on the old strings. Can't you see my position?"

"And his too," said Kemp.

The Invisible Man stood up sharply. "What do you mean to say?"

Kemp's face grew a trifle hard. He was about to speak and checked himself. "I suppose, after all," he said with a sudden change of manner, "the thing had to be done. You were in a fix. But still—"

"Of course I was in a fix—an infernal fix. And he made me wild too—hunting me about the house, fooling about with his revolver, locking and unlocking doors. He was simply exasperating. You don't blame me, do you? You don't blame me?"

"I never blame anyone," said Kemp. "It's quite out of fashion. What did you do next?"

"I was hungry. Downstairs I found a loaf and some rank cheese—more than sufficient to satisfy my hunger. I took some brandy and water, and then went up past my impromptu bag—he was lying quite still—to the room containing the old clothes. This looked out upon the street, two lace curtains brown with dirt guarding the window. I went and peered out through their interstices. Outside the day was bright—by contrast with the brown shadows of the dismal house in which I found myself, dazzlingly bright. A brisk traffic was going by, fruit carts, a hansom, a four-wheeler with a pile of boxes, a fishmonger's cart. I turned with spots of colour swimming before my eyes to the shadowy fixtures behind me. My excitement was giving place to a clear apprehension of my position again. The room was full of a faint scent of benzoline, used, I suppose, in cleaning the garments.

"I began a systematic search of the place. I should judge the hunchback had been alone in the house for some time. He was a curious person. Everything that could possibly be of service to me I collected in the clothes storeroom, and then I made a deliberate selection. I found a handbag I thought a suitable possession, and some powder, rouge, and sticking-plaster.

"I had thought of painting and powdering my face and all that there was to show of me, in order to render myself visible, but the disadvantage of this lay in the fact that I should require turpentine and other appliances and a considerable amount of time before I could vanish again. Finally I chose a mask of the better type, slightly grotesque but not more so than many human beings, dark glasses, greyish whiskers, and a wig. I could find no underclothing, but that I could buy subsequently, and for the time I swathed myself in calico dominoes and some white cashmere scarfs. I could find no socks, but the hunchback's boots were rather a loose fit and sufficed. In a desk in the shop were three sovereigns and about thirty shillings' worth of silver, and in a locked cupboard I burst in the inner room were eight pounds in gold. I could go forth into the world again, equipped.

"Then came a curious hesitation. Was my appearance really—credible? I tried myself with a little bedroom looking-glass, inspecting myself from every point of view to discover any forgotten chink, but it all seemed sound. I was grotesque to the theatrical pitch, a stage miser, but I was certainly not a physical impossibility. Gathering confidence, I took my looking-glass down into the shop, pulled down the shop blinds, and surveyed myself from every point of view with the help of the cheval glass in the corner.

"I spent some minutes screwing up my courage and then unlocked the shop door and marched out into the street, leaving the little man to get out of his sheet again when he liked. In five minutes a dozen turnings intervened between me and the costumier's shop. No one appeared to notice me very pointedly. My last difficulty seemed overcome."

He stopped again.

"And you troubled no more about the hunchback?" said Kemp.

"No," said the Invisible Man. "Nor have I heard what became of him. I suppose he untied himself or kicked himself out. The knots were pretty tight."

He became silent and went to the window and stared out.

"What happened when you went out into the Strand?"

"Oh!—disillusionment again. I thought my troubles were over. Practically I thought I had impunity to do whatever I chose, everything—save to give away my secret. So I thought. Whatever I did, whatever the consequences might be, was nothing to me. I had merely to fling aside my garments and vanish. No person could hold me. I could take my money where I found it. I decided to treat myself to a sumptuous feast, and then put up at a good hotel, and accumulate a new outfit of property. I felt amazingly confident,—it's not particularly pleasant recalling that I was an ass. I went into a place and was already ordering a lunch, when it occurred to me that I could not eat unless I exposed my invisible face. I finished ordering the lunch, told the man I should be back in ten minutes, and went out exasperated. I don't know if you have ever been disappointed in your appetite."

"Not quite so badly," said Kemp, "but I can imagine it."

"I could have smashed the silly devils. At last, faint with the desire for tasteful food, I went into another place and demanded a private room. 'I am disfigured,' I said. 'Badly.' They looked at me curiously, but of course it was not their affair—and so at last I got my lunch. It was not particularly well served, but it sufficed; and when I had had it, I sat over a cigar, trying to plan my line of action. And outside a snowstorm was beginning.

"The more I thought it over, Kemp, the more I realised what a helpless absurdity an Invisible Man was,—in a cold and dirty climate and a crowded civilised city. Before I made this mad experiment I had dreamt of a thousand advantages. That afternoon it seemed all disappointment. I went over the heads of the things a man reckons desirable. No doubt invisibility made it possible to get them, but it made it impossible to enjoy them when they are got. Ambition—what is the good of pride of place when you cannot appear there? What is the good of the love of woman when her name must needs be Delilah? I have no taste for politics, for the blackguardisms of fame, for philanthropy, for sport. What was I to do? And for this I had become a wrapped-up mystery, a swathed and bandaged caricature of a man!"

He paused, and his attitude suggested a roving glance at the window.

"But how did you get to Iping?" said Kemp, anxious to keep his guest busy talking.

"I went there to work. I had one hope. It was a half idea! I have it still. It is a full blown idea now. A way of getting back! Of restoring what I have done. When I choose. When I have done all I mean to do invisibly. And that is what I chiefly want to talk to you about now."

"You went straight to Iping?"

"Yes. I had simply to get my three volumes of memoranda and my cheque-book, my luggage and underclothing, order a quantity of chemicals to work out this idea of mine,—I will show you the calculations as soon as I get my books,—and then I started. Jove! I remember the snowstorm now, and the accursed bother it was to keep the snow from damping my pasteboard nose."

"At the end," said Kemp, "the day before yesterday, when they found you out, you rather—to judge by the papers—"

"I did. Rather. Did I kill that fool of a constable?"

"No," said Kemp. "He's expected to recover."

"That's his luck, then. I clean lost my temper, the fools! Why couldn't they leave me alone? And that grocer lout?"

"There are no deaths expected," said Kemp.

"I don't know about that tramp of mine," said the Invisible Man, with an unpleasant laugh.

"By Heaven, Kemp, you don't know what rage *is!* To have worked for years, to have planned and plotted, and then to get some fumbling purblind idiot messing across your course! Every conceivable sort of silly creature that has ever been created has been sent to cross me.

"If I have much more of it, I shall go wild,—I shall start mowing 'em.

"As it is, they've made things a thousand times more difficult."

"No doubt it's exasperating," said Kemp, drily.

# XXIV. THE PLAN THAT FAILED

"But now," said Kemp, with a side glance out of the window, "what are we to do?"

He moved nearer his guest as he spoke in such a manner as to prevent the possibility of a sudden glimpse of the three men who were advancing up the hill road—with an intolerable slowness, as it seemed to Kemp.

"What were you planning to do when you were heading for Port Burdock? *Had* you any plan?"

"I was going to clear out of the country. But I have altered that plan rather since seeing you. I thought it would be wise, now the weather is hot and invisibility possible, to make for the South. Especially as my secret was known, and everyone would be on the lookout for a masked and muffled man. You have a line of steamers from here to France. My idea was to get aboard one and run the risks of the passage. Thence I could go by train into Spain, or else get to Algiers. It would not be difficult. There a man might always be invisible—and yet live. And do things. I was using that tramp as a money box and luggage carrier, until I decided how to get my books and things sent over to meet me."

"That's clear."

"And then the filthy brute must needs try and rob me! He has hidden my books, Kemp. Hidden my books! If I can lay my hands on him!"

"Best plan to get the books out of him first."

"But where is he? Do you know?"

"He's in the town police station, locked up, by his own request, in the strongest cell in the place."

"Cur!" said the Invisible Man.

"But that hangs up your plans a little."

"We must get those books; those books are vital."

"Certainly," said Kemp, a little nervously, wondering if he heard footsteps outside. "Certainly we must get those books. But that won't be difficult, if he doesn't know they're for you."

"No," said the Invisible Man, and thought.

Kemp tried to think of something to keep the talk going, but the Invisible Man resumed of his own accord.

"Blundering into your house, Kemp," he said, "changes all my plans. For you are a man that can understand. In spite of all that has happened, in spite of this publicity, of the loss of my books, of what I have suffered, there still remain great possibilities, huge possibilities—"

"You have told no one I am here?" he asked abruptly.

Kemp hesitated. "That was implied," he said.

"No one?" insisted Griffin.

"Not a soul."

"Ah! Now—" The Invisible Man stood up, and sticking his arms akimbo began to pace the study.

"I made a mistake, Kemp, a huge mistake, in carrying this thing through alone. I have wasted strength, time, opportunities. Alone—it is wonderful how little a man can do alone! To rob a little, to hurt a little, and there is the end.

"What I want, Kemp, is a goal-keeper, a helper, and a hiding-place, an arrangement whereby I can sleep and eat and rest in peace, and unsuspected. I must have a confederate. With a confederate, with food and rest—a thousand things are possible.

"Hitherto I have gone on vague lines. We have to consider all that invisibility means, all that it does not mean. It means little advantage for eavesdropping and so forth—one makes sounds. It's of little help, a little help perhaps—in housebreaking and so forth. Once you've caught me you could easily imprison me. But on the other hand I am hard to catch. This invisibility, in fact, is only good in two cases: It's useful in getting away, it's useful in approaching. It's particularly useful, therefore, in killing. I can walk round a man, whatever weapon he has, choose my point, strike as I like. Dodge as I like. Escape as I like."

Kemp's hand went to his moustache. "Was that a movement downstairs?

"And it is killing we must do, Kemp."

"It is killing we must do," repeated Kemp. "I'm listening to your plan, Griffin, but I'm not agreeing, mind. *Why* killing?"

"Not wanton killing, but a judicious slaying. The point is, they know there is an Invisible Man—as well as we know there is an Invisible Man. And that Invisible Man, Kemp, must now establish a Reign of Terror. Yes—no doubt it's startling. But I mean it. A Reign of Terror. He must take some town like your Burdock and terrify and dominate it. He must issue his orders. He can do that in a thousand ways—scraps of paper thrust under doors would suffice. And all who disobey his orders he must kill, and kill all who would defend them."

"Humph!" said Kemp, no longer listening to Griffin but to the sound of his front door opening and closing.

"It seems to me, Griffin," he said, to cover his wandering attention, "that your confederate would be in a difficult position."

"No one would know he was a confederate," said the Invisible Man, eagerly. And then suddenly, "*Hush!* What's that downstairs?"

"Nothing," said Kemp, and suddenly began to speak loud and fast. "I don't agree to this, Griffin," he said. "Understand me, I don't agree to this. Why dream of playing a game against the race? How can you hope to gain happiness? Don't be a lone wolf. Publish your results; take the world—take the nation at least—into your confidence. Think what you might do with a million helpers—"

The Invisible Man interrupted Kemp—arms extended. "There are footsteps coming upstairs," he said in a low voice.

"Nonsense," said Kemp.

"Let me see," said the Invisible Man, and advanced, arm extended, to the door.

And then things happened very swiftly. Kemp hesitated for a second and then moved to intercept him. The Invisible Man started and stood still. "Traitor!" cried the Voice, and suddenly the dressing-gown opened, and sitting down the Unseen began to disrobe. Kemp made three swift steps to the door, and forthwith the Invisible Man—his legs had vanished—sprang to his feet with a shout. Kemp flung the door open.

As it opened, there came a sound of hurrying feet downstairs and voices.

With a quick movement Kemp thrust the Invisible Man back, sprang aside, and slammed the door. The key was outside and ready. In another moment Griffin would have been alone in the belvedere study, a prisoner. Save for one little thing. The key had been slipped in hastily that morning. As Kemp slammed the door it fell noisily upon the carpet.

Kemp's face became white. He tried to grip the door handle with both hands. For a moment he stood lugging. Then the door gave six inches. But he got it closed again. The second time it was jerked a foot wide, and the dressing-gown came wedging itself into the opening. His throat was gripped by invisible fingers, and he left his hold on the handle to defend himself. He was forced back, tripped and pitched heavily into the corner of the landing. The empty dressing-gown was flung on the top of him.

Halfway up the staircase was Colonel Adye, the recipient of Kemp's letter, the chief of the Burdock police. He was staring aghast at the sudden appearance of Kemp, followed by the extraordinary sight of clothing tossing empty in the air. He saw Kemp felled, and struggling to his feet. He saw him rush forward, and go down again, felled like an ox.

Then suddenly he was struck violently. By nothing! A vast weight, it seemed, leapt upon him, and he was hurled headlong down the staircase, with the grip at his throat and a knee in his groin. An invisible foot trod on his back, a ghostly patter passed downstairs, he heard the two police officers in the hall shout and run, and the front door of the house slammed violently.

He rolled over and sat up staring. He saw, staggering down the staircase, Kemp, dusty and dishevelled, one side of his face white from a blow, his lip bleeding, and a pink dressing-gown and some underclothing held in his arms.

"My God!" cried Kemp, "the game's up! He's gone!"

## XXV. THE HUNTING OF THE INVISIBLE MAN

For a space Kemp was too inarticulate to make Adye understand the swift things that had just happened. They stood on the landing, Kemp speaking swiftly, the grotesque swathings of Griffin still on his arm. But presently Adye began to grasp something of the situation.

"He is mad," said Kemp; "inhuman. He is pure selfishness. He thinks of nothing but his own advantage, his own safety. I have listened to such a story this morning of brutal self-seeking! He has wounded men. He will kill them unless we can prevent him. He will create a panic. Nothing can stop him. He is going out now—furious!"

"He must be caught," said Adye. "That is certain."

"But how?" cried Kemp, and suddenly became full of ideas. "You must begin at once. You must set every available man to work. You must prevent his leaving this district. Once he gets away, he may go through the countryside as he wills, killing and maiming. He dreams of a reign of terror! A reign of terror, I tell you. You must set a watch on trains and roads and shipping. The garrison must help. You must wire for help. The only thing that may keep him here is the thought of recovering some books of notes he counts of value. I will tell you of that! There is a man in your police station,—Marvel."

"I know," said Adye, "I know. Those books—yes."

"And you must prevent him from eating or sleeping; day and night the country must be astir for him. Food must be locked up and secured, all food, so that he will have to break his way to it. The houses everywhere must be barred against him. Heaven send us cold nights and rain! The whole country-side must begin hunting and keep hunting. I tell you, Adye, he is a danger, a disaster; unless he is pinned and secured, it is frightful to think of the things that may happen."

"What else can we do?" said Adye. "I must go down at once and begin organising. But why not come? Yes—you come too! Come, and we must hold a sort of council of war,—get Hopps to help—and the railway managers. By Jove! it's urgent. Come along—tell me as we go. What else is there we can do? Put that stuff down."

In another moment Adye was leading the way downstairs. They found the front door open and the policemen standing outside staring at empty air. "He's got away, sir," said one.

"We must go to the central station at once," said Adye. "One of you go on down and get a cab to come up and meet us—quickly. And now, Kemp, what else?"

"Dogs," said Kemp. "Get dogs. They don't see him, but they wind him. Get dogs."

"Good," said Adye. "It's not generally known, but the prison officials over at Halstead know a man with bloodhounds. Dogs. What else?"

"Bear in mind," said Kemp, "his food shows. After eating, his food shows until it is assimilated. So that he has to hide after eating. You must keep on beating,—every thicket, every quiet corner. And put all weapons, all implements that might be weapons, away. He can't carry such things for long. And what he can snatch up and strike men with must be hidden away."

"Good again," said Adye. "We shall have him yet!"

"And on the roads," said Kemp, and hesitated.

"Yes?" said Adye.

"Powdered glass," said Kemp. "It's cruel, I know. But think of what he may do!"

Adye drew the air in sharply between his teeth. "It's unsportsmanlike. I don't know. But I'll have powdered glass got ready. If he goes too far—"

"The man's become inhuman, I tell you," said Kemp. "I am as sure he will establish a reign of terror—so soon as he has got over the emotions of this escape—as I am sure I am talking to you. Our only chance is to be ahead. He has cut himself off from his kind. His blood be upon his own head."

## XXVI. THE WICKSTEED MURDER

The Invisible Man seems to have rushed out of Kemp's house in a state of blind fury. A little child playing near Kemp's gateway was violently caught up and thrown aside, so that its ankle was broken, and thereafter for some hours the Invisible Man passed out of human perceptions. No one knows where he went nor what he did. But one can imagine him hurrying through the hot June forenoon, up the hill and on to the open downland behind Port Burdock, raging and despairing at his intolerable fate, and sheltering at last, heated and weary, amid the thickets of Hintondean, to piece together again his shattered schemes against his species. That seems the most probable refuge for him, for there it was he re-asserted himself in a grimly tragical manner about two in the afternoon.

One wonders what his state of mind may have been during that time, and what plans he devised. No doubt he was almost ecstatically exasperated by Kemp's treachery, and though we may be able to understand the motives that led to that deceit, we may still imagine and even sympathise a little with the fury the attempted surprise must have occasioned. Perhaps something of the stunned astonishment of his Oxford Street experiences may have returned to him, for he had evidently counted on Kemp's co-operation in his brutal dream of a terrorised world. At any rate he vanished from human ken about midday, and no living witness can tell what he did until about half-past two. It was a fortunate thing, perhaps, for humanity, but for him it was a fatal inaction.

During that time a growing multitude of men scattered over the countryside were busy. In the morning he had still been simply a legend, a terror; in the afternoon, by virtue chiefly of Kemp's drily worded proclamation, he was presented as a tangible antagonist, to be wounded, captured, or overcome, and the countryside began organising itself with inconceivable rapidity. By two o'clock even he might still have removed himself out of the district by getting aboard a train, but after two that became impossible. Every passenger train along the lines on a great parallelogram between Southhampton, Manchester, Brighton, and Horshman, travelled with locked doors, and the goods traffic was almost entirely suspended. And in a great circle of twenty miles round Port Burdock, men armed with guns and bludgeons were presently setting out in groups of three and four, with dogs, to beat the roads and fields.

Mounted policemen rode along the country lanes, stopping at every cottage and warning the people to lock up their houses, and keep indoors unless they were armed, and all the elementary schools had broken up by three o'clock, and the children, scared and keeping together in groups, were hurrying home. Kemp's proclamation—signed indeed by Adye—was posted over almost the whole district by four or five o'clock in the afternoon. It gave briefly but clearly all the conditions of the struggle, the necessity of keeping the Invisible Man from food and sleep, the necessity for incessant watchfulness and for a prompt attention to any evidence of his movements. And so swift and decided was the action of the authorities, so prompt and universal was the belief in this strange being, that before nightfall an area of several hundred square miles was in a stringent state of siege. And before nightfall, too, a thrill of horror went through the whole watching nervous countryside. Going from whispering mouth to mouth, swift and certain over the length and breadth of the county, passed the story of the murder of Mr. Wicksteed.

If our supposition that the Invisible Man's refuge was the Hintondean thickets, then we must suppose that in the early afternoon he sallied out again bent upon some project that involved the use of a weapon. We cannot know what the project was, but the evidence that he had the iron rod in hand before he met Wicksteed is to me at least overwhelming.

Of course we can know nothing of the details of the encounter. It occurred on the edge of a gravel pit, not two hundred yards from Lord Burdock's Lodge gate. Everything points to a desperate struggle,—the trampled ground, the numerous wounds Mr. Wicksteed received, his splintered walking-stick; but why the attack was made—save in a murderous frenzy—it is impossible to imagine. Indeed the theory of madness is almost unavoidable. Mr. Wicksteed was a man of forty-five or forty-six, steward to Lord Burdock, of inoffensive habits and appearance, the very last person in the world to provoke such a terrible antagonist. Against him it would seem the Invisible Man used an iron rod dragged from a broken piece of fence. He stopped this quiet man, going quietly home to his midday meal, attacked him, beat down his feeble defences, broke his arm, felled him, and smashed his head to a jelly.

Of course he must have dragged this rod out of the fencing before he met his victim; he must have been carrying it ready in his hand. Only two details beyond what has already been stated seem to bear on the matter. One is the circumstance that the gravel pit was not in Mr. Wicksteed's direct path home, but nearly a couple of hundred yards out of his way. The other is the assertion of a little girl to the effect that, going to her afternoon school, she saw the murdered man "*trotting*" in a peculiar manner across a field towards the gravel pit. Her pantomime of his action suggests a man pursuing something on the ground before him and striking at it ever and again with his walking-stick. She was the last person to see him alive. He passed out of her sight to his death, the struggle being hidden from her only by a clump of beech trees and a slight depression in the ground.

Now this, to the present writer's mind at least, lifts the murder out of the realm of the absolutely wanton. We may imagine that Griffin had taken the rod as a weapon indeed, but without any deliberate intention of using it in murder. Wicksteed may then have come by and noticed this rod inexplicably moving through the air. Without any thought of the Invisible Man—for Port Burdock is ten miles away—he may have pursued it. It is quite conceivable that he may not even have heard of the Invisible Man. One can then imagine the Invisible Man making off—quietly in order to avoid discovering his presence in the neighbourhood, and Wicksteed, excited and curious, pursuing this unaccountably locomotive object,—finally striking at it.

No doubt the Invisible Man could easily have distanced his middle-aged pursuer under ordinary circumstances, but the position in which Wicksteed's body was found suggests that he had the ill luck to drive his quarry into a corner between a drift of stinging nettles and the gravel pit. To those who appreciate the extraordinary irascibility of the Invisible Man, the rest of the encounter will be easy to imagine.

But this is pure hypothesis. The only undeniable facts—for stories of children are often unreliable—are the discovery of Wicksteed's body, done to death, and of the blood-stained iron rod flung among the nettles. The abandonment of the rod by Griffin, suggests that in the emotional excitement of the affair, the purpose for which he took it—if he had a purpose—was abandoned. He was certainly an intensely egotistical and unfeeling man, but the sight of his victim, his first victim, bloody and pitiful at his feet, may have released some long pent fountain of remorse which for a time may have flooded whatever scheme of action he had contrived.

After the murder of Mr. Wicksteed, he would seem to have struck across the country towards the downland. There is a story of a voice heard about sunset by a couple of men in a field near Fern Bottom. It was wailing and laughing, sobbing and groaning, and ever and again it shouted. It must have been queer hearing. It drove up across the middle of a clover field and died away towards the hills.

That afternoon the Invisible Man must have learnt something of the rapid use Kemp had made of his confidences. He must have found houses locked and secured; he may have loitered about railway stations and prowled about inns, and no doubt he read the proclamations and realised something of the nature of the campaign against him. And as the evening advanced, the fields became dotted here and there with groups of three or four men, and noisy with the yelping of dogs. These men-hunters had particular instructions in the case of an encounter as to the way they should support one another. He avoided them all. We may understand something of his exasperation, and it could have been none the less because he himself had supplied the information that was being used so remorselessly against him. For that day at least he lost heart; for nearly twenty-four hours, save when he turned on Wicksteed, he was a hunted man. In the night, he must have eaten and slept; for in the morning he was himself again, active, powerful, angry, and malignant, prepared for his last great struggle against the world.

## XXVII. THE SIEGE OF KEMP'S HOUSE

Kemp read a strange missive, written in pencil on a greasy sheet of paper.

"You have been amazingly energetic and clever," this letter ran, "though what you stand to gain by it I cannot imagine. You are against me. For a whole day you have chased me; you have tried to rob me of a night's rest. But I have had food in spite of you, I have slept in spite of you, and the game is only beginning. The game is only beginning. There is nothing for it, but to start the Terror. This announces the first day of the Terror. Port Burdock is no longer under the Queen, tell your Colonel of Police, and the rest of them; it is under me—the Terror! This is day one of year one of the new epoch,—the Epoch of the Invisible Man. I am Invisible Man the First. To begin with the rule will be easy. The first day there will be one execution for the sake of example,—a man named Kemp. Death starts for him to-day. He may lock himself away, hide himself away, get guards about him, put on armour if he likes; Death, the unseen Death, is coming. Let him take precautions; it will impress my people. Death starts from the pillar box by midday. The letter will fall in as the postman comes along, then off! The game begins. Death starts. Help him not, my people, lest Death fall upon you also. To-day Kemp is to die."

When Kemp read this letter twice, "It's no hoax," he said. "That's his voice! And he means it."

He turned the folded sheet over and saw on the addressed side of it the postmark Hintondean, and the prosaic detail *"2d. to pay."*

He got up slowly, leaving his lunch unfinished,—the letter had come by the one o'clock post,—and went into his study. He rang for his housekeeper, and told her to go round the house at once, examine all the fastenings of the windows, and close all the shutters. He closed the shutters of his study himself. From a locked drawer in his bedroom he took a little revolver, examined it carefully, and put it into the pocket of his lounge jacket. He wrote a number of brief notes, one to Colonel Adye, gave them to his servant to take, with explicit instructions as to her way of leaving the house. "There is no danger," he said, and added a mental reservation, "to you." He remained meditative for a space after doing this, and then returned to his cooling lunch.

He ate with gaps of thought. Finally he struck the table sharply. "We will have him!" he said; "and I am the bait. He will come too far."

He went up to the belvedere, carefully shutting every door after him. "It's a game," he said, "an odd game—but the chances are all for me, Mr. Griffin, in spite of your invisibility. Griffin *contra mundum*—with a vengeance."

He stood at the window staring at the hot hillside. "He must get food every day—and I don't envy him. Did he really sleep last night? Out in the open somewhere—secure from collisions. I wish we could get some good cold wet weather instead of the heat.

"He may be watching me now."

He went close to the window. Something rapped smartly against the brickwork over the frame, and made him start violently back.

"I'm getting nervous," said Kemp. But it was five minutes before he went to the window again. "It must have been a sparrow," he said.

Presently he heard the front-door bell ringing, and hurried downstairs. He unbolted and unlocked the door, examined the chain, put it up, and opened cautiously without showing himself. A familiar voice hailed him. It was Adye.

"Your servant's been assaulted, Kemp," he said round the door.

"What!" exclaimed Kemp.

"Had that note of yours taken away from her. He's close about here. Let me in."

Kemp released the chain, and Adye entered through as narrow an opening as possible. He stood in the hall, looking with infinite relief at Kemp refastening the door. "Note was snatched out of her hand. Scared her horribly. She's down at the station. Hysterics. He's close here. What was it about?"

Kemp swore.

"What a fool I was," said Kemp. "I might have known. It's not an hour's walk from Hintondean. Already!"

"What's up?" said Adye.

"Look here!" said Kemp, and led the way into his study. He handed Adye the Invisible Man's letter. Adye read it and whistled softly. "And you—?" said Adye.

"Proposed a trap—like a fool," said Kemp, "and sent my proposal out by a maid servant. To him."

Adye followed Kemp's profanity.

"He'll clear out," said Adye.

"Not he," said Kemp.

A resounding smash of glass came from upstairs. Adye had a silvery glimpse of a little revolver half out of Kemp's pocket. "It's a window, upstairs!" said Kemp, and led the way up. There came a second smash while they were still on the staircase. When they reached the study they found two of the three windows smashed, half the room littered with splintered glass, and one big flint lying on the writing table. The two men stopped in the doorway, contemplating the wreckage. Kemp swore again, and as he did so the third window went with a snap like a pistol, hung starred for a moment, and collapsed in jagged, shivering triangles into the room.

"What's this for?" said Adye.

"It's a beginning," said Kemp.

"There's no way of climbing up here?"

"Not for a cat," said Kemp.

"No shutters?"

"Not here. All the downstairs rooms—Hullo!"

Smash, and then whack of boards hit hard came from downstairs. "Confound him!" said Kemp. "That must be—yes—it's one of the bedrooms. He's going to do all the house. But he's a fool. The shutters are up, and the glass will fall outside. He'll cut his feet."

Another window proclaimed its destruction. The two men stood on the landing perplexed. "I have it!" said Adye. "Let me have a stick or something, and I'll go down to the station and get the bloodhounds put on. That ought to settle him! They're hard by—not ten minutes—"

Another window went the way of its fellows.

"You haven't a revolver?" asked Adye.

Kemp's hand went to his pocket. Then he hesitated. "I haven't one —at least to spare."

"I'll bring it back," said Adye, "you'll be safe here."

Kemp, ashamed of his momentary lapse from truthfulness, handed him the weapon.

"Now for the door," said Adye.

As they stood hesitating in the hall, they heard one of the first-floor bedroom windows crack and clash. Kemp went to the door and began to slip the bolts as silently as possible. His face was a little paler than usual. "You must step straight out," said Kemp. In another moment Adye was on the doorstep and the bolts were dropping back into the staples. He hesitated for a moment, feeling more comfortable with his back against the door. Then he marched, upright and square, down the steps. He crossed the lawn and approached the gate. A little breeze seemed to ripple over the grass. Something moved near him. "Stop a bit," said a Voice, and Adye stopped dead and his hand tightened on the revolver.

"Well?" said Adye, white and grim, and every nerve tense.

"Oblige me by going back to the house," said the Voice, as tense and grim as Adye's.

"Sorry," said Adye a little hoarsely, and moistened his lips with his tongue. The Voice was on his left front, he thought. Suppose he were to take his luck with a shot?

"What are you going for?" said the Voice, and there was a quick movement of the two, and a flash of sunlight from the open lip of Adye's pocket.

Adye desisted and thought. "Where I go," he said slowly, "is my own business." The words were still on his lips, when an arm came round his neck, his back felt a knee, and he was sprawling backward. He drew clumsily and fired absurdly, and in another moment he was struck in the mouth and the revolver wrested from his grip. He made a vain clutch at a slippery limb, tried to struggle up and fell back. "Damn!" said Adye. The Voice laughed. "I'd kill you now if it wasn't the waste of a bullet," it said. He saw the revolver in mid-air, six feet off, covering him.

"Well?" said Adye, sitting up.

"Get up," said the Voice.

Adye stood up.

"Attention," said the Voice, and then fiercely, "Don't try any games.

Remember I can see your face if you can't see mine. You've got to go back to the house."

"He won't let me in," said Adye.

"That's a pity," said the Invisible Man. "I've got no quarrel with you."

Adye moistened his lips again. He glanced away from the barrel of the revolver and saw the sea far off very blue and dark under the midday sun, the smooth green down, the white cliff of the Head, and the multitudinous town, and suddenly he knew that life was very sweet. His eyes came back to this little metal thing hanging between heaven and earth, six yards away. "What am I to do?" he said sullenly.

"What am *I* to do?" asked the Invisible Man. "You will get help. The only thing is for you to go back."

"I will try. If he lets me in will you promise not to rush the door?"

"I've got no quarrel with you," said the Voice.

Kemp had hurried upstairs after letting Adye out, and now crouching among the broken glass and peering cautiously over the edge of the study window sill, he saw Adye stand parleying with the Unseen. "Why doesn't he fire?" whispered Kemp to himself. Then the revolver moved a little and the glint of the sunlight flashed in Kemp's eyes. He shaded his eyes and tried to see the source of the blinding beam.

"Surely!" he said, "Adye has given up the revolver."

"Promise not to rush the door," Adye was saying. "Don't push a winning game too far. Give a man a chance."

"You go back to the house. I tell you flatly I will not promise anything."

Adye's decision seemed suddenly made. He turned towards the house, walking slowly with his hands behind him. Kemp watched him —puzzled. The revolver vanished, flashed again into sight, vanished again, and became evident on a closer scrutiny as a little dark object following Adye. Then things happened very quickly. Adye leapt backwards, swung round, clutched at this little object, missed it, threw up his hands and fell forward on his face, leaving a little puff of blue in the air. Kemp did not hear the sound of the shot. Adye writhed, raised himself on one arm, fell forward, and lay still.

For a space Kemp remaining staring at the quiet carelessness of Adye's attitude. The afternoon was very hot and still, nothing seemed stirring in all the world save a couple of yellow butterflies chasing each other through the shrubbery between the house and the road gate. Adye lay on the lawn near the gate. The blinds of all the villas down the hill-road were drawn, but in one little green summer-house was a white figure, apparently an old man asleep. Kemp scrutinized the surroundings of the house for a glimpse of the revolver, but it had vanished. His eyes came back to Adye. The game was opening well.

Then came a ringing and knocking at the front door, that grew at last tumultuous, but pursuant to Kemp's instructions the servants had locked themselves into their rooms. This was followed by a silence. Kemp sat listening and then began peering cautiously out of the three windows, one after another. He went to the staircase head and stood listening uneasily. He armed himself with his bedroom poker, and went to examine the interior fastenings of the ground-floor windows again. Everything was safe and quiet. He returned to the belvedere. Adye lay motionless over the edge of the gravel just as he had fallen. Coming along the road by the villas were the housemaid and two policemen.

Everything was deadly still. The three people seemed very slow in approaching. He wondered what his antagonist was doing.

He started. There was a smash from below. He hesitated and went downstairs again. Suddenly the house resounded with heavy blows and the splintering of wood. He heard a smash and the destructive clang of the iron fastenings of the shutters. He turned the key and opened the kitchen door. As he did so, the shutters, split and splintering, came flying inward. He stood aghast. The window frame, save for one crossbar, was still intact, but only little teeth of glass remained in the frame. The shutters had been driven in with an axe, and now the axe was descending in sweeping blows upon the window frame and the iron bars defending it. Then suddenly it leapt aside and vanished. He saw the revolver lying on the path outside, and then the little weapon sprang into the air. He dodged back. The revolver cracked just too late, and a splinter from the edge of the closing door flashed over his head. He slammed and locked the door, and as he stood outside he heard Griffin shouting and laughing. Then the blows of the axe with its splitting and smashing consequences, were resumed.

Kemp stood in the passage trying to think. In a moment the Invisible Man would be in the kitchen. This door would not keep him a moment, and then—

A ringing came at the front door again. It would be the policemen. He ran into the hall, put up the chain, and drew the bolts. He made the girl speak before he dropped the chain, and the three people blundered into the house in a heap, and Kemp slammed the door again.

"The Invisible Man!" said Kemp. "He has a revolver, with two shots—left. He's killed Adye. Shot him anyhow. Didn't you see him on the lawn? He's lying there."

"Who?" said one of the policemen.

"Adye," said Kemp.

"We came in the back way," said the girl.

"What's that smashing?" asked one of the policemen.

"He's in the kitchen—or will be. He has found an axe—"

Suddenly the house was full of the Invisible Man's resounding blows on the kitchen door. The girl stared towards the kitchen, shuddered, and retreated into the dining-room. Kemp tried to explain in broken sentences. They heard the kitchen door give.

"This way," cried Kemp, starting into activity, and bundled the policemen into the dining-room doorway.

"Poker," said Kemp, and rushed to the fender. He handed the poker he had carried to the policeman and the dining-room one to the other. He suddenly flung himself backward.

"Whup!" said one policeman, ducked, and caught the axe on his poker. The pistol snapped its penultimate shot and ripped a valuable Sidney Cooper. The second policeman brought his poker down on the little weapon, as one might knock down a wasp, and sent it rattling to the floor.

At the first clash the girl screamed, stood screaming for a moment by the fireplace, and then ran to open the shutters—possibly with an idea of escaping by the shattered window.

The axe receded into the passage, and fell to a position about two feet from the ground. They could hear the Invisible Man breathing. "Stand away, you two," he said. "I want that man Kemp."

"We want you," said the first policeman, making a quick step forward and wiping with his poker at the Voice. The Invisible Man must have started back, and he blundered into the umbrella stand. Then, as the policeman staggered with the swing of the blow he had aimed, the Invisible Man countered with the axe, the helmet crumpled like paper, and the blow sent the man spinning to the floor at the head of the kitchen stairs. But the second policeman, aiming behind the axe with his poker, hit something soft that snapped. There was a sharp exclamation of pain and then the axe fell to the ground. The policeman wiped again at vacancy and hit nothing; he put his foot on the axe, and struck again. Then he stood, poker clubbed, listening intent for the slightest movement.

He heard the dining-room window open, and a quick rush of feet within. His companion rolled over and sat up, with the blood running down between his eye and ear. "Where is he?" asked the man on the floor.

"Don't know. I've hit him. He's standing somewhere in the hall. Unless he's slipped past you. Doctor Kemp—sir."

Pause.

"Doctor Kemp," cried the policeman again.

The second policeman began struggling to his feet. He stood up. Suddenly the faint pad of bare feet on the kitchen stairs could be heard. "Yap!" cried the first policeman, and incontinently flung his poker. It smashed a little gas bracket.

He made as if he would pursue the Invisible Man downstairs. Then he thought better of it and stepped into the dining-room.

"Doctor Kemp," he began, and stopped short—

"Doctor Kemp's in here," he said, as his companion looked over his shoulder.

The dining-room window was wide open, and neither housemaid nor Kemp was to be seen.

The second policeman's opinion of Kemp was terse and vivid.

## XXVIII. THE HUNTER HUNTED

Mr. Heelas, Mr. Kemp's nearest neighbour among the villa holders, was asleep in his summer house when the siege of Kemp's house began. Mr. Heelas was one of the sturdy minority who refused to believe "in all this nonsense" about an Invisible Man. His wife, however, as he was subsequently to be reminded, did. He insisted upon walking about his garden just as if nothing was the matter, and he went to sleep in the afternoon in accordance with the custom of years. He slept through the smashing of the windows, and then woke up suddenly with a curious persuasion of something wrong. He looked across at Kemp's house, rubbed his eyes and looked again. Then he put his feet to the ground, and sat listening. He said he was damned, and still the strange thing was visible. The house looked as though it had been deserted for weeks—after a violent riot. Every window was broken, and every window, save those of the belvedere study, was blinded by the internal shutters.

"I could have sworn it was all right"—he looked at his watch—"twenty minutes ago."

He became aware of a measured concussion and the clash of glass, far away in the distance. And then, as he sat open-mouthed, came a still more wonderful thing. The shutters of the drawing-room window were flung open violently, and the housemaid in her outdoor hat and garments, appeared struggling in a frantic manner to throw up the sash. Suddenly a man appeared beside her, helping her,—Dr.

Kemp! In another moment the window was open, and the housemaid was struggling out; she pitched forward and vanished among the shrubs. Mr. Heelas stood up, exclaiming vaguely and vehemently at all these wonderful things. He saw Kemp stand on the sill, spring from the window, and reappear almost instantaneously running along a path in the shrubbery and stooping as he ran, like a man who evades observation. He vanished behind a laburnum, and appeared again clambering a fence that abutted on the open down. In a second he had tumbled over and was running at a tremendous pace down the slope towards Mr. Heelas.

"Lord!" cried Mr. Heelas, struck with an idea; "it's that Invisible Man brute! It's right, after all!"

With Mr. Heelas to think things like that was to act, and his cook watching him from the top window was amazed to see him come pelting towards the house at a good nine miles an hour. "Thought he wasn't afraid," said the cook. "Mary, just come here!" There was a slamming of doors, a ringing of bells, and the voice of Mr. Heelas bellowing like a bull. "Shut the doors, shut the windows, shut everything! the Invisible Man is coming!" Instantly the house was full of screams and directions, and scurrying feet. He ran himself to shut the French windows that opened on the veranda; as he did so Kemp's head and shoulders and knee appeared over the edge of the garden fence. In another moment Kemp had ploughed through the asparagus, and was running across the tennis lawn to the house.

"You can't come in," said Mr. Heelas, shutting the bolts. "I'm very sorry if he's after you, but you can't come in!"

Kemp appeared with a face of terror close to the glass, rapping and then shaking frantically at the French window. Then, seeing his efforts were useless, he ran along the veranda, vaulted the end, and went to hammer at the side door. Then he ran round by the side gate to the front of the house, and so into the hill-road. And Mr. Heelas staring from his window—a face of horror—had scarcely witnessed Kemp vanish, ere the asparagus was being trampled this way and that by feet unseen. At that Mr. Heelas fled precipitately upstairs, and the rest of the chase is beyond his purview. But as he passed the staircase window, he heard the side gate slam.

Emerging into the hill-road, Kemp naturally took the downward direction, and so it was he came to run in his own person the very race he had watched with such a critical eye from the belvedere study only four days ago. He ran it well, for a man out of training, and though his face was white and wet, his wits were cool to the last. He ran with wide strides, and wherever a patch of rough ground intervened, wherever there came a patch of raw flints, or a bit of broken glass shone dazzling, he crossed it and left the bare invisible feet that followed to take what line they would.

For the first time in his life Kemp discovered that the hill-road was indescribably vast and desolate, and that the beginnings of the town far below at the hill foot were strangely remote. Never had there been a slower or more painful method of progression than running. All the gaunt villas, sleeping in the afternoon sun, looked locked and barred; no doubt they were locked and barred—by his own orders. But at any rate they might have kept a lookout for an eventuality like this! The town was rising up now, the sea had dropped out of sight behind it, and people down below were stirring. A tram was just arriving at the hill foot. Beyond that was the police station. Was that footsteps he heard behind him? Spurt.

The people below were staring at him, one or two were running, and his breath was beginning to saw in his throat. The tram was quite near now, and the Jolly Cricketers was noisily barring its doors. Beyond the tram were posts and heaps of gravel,—the drainage works. He had a transitory idea of jumping into the tram and slamming the doors, and then he resolved to go for the police station. In another moment he had passed the door of the Jolly Cricketers, and was in the blistering fag end of street, with human beings about him. The tram driver and his helper—arrested by the sight of his furious haste—stood staring with the tram horses unhitched. Further on the astonished features of navvies appeared above the mounds of gravel.

His pace broke a little, and then he heard the swift pad of his pursuer, and leapt forward again. "The Invisible Man!" he cried to the navvies, with a vague indicative gesture, and by an inspiration leapt the excavation and placed a burly group between him and the chase. Then abandoning the idea of the police station he turned into a little side street, rushed by a greengrocer's cart, hesitated for the tenth of a second at the door of a sweetstuff shop, and then made for the mouth of an alley that ran back into the main Hill Street again. Two or three little children were playing here, and shrieked and scattered at his apparition, and forthwith doors and windows opened and excited mothers revealed their hearts. Out he shot into Hill Street again, three hundred yards from the tram-line end, and immediately he became aware of a tumultuous vociferation and running people.

He glanced up the street towards the hill. Hardly a dozen yards off ran a huge navvy, cursing in fragments and slashing viciously with a spade, and hard behind him came the tram conductor with his fists clenched. Up the street others followed these two, striking and shouting. Down towards the town, men and women were running, and he noticed clearly one man coming out of a shop-door with a stick in his hand. "Spread out! Spread out!" cried some one. Kemp suddenly grasped the altered condition of the chase. He stopped, and looked round, panting. "He's close here!" he cried. "Form a line across—"

"Aha!" shouted a voice.

He was hit hard under the ear, and went reeling, trying to face round towards his unseen antagonist. He just managed to keep his feet, and he struck a vain counter in the air. Then he was hit again under the jaw, and sprawled headlong on the ground. In another moment a knee compressed his diaphragm, and a couple of eager hands gripped his throat, but the grip of one was weaker than the other; he grasped the wrists, heard a cry of pain from his assailant, and then the spade of the navvy came whirling through the air above him, and struck something with a dull thud. He felt a drop of moisture on his face. The grip at his throat suddenly relaxed, and with a convulsive effort, Kemp loosed himself, grasped a limp shoulder, and rolled uppermost. He gripped the unseen elbows near the ground. "I've got him!" screamed Kemp. "Help! Help hold! He's down! Hold his feet!"

In another second there was a simultaneous rush upon the struggle, and a stranger coming into the road suddenly might have thought an exceptionally savage game of Rugby football was in progress. And there was no shouting after Kemp's cry,—only a sound of blows and feet and a heavy breathing.

Then came a mighty effort, and the Invisible Man threw off a couple of his antagonists and rose to his knees. Kemp clung to him in front like a hound to a stag, and a dozen hands gripped, clutched, and tore at the Unseen. The tram conductor suddenly got the neck and shoulders and lugged him back.

Down went the heap of struggling men again and rolled over. There was, I am afraid, some savage kicking. Then suddenly a wild scream of "Mercy! Mercy!" that died down swiftly to a sound like choking.

"Get back, you fools!" cried the muffled voice of Kemp, and there was a vigorous shoving back of stalwart forms. "He's hurt, I tell you. Stand back!"

There was a brief struggle to clear a space, and then the circle of eager faces saw the doctor kneeling, as it seemed, fifteen inches in the air, and holding invisible arms to the ground. Behind him a constable gripped invisible ankles.

"Don't you leave go of en," cried the big navvy, holding a blood-stained spade; "he's shamming."

"He's not shamming," said the doctor, cautiously raising his knee; "and I'll hold him." His face was bruised and already going red; he spoke thickly because of a bleeding lip. He released one hand and seemed to be feeling at the face. "The mouth's all wet," he said. And then, "Good God!"

He stood up abruptly and then knelt down on the ground by the side of the thing unseen. There was a pushing and shuffling, a sound of heavy feet as fresh people turned up to increase the pressure of the crowd. People now were coming out of the houses. The doors of the Jolly Cricketers were suddenly wide open. Very little was said.

Kemp felt about, his hand seeming to pass through empty air. "He's not breathing," he said, and then, "I can't feel his heart. His side—ugh!"

Suddenly an old woman, peering under the arm of the big navvy, screamed sharply. "Looky there!" she said, and thrust out a wrinkled finger.

And looking where she pointed, everyone saw, faint and transparent as though it was made of glass, so that veins and arteries and bones and nerves could be distinguished, the outline of a hand, a hand limp and prone. It grew clouded and opaque even as they stared.

"Hullo!" cried the constable. "Here's his feet a-showing!"

And so, slowly, beginning at his hands and feet and creeping along his limbs to the vital centres of his body, that strange change continued. It was like the slow spreading of a poison. First came the little white nerves, a hazy grey sketch of a limb, then the glassy bones and intricate arteries, then the flesh and skin, first a faint fogginess, and then growing rapidly dense and opaque. Presently they could see his crushed chest and his shoulders, and the dim outline of his drawn and battered features.

When at last the crowd made way for Kemp to stand erect, there lay, naked and pitiful on the ground, the bruised and broken body of a young man about thirty. His hair and beard were white,—not grey with age, but white with the whiteness of albinism, and his eyes were like garnets. His hands were clenched, his eyes wide open, and his expression was one of anger and dismay.

"Cover his face!" said a man. "For Gawd's sake, cover that face!" and three little children, pushing forward through the crowd, were suddenly twisted round and sent packing off again.

Someone brought a sheet from the Jolly Cricketers, and having covered him, they carried him into that house.

# THE EPILOGUE

So ends the story of the strange and evil experiment of the Invisible Man. And if you would learn more of him you must go to a little inn near Port Stowe and talk to the landlord. The sign of the inn is an empty board save for a hat and boots, and the name is the title of this story. The landlord is a short and corpulent little man with a nose of cylindrical protrusion, wiry hair, and a sporadic rosiness of visage. Drink generously, and he will tell you generously of all the things that happened to him after that time, and of how the lawyers tried to do him out of the treasure found upon him.

"When they found they couldn't prove who's money was which, I'm blessed," he says, "if they didn't try to make me out a blooming treasure trove! Do I *look* like a Treasure Trove? And then a gentleman gave me a guinea a night to tell the story at the Empire Music'all—just to tell 'em in my own words—barring one."

And if you want to cut off the flow of his reminiscences abruptly, you can always do so by asking if there weren't three manuscript books in the story. He admits there were and proceeds to explain, with asseverations that everybody thinks *he* has 'em! But bless you! he hasn't. "The Invisible Man it was took 'em off to hide 'em when I cut and ran for Port Stowe. It's that Mr. Kemp put people on with the idea of *my* having 'em."

And then he subsides into a pensive state, watches you furtively, bustles nervously with glasses, and presently leaves the bar.

He is a bachelor man—his tastes were ever bachelor, and there are no women folk in the house. Outwardly he buttons—it is expected of him—but in his more vital privacies, in the matter of braces for example, he still turns to string. He conducts his house without enterprise, but with eminent decorum. His movements are slow, and he is a great thinker. But he has a reputation for wisdom and for a respectable parsimony in the village, and his knowledge of the roads of the South of England would beat Cobbett.

And on Sunday mornings, every Sunday morning, all the year round, while he is closed to the outer world, and every night after ten, he goes into his bar parlour, bearing a glass of gin faintly tinged with water, and having placed this down, he locks the door and examines the blinds, and even looks under the table. And then, being satisfied of his solitude, he unlocks the cupboard and a box in the cupboard and a drawer in that box, and produces three volumes bound in brown leather, and places them solemnly in the middle of the table. The covers are weather-worn and tinged with an algal green for once they sojourned in a ditch and some of the pages have been washed blank by dirty water. The landlord sits down in an armchair, fills a long clay pipe slowly—gloating over the books the while. Then he pulls one towards him and opens it, and begins to study it—turning over the leaves backwards and forwards.

His brows are knit and his lips move painfully. "Hex, little two up in the air, cross and a fiddle-de-dee. Lord! what a one he was for intellect!"

Presently he relaxes and leans back, and blinks through his smoke across the room at things invisible to other eyes. "Full of secrets," he says. "Wonderful secrets!

"Once I get the haul of them—*Lord!*

"I wouldn't do what *he* did; I'd just—well!" He pulls at his pipe.

So he lapses into a dream, the undying wonderful dream of his life. And though Kemp has fished unceasingly, and Adye has questioned closely, no human being save the landlord knows those books are there, with the subtle secret of invisibility and a dozen other strange secrets written therein. And none other will know of them until he dies.

# THE CRYSTAL EGG

There was, until a year ago, a little and very grimy-looking shop near Seven Dials, over which, in weather-worn yellow lettering, the name of "C. Cave, Naturalist and Dealer in Antiquities," was inscribed. The contents of its window were curiously variegated. They comprised some elephant tusks and an imperfect set of chessmen, beads and weapons, a box of eyes, two skulls of tigers and one human, several moth-eaten stuffed monkeys (one holding a lamp), an old-fashioned cabinet, a flyblown ostrich egg or so, some fishing-tackle, and an extraordinarily dirty, empty glass fishtank. There was also, at the moment the story begins, a mass of crystal, worked into the shape of an egg and brilliantly polished. And at that two people, who stood outside the window, were looking, one of them a tall, thin clergyman, the other a black-bearded young man of dusky complexion and unobtrusive costume. The dusky young man spoke with eager gesticulation, and seemed anxious for his companion to purchase the article.

While they were there, Mr. Cave came into his shop, his beard still wagging with the bread and butter of his tea. When he saw these men and the object of their regard, his countenance fell. He glanced guiltily over his shoulder, and softly shut the door. He was a little old man, with pale face and peculiar watery blue eyes; his hair was a dirty grey, and he wore a shabby blue frock-coat, an ancient silk hat, and carpet slippers very much down at heel. He remained watching the two men as they talked. The clergyman went deep into his trouser pocket, examined a handful of money, and showed his teeth in an agreeable smile. Mr. Cave seemed still more depressed when they came into the shop.

The clergyman, without any ceremony, asked the price of the crystal egg. Mr. Cave glanced nervously towards the door leading into the parlour, and said five pounds. The clergyman protested that the price was high, to his companion as well as to Mr. Cave—it was, indeed, very much more than Mr. Cave had intended to ask, when he had stocked the article—and an attempt at bargaining ensued. Mr. Cave stepped to the shop-door, and held it open. "Five pounds is my price," he said, as though he wished to save himself the trouble of unprofitable discussion. As he did so, the upper portion of a woman's face appeared above the blind in the glass upper panel of the door leading into the parlour, and stared curiously at the two customers. "Five pounds is my price," said Mr. Cave, with a quiver in his voice.

The swarthy young man had so far remained a spectator, watching Cave keenly. Now he spoke. "Give him five pounds," he said. The clergyman glanced at him to see if he were in earnest, and, when he looked at Mr. Cave again, he saw that the latter's face was white. "It's a lot of money," said the clergyman, and, diving into his pocket, began counting his resources. He had little more than thirty shillings, and he appealed to his companion, with whom he seemed to be on terms of considerable intimacy. This gave Mr. Cave an opportunity of collecting his thoughts, and he began to explain in an agitated manner that the crystal was not, as a matter of fact, entirely free for sale. His two customers were naturally surprised at this, and inquired why he had not thought of that before he began to bargain. Mr. Cave became confused, but he stuck to his story, that the crystal was not in the market that afternoon, that a probable purchaser of it had already appeared. The two, treating this as an attempt to raise the price still further, made as if they would leave the shop. But at this point the parlour door opened, and the owner of the dark fringe and the little eyes appeared.

She was a coarse-featured, corpulent woman, younger and very much larger than Mr. Cave; she walked heavily, and her face was flushed. "That crystal *is* for sale, she said. "And five pounds is a good enough price for it. I can't think what you're about, Cave, not to take the gentleman's offer!"

Mr. Cave, greatly perturbed by the irruption, looked angrily at her over the rims of his spectacles, and, without excessive assurance, asserted his right to manage his business in his own way. An altercation began. The two customers watched the scene with interest and some amusement, occasionally assisting Mrs. Cave with suggestions. Mr. Cave, hard driven, persisted in a confused and impossible story of an enquiry for the crystal that morning, and his agitation became painful. But he stuck to his point with extraordinary persistence. It was the young Oriental who ended this curious controversy. He proposed that they should call again in the course of two days—so as to give the alleged enquirer a fair chance. "And then we must insist," said the clergyman. "Five pounds." Mrs. Cave took it on herself to apologise for her husband, explaining that he was sometimes "a little odd," and as the two customers left, the couple prepared for a free discussion of the incident in all its bearings.

Mrs. Cave talked to her husband with singular directness. The poor little man, quivering with emotion, muddled himself between his stories, maintaining on the one hand that he had another customer in view, and on the other asserting that the crystal was honestly worth ten guineas. "Why did you ask five pounds?" said his wife. "*Do* let me manage my business my own way!" said Mr. Cave.

Mr. Cave had living with him a step-daughter and a step-son, and at supper that night the transaction was re-discussed. None of them had a high opinion of Mr. Cave's business methods, and this action seemed a culminating folly.

"It's my opinion he's refused that crystal before," said the step-son, a loose-limbed lout of eighteen.

"But *Five Pounds!*" said the step-daughter, an argumentative young woman of six-and-twenty.

Mr. Cave's answers were wretched; he could only mumble weak assertions that he knew his own business best. They drove him from his half-eaten supper into the shop, to close it for the night, his ears aflame and tears of vexation behind his spectacles. "Why had he left the crystal in the window so long? The folly of it!" That was the trouble closest in his mind. For a time he could see no way of evading sale.

After supper his step-daughter and step-son smartened themselves up and went out and his wife retired upstairs to reflect upon the business aspects of the crystal, over a little sugar and lemon and so forth in hot water. Mr. Cave went into the shop, and stayed there until late, ostensibly to make ornamental rockeries for gold-fish cases but really for a private purpose that will be better explained later. The next day Mrs. Cave found that the crystal had been removed from the window, and was lying behind some second-hand books on angling. She replaced it in a conspicuous position. But she did not argue further about it, as a nervous headache disinclined her from debate. Mr. Cave was always disinclined. The day passed disagreeably. Mr. Cave was, if anything, more absent-minded than usual, and uncommonly irritable withal. In the afternoon, when his wife was taking her customary sleep, he removed the crystal from the window again.

The next day Mr. Cave had to deliver a consignment of dog-fish at one of the hospital schools, where they were needed for dissection. In his absence Mrs. Cave's mind reverted to the topic of the crystal, and the methods of expenditure suitable to a windfall of five pounds. She had already devised some very agreeable expedients, among others a dress of green silk for herself and a trip to Richmond, when a jangling of the front door bell summoned her into the shop. The customer was an examination coach who came to complain of the non-delivery of certain frogs asked for the previous day. Mrs. Cave did not approve of this particular branch of Mr. Cave's business, and the gentleman, who had called in a somewhat aggressive mood, retired after a brief exchange of words—entirely civil so far as he was concerned. Mrs. Cave's eye then naturally turned to the window; for the sight of the crystal was an assurance of the five pounds and of her dreams. What was her surprise to find it gone!

She went to the place behind the locker on the counter, where she had discovered it the day before. It was not there; and she immediately began an eager search about the shop.

When Mr. Cave returned from his business with the dog-fish, about a quarter to two in the afternoon, he found the shop in some confusion, and his wife, extremely exasperated and on her knees behind the counter, routing among his taxidermic material. Her face came up hot and angry over the counter, as the jangling bell announced his return, and she forthwith accused him of "hiding it."

"Hid *what?*" asked Mr. Cave.

"The crystal!"

At that Mr. Cave, apparently much surprised, rushed to the window. "Isn't it here?" he said. "Great Heavens! what has become of it?"

Just then, Mr. Cave's step-son re-entered the shop from the inner room—he had come home a minute or so before Mr. Cave—and he was blaspheming freely. He was apprenticed to a second-hand furniture dealer down the road, but he had his meals at home, and he was naturally annoyed to find no dinner ready.

But, when he heard of the loss of the crystal, he forgot his meal, and his anger was diverted from his mother to his step-father. Their first idea, of course, was that he had hidden it. But Mr. Cave stoutly denied all knowledge of its fate—freely offering his bedabbled affidavit in the matter—and at last was worked up to the point of accusing, first, his wife and then his step-son of having taken it with a view to a private sale. So began an exceedingly acrimonious and emotional discussion, which ended for Mrs. Cave in a peculiar nervous condition midway between hysterics and amuck, and caused the step-son to be half-an-hour late at the furniture establishment in the afternoon. Mr. Cave took refuge from his wife's emotions in the shop.

In the evening the matter was resumed, with less passion and in a judicial spirit, under the presidency of the step-daughter. The supper passed unhappily and culminated in a painful scene. Mr. Cave gave way at last to extreme exasperation, and went out banging the front door violently. The rest of the family, having discussed him with the freedom his absence warranted, hunted the house from garret to cellar, hoping to light upon the crystal.

The next day the two customers called again. They were received by Mrs. Cave almost in tears. It transpired that no one *could* imagine all that she had stood from Cave at various times in her married pilgrimage. . . . . She also gave a garbled account of the disappearance. The clergyman and the Oriental laughed silently at one another, and said it was very extraordinary. As Mrs. Cave seemed disposed to give them the complete history of her life they made to leave the shop. Thereupon Mrs. Cave, still clinging to hope, asked for the clergyman's address, so that, if she could get anything out of Cave, she might communicate it. The address was duly given, but apparently was afterwards mislaid. Mrs. Cave can remember nothing about it.

In the evening of that day, the Caves seem to have exhausted their emotions, and Mr. Cave, who had been out in the afternoon, supped in a gloomy isolation that contrasted pleasantly with the impassioned controversy of the previous days. For some time matters were very badly strained in the Cave household, but neither crystal nor customer reappeared.

Now, without mincing the matter, we must admit that Mr. Cave was a liar. He knew perfectly well where the crystal was. It was in the rooms of Mr. Jacoby Wace, Assistant Demonstrator at St. Catherine's Hospital, Westbourne Street. It stood on the sideboard partially covered by a black velvet cloth, and beside a decanter of American whisky. It is from Mr. Wace, indeed, that the particulars upon which this narrative is based were derived. Cave had taken off the thing to the hospital hidden in the dog-fish sack, and there had pressed the young investigator to keep it for him. Mr. Wace was a little dubious at first. His relationship to Cave was peculiar. He had a taste for singular characters, and he had more than once invited the old man to smoke and drink in his rooms, and to unfold his rather amusing views of life in general and of his wife in particular. Mr. Wace had encountered Mrs. Cave, too, on occasions when Mr. Cave was not at home to attend to him. He knew the constant interference to which Cave was subjected, and having weighed the story judicially, he decided to give the crystal a refuge. Mr. Cave promised to explain the reasons for his remarkable affection for the crystal more fully on a later occasion, but he spoke distinctly of seeing visions therein. He called on Mr. Wace the same evening.

He told a complicated story. The crystal he said had come into his possession with other oddments at the forced sale of another curiosity dealer's effects, and not knowing what its value might be, he had ticketed it at ten shillings. It had hung upon his hands at that price for some months, and he was thinking of "reducing the figure," when he made a singular discovery.

At that time his health was very bad—and it must be borne in mind that, throughout all this experience, his physical condition was one of ebb—and he was in considerable distress by reason of the negligence, the positive ill-treatment even, he received from his wife and step-children. His wife was vain, extravagant, unfeeling and had a growing taste for private drinking; his step-daughter was mean and over-reaching; and his step-son had conceived a violent dislike for him, and lost no chance of showing it. The requirements of his business pressed heavily upon him, and Mr. Wace does not think that he was altogether free from occasional intemperance. He had begun life in a comfortable position, he was a man of fair education, and he suffered, for weeks at a stretch, from melancholia and insomnia. Afraid to disturb his family, he would slip quietly from his wife's side, when his thoughts became intolerable, and wander about the house. And about three o'clock one morning, late in August, chance directed him into the shop.

The dirty little place was impenetrably black except in one spot, where he perceived an unusual glow of light. Approaching this, he discovered it to be the crystal egg, which was standing on the corner of the counter towards the window. A thin ray smote through a crack in the shutters, impinged upon the object, and seemed as it were to fill its entire interior.

It occurred to Mr. Cave that this was not in accordance with the laws of optics as he had known them in his younger days. He could understand the rays being refracted by the crystal and coming to a focus in its interior, but this diffusion jarred with his physical conceptions. He approached the crystal nearly, peering into it and round it, with a transient revival of the scientific curiosity that in his youth had determined his choice of a calling. He was surprised to find the light not steady, but writhing within the substance of the egg, as though that object was a hollow sphere of some luminous vapour. In moving about to get different points of view, he suddenly found that he had come between it and the ray, and that the crystal none the less remained luminous. Greatly astonished, he lifted it out of the light ray and carried it to the darkest part of the shop. It remained bright for some four or five minutes, when it slowly faded and went out. He placed it in the thin streak of daylight, and its luminousness was almost immediately restored.

So far, at least, Mr. Wace was able to verify the remarkable story of Mr. Cave. He has himself repeatedly held this crystal in a ray of light (which had to be of a less diameter than one millimetre). And in a perfect darkness, such as could be produced by velvet wrapping, the crystal did undoubtedly appear very faintly phosphorescent. It would seem, however, that the luminousness was of some exceptional sort, and not equally visible to all eyes; for Mr. Harbinger—whose name will be familiar to the scientific reader in connection with the Pasteur Institute—was quite unable to see any light whatever. And Mr. Wace's own capacity for its appreciation was out of comparison inferior to that of Mr. Cave's. Even with Mr. Cave the power varied very considerably: his vision was most vivid during states of extreme weakness and fatigue.

Now, from the outset this light in the crystal exercised a curious fascination upon Mr. Cave. And it says more for his loneliness of soul than a volume of pathetic writing could do, that he told no human being of his curious observations. He seems to have been living in such an atmosphere of petty spite that to admit the existence of a pleasure would have been to risk the loss of it. He found that as the dawn advanced, and the amount of diffused light increased, the crystal became to all appearance non-luminous. And for some time he was unable to see anything in it, except at night-time, in dark corners of the shop.

But the use of an old velvet cloth, which he used as a background for a collection of minerals, occurred to him, and by doubling this, and putting it over his head and hands, he was able to get a sight of the luminous movement within the crystal even in the day-time. He was very cautious lest he should be thus discovered by his wife, and he practised this occupation only in the afternoons, while she was asleep upstairs, and then circumspectly in a hollow under the counter. And one day, turning the crystal about in his hands, he saw something. It came and went like a flash, but it gave him the impression that the object had for a moment opened to him the view of a wide and spacious and strange country; and, turning it about, he did, just as the light faded, see the same vision again.

Now, it would be tedious and unnecessary to state all the phases of Mr. Cave's discovery from this point. Suffice that the effect was this: the crystal, being peered into at an angle of about 137 degrees from the direction of the illuminating ray, gave a clear and consistent picture of a wide and peculiar country-side. It was not dream-like at all: it produced a definite impression of reality, and the better the light the more real and solid it seemed. It was a moving picture: that is to say, certain objects moved in it, but slowly in an orderly manner like real things, and, according as the direction of the lighting and vision changed, the picture changed also. It must, indeed, have been like looking through an oval glass at a view, and turning the glass about to get at different aspects.

Mr. Cave's statements, Mr. Wace assures me, were extremely circumstantial, and entirely free from any of that emotional quality that taints hallucinatory impressions. But it must be remembered that all the efforts of Mr. Wace to see any similar clarity in the faint opalescence of the crystal were wholly unsuccessful, try as he would. The difference in intensity of the impressions received by the two men was very great, and it is quite conceivable that what was a view to Mr. Cave was a mere blurred nebulosity to Mr. Wace.

The view, as Mr. Cave described it, was invariably of an extensive plain, and he seemed always to be looking at it from a considerable height, as if from a tower or a mast. To the east and to the west the plain was bounded at a remote distance by vast reddish cliffs, which reminded him of those he had seen in some picture; but what the picture was Mr. Wace was unable to ascertain. These cliffs passed north and south–he could tell the points of the compass by the stars that were visible of a night– receding in an almost illimitable perspective and fading into the mists of the distance before they met. He was nearer the eastern set of cliffs, on the occasion of his first vision the sun was rising over them, and black against the sunlight and pale against their shadow appeared a multitude of soaring forms that Mr. Cave regarded as birds. A vast range of buildings spread below him; he seemed to be looking down upon them; and, as they approached the blurred and refracted edge of the picture, they became indistinct. There were also trees curious in shape, and in colouring, a deep mossy green and an exquisite grey, beside a wide and shining canal. And something great and brilliantly coloured flew across the picture. But the first time Mr. Cave saw these pictures he saw only in flashes, his hands shook, his head moved, the vision came and went, and grew foggy and indistinct. And at first he had the greatest difficulty in finding the picture again once the direction of it was lost.

His next clear vision, which came about a week after the first, the interval having yielded nothing but tantalising glimpses and some useful experience, showed him the view down the length of the valley. The view was different, but he had a curious persuasion, which his subsequent observations abundantly confirmed, that he was regarding this strange world from exactly the same spot, although he was looking in a different direction. The long façade of the great building, whose roof he had looked down upon before, was now receding in perspective. He recognised the roof. In the front of the façade was a terrace of massive proportions and extraordinary length, and down the middle of the terrace, at certain intervals, stood huge but very graceful masts, bearing small shiny objects which reflected the setting sun. The import of these small objects did not occur to Mr. Cave until some time after, as he was describing the scene to Mr. Wace. The terrace overhung a thicket of the most luxuriant and graceful vegetation, and beyond this was a wide grassy lawn on which certain broad creatures, in form like beetles but enormously larger, reposed. Beyond this again was a richly decorated causeway of pinkish stone; and beyond that, and lined with dense *red* weeds, and passing up the valley exactly parallel with the distant cliffs, was a broad and mirror-like expanse of water. The air seemed full of squadrons of great birds, manœuvring in stately curves; and across the river was a multitude of splendid buildings, richly coloured and glittering with metallic tracery and facets, among a forest of moss-like and lichenous trees. And suddenly something flapped repeatedly across the vision, like the fluttering of a jewelled fan or the beating of a wing, and a face, or rather the upper part of a face with very large eyes, came as it were close to his own and as if on the other side of the crystal. Mr. Cave was so startled and so impressed by the absolute reality of these eyes, that he drew his head back from the crystal to look behind it. He had become so absorbed in watching that he was quite surprised to find himself in the cool darkness of his little shop, with its familiar odour of methyl, mustiness, and decay. And, as he blinked about him, the glowing crystal faded, and went out.

Such were the first general impressions of Mr. Cave. The story is curiously direct and circumstantial. From the outset, when the valley first flashed momentarily on his senses, his imagination was strangely affected, and, as he began to appreciate the details of the scene he saw, his wonder rose to the point of a passion. He went about his business listless and distraught, thinking only of the time when he should be able to return to his watching. And then a few weeks after his first sight of the valley came the two customers, the stress and excitement of their offer, and the narrow escape of the crystal from sale, as I have already told.

Now, while the thing was Mr. Cave's secret, it remained a mere wonder, a thing to creep to covertly and peep at, as a child might peep upon a forbidden garden. But Mr. Wace has, for a young scientific investigator, a particularly lucid and consecutive habit of mind. Directly the crystal and its story came to him, and he had satisfied himself, by seeing the phosphorescence with his own eyes, that there really was a certain evidence for Mr. Cave's statements, he proceeded to develop the matter systematically. Mr. Cave was only too eager to come and feast his eyes on this wonderland he saw, and he came every night from half-past eight until half-past ten, and sometimes, in Mr. Wace's absence, during the day. On Sunday afternoons, also, he came. From the outset Mr. Wace made copious notes, and it was due to his scientific method that the relation between the direction from which the initiating ray entered the crystal and the orientation of the picture were proved. And, by covering the crystal in a box perforated only with a small aperture to admit the exciting ray, and by substituting black holland for his buff blinds, he greatly improved the conditions of the observations; so that in a little while they were able to survey the valley in any direction they desired.

So having cleared the way, we may give a brief account of this visionary world within the crystal. The things were in all cases seen by Mr. Cave, and the method of working was invariably for him to watch the crystal and report what he saw, while Mr. Wace (who as a science student had learnt the trick of writing in the dark) wrote a brief note of his report. When the crystal faded, it was put into its box in the proper position and the electric light turned on. Mr. Wace asked questions, and suggested observations to clear up difficult points. Nothing, indeed, could have been less visionary and more matter-of-fact.

The attention of Mr. Cave had been speedily directed to the bird-like creatures he had seen so abundantly present in each of his earlier visions. His first impression was soon corrected, and he considered for a time that they might represent a diurnal species of bat. Then he thought, grotesquely enough, that they might be cherubs. Their heads were round, and curiously human, and it was the eyes of one of them that had so startled him on his second observation. They had broad, silvery wings, not feathered, but glistening almost as brilliantly as new-killed fish and with the same subtle play of colour, and these wings were not built on the plan of a bird-wing or bat, Mr. Wace learned, but supported by curved ribs radiating from the body. (A sort of butterfly wing with curved ribs seems best to express their appearance.) The body was small, but fitted with two bunches of prehensile organs, like long tentacles, immediately under the mouth. Incredible as it appeared to Mr. Wace, the persuasion at last became irresistible, that it was these creatures which owned the great quasi-human buildings and the magnificent garden that made the broad valley so splendid. And Mr. Cave perceived that the buildings, with other peculiarities, had no doors, but that the great circular windows, which opened freely, gave the creatures egress and entrance. They would alight upon their tentacles, fold their wings to a smallness almost rod-like, and hop into the interior. But among them was a multitude of smaller-winged creatures, like great dragon-flies and moths and flying beetles, and across the greensward brilliantly-coloured gigantic ground-beetles crawled lazily to and fro. Moreover, on the causeways and terraces, large-headed creatures similar to the greater winged flies, but wingless, were visible, hopping busily upon their hand-like tangle of tentacles.

Allusion has already been made to the glittering objects upon masts that stood upon the terrace of the nearer building. It dawned upon Mr. Cave, after regarding one of these masts very fixedly on one particularly vivid day, that the glittering object there was a crystal exactly like that into which he peered. And a still more careful scrutiny convinced him that each one in a vista of nearly twenty carried a similar object.

Occasionally one of the large flying creatures would flutter up to one, and, folding its wings and coiling a number of its tentacles about the mast, would regard the crystal fixedly for a space,—sometimes for as long as fifteen minutes. And a series of observations, made at the suggestion of Mr. Wace, convinced both watchers that, so far as this visionary world was concerned, the crystal into which they peered actually stood at the summit of the end-most mast on the terrace, and that on one occasion at least one of these inhabitants of this other world had looked into Mr. Cave's face while he was making these observations.

So much for the essential facts of this very singular story. Unless we dismiss it all as the ingenious fabrication of Mr. Wace, we have to believe one of two things: either that Mr. Cave's crystal was in two worlds at once, and that, while it was carried about in one, it remained stationary in the other, which seems altogether absurd; or else that it had some peculiar relation of sympathy with another and exactly similar crystal in this other world, so that what was seen in the interior of the one in this world, was, under suitable conditions, visible to an observer in the corresponding crystal in the other world; and *vice versa.* At present, indeed, we do not know of any way in which two crystals could so come *en rapport,* but nowadays we know enough to understand that the thing is not altogether impossible. This view of the crystals as *en rapport* was the supposition that occurred to Mr. Wace, and to me at least it seems extremely plausible. . . . .

And where was this other world? On this, also, the alert intelligence of Mr. Wace speedily threw light. After sunset, the sky darkened rapidly—there was a very brief twilight interval indeed—and the stars shone out. They were recognisably the same as those we see, arranged in the same constellations. Mr. Cave recognised the Bear, the Pleiades, Aldebaran, and Sirius: so that the other world must be somewhere in the solar system, and, at the utmost, only a few hundreds of millions of miles from our own. Following up this clue, Mr. Wace learned that the midnight sky was a darker blue even than our midwinter sky, and that the sun seemed a little smaller. *And there were two small moons!* "like our moon but smaller, and quite differently marked" one of which moved so rapidly that its motion was clearly visible as one regarded it. These moons were never high in the sky, but vanished as they rose: that is, every time they revolved they were eclipsed because they were so near their primary planet. And all this answers quite completely, although Mr. Cave did not know it, to what must be the condition of things on Mars.

Indeed, it seems an exceedingly plausible conclusion that peering into this crystal Mr. Cave did actually see the planet Mars and its inhabitants. And, if that be the case, then the evening star that shone so brilliantly in the sky of that distant vision, was neither more nor less than our own familiar earth.

For a time the Martians—if they were Martians—do not seem to have known of Mr. Cave's inspection. Once or twice one would come to peer, and go away very shortly to some other mast, as though the vision was unsatisfactory. During this time Mr. Cave was able to watch the proceedings of these winged people without being disturbed by their attentions, and, although his report is necessarily vague and fragmentary, it is nevertheless very suggestive. Imagine the impression of humanity a Martian observer would get who, after a difficult process of preparation and with considerable fatigue to the eyes, was able to peer at London from the steeple of St. Martin's Church for stretches, at longest, of four minutes at a time. Mr. Cave was unable to ascertain if the winged Martians were the same as the Martians who hopped about the causeways and terraces, and if the latter could put on wings at will. He several times saw certain clumsy bipeds, dimly suggestive of apes, white and partially translucent, feeding among certain of the lichenous trees, and once some of these fled before one of the hopping, round-headed Martians. The latter caught one in its tentacles, and then the picture faded suddenly and left Mr. Cave most tantalisingly in the dark. On another occasion a vast thing, that Mr. Cave thought at first was some gigantic insect, appeared advancing along the causeway beside the canal with extraordinary rapidity. As this drew nearer Mr. Cave perceived that it was a mechanism of shining metals and of extraordinary complexity. And then, when he looked again, it had passed out of sight.

After a time Mr. Wace aspired to attract the attention of the Martians, and the next time that the strange eyes of one of them appeared close to the crystal Mr. Cave cried out and sprang away, and they immediately turned on the light and began to gesticulate in a manner suggestive of signalling. But when at last Mr. Cave examined the crystal again the Martian had departed.

Thus far these observations had progressed in early November, and then Mr. Cave, feeling that the suspicions of his family about the crystal were allayed, began to take it to and fro with him in order that, as occasion arose in the daytime or night, he might comfort himself with what was fast becoming the most real thing in his existence.

In December Mr. Wace's work in connection with a forthcoming examination became heavy, the sittings were reluctantly suspended for a week, and for ten or eleven days—he is not quite sure which—he saw nothing of Cave. He then grew anxious to resume these investigations, and, the stress of his seasonal labours being abated, he went down to Seven Dials. At the corner he noticed a shutter before a bird fancier's window, and then another at a cobbler's. Mr. Cave's shop was closed.

He rapped and the door was opened by the step-son in black. He at once called Mrs. Cave, who was, Mr. Wace could not but observe, in cheap but ample widow's weeds of the most imposing pattern. Without any very great surprise Mr. Wace learnt that Cave was dead and already buried. She was in tears, and her voice was a little thick. She had just returned from Highgate. Her mind seemed occupied with her own prospects and the honourable details of the obsequies, but Mr. Wace was at last able to learn the particulars of Cave's death. He had been found dead in his shop in the early morning, the day after his last visit to Mr. Wace, and the crystal had been clasped in his stone-cold hands. His face was smiling, said Mrs. Cave, and the velvet cloth from the minerals lay on the floor at his feet. He must have been dead five or six hours when he was found.

This came as a great shock to Wace, and he began to reproach himself bitterly for having neglected the plain symptoms of the old man's ill-health. But his chief thought was of the crystal. He approached that topic in a gingerly manner, because he knew Mrs. Cave's peculiarities. He was dumbfoundered to learn that it was sold.

Mrs. Cave's first impulse, directly Cave's body had been taken upstairs, had been to write to the mad clergyman who had offered five pounds for the crystal, informing him of its recovery; but after a violent hunt in which her daughter joined her, they were convinced of the loss of his address. As they were without the means required to mourn and bury Cave in the elaborate style the dignity of an old Seven Dials inhabitant demands, they had appealed to a friendly fellow-tradesman in Great Portland Street. He had very kindly taken over a portion of the stock at a valuation. The valuation was his own and the crystal egg was included in one of the lots. Mr. Wace, after a few suitable consolatory observations, a little off-handedly proffered perhaps, hurried at once to Great Portland Street. But there he learned that the crystal egg had already been sold to a tall, dark man in grey. And there the material facts in this curious, and to me at least very suggestive, story come abruptly to an end. The Great Portland Street dealer did not know who the tall dark man in grey was, nor had he observed him with sufficient attention to describe him minutely. He did not even know which way this person had gone after leaving the shop. For a time Mr. Wace remained in the shop, trying the dealer's patience with hopeless questions, venting his own exasperation. And at last, realising abruptly that the whole thing had passed out of his hands, had vanished like a vision of the night, he returned to his own rooms, a little astonished to find the notes he had made still tangible and visible upon his untidy table.

His annoyance and disappointment were naturally very great. He made a second call (equally ineffectual) upon the Great Portland Street dealer, and he resorted to advertisements in such periodicals as were likely to come into the hands of a *bric-a-brac* collector. He also wrote letters to *The Daily Chronicle* and *Nature,* but both those periodicals, suspecting a hoax, asked him to reconsider his action before they printed, and he was advised that such a strange story, unfortunately so bare of supporting evidence, might imperil his reputation as an investigator. Moreover, the calls of his proper work were urgent. So that after a month or so, save for an occasional reminder to certain dealers, he had reluctantly to abandon the quest for the crystal egg, and from that day to this it remains undiscovered. Occasionally, however, he tells me, and I can quite believe him, he has bursts of zeal, in which he abandons his more urgent occupation and resumes the search.

Whether or not it will remain lost for ever, with the material and origin of it, are things equally speculative at the present time. If the present purchaser is a collector, one would have expected the enquiries of Mr. Wace to have reached him through the dealers. He has been able to discover Mr. Cave's clergyman and "Oriental"—no other than the Rev. James Parker and the young Prince of Bosso-Kuni in Java. I am obliged to them for certain particulars. The object of the Prince was simply curiosity—and extravagance. He was so eager to buy, because Cave was so oddly reluctant to sell. It is just as possible that the buyer in the second instance was simply a casual purchaser and not a collector at all, and the crystal egg, for all I know, may at the present moment be within a mile of me, decorating a drawing-room or serving as a paper-weight—its remarkable functions all unknown. Indeed, it is partly with the idea of such a possibility that I have thrown this narrative into a form that will give it a chance of being read by the ordinary consumer of fiction.

My own ideas in the matter are practically identical with those of Mr. Wace. I believe the crystal on the mast in Mars and the crystal egg of Mr. Cave's to be in some physical, but at present quite inexplicable, way *en rapport*, and we both believe further that the terrestrial crystal must have been—possibly at some remote date—sent hither from that planet, in order to give the Martians a near view of our affairs. Possibly the fellows to the crystals in the other masts are also on our globe. No theory of hallucination suffices for the facts.

# THE MAN WHO COULD WORK MIRACLES

## A PANTOUM IN PROSE

It is doubtful whether the gift was innate. For my own part, I think it came to him suddenly. Indeed, until he was thirty he was a sceptic, and did not believe in miraculous powers. And here, since it is the most convenient place, I must mention that he was a little man, and had eyes of a hot brown, very erect red hair, a moustache with ends that he twisted up, and freckles. His name was George McWhirter Fotheringay—not the sort of name by any means to lead to any expectation of miracles—and he was clerk at Gomshott's. He was greatly addicted to assertive argument. It was while he was asserting the impossibility of miracles that he had his first intimation of his extraordinary powers. This particular argument was being held in the bar of the Long Dragon, and Toddy Beamish was conducting the opposition by a monotonous but effective "So *you* say," that drove Mr. Fotheringay to the very limit of his patience.

There were present, besides these two, a very dusty cyclist, landlord Cox, and Miss Maybridge, the perfectly respectable and rather portly barmaid of the Dragon. Miss Maybridge was standing with her back to Mr. Fotheringay, washing glasses; the others were watching him, more or less amused by the present ineffectiveness of the assertive method. Goaded by the Torres Vedras tactics of Mr. Beamish, Mr. Fotheringay determined to make an unusual rhetorical effort. "Looky here, Mr. Beamish," said Mr. Fotheringay. "Let us clearly understand what a miracle is. It's something contrariwise to the course of nature done by power of Will, something what couldn't happen without being specially willed."

"So *you* say," said Mr. Beamish, repulsing him.

Mr. Fotheringay appealed to the cyclist, who had hitherto been a silent auditor, and received his assent—given with a hesitating cough and a glance at Mr. Beamish. The landlord would express no opinion, and Mr. Fotheringay, returning to Mr. Beamish, received the unexpected concession of a qualified assent to his definition of a miracle.

"For instance," said Mr. Fotheringay, greatly encouraged. "Here would be a miracle. That lamp, in the natural course of nature, couldn't burn like that upsy-down, could it, Beamish?"

"*You* say it couldn't," said Beamish.

"And you?" said Fotheringay. "You don't mean to say—eh?"

"No," said Beamish reluctantly. "No, it couldn't."

"Very well," said Mr. Fotheringay. "Then here comes someone, as it might be me, along here, and stands as it might be here, and says to that lamp, as I might do, collecting all my will—Turn upsy-down without breaking, and go on burning steady, and—Hullo!"

It was enough to make anyone say "Hullo!" The impossible, the incredible, was visible to them all. The lamp hung inverted in the air, burning quietly with its flame pointing down. It was as solid, as indisputable as ever a lamp was, the prosaic common lamp of the Long Dragon bar.

Mr. Fotheringay stood with an extended forefinger and the knitted brows of one anticipating a catastrophic smash. The cyclist, who was sitting next the lamp, ducked and jumped across the bar. Everybody jumped, more or less. Miss Maybridge turned and screamed. For nearly three seconds the lamp remained still. A faint cry of mental distress came from Mr. Fotheringay. "I can't keep it up," he said, "any longer." He staggered back, and the inverted lamp suddenly flared, fell against the corner of the bar, bounced aside, smashed upon the floor, and went out.

It was lucky it had a metal receiver, or the whole place would have been in a blaze. Mr. Cox was the first to speak, and his remark, shorn of needless excrescences, was to the effect that Fotheringay was a fool. Fotheringay was beyond disputing even so fundamental a proposition as that! He was astonished beyond measure at the thing that had occurred. The subsequent conversation threw absolutely no light on the matter so far as Fotheringay was concerned; the general opinion not only followed Mr. Cox very closely but very vehemently. Everyone accused Fotheringay of a silly trick, and presented him to himself as a foolish destroyer of comfort and security. His mind was in a tornado of perplexity, he was himself inclined to agree with them, and he made a remarkably ineffectual opposition to the proposal of his departure.

He went home flushed and heated, coat-collar crumpled, eyes smarting and ears red. He watched each of the ten street lamps nervously as he passed it. It was only when he found himself alone in his little bed-room in Church Row that he was able to grapple seriously with his memories of the occurrence, and ask, "What on earth happened?"

He had removed his coat and boots, and was sitting on the bed with his hands in his pockets repeating the text of his defence for the seventeenth time, "*I* didn't want the confounded thing to upset," when it occurred to him that at the precise moment he had said the commanding words he had inadvertently willed the thing he said, and that when he had seen the lamp in the air he had felt it depended on him to maintain it there without being clear how this was to be done. He had not a particularly complex mind, or he might have stuck for a time at that "inadvertently willed," embracing, as it does, the abstrusest problems of voluntary action; but as it was, the idea came to him with a quite acceptable haziness. And from that, following, as I must admit, no clear logical path, he came to the test of experiment.

He pointed resolutely to his candle and collected his mind, though he felt he did a foolish thing. "Be raised up," he said. But in a second that feeling vanished. The candle was raised, hung in the air one giddy moment, and as Mr. Fotheringay gasped, fell with a smash on his toilet-table, leaving him in darkness save for the expiring glow of its wick.

For a time Mr. Fotheringay sat in the darkness, perfectly still. "It did happen, after all," he said. "And 'ow *I'm* to explain it I *don't* know." He sighed heavily, and began feeling in his pockets for a match. He could find none, and he rose and groped about the toilet-table. "I wish I had a match," he said. He resorted to his coat, and there was none there, and then it dawned upon him that miracles were possible even with matches. He extended a hand and scowled at it in the dark. "Let there be a match in that hand," he said. He felt some light object fall across his palm, and his fingers closed upon a match.

After several ineffectual attempts to light this, he discovered it was a safety-match. He threw it down, and then it occurred to him that he might have willed it lit. He did, and perceived it burning in the midst of his toilet-table mat. He caught it up hastily, and it went out. His perception of possibilities enlarged, and he felt for and replaced the candle in its candlestick. "Here! *you* be lit," said Mr. Fotheringay, and forthwith the candle was flaring, and he saw a little black hole in the toilet-cover, with a wisp of smoke rising from it. For a time he stared from this to the little flame and back, and then looked up and met his own gaze in the looking glass. By this help he communed with himself in silence for a time.

"How about miracles now?" said Mr. Fotheringay at last, addressing his reflection.

The subsequent meditations of Mr. Fotheringay were of a severe but confused description. So far, he could see it was a case of pure willing with him. The nature of his experiences so far disinclined him for any further experiments, at least until he had reconsidered them. But he lifted a sheet of paper, and turned a glass of water pink and then green, and he created a snail, which he miraculously annihilated, and got himself a miraculous new tooth-brush. Somewhen in the small hours he had reached the fact that his will-power must be of a particularly rare and pungent quality, a fact of which he had certainly had inklings before, but no certain assurance. The scare and perplexity of his first discovery was now qualified by pride in this evidence of singularity and by vague intimations of advantage. He became aware that the church clock was striking one, and as it did not occur to him that his daily duties at Gomshott's might be miraculously dispensed with, he resumed undressing, in order to get to bed without further delay. As he struggled to get his shirt over his head, he was struck with a brilliant idea. "Let me be in bed," he said, and found himself so. "Undressed," he stipulated; and, finding the sheets cold, added hastily, "and in my nightshirt—no, in a nice soft woollen nightshirt. Ah!" he said with immense enjoyment. "And now let me be comfortably asleep. . . . ."

He awoke at his usual hour and was pensive all through breakfast-time, wondering whether his overnight experience might not be a particularly vivid dream. At length his mind turned again to cautious experiments. For instance, he had three eggs for breakfast; two his landlady had supplied, good, but shoppy, and one was a delicious fresh goose-egg, laid, cooked, and served by his extraordinary will. He hurried off to Gomshott's in a state of profound but carefully concealed excitement, and only remembered the shell of the third egg when his landlady spoke of it that night. All day he could do no work because of this astonishingly new self-knowledge, but this caused him no inconvenience, because he made up for it miraculously in his last ten minutes.

As the day wore on his state of mind passed from wonder to elation, albeit the circumstances of his dismissal from the Long Dragon were still disagreeable to recall, and a garbled account of the matter that had reached his colleagues led to some badinage. It was evident he must be careful how he lifted frangible articles, but in other ways his gift promised more and more as he turned it over in his mind.

He intended among other things to increase his personal property by unostentatious acts of creation. He called into existence a pair of very splendid diamond studs, and hastily annihilated them again as young Gomshott came across the counting-house to his desk. He was afraid young Gomshott might wonder how he had come by them. He saw quite clearly the gift required caution and watchfulness in its exercise, but so far as he could judge the difficulties attending its mastery would be no greater than those he had already faced in the study of cycling. It was that analogy, perhaps, quite as much as the feeling that he would be unwelcome in the Long Dragon, that drove him out after supper into the lane beyond the gas-works, to rehearse a few miracles in private.

There was possibly a certain want of originality in his attempts, for apart from his will-power Mr. Fotheringay was not a very exceptional man. The miracle of Moses' rod came to his mind, but the night was dark and unfavourable to the proper control of large miraculous snakes. Then he recollected the story of "Tannhäuser" that he had read on the back of the Philharmonic programme. That seemed to him singularly attractive and harmless. He stuck his walking-stick—a very nice Poona-Penang lawyer—into the turf that edged the footpath, and commanded the dry wood to blossom. The air was immediately full of the scent of roses, and by means of a match he saw for himself that this beautiful miracle was indeed accomplished. His satisfaction was ended by advancing footsteps. Afraid of a premature discovery of his powers, he addressed the blossoming stick hastily: "Go back." What he meant was "Change back;" but of course he was confused. The stick receded at a considerable velocity, and incontinently came a cry of anger and a bad word from the approaching person. "Who are you throwing brambles at, you fool?" cried a voice. "That got me on the shin."

"I'm sorry, old chap," said Mr. Fotheringay, and then realising the awkward nature of the explanation, caught nervously at his moustache. He saw Winch, one of the three Immering constables, advancing.

"What d'yer mean by it?" asked the constable. "Hullo! It's you, is it? The gent that broke the lamp at the Long Dragon!"

"I don't mean anything by it," said Mr. Fotheringay. "Nothing at all."

"What d'yer do it for then?"

"Oh, bother!" said Mr. Fotheringay.

"Bother indeed! D'yer know that stick hurt? What d'yer do it for, eh?"

For the moment Mr. Fotheringay could not think what he had

done it for. His silence seemed to irritate Mr. Winch. "You've been assaulting the police, young man, this time. That's what *you* done."

"Look here, Mr. Winch," said Mr. Fotheringay, annoyed and confused, "I'm very sorry. The fact is——"

"Well?"

He could think of no way but the truth. "I was working a miracle." He tried to speak in an off-hand way, but try as he would he couldn't.

"Working a——! 'Ere, don't you talk rot. Working a miracle, indeed! Miracle! Well, that's downright funny! Why, you's the chap that don't believe in miracles. . . . . Fact is, this is another of your silly conjuring tricks—that's what this is. Now, I tell you——"

But Mr. Fotheringay never heard what Mr. Winch was going to tell him. He realised he had given himself away, flung his valuable secret to all the winds of heaven. A violent gust of irritation swept him to action. He turned on the constable swiftly and fiercely. "Here," he said, "I've had enough of this, I have! I'll show you a silly conjuring trick, I will! Go to Hades! Go, now!"

He was alone!

Mr. Fotheringay performed no more miracles that night nor did he trouble to see what had become of his flowering stick. He returned to the town, scared and very quiet, and went to his bed-room. "Lord!" he said, "it's a powerful gift—an extremely powerful gift. I didn't hardly mean as much as that. Not really. . . . I wonder what Hades is like!"

He sat on the bed taking off his boots. Struck by a happy thought he transferred the constable to San Francisco, and without any more interference with normal causation went soberly to bed. In the night he dreamt of the anger of Winch.

The next day Mr. Fotheringay heard two interesting items of news. Someone had planted a most beautiful climbing rose against the elder Mr. Gomshott's private house in the Lullaborough Road, and the river as far as Rawling's Mill was to be dragged for Constable Winch.

Mr. Fotheringay was abstracted and thoughtful all that day, and performed no miracles except certain provisions for Winch, and the miracle of completing his day's work with punctual perfection in spite of all the bee-swarm of thoughts that hummed through his mind. And the extraordinary abstraction and meekness of his manner was remarked by several people, and made a matter for jesting. For the most part he was thinking of Winch.

On Sunday evening he went to chapel, and oddly enough, Mr. Maydig, who took a certain interest in occult matters, preached about "things that are not lawful." Mr. Fotheringay was not a regular chapel goer, but the system of assertive scepticism, to which I have already alluded, was now very much shaken. The tenor of the sermon threw an entirely new light on these novel gifts, and he suddenly decided to consult Mr. Maydig immediately after the service. So soon as that was determined, he found himself wondering why he had not done so before.

Mr. Maydig, a lean, excitable man with quite remarkably long wrists and neck, was gratified at a request for a private conversation from a young man whose carelessness in religious matters was a subject for general remark in the town. After a few necessary delays, he conducted him to the study of the Manse, which was contiguous to the chapel, seated him comfortably, and, standing in front of a cheerful fire—his legs threw a Rhodian arch of shadow on the opposite wall—requested Mr. Fotheringay to state his business.

At first Mr. Fotheringay was a little abashed, and found some difficulty in opening the matter. "You will scarcely believe me, Mr. Maydig, I am afraid"—and so forth for some time. He tried a question at last, and asked Mr. Maydig his opinion of miracles.

Mr. Maydig was still saying "Well" in an extremely judicial tone, when Mr. Fotheringay interrupted again: "You don't believe, I suppose, that some common sort of person—like myself, for instance—as it might be sitting here now, might have some sort of twist inside him that made him able to do things by his will."

"It's possible," said Mr. Maydig. "Something of the sort, perhaps, is possible."

"If I might make free with something here, I think I might show you by a sort of experiment," said Mr. Fotheringay. "Now, take that tobacco-jar on the table, for instance. What I want to know is whether what I am going to do with it is a miracle or not. Just half a minute, Mr. Maydig, please."

He knitted his brows, pointed to the tobacco-jar and said: "Be a bowl of vi'lets."

The tobacco-jar did as it was ordered.

Mr. Maydig started violently at the change, and stood looking from the thaumaturgist to the bowl of flowers. He said nothing. Presently he ventured to lean over the table and smell the violets; they were fresh-picked and very fine ones. Then he stared at Mr. Fotheringay again.

"How did you do that?" he asked.

Mr. Fotheringay pulled his moustache. "Just told it—and there you are. Is that a miracle, or is it black art, or what is it? And what do you think's the matter with me? That's what I want to ask."

"It's a most extraordinary occurrence."

"And this day last week I knew no more that I could do things like that than you did. It came quite sudden. It's something odd about my will, I suppose, and that's as far as I can see."

"Is *that*—the only thing? Could you do other things besides that?"

"Lord, yes! said Mr. Fotheringay. "Just anything." He thought, and suddenly recalled a conjuring entertainment he had seen. "Here!" He pointed. "Change into a bowl of fish—no, not that—change into a glass bowl full of water with goldfish swimming in it. That's better! You see that, Mr. Maydig?"

"It's astonishing. It's incredible. You are either a most extraordinary . . . But no——"

"I could change it into anything," said Mr. Fotheringay. "Just anything. Here! be a pigeon, will you?"

In another moment a blue pigeon was fluttering round the room and making Mr. Maydig duck every time it came near him. "Stop there, will you," said Mr. Fotheringay; and the pigeon hung motionless in the air. "I could change it back to a bowl of flowers," he said, and after replacing the pigeon on the table worked that miracle. "I expect you will want your pipe in a bit," he said, and restored the tobacco-jar.

Mr. Maydig had followed all these later changes in a sort of ejaculatory silence. He stared at Mr. Fotheringay and, in a very gingerly manner, picked up the tobacco-jar, examined it, replaced it on the table. "*Well!*" was the only expression of his feelings.

"Now, after that it's easier to explain what I came about," said Mr. Fotheringay; and proceeded to a lengthy and involved narrative of his strange experiences, beginning with the affair of the lamp in the Long Dragon and complicated by persistent allusions to Winch. As he went on, the transient pride Mr. Maydig's consternation had caused passed away; he became the very ordinary Mr. Fotheringay of everyday intercourse again. Mr. Maydig listened intently, the tobacco-jar in his hand, and his bearing changed also with the course of the narrative. Presently, while Mr. Fotheringay was dealing with the miracle of the third egg, the minister interrupted with a fluttering extended hand—

"It is possible," he said. "It is credible. It is amazing, of course, but it reconciles a number of amazing difficulties. The power to work miracles is a gift—a peculiar quality like genius or second sight—hitherto it has come very rarely and to exceptional people. But in this case . . . I have always wondered at the miracles of Mahomet, and at Yogi's miracles, and the miracles of Madame Blavatsky. But, of course! Yes, it is simply a gift! It carries out so beautifully the arguments of that great thinker"—Mr. Maydig's voice sank—"his Grace the

Duke of Argyll. Here we plumb some profounder law—deeper than the ordinary laws of nature. Yes—yes. Go on. Go on!"

Mr. Fotheringay proceeded to tell of his misadventure with Winch, and Mr. Maydig, no longer overawed or scared, began to jerk his limbs about and interject astonishment. "It's this what troubled me most," proceeded Mr. Fotheringay; "it's this I'm most mijitly in want of advice for; of course he's at San Francisco—wherever San Francisco may be—but of course it's awkward for both of us, as you'll see, Mr. Maydig. I don't see how he can understand what has happened, and I daresay he's scared and exasperated something tremendous, and trying to get at me. I daresay he keeps on starting off to come here. I send him back, by a miracle, every few hours, when I think of it. And of course, that's a thing he won't be able to understand, and it's bound to annoy him; and, of course, if he takes a ticket every time it will cost him a lot of money. I done the best I could for him, but of course it's difficult for him to put himself in my place. I thought afterwards that his clothes might have got scorched, you know—if Hades is all it's supposed to be—before I shifted him. In that case I suppose they'd have locked him up in San Francisco. Of course I willed him a new suit of clothes on him directly I thought of it. But, you see, I'm already in a deuce of a tangle——"

Mr. Maydig looked serious. "I see you are in a tangle. Yes, it's a difficult position. How you are to end it . . ." He became diffuse and inconclusive.

"However, we'll leave Winch for a little and discuss the larger question. I don't think this is a case of the black art or anything of the sort. I don't think there is any taint of criminality about it at all, Mr. Fotheringay—none whatever, unless you are suppressing material facts. No, it's miracles—pure miracles—miracles, if I may say so, of the very highest class."

He began to pace the hearthrug and gesticulate, while Mr. Fotheringay sat with his arm on the table and his head on his arm, looking worried. "I don't see how I'm to manage about Winch," he said.

"A gift of working miracles—apparently a very powerful gift," said Mr. Maydig, "will find a way about Winch—never fear. My dear Sir, you are a most important man—a man of the most astonishing possibilities. As evidence, for example! And in other ways, the things you may do . . . ."

"Yes, *I've* thought of a thing or two," said Mr. Fotheringay. "But —some of the things came a bit twisty. You saw that fish at first? Wrong sort of bowl and wrong sort of fish. And I thought I'd ask someone."

"A proper course," said Mr. Maydig, "a very proper course—altogether the proper course." He stopped and looked at Mr. Fotheringay. "It's practically an unlimited gift. Let us test your powers, for instance. If they really *are* . . . If they really are all they seem to be."

And so, incredible as it may seem, in the study of the little house behind the Congregational Chapel, on the evening of Sunday, Nov. 10, 1896, Mr. Fotheringay, egged on and inspired by Mr. Maydig, began to work miracles. The reader's attention is specially and definitely called to the date. He will object, probably has already objected, that certain points in this story are improbable, that if any things of the sort already described had indeed occurred, they would have been in all the papers a year ago. The details immediately following he will find particularly hard to accept, because among other things they involve the conclusion that he or she, the reader in question, must have been killed in a violent and unprecedented manner more than a year ago. Now a miracle is nothing if not improbable, and as a matter of fact the reader *was* killed in a violent and unprecedented manner a year ago. In the subsequent course of this story that will become perfectly clear and credible, as every right-minded and reasonable reader will admit. But this is not the place for the end of the story, being but little beyond the hither side of the middle. And at first the miracles worked by Mr. Fotheringay were timid little miracles—little things with the cups and parlour fitments. as feeble as the miracles of Theosophists, and, feeble as they were, they were received with awe by his collaborator. He would have preferred to settle the Winch business out of hand, but Mr. Maydig would not let him. But after they had worked a dozen of these domestic trivialities, their sense of power grew, their imagination began to show signs of stimulation, and their ambition enlarged. Their first larger enterprise was due to hunger and the negligence of Mrs. Minchin, Mr. Maydig's housekeeper. The meal to which the minister conducted Mr. Fotheringay was certainly ill-laid and uninviting as refreshment for two industrious miracle-workers; but they were seated, and Mr. Maydig was descanting in sorrow rather than in anger upon his housekeeper's shortcomings, before it occurred to Mr. Fotheringay that an opportunity lay before him. "Don't you think, Mr. Maydig," he said; "if it isn't a liberty, *I*——"

"My dear Mr. Fotheringay! Of course! No—I didn't think."

Mr. Fotheringay waved his hand. "What shall we have?" he said, in a large, inclusive spirit, and, at Mr. Maydig's order, revised the supper very thoroughly. "As for me," he said, eyeing Mr. Maydig's selection, "I am always particularly fond of a tankard of stout and a nice Welsh rarebit, and I'll order that. I ain't much given to Burgundy," and forthwith stout and Welsh rarebit promptly appeared at his command. They sat long at their supper, talking like equals, as Mr. Fotheringay presently perceived, with a glow of surprise and gratification, of all the miracles they would presently do. "And, by the bye, Mr. Maydig," said Mr. Fotheringay, "I might perhaps be able to help you—in a domestic way."

"Don't quite follow," said Mr. Maydig pouring out a glass of miraculous old Burgundy.

Mr. Fotheringay helped himself to a second Welsh rarebit out of vacancy, and took a mouthful. "I was thinking," he said, "I might be able (*chum, chum*) to work (*chum, chum*) a miracle with Mrs. Minchin (*chum, chum*)—make her a better woman."

Mr. Maydig put down the glass and looked doubtful. "She's—— She strongly objects to interference, you know, Mr. Fotheringay. And—as a matter of fact—it's well past eleven and she's probably in bed and asleep. Do you think, on the whole——"

Mr. Fotheringay considered these objections. "I don't see that it shouldn't be done in her sleep."

For a time Mr. Maydig opposed the idea, and then he yielded. Mr. Fotheringay issued his orders, and a little less at their ease, perhaps, the two gentlemen proceeded with their repast. Mr. Maydig was enlarging on the changes he might expect in his housekeeper next day, with an optimism that seemed even to Mr. Fotheringay's supper senses a little forced and hectic, when a series of confused noises from upstairs began. Their eyes exchanged interrogations, and Mr. Maydig left the room hastily. Mr. Fotheringay heard him calling up to his housekeeper and then his footsteps going softly up to her.

In a minute or so the minister returned, his step light, his face radiant. "Wonderful!" he said, "and touching! Most touching!"

He began pacing the hearthrug. "A repentance—a most touching repentance—through the crack of the door. Poor woman! A most wonderful change! She had got up. She must have got up at once. She had got up out of her sleep to smash a private bottle of brandy in her box. And to confess it too! . . . But this gives us—it opens—a most amazing vista of possibilities. If we can work this miraculous change in *her*. . . ."

"The thing's unlimited seemingly," said Mr. Fotheringay. "And about Mr. Winch—"

"Altogether unlimited." And from the hearthrug Mr. Maydig, waving the Winch difficulty aside, unfolded a series of wonderful proposals—proposals he invented as he went along.

Now what those proposals were does not concern the essentials of this story. Suffice it that they were designed in a spirit of infinite benevolence, the sort of benevolence that used to be called post-prandial. Suffice it, too, that the problem of Winch remained unsolved. Nor is it necessary to describe how far that series got to its fulfilment. There were astonishing changes. The small hours found Mr. Maydig and Mr. Fotheringay careering across the chilly market-square under the still moon, in a sort of ecstasy of thaumaturgy, Mr. Maydig all flap and gesture, Mr. Fotheringay short and bristling, and no longer abashed at his greatness. They had reformed every drunkard in the Parliamentary division, changed all the beer and alcohol to water (Mr. Maydig had overruled Mr. Fotheringay on this point); they had, further, greatly improved the railway communication of the place, drained Flinder's swamp, improved the soil of One Tree Hill, and cured the Vicar's wart. And they were going to see what could be done with the injured pier at South Bridge. "The place," gasped Mr. Maydig, "won't be the same place to-morrow. How surprised and thankful everyone will be!" And just at that moment the church clock struck three.

"I say," said Mr. Fotheringay, "that's three o'clock! I must be getting back. I've got to be at business by eight. And besides, Mrs. Wimms—"

"We're only beginning," said Mr. Maydig, full of the sweetness of unlimited power. "We're only beginning. Think of all the good we're doing. When people wake—"

"But—," said Mr. Fotheringay.

Mr. Maydig gripped his arm suddenly. His eyes were bright and wild. "My dear chap," he said, "there's no hurry. "Look"—he pointed to the moon at the zenith—"Joshua!"

"Joshua?" said Mr. Fotheringay.

"Joshua," said Mr. Maydig. "Why not? Stop it."

Mr. Fotheringay looked at the moon.

"That's a bit tall," he said after a pause.

"Why not?" said Mr. Maydig. "Of course it doesn't stop. You stop the rotation of the earth, you know. Time stops. It isn't as if we were doing harm."

"H'm!" said Mr. Fotheringay. "Well." He sighed. "I'll try. Here—"

He buttoned up his jacket and addressed himself to the habitable globe, with as good an assumption of confidence as lay in his power. "Jest stop rotating, will you," said Mr. Fotheringay.

Incontinently he was flying head over heels through the air at the rate of dozens of miles a minute. In spite of the innumerable circles he was describing per second, he thought; for thought is wonderful—sometimes as sluggish as flowing pitch, sometimes as instantaneous as light. He thought in a second, and willed. "Let me come down safe and sound. Whatever else happens, let me down safe and sound."

He willed it only just in time, for his clothes, heated by his rapid flight through the air, were already beginning to singe. He came down with a forcible, but by no means injurious bump in what appeared to be a mound of fresh-turned earth. A large mass of metal and masonry, extraordinarily like the clock-tower in the middle of the market-square, hit the earth near him, ricochetted over him, and flew into stonework, bricks, and masonry, like a bursting bomb. A hurtling cow hit one of the larger blocks and smashed like an egg. There was a crash that made all the most violent crashes of his past life seem like the sound of falling dust, and this was followed by a descending series of lesser crashes. A vast wind roared throughout earth and heaven, so that he could scarcely lift his head to look. For a while he was too breathless and astonished even to see where he was or what had happened. And his first movement was to feel his head and reassure himself that his streaming hair was still his own.

"Lord!" gasped Mr. Fotheringay, scarce able to speak for the gale, "I've had a squeak! What's gone wrong? Storms and thunder. And only a minute ago a fine night. It's Maydig set me on to this sort of thing. *What* a wind! If I go on fooling in this way I'm bound to have a thundering accident! . . .

"Where's Maydig?

"What a confounded mess everything's in!"

He looked about him so far as his flapping jacket would permit. The appearance of things was really extremely strange. "The sky's all right anyhow," said Mr. Fotheringay. "And that's about all that is all right. And even there it looks like a terrific gale coming up. But there's the moon overhead. Just as it was just now. Bright as midday. But as for the rest—Where's the village? Where's—where's anything? And what on earth set this wind ablowing? *I* didn't order no wind."

Mr. Fotheringay struggled to get to his feet in vain, and after one failure, remained on all fours, holding on. He surveyed the moonlit world to leeward, with the tails of his jacket streaming over his head. "There's something seriously wrong," said Mr. Fotheringay. "And what it is—goodness knows."

Far and wide nothing was visible in the white glare through the haze of dust that drove before a screaming gale but tumbled masses of earth and heaps of inchoate ruins, no trees, no houses, no familiar shapes, only a wilderness of disorder vanishing at last into the darkness beneath the whirling columns and streamers, the lightnings and thunderings of a swiftly rising storm. Near him in the livid glare was something that might once have been an elm-tree, a smashed mass of splinters, shivered from boughs to base, and further a twisted mass of iron girders—only too evidently the viaduct—rose out of the piled confusion.

You see, when Mr. Fotheringay had arrested the rotation of the solid globe, he had made no stipulation concerning the trifling movables upon its surface. And the earth spins so fast that the surface at its equator is travelling at rather more than a thousand miles an hour, and in these latitudes at more than half that pace. So that the village, and Mr. Maydig, and Mr. Fotheringay, and everybody and everything had been jerked violently forward at about nine miles per second—that is to say, much more violently than if they had been fired out of a cannon. And every human being, every living creature, every house, and every tree—all the world as we know it—had been so jerked and smashed and utterly destroyed. That was all.

These things Mr. Fotheringay did not, of course, fully appreciate. But he perceived that his miracle had miscarried, and with that a great disgust of miracles came upon him. He was in darkness now, for the clouds had swept together and blotted out his momentary glimpse of the moon, and the air was full of fitful struggling tortured wraiths of hail. A great roaring of wind and waters filled earth and sky, and, peering under his hand through the dust and sleet to windward, he saw by the play of the lightnings a vast wall of water pouring towards him.

"Maydig!" screamed Mr. Fotheringay's feeble voice amid the elemental uproar. "Here!—Maydig!"

"Stop!" cried Mr. Fotheringay to the advancing water. "Oh, for goodness' sake, stop!"

"Just a moment," said Mr. Fotheringay to the lightnings and thunder. "Stop jest a moment while I collect my thoughts. . . . And now what shall I do?" he said. "What *shall* I do? Lord! I wish Maydig was about."

"I know," said Mr. Fotheringay. "And for goodness' sake let's have it right *this* time."

He remained on all fours, leaning against the wind, very intent to have everything right.

"Ah!" he said. "Let nothing what I'm going to order happen until I say 'Off!' . . . Lord! I wish I'd thought of that before!"

He lifted his little voice against the whirlwind, shouting louder and louder in the vain desire to hear himself speak. "Now then!—here goes! Mind about that what I said just now. In the first place, when all I've got to say is done, let me lose my miraculous power, let my will become just like anybody else's will, and all these dangerous miracles be stopped. I don't like them. I'd rather I didn't work 'em. Ever so much. That's the first thing. And the second is—let me be back just before the miracles begin; let everything be just as it was before that blessed lamp turned up. It's a big job, but it's the last. Have you got it? No more miracles, everything as it was—me back in the Long Dragon just before I drank my half-pint. That's it! Yes."

He dug his fingers into the mould, closed his eyes, and said "Off!"

Everything became perfectly still. He perceived that he was standing erect.

"So *you* say," said a voice.

He opened his eyes. He was in the bar of the Long Dragon, arguing about miracles with Toddy Beamish. He had a vague sense of some great thing forgotten that instantaneously passed. You see, except for the loss of his miraculous powers, everything was back as it had been; his mind and memory therefore were now just as they had been at the time when this story began. So that he knew absolutely nothing of all that is told here, knows nothing of all that is told here to this day. And among other things, of course, he still did not believe in miracles.

"I tell you that miracles, properly speaking, can't possibly happen," he said, "whatever you like to hold. And I'm prepared to prove it up to the hilt."

"That's what *you* think," said Toddy Beamish, and "Prove it if you can."

"Looky here, Mr. Beamish," said Mr. Fotheringay. "Let us clearly understand what a miracle is. It's something contrariwise to the course of nature done by power of Will . . ."

# THE PLATTNER STORY

Whether the story of Gottfried Plattner is to be credited or not, is a pretty question in the value of evidence. On the one hand, we have seven witnesses—to be perfectly exact, we have six and a half pairs of eyes, and one undeniable fact; and on the other we have—what is it? —prejudice, common sense, the inertia of opinion. Never were there seven more honest-seeming witnesses; never was there a more undeniable fact than the inversion of Gottfried Plattner's anatomical structure, and—never was there a more preposterous story than the one they have to tell! The most preposterous part of the story is the worthy Gottfried's contribution (for I count him as one of the seven). Heaven forbid that I should be led into giving countenance to superstition by a passion for impartiality, and so come to share the fate of Eusapia's patrons! Frankly, I believe there is something crooked about this business of Gottfried Plattner; but what that crooked factor is, I will admit as frankly, I do not know. I have been surprised at the credit accorded to the story in the most unexpected and authoritative quarters. The fairest way to the reader, however, will be for me to tell it without further comment.

Gottfried Plattner is, in spite of his name, a freeborn Englishman. His father was an Alsatian who came to England in the Sixties, married a respectable English girl of unexceptionable antecedents, and died, after a wholesome and uneventful life (devoted, I understand, chiefly to the laying of parquet flooring), in 1887. Gottfried's age is seven-and-twenty. He is, by virtue of his heritage of three languages, Modern Languages Master in a small private school in the South of England. To the casual observer he is singularly like any other Modern Languages Master in any other small private school. His costume is neither very costly nor very fashionable, but, on the other hand, it is not markedly cheap or shabby; his complexion, like his height and his bearing, is inconspicuous. You would notice, perhaps, that, like the majority of people, his face was not absolutely symmetrical, his right eye a little larger than the left, and his jaw a trifle heavier on the right side. If you, as an ordinary careless person, were to bare his chest and feel his heart beating, you would probably find it quite like the heart of any one else. But here you and the trained observer would part company. If you found his heart quite ordinary, the trained observer would find it quite otherwise. And once the thing was pointed out to you, you too would perceive the peculiarity easily enough. It is that Gottfried's heart beats on the right side of his body.

Now, that is not the only singularity of Gottfried's structure, although it is the only one that would appeal to the untrained mind. Careful sounding of Gottfried's internal arrangements, by a well-known surgeon, seems to point to the fact that all the other unsymmetrical parts of his body are similarly misplaced. The right lobe of his liver is on the left side, the left on his right; while his lungs, too, are similarly contraposed. What is still more singular, unless Gottfried is a consummate actor, we must believe that his right hand has recently become his left. Since the occurrences we are about to consider (as impartially as possible), he has found the utmost difficulty in writing, except from right to left across the paper with his left hand. He cannot throw with his right hand, he is perplexed at meal times between knife and fork, and his ideas of the rule of the road—he is a cyclist—are still a dangerous confusion. And there is not a scrap of evidence to show that before these occurrences Gottfried was at all left-handed.

There is yet another wonderful fact in this preposterous business. Gottfried produces three photographs of himself. You have him at the age of five or six, thrusting fat legs at you from under a plaid frock, and scowling. In that photograph his left eye is a little larger than his right, and his jaw is a trifle heavier on the left side. This is the reverse of his present living conditions. The photograph of Gottfried at fourteen seems to contradict these facts, but that is because it is one of those cheap "Gem" photographs that were then in vogue, taken direct upon metal, and therefore reversing things just as a looking-glass would. The third photograph represents him at one-and-twenty, and confirms the record of the others. There seems here evidence of the strongest confirmatory character that Gottfried has exchanged his left side for his right. Yet how a human being can be so changed, short of a fantastic and pointless miracle, it is exceedingly hard to suggest.

In one way, of course, these facts might be explicable on the supposition that Plattner has undertaken an elaborate mystification, on the strength of his heart's displacement. Photographs may be fudged, and left-handedness imitated. But the character of the man does not lend itself to any such theory. He is quiet, practical, unobtrusive, and thoroughly sane, from the Nordau standpoint. He likes beer, and smokes moderately, takes walking exercise daily, and has a healthily high estimate of the value of his teaching. He has a good but untrained tenor voice, and takes a pleasure in singing airs of a popular and cheerful character. He is fond, but not morbidly fond, of reading,—chiefly fiction pervaded with a vaguely pious optimism,—sleeps well, and rarely dreams. He is, in fact, the very last person to evolve a fantastic fable. Indeed, so far from forcing this story upon the world, he has been singularly reticient on the matter. He meets enquirers with a certain engaging—bashfulness is almost the word, that disarms the most suspicious. He seems genuinely ashamed that anything so unusual has occurred to him.

It is to be regretted that Plattner's aversion to the idea of postmortem dissection may postpone, perhaps for ever, the positive proof that his entire body has had its left and right sides transposed. Upon that fact mainly the credibility of his story hangs. There is no way of taking a man and moving him about *in space,* as ordinary people understand space, that will result in our changing his sides. Whatever you do, his right is still his right, his left his left. You can do that with a perfectly thin and flat thing, of course. If you were to cut a figure out of paper, any figure with a right and left side, you could change its sides simply by lifting it up and turning it over. But with a solid it is different. Mathematical theorists tell us that the only way in which the right and left sides of a solid body can be changed is by taking that body clean out of space as we know it,—taking it out of ordinary existence, that is, and turning it somewhere outside space. This is a little abstruse, no doubt, but any one with any knowledge of mathematical theory will assure the reader of its truth. To put the thing in technical language, the curious inversion of Plattner's right and left sides is proof that he has moved out of our space into what is called the Fourth Dimension, and that he has returned again to our world. Unless we choose to consider ourselves the victims of an elaborate and motiveless fabrication, we are almost bound to believe that this has occurred.

So much for the tangible facts. We come now to the account of the phenomena that attended his temporary disappearance from the world. It appears that in the Sussexville Proprietary School Plattner not only discharged the duties of Modern Languages Master, but also taught chemistry, commercial geography, book-keeping, shorthand, drawing, and any other additional subject to which the changing fancies of the boys' parents might direct attention. He knew little or nothing of these various subjects, but in secondary as distinguished from Board or elementary schools, knowledge in the teacher is, very properly, by no means so necessary as high moral character and gentlemanly tone. In chemistry he was particularly deficient, knowing, he says, nothing beyond the Three Gases (whatever the three gases may be). As, however, his pupils began by knowing nothing, and derived all their information from him, this caused him (or any one) but little inconvenience for several terms. Then a little boy named Whibble joined the school, who had been educated (it seems) by some mischievous relative into an enquiring habit of mind. This little boy followed Plattner's lessons with marked and sustained interest, and in order to exhibit his zeal on the subject, brought, at various times, substances for Plattner to analyse. Plattner, flattered by this evidence of his power of awakening interest, and trusting to the boy's ignorance, analysed these, and even made general statements as to their composition. Indeed, he was so far stimulated by his pupil as to obtain a work upon analytical chemistry and study it during his supervision of the evening's preparation. He was surprised to find chemistry quite an interesting subject.

So far the story is absolutely commonplace. But now the greenish powder comes upon the scene. The source of that greenish powder seems, unfortunately, lost. Master Whibble tells a tortuous story of finding it done up in a packet in a disused limekiln near the downs. It would have been an excellent thing for Plattner, and possibly for Master Whibble's family, if a match could have been applied to that powder there and then. The young gentleman certainly did not bring it to school in a packet, but in a common eight-ounce graduated medicine bottle, plugged with masticated newspaper. He gave it to Plattner at the end of the afternoon school. Four boys had been detained after school prayers in order to complete some neglected tasks, and Plattner was supervising these in the small classroom in which the chemical teaching was conducted. The appliances for the practical teaching of chemistry in the Sussexville Proprietary School, as in most small schools in this country, are characterised by a severe simplicity. They are kept in a small cupboard standing in a recess, and having about the same capacity as a common travelling trunk. Plattner, being bored with his passive superintendence, seems to have welcomed the intervention of Whibble with his green powder as an agreeable diversion, and, unlocking this cupboard, proceeded at once with his analytical experiments. Whibble sat, luckily for himself, at a safe distance, regarding him. The four malefactors, feigning a profound absorption in their work, watched him furtively with the keenest interest. For even within the limits of the Three Gases, Plattner's practical chemistry was, I understand, temerarious.

They are practically unanimous in their account of Plattner's proceedings. He poured a little of the green powder into a test-tube, and tried the substance with water, hydrochloric acid, nitric acid, and sulphuric acid in succession. Getting no result, he emptied out a little heap—nearly half the bottleful, in fact—upon a slate and tried a match. He held the medicine bottle in his left hand. The stuff began to smoke and melt, and then—exploded with deafening violence and a blinding flash.

The five boys, seeing the flash and being prepared for catastrophes, ducked below their desks, and were none of them seriously hurt. The window was blown out into the playground, and the blackboard on its easel was upset. The slate was smashed to atoms. Some plaster fell from the ceiling. No other damage was done to the school edifice or appliances, and the boys at first, seeing nothing of Plattner, fancied he was knocked down and lying out of their sight below the desks. They jumped out of their places to go to his assistance, and were amazed to find the space empty. Being still confused by the sudden violence of the report, they hurried to the open door, under the impression that he must have been hurt, and have rushed out of the room. But Carson, the foremost, nearly collided in the doorway with the principal, Mr. Lidgett.

Mr. Lidgett is a corpulent, excitable man with one eye. The boys describe him as stumbling into the room mouthing some of those tempered expletives irritable schoolmasters accustom themselves to use —lest worse befall. "Wretched mumchancer!" he said. "Where's Mr. Plattner?" The boys are agreed on the very words. ("Wobbler," "snivelling puppy," and "mumchancer" are, it seems, among the ordinary small change of Mr. Lidgett's scholastic commerce.)

Where's Mr. Plattner? That was a question that was to be repeated many times in the next few days. It really seemed as though that frantic hyperbole, "blown to atoms," had for once realised itself. There was not a visible particle of Plattner to be seen; not a drop of blood nor a stitch of clothing to be found. Apparently he had been blown clean out of existence and left not a wrack behind. Not so much as would cover a sixpenny piece, to quote a proverbial expression! The evidence of his absolute disappearance, as a consequence of that explosion, is indubitable.

It is not necessary to enlarge here upon the commotion excited in the Sussexville Proprietary School, and in Sussexville and elsewhere, by this event. It is quite possible, indeed, that some of the readers of these pages may recall the hearing of some remote and dying version of that excitement during the last summer holidays. Lidgett, it would seem, did everything in his power to suppress and minimise the story. He instituted a penalty of twenty-five lines for any mention of Plattner's name among the boys, and stated in the schoolroom that he was clearly aware of his assistant's whereabouts. He was afraid, he explains, that the possibility of an explosion happening, in spite of the elaborate precautions taken to minimise the practical teaching of chemistry, might injure the reputation of the school; and so might any mysterious quality in Plattner's departure. Indeed, he did everything in his power to make the occurrence seem as ordinary as possible. In particular, he cross-examined the five eye-witnesses of the occurrence so searchingly that they began to doubt the plain evidence of their senses. But, in spite of these efforts, the tale, in a magnified and distorted state, made a nine days' wonder in the district, and several parents withdrew their sons on colourable pretexts. Not the least remarkable point in the matter is the fact that a large number of people in the neighbourhood dreamed singularly vivid dreams of Plattner during the period of excitement before his return, and that these dreams had a curious uniformity. In almost all of them Plattner was seen, sometimes singly, sometimes in company, wandering about through a coruscating iridescence. In all cases his face was pale and distressed, and in some he gesticulated towards the dreamer. One or two of the boys, evidently under the influence of nightmare, fancied that Plattner approached them with remarkable swiftness, and seemed to look closely into their very eyes. Others fled with Plattner from the pursuit of vague and extraordinary creatures of a globular shape. But all these fancies were forgotten in enquiries and speculations when, on the Wednesday next but one after the Monday of the explosion, Plattner returned.

The circumstances of his return were as singular as those of his departure. So far as Mr. Lidgett's somewhat choleric outline can be filled in from Plattner's hesitating statements, it would appear that on Wednesday evening, towards the hour of sunset, the former gentleman, having dismissed evening preparation, was engaged in his garden, picking and eating strawberries, a fruit of which he is inordinately fond. It is a large old-fashioned garden, secured from observation, fortunately, by a high and ivy-covered red-brick wall. Just as he was stooping over a particularly prolific plant, there was a flash in the air and a heavy thud, and before he could look round, some heavy body struck him violently from behind. He was pitched forward, crushing the strawberries he held in his hand, and that so roughly, that his silk hat—Mr. Lidgett adheres to the older ideas of scholastic costume—was driven violently down upon his forehead, and almost over one eye. This heavy missile, which slid over him sideways and collapsed into a sitting posture among the strawberry plants, proved to be our long-lost Mr. Gottfried Plattner, in an extremely dishevelled condition. He was collarless and hatless, his linen was dirty, and there was blood upon his hands. Mr. Lidgett was so indignant and surprised that he remained on all-fours, and with his hat jammed down on his eye, while he expostulated vehemently with Plattner for his disrespectful and unaccountable conduct.

This scarcely idyllic scene completes what I may call the exterior version of the Plattner story—its exoteric aspect. It is quite unnecessary to enter here into all the details of his dismissal by Mr. Lidgett. Such details, with the full names and dates and references, will be found in the larger report of these occurrences that was laid before the Society for the Investigation of Abnormal Phenomena. The singular transposition of Plattner's right and left sides was scarcely observed for the first day or so, and then first in connection with his disposition to write from right to left across the blackboard. He concealed rather than ostended this curious confirmatory circumstance, as he considered it would unfavourably affect his prospects in a new situation. The displacement of his heart was discovered some months after, when he was having a tooth extracted under anæsthetics. He then, very unwillingly, allowed a cursory surgical examination to be made of himself, with a view to a brief account in the *Journal of Anatomy*. That exhausts the statement of the material facts; and we may now go on to consider Plattner's account of the matter.

But first let us clearly differentiate between the preceding portion of this story and what is to follow. All I have told thus far is established by such evidence as even a criminal lawyer would approve. Every one of the witnesses is still alive; the reader, if he have the leisure, may hunt the lads out to-morrow, or even brave the terrors of the redoubtable Lidgett, and cross-examine and trap and test to his heart's content; Gottfried Plattner, himself, and his twisted heart and his three photographs are producible. It may be taken as proved that he did disappear for nine days as the consequence of an explosion; that he returned almost as violently, under circumstances in their nature annoying to Mr. Lidgett, whatever the details of those circumstances may be; and that he returned inverted, just as a reflection returns from a mirror. From the last fact, as I have already stated, it follows almost inevitably that Plattner, during those nine days, must have been in some state of existence altogether out of space. The evidence to these statements is, indeed, far stronger than that upon which most murderers are hanged. But for his own particular account of where he had been, with its confused explanations and well-nigh self-contradictory details, we have only Mr. Gottfried Plattner's word. I do not wish to discredit that, but I must point out—what so many writers upon obscure psychic phenomena fail to do—that we are passing here from the practically undeniable to that kind of matter which any reasonable man is entitled to believe or reject as he thinks proper. The previous statements render it plausible; its discordance with common experience tilts it towards the incredible. I would prefer not to sway the beam of the reader's judgment either way, but simply to tell the story as Plattner told it me.

He gave me his narrative, I may state, at my house at Chislehurst, and so soon as he had left me that evening, I went into my study and wrote down everything as I remembered it. Subsequently he was good enough to read over a type-written copy, so that its substantial correctness is undeniable.

He states that at the moment of the explosion he distinctly thought he was killed. He felt lifted off his feet and driven forcibly backward. It is a curious fact for psychologists that he thought clearly during his backward flight, and wondered whether he should hit the chemistry cupboard or the blackboard easel. His heels struck ground, and he staggered and fell heavily into a sitting position on something soft and firm. For a moment the concussion stunned him. He became aware at once of a vivid scent of singed hair, and he seemed to hear the voice of Lidgett asking for him. You will understand that for a time his mind was greatly confused.

At first he was distinctly under the impression that he was still in the classroom. He perceived quite distinctly the surprise of the boys and the entry of Mr. Lidgett. He is quite positive upon that score. He did not hear their remarks; but that he ascribed to the deafening effect of the experiment. Things about him seemed curiously dark and faint, but his mind explained that on the obvious but mistaken idea that the explosion had engendered a huge volume of dark smoke. Through the dimness the figures of Lidgett and the boys moved, as faint and silent as ghosts. Plattner's face still tingled with the stinging heat of the flash. He was, he says, "all muddled." His first definite thoughts seem to have been of his personal safety. He thought he was perhaps blinded and deafened. He felt his limbs and face in a gingerly manner. Then his perceptions grew clearer, and he was astonished to miss the old familiar desks and other schoolroom furniture about him. Only dim, uncertain, grey shapes stood in the place of these. Then came a thing that made him shout aloud, and awoke his stunned faculties to instant activity. *Two of the boys, gesticulating, walked one after the other clean through him!* Neither manifested the slightest consciousness of his presence. It is difficult to imagine the sensation he felt. They came against him, he says, with no more force than a wisp of mist.

Plattner's first thought after that was that he was dead. Having been brought up with thoroughly sound views in these matters, however, he was a little surprised to find his body still about him. His second conclusion was that he was not dead, but that the others were: that the explosion had destroyed the Sussexville Proprietary School and every soul in it except himself. But that, too, was scarcely satisfactory. He was thrown back upon astonished observation.

Everything about him was extraordinarily dark: at first it seemed to have an altogether ebony blackness. Overhead was a black firmament. The only touch of light in the scene was a faint greenish glow at the edge of the sky in one direction, which threw into prominence a horizon of undulating black hills. This, I say, was his impression at first. As his eye grew accustomed to the darkness, he began to distinguish a faint quality of differentiating greenish colour in the circumambient night. Against this background the furniture and occupants of the classroom, it seems, stood out like phosphorescent spectres, faint and impalpable. He extended his hand, and thrust it without an effort through the wall of the room by the fireplace.

He describes himself as making a strenuous effort to attract attention. He shouted to Lidgett, and tried to seize the boys as they went to and fro. He only desisted from these attempts when Mrs. Lidgett, whom he (as an Assistant Master) naturally disliked, entered the room. He says the sensation of being in the world, and yet not a part of it, was an extraordinarily disagreeable one. He compared his feelings, not inaptly, to those of a cat watching a mouse through a window. Whenever he made a motion to communicate with the dim, familiar world about him, he found an invisible, incomprehensible barrier preventing intercourse.

He then turned his attention to his solid environment. He found the medicine bottle still unbroken in his hand, with the remainder of the green powder therein. He put this in his pocket, and began to feel about him. Apparently, he was sitting on a boulder of rock covered with a velvety moss. The dark country about him he was unable to see, the faint, misty picture of the schoolroom blotting it out, but he had a feeling (due perhaps to a cold wind) that he was near the crest of a hill, and that a steep valley fell away beneath his feet. The green glow along the edge of the sky seemed to be growing in extent and intensity. He stood up, rubbing his eyes.

It would seem that he made a few steps, going steeply downhill, and then stumbled, nearly fell, and sat down again upon a jagged mass of rock to watch the dawn. He became aware that the world about him was absolutely silent. It was as still as it was dark, and though there was a cold wind blowing up the hill-face, the rustle of grass, the soughing of the boughs that should have accompanied it, were absent. He could hear, therefore, if he could not see, that the hillside upon which he stood was rocky and desolate. The green grew brighter every moment, and as it did so, a faint, transparent blood-red mingled with, but did not mitigate, the blackness of the sky overhead and the rocky desolations about him. Having regard to what follows, I am inclined to think that that redness may have been an optical effect due to contrast. Something black fluttered momentarily against the livid yellow-green of the lower sky, and then the thin and penetrating voice of a bell rose out of the black gulf below him. An oppressive expectation grew with the growing light.

It is probable that an hour or more elapsed while he sat there, the strange green light growing brighter every moment, and spreading slowly, in flamboyant fingers, upward towards the zenith. As it grew, the spectral vision of *our* world became relatively or absolutely fainter. Probably both, for the time must have been about that of our earthly sunset. So far as his vision of our world went, Plattner, by his few steps downhill, had passed through the floor of the classroom, and was now, it seemed, sitting in mid-air in the larger schoolroom downstairs. He saw the boarders distinctly, but much more faintly than he had seen Lidgett. They were preparing their evening tasks, and he noticed with interest that several were cheating with their Euclid riders by means of a crib, a compilation whose existence he had hitherto never suspected. As the time passed, they faded steadily, as steadily as the light of the green dawn increased.

Looking down into the valley, he saw that the light had crept far down its rocky sides, and that the profound blackness of the abyss was now broken by a minute green glow, like the light of a glowworm. And almost immediately the limb of a huge heavenly body of blazing green rose over the basaltic undulations of the distant hills, and the monstrous hill-masses about him came out gaunt and desolate, in green light and deep, ruddy black shadows. He became aware of a vast number of ball-shaped objects drifting as thistledown drifts over the high ground. There were none of these nearer to him than the opposite side of the gorge. The bell below twanged quicker and quicker, with something like impatient insistence, and several lights moved hither and thither. The boys at work at their desks were now almost imperceptibly faint.

This extinction of our world, when the green sun of this other universe rose, is a curious point upon which Plattner insists. During the Other-World night, it is difficult to move about, on account of the vividness with which the things of this world are visible. It becomes a riddle to explain why, if this is the case, we in this world catch no glimpse of the Other-World. It is due, perhaps, to the comparatively vivid illumination of this world of ours. Plattner describes the midday of the Other-World, at its brightest, as not being nearly so bright as this world at full moon, while its night is profoundly black. Consequently, the amount of light, even in an ordinary dark room, is sufficient to render the things of the Other-World invisible, on the same principle that faint phosphorescence is only visible in the profoundest darkness. I have tried, since he told me his story, to see something of the Other-World by sitting for a long space in a photographer's dark room at night. I have certainly seen indistinctly the form of greenish slopes and rocks, but only, I must admit, very indistinctly indeed. The reader may possibly be more successful. Plattner tells me that since his return he has dreamt and seen and recognised places in the Other-World, but this is probably due to his memory of these scenes. It seems quite possible that people with unusually keen eyesight may occasionally catch a glimpse of this strange Other-World about us.

However, this is a digression. As the green sun rose, a long street of black buildings became perceptible, though only darkly and indistinctly, in the gorge, and, after some hesitation, Plattner began to clamber down the precipitous descent towards them. The descent was long and exceedingly tedious, being so not only by the extraordinary steepness, but also by reason of the looseness of the boulders with which the whole face of the hill was strewn. The noise of his descent—now and then his heels struck fire from the rocks—seemed now the only sound in the universe, for the beating of the bell had ceased. As he drew nearer, he perceived that the various edifices had a singular resemblance to tombs and mausoleums and monuments, saving only that they were all uniformly black instead of being white, as most sepulchres are. And then he saw, crowding out of the largest building, very much as people disperse from church, a number of pallid, rounded, pale-green figures. These dispersed in several directions about the broad street of the place, some going through side alleys and reappearing upon the steepness of the hill, others entering some of the small black buildings which lined the way.

At the sight of these things drifting up towards him, Plattner stopped, staring. They were not walking, they were indeed limbless, and they had the appearance of human heads, beneath which a tadpole-like body swung. He was too astonished at their strangeness, too full, indeed, of strangeness, to be seriously alarmed by them. They drove towards him, in front of the chill wind that was blowing uphill, much as soap-bubbles drive before a draught. And as he looked at the nearest of those approaching, he saw it was indeed a human head, albeit with singularly large eyes, and wearing such an expression of distress and anguish as he had never seen before upon mortal countenance. He was surprised to find that it did not turn to regard him, but seemed to be watching and following some unseen moving thing. For a moment he was puzzled, and then it occurred to him that this creature was watching with its enormous eyes something that was happening in the world he had just left. Nearer it came, and nearer, and he was too astonished to cry out. It made a very faint fretting sound as it came close to him. Then it struck his face with a gentle pat,—its touch was very cold,—and drove past him, and upward towards the crest of the hill.

An extraordinary conviction flashed across Plattner's mind that this head had a strong likeness to Lidgett. Then he turned his attention to the other heads that were now swarming thickly up the hillside. None made the slightest sign of recognition. One or two, indeed, came close to his head and almost followed the example of the first, but he dodged convulsively out of the way. Upon most of them he saw the same expression of unavailing regret he had seen upon the first, and heard the same faint sounds of wretchedness from them. One or two wept, and one rolling swiftly uphill wore an expression of diabolical rage. But others were cold, and several had a look of gratified interest in their eyes. One, at least, was almost in an ecstasy of happiness. Plattner does not remember that he recognised any more likenesses in those he saw at this time.

For several hours, perhaps, Plattner watched these strange things dispersing themselves over the hills, and not till long after they had ceased to issue from the clustering black buildings in the gorge, did he resume his downward climb. The darkness about him increased so much that he had a difficulty in stepping true. Overhead the sky was now a bright, pale green. He felt neither hunger nor thirst. Later, when he did, he found a chilly stream running down the centre of the gorge, and the rare moss upon the boulders, when he tried it at last in desperation, was good to eat.

He groped about among the tombs that ran down the gorge, seeking vaguely for some clue to these inexplicable things. After a long time he came to the entrance of the big mausoleum-like building from which the heads had issued. In this he found a group of green lights burning upon a kind of basaltic altar, and a bell-rope from a belfry overhead hanging down into the centre of the place. Round the wall ran a lettering of fire in a character unknown to him. While he was still wondering at the purport of these things, he heard the receding tramp of heavy feet echoing far down the street. He ran out into the darkness again, but he could see nothing. He had a mind to pull the bell-rope, and finally decided to follow the footsteps. But, although he ran far, he never overtook them; and his shouting was of no avail. The gorge seemed to extend an interminable distance. It was as dark as earthly starlight throughout its length, while the ghastly green day lay along the upper edge of its precipices. There were none of the heads, now, below. They were all, it seemed, busily occupied along the upper slopes. Looking up, he saw them drifting hither and thither, some hovering stationary, some flying swiftly through the air. It reminded him, he said, of "big snowflakes;" only these were black and pale green.

In pursuing the firm, undeviating footsteps that he never overtook, in groping into new regions of this endless devil's dyke, in clambering up and down the pitiless heights, in wandering about the summits, and in watching the drifting faces, Plattner states that he spent the better part of seven or eight days. He did not keep count, he says. Though once or twice he found eyes watching him, he had word with no living soul. He slept among the rocks on the hillside. In the gorge things earthly were invisible, because, from the earthly standpoint, it was far underground. On the altitudes, so soon as the earthly day began, the world became visible to him. He found himself sometimes stumbling over the dark-green rocks, or arresting himself on a precipitous brink, while all about him the green branches of the Sussexville lanes were swaying; or, again, he seemed to be walking through the Sussexville streets, or watching unseen the private business of some household. And then it was he discovered, that to almost every human being in our world there pertained some of these drifting heads: that every one in the world is watched intermittently by these helpless disembodiments.

What are they—these Watchers of the Living? Plattner never learned. But two, that presently found and followed him, were like his childhood's memory of his father and mother. Now and then other faces turned their eyes upon him: eyes like those of dead people who had swayed him, or injured him, or helped him in his youth and manhood. Whenever they looked at him, Plattner was overcome with a strange sense of responsibility. To his mother he ventured to speak;

but she made no answer. She looked sadly, steadfastly, and tenderly—a little reproachfully, too, it seemed—into his eyes.

He simply tells this story: he does not endeavour to explain. We are left to surmise who these Watchers of the Living may be, or if they are indeed the Dead, why they should so closely and passionately watch a world they have left for ever. It may be—indeed to my mind it seems just—that, when our life has closed, when evil or good is no longer a choice for us, we may still have to witness the working out of the train of consequences we have laid. If human souls continue after death, then surely human interests continue after death. But that is merely my own guess at the meaning of the things seen. Plattner offers no interpretation, for none was given him. It is well the reader should understand this clearly. Day after day, with his head reeling, he wandered about this strange-lit world outside the world, weary and, towards the end, weak and hungry. By day—by our earthly day, that is—the ghostly vision of the old familiar scenery of Sussexville, all about him, irked and worried him. He could not see where to put his feet, and ever and again with a chilly touch one of these Watching Souls would come against his face. And after dark the multitude of these Watchers about him, and their intent distress, confused his mind beyond describing. A great longing to return to the earthly life that was so near and yet so remote consumed him. The unearthliness of things about him produced a positively painful mental distress. He was worried beyond describing by his own particular followers. He would shout at them to desist from staring at him, scold at them, hurry away from them. They were always mute and intent. Run as he might over the uneven ground, they followed his destinies.

On the ninth day, towards evening, Plattner heard the invisible footsteps approaching, far away down the gorge. He was then wandering over the broad crest of the same hill upon which he had fallen in his entry into this strange Other-World of his. He turned to hurry down into the gorge, feeling his way hastily, and was arrested by the sight of the thing that was happening in a room in a back street near the school. Both of the people in the room he knew by sight. The windows were open, the blinds up, and the setting sun shone clearly into it, so that it came out quite brightly at first, a vivid oblong of room, lying like a magic-lantern picture upon the black landscape and the livid green dawn. In addition to the sunlight, a candle had just been lit in the room.

On the bed lay a lank man, his ghastly white face terrible upon the tumbled pillow. His clenched hands were raised above his head. A little table beside the bed carried a few medicine bottles, some toast and water, and an empty glass. Every now and then the lank man's lips fell apart, to indicate a word he could not articulate. But the woman did not notice that he wanted anything, because she was busy turning out papers from an old-fashioned bureau in the opposite corner of the room. At first the picture was very vivid indeed, but as the green dawn behind it grew brighter and brighter, so it became fainter and more and more transparent.

As the echoing footsteps paced nearer and nearer, those footsteps that sound so loud in that Other-World and come so silently in this, Plattner perceived about him a great multitude of dim faces gathering together out of the darkness and watching the two people in the room. Never before had he seen so many of the Watchers of the Living. A multitude had eyes only for the sufferer in the room, another multitude, in infinite anguish, watched the woman as she hunted with greedy eyes for something she could not find. They crowded about Plattner, they came across his sight and buffeted his face, the noise of their unavailing regrets was all about him. He saw clearly only now and then. At other times the picture quivered dimly, through the veil of green reflections upon their movements. In the room it must have been very still, and Plattner says the candle flame streamed up into a perfectly vertical line of smoke, but in his ears each footfall and its echoes beat like a clap of thunder. And the faces! Two, more particularly near the woman's: one a woman's also, white and clear-featured, a face which might have once been cold and hard, but which was now softened by the touch of a wisdom strange to earth. The other might have been the woman's father. Both were evidently absorbed in the contemplation of some act of hateful meanness, so it seemed, which they could no longer guard against and prevent. Behind were others, teachers, it may be, who had taught ill, friends whose influence had failed. And over the man, too—a multitude, but none that seemed to be parents or teachers! Faces that might once have been coarse, now purged to strength by sorrow! And in the forefront one face, a girlish one, neither angry nor remorseful, but merely patient and weary, and, as it seemed to Plattner, waiting for relief. His powers of description fail him at the memory of this multitude of ghastly countenances. They gathered on the stroke of the bell. He saw them all in the space of a second. It would seem that he was so worked on by his excitement that, quite involuntarily, his restless fingers took the bottle of green powder out of his pocket and held it before him. But he does not remember that.

Abruptly the footsteps ceased. He waited for the next, and there was silence, and then suddenly, cutting through the unexpected stillness like a keen, thin blade, came the first stroke of the bell. At that the multitudinous faces swayed to and fro and a louder crying began all about him. The woman did not hear; she was burning something now in the candle flame. At the second stroke everything grew dim, and a breath of wind, icy cold, blew through the host of watchers. They swirled about him like an eddy of dead leaves in the spring, and at the third stroke something was extended through them to the bed. You have heard of a beam of light. This was like a beam of darkness, and looking again at it, Plattner saw that it was a shadowy arm and hand.

The green sun was now topping the black desolations of the horizon, and the vision of the room was very faint. Plattner could see that the white of the bed struggled, and was convulsed; and that the woman looked round over her shoulder at it, startled.

The cloud of watchers lifted high like a puff of green dust before the wind, and swept swiftly downward towards the temple in the gorge. Then suddenly Plattner understood the meaning of the shadowy black arm that stretched across his shoulder and clutched its prey. He did not dare turn his head to see the Shadow behind the arm. With a violent effort, and covering his eyes, he set himself to run, made, perhaps, twenty strides, then slipped on a boulder, and fell. He fell forward on his hands; and the bottle smashed and exploded as he touched the ground.

In another moment he found himself, stunned and bleeding, sitting face to face with Lidgett in the old walled garden behind the school.

There the story of Plattner's experiences ends. I have resisted, I believe successfully, the natural disposition of a writer of fiction to dress up incidents of this sort. I have told the thing as far as possible in the order in which Plattner told it to me. I have carefully avoided any attempt at style, effect, or construction. It would have been easy, for instance, to have worked the scene of the death-bed into a kind of plot in which Plattner might have been involved. But, quite apart from the objectionableness of falsifying a most extraordinary true story, any such trite devices would spoil, to my mind, the peculiar effect of this dark world, with its livid green illumination and its drifting Watchers of the Living, which, unseen and unapproachable to us, is yet lying all about us.

It remains to add, that a death did actually occur in Vincent Terrace, just beyond the school garden, and, so far as can be proved, at the moment of Plattner's return. Deceased was a rate-collector and insurance agent. His widow, who was much younger than himself, married last month a Mr. Whymper, a veterinary surgeon of Allbeeding. As the portion of this story given here has in various forms circulated orally in Sussexville, she has consented to my use of her name, on condition that I make it distinctly known that she emphatically contradicts every detail of Plattner's account of her husbands last moments. She burnt no will, she says, although Plattner never accused her of doing so; her husband made but one will, and that just after their marriage. Certainly, from a man who had never seen it, Plattner's account of the furniture of the room was curiously accurate.

One other thing, even at the risk of an irksome repetition, I must insist upon, lest I seem to favour the credulous, superstitious view. Plattner's absence from the world for nine days is, I think, proved. But that does not prove his story. It is quite conceivable that even outside space hallucinations may be possible. That, at least, the reader must bear distinctly in mind.

# THE STRANGE ORCHID

The buying of orchids always has in it a certain speculative flavour. You have before you the brown shrivelled lump of tissue, and for the rest you must trust your judgment, or the auctioneer, or your good-luck, as your taste may incline. The plant may be moribund or dead, or it may be just a respectable purchase, fair value for your money, or perhaps—for the thing has happened again and again—there slowly unfolds before the delighted eyes of the happy purchaser, day after day, some new variety, some novel richness, a strange twist of the labellum, or some subtler colouration or unexpected mimicry. Pride, beauty, and profit blossom together on one delicate green spike, and it may be, even immortality. For the new miracle of Nature may stand in need of a new specific name, and what so convenient as that of its discoverer? "Johnsmithia"! There have been worse names.

It was perhaps the hope of some such happy discovery that made Winter-Wedderburn such a frequent attendant at these sales—that hope, and also, maybe, the fact that he had nothing else of the slightest interest to do in the world. He was a shy, lonely, rather ineffectual man, provided with just enough income to keep off the spur of necessity, and not enough nervous energy to make him seek any exacting employments. He might have collected stamps or coins, or translated Horace, or bound books, or invented new species of diatoms. But, as it happened, he grew orchids, and had one ambitious little hot-house.

"I have a fancy," he said over his coffee, "that something is going to happen to me to-day." He spoke—as he moved and thought—slowly.

"Oh, don't say *that!*" said his housekeeper—who was also his remote cousin. For "something happening" was a euphemism that meant only one thing to her.

"You misunderstand me. I mean nothing unpleasant—though what I do mean I scarcely know.

"To-day," he continued after a pause, "Peters are going to sell a batch of plants from the Andamans and the Indies. I shall go up and see what they have. It may be I shall buy something good, unawares. That may be it."

He passed his cup for his second cupful of coffee.

"Are these the things collected by that poor young fellow you told me of the other day?" asked his cousin as she filled his cup.

"Yes," he said, and became meditative over a piece of toast.

"Nothing ever does happen to me," he remarked presently, beginning to think aloud. "I wonder why? Things enough happen to other people. There is Harvey. Only the other week, on Monday he picked up sixpence, on Wednesday his chicks all had the staggers, on Friday his cousin came home from Australia, and on Saturday he broke his ankle. What a whirl of excitement!—compared to me."

"I think I would rather be without so much excitement," said his housekeeper. "It can't be good for you."

"I suppose it's troublesome. Still—you see, nothing ever happens to me. When I was a little boy I never had accidents. I never fell in love as I grew up. Never married—I wonder how it feels to have something happen to you, something really remarkable.

"That orchid-collector was only thirty-six—twenty years younger than myself—when he died. And he had been married twice and divorced once; he had had malarial fever four times, and once he broke his thigh. He killed a Malay once, and once he was wounded by a poisoned dart. And in the end he was killed by jungle-leeches. It must have all been very troublesome, but then it must have been very interesting, you know—except, perhaps, the leeches."

"I am sure it was not good for him," said the lady, with conviction.

"Perhaps not." And then Wedderburn looked at his watch. "Twenty-three minutes past eight. I am going up by the quarter to twelve train, so that there is plenty of time. I think I shall wear my alpaca jacket —it is quite warm enough—and my grey felt hat and brown shoes. I suppose—"

He glanced out of the window at the serene sky and sunlit garden, and then nervously at his cousin's face.

"I think you had better take an umbrella if you are going to London," she said in a voice that admitted of no denial. "There's all between here and the station coming back."

When he returned he was in a state of mild excitement. He had made a purchase. It was rare that he could make up his mind quickly enough to buy, but this time he had done so.

"There are Vandas," he said, "and a Dendrobe and some Palæonophis." He surveyed his purchases lovingly as he consumed his soup. They were laid out on the spotless tablecloth before him, and he was telling his cousin all about them as he slowly meandered through his dinner. It was his custom to live all his visits to London over again in the evening for her and his own entertainment.

"I knew something would happen to-day. And I have bought all these. Some of them—some of them—I feel sure, do you know, that some of them will be remarkable. I don't know how it is, but I feel just as sure as if some one had told me that some of these will turn out remarkable.

"That one"—he pointed to a shrivelled rhizome—"was not identified. It may be a Palæonophis—or it may not. It may be a new species, or even a new genus. And it was the last that poor Batten ever collected."

"I don't like the look of it," said his housekeeper. "It's such an ugly shape."

"To me it scarcely seems to have a shape."

"I don't like those things that stick out," said his housekeeper.

"It shall be put away in a pot to-morrow."

"It looks," said the housekeeper, "like a spider shamming dead."

Wedderburn smiled and surveyed the root with his head on one side. "It is certainly not a pretty lump of stuff. But you can never judge of these things from their dry appearance. It may turn out to be a very beautiful orchid indeed. How busy I shall be to-morrow! I must see tonight just exactly what to do with these things, and to-morrow I shall set to work.

"They found poor Batten lying dead, or dying, in a mangrove swamp—I forget which," he began again presently, "with one of these very orchids crushed up under his body. He had been unwell for some days with some kind of native fever, and I suppose he fainted. These mangrove swamps are very unwholesome. Every drop of blood, they say, was taken out of him by the jungle-leeches. It may be that very plant that cost him his life to obtain."

"I think none the better of it for that."

"Men must work though women may weep," said Wedderburn, with profound gravity.

"Fancy dying away from every comfort in a nasty swamp! Fancy being ill of fever with nothing to take but chlorodyne and quinine—if men were left to themselves they would live on chlorodyne and quinine—and no one round you but horrible natives! They say the

Andaman islanders are most disgusting wretches—and, anyhow, they can scarcely make good nurses, not having the necessary training. And just for people in England to have orchids!"

"I don't suppose it was comfortable, but some men seem to enjoy that kind of thing," said Wedderburn. "Anyhow, the natives of his party were sufficiently civilised to take care of all his collection until his colleague, who was an ornithologist, came back again from the interior; though they could not tell the species of the orchid, and had let it wither. And it makes these things more interesting."

"It makes them disgusting. I should be afraid of some of the malaria clinging to them. And just think, there has been a dead body lying across that ugly thing! I never thought of that before. There! I declare I cannot eat another mouthful of dinner."

"I will take them off the table if you like, and put them in the window-seat. I can see them just as well there."

The next few days he was indeed singularly busy in his steamy little hothouse, fussing about with charcoal, lumps of teak, moss, and all the other mysteries of the orchid cultivator. He considered he was having a wonderfully eventful time. In the evening he would talk about these new orchids to his friends, and over and over again he reverted to his expectation of something strange.

Several of the Vandas and the Dendrobium died under his care, but presently the strange orchid began to show signs of life. He was delighted, and took his housekeeper right away from jam-making to see it at once, directly he made the discovery.

"That is a bud," he said, "and presently there will be a lot of leaves there, and those little things coming out here are aërial rootlets."

"They look to me like little white fingers poking out of the brown. I don't like them," said his housekeeper.

"Why not?"

"I don't know. They look like fingers trying to get at you. I can't help my likes and dislikes."

"I don't know for certain, but I don't *think* there are any orchids I know that have aërial rootlets quite like that. It may be my fancy, of course. You see they are a little flattened at the ends."

"I don't like 'em," said his housekeeper, suddenly shivering and turning away. "I know it's very silly of me—and I'm very sorry, particularly as you like the thing so much. But I can't help thinking of that corpse."

"But it may not be that particular plant. That was merely a guess of mine."

His housekeeper shrugged her shoulders.

"Anyhow I don't like it," she said.

Wedderburn felt a little hurt at her dislike to the plant. But that did not prevent his talking to her about orchids generally, and this orchid in particular, whenever he felt inclined.

"There are such queer things about orchids," he said one day; "such possibilities of surprises. You know, Darwin studied their fertilisation, and showed that the whole structure of an ordinary orchid-flower was contrived in order that moths might carry the pollen from plant to plant. Well, it seems that there are lots of orchids known the flower of which cannot possibly be used for fertilisation in that way. Some of the Cypripediums, for instance; there are no insects known that can possibly fertilise them, and some of them have never been found with seed."

"But how do they form new plants?"

"By runners and tubers, and that kind of outgrowth. That is easily explained. The puzzle is, what are the flowers for?

"Very likely," he added, "*my* orchid may be something extraordinary in that way. If so, I shall study it. I have often thought of making researches as Darwin did. But hitherto I have not found the time, or something else has happened to prevent it. The leaves are beginning to unfold now. I do wish you would come and see them!"

But she said that the orchid-house was so hot it gave her the headache. She had seen the plant once again, and the aërial rootlets, which were now some of them more than a foot long, had unfortunately reminded her of tentacles reaching out after something; and they got into her dreams, growing after her with incredible rapidity. So that she had settled to her entire satisfaction that she would not see that plant again, and Wedderburn had to admire its leaves alone. They were of the ordinary broad form, and a deep glossy green, with splashes and dots of deep red towards the base. He knew of no other leaves quite like them. The plant was placed on a low bench near the thermometer, and close by was a simple arrangement by which a tap dripped on the hot-water pipes and kept the air steamy. And he spent his afternoons now with some regularity meditating on the approaching flowering of this strange plant.

And at last the great thing happened. Directly he entered the little glass house he knew that the spike had burst out, although his great *Palæonophis Lowii* hid the corner where his new darling stood. There was a new odour in the air, a rich, intensely sweet scent, that overpowered every other in that crowded, steaming little greenhouse.

Directly he noticed this he hurried down to the strange orchid. And, behold! the trailing green spikes bore now three great splashes of blossom, from which this overpowering sweetness proceeded. He stopped before them in an ecstasy of admiration.

The flowers were white, with streaks of golden orange upon the petals; the heavy labellum was coiled into an intricate projection, and a wonderful bluish purple mingled there with the gold. He could see at once that the genus was altogether a new one. And the insufferable scent! How hot the place was! The blossoms swam before his eyes.

He would see if the temperature was right. He made a step towards the thermometer. Suddenly everything appeared unsteady. The bricks on the floor were dancing up and down. Then the white blossoms, the green leaves behind them, the whole greenhouse, seemed to sweep sideways, and then in a curve upward.

A half-past four his cousin made the tea, according to their invariable custom. But Wedderburn did not come in for his tea.

"He is worshipping that horrid orchid," she told herself, and waited ten minutes. "His watch must have stopped. I will go and call him."

She went straight to the hothouse, and, opening the door, called his name. There was no reply. She noticed that the air was very close, and loaded with an intense perfume. Then she saw something lying on the bricks between the hot-water pipes.

For a minute, perhaps, she stood motionless.

He was lying, face upward, at the foot of the strange orchid. The tentacle-like aërial rootlets no longer swayed freely in the air, but were crowded together, a tangle of grey ropes, and stretched tight with their ends closely applied to his chin and neck and hands.

She did not understand. Then she saw from under one of the exultant tentacles upon his cheek there trickled a little thread of blood.

With an inarticulate cry she ran towards him, and tried to pull him away from the leech-like suckers. She snapped two of these tentacles, and their sap dripped red.

Then the overpowering scent of the blossom began to make her head reel. How they clung to him! She tore at the tough ropes, and he and the white inflorescence swam about her. She felt she was fainting, knew she must not. She left him and hastily opened the nearest door, and, after she had panted for a moment in the fresh air, she had a brilliant inspiration. She caught up a flower-pot and smashed in the windows at the end of the greenhouse. Then she re-entered. She tugged now with renewed strength at Wedderburn's motionless body, and brought the strange orchid crashing to the floor. It still clung with the grimmest tenacity to its victim. In a frenzy, she lugged it and him into the open air.

Then she thought of tearing through the sucker rootlets one by one, and in another minute she had released him and was dragging him away from the horror.

He was white and bleeding from a dozen circular patches.

The odd-job man was coming up the garden, amazed at the smashing of glass, and saw her emerge, hauling the inanimate body with red-stained hands. For a moment he thought impossible things.

"Bring some water!" she cried, and her voice dispelled his fancies. When, with unnatural alacrity, he returned with the water, he found her weeping with excitement, and with Wedderburn's head upon her knee, wiping the blood from his face.

"What's the matter?" said Wedderburn, opening his eyes feebly, and closing them again at once.

"Go and tell Annie to come out here to me, and then go for Dr. Haddon at once," she said to the odd-job man so soon as he brought the water; and added, seeing he hesitated, "I will tell you all about it when you come back."

Presently Wedderburn opened his eyes again, and, seeing that he was troubled by the puzzle of his position, she explained to him, "You fainted in the hothouse."

"And the orchid?"

"I will see to that," she said.

Wedderburn had lost a good deal of blood, but beyond that he had suffered no very great injury. They gave him brandy mixed with some pink extract of meat, and carried him upstairs to bed. His housekeeper told her incredible story in fragments to Dr. Haddon. "Come to the orchid-house and see," she said.

The cold outer air was blowing in through the open door, and the sickly perfume was almost dispelled. Most of the torn aërial rootlets lay already withered amidst a number of dark stains upon the bricks. The stem of the inflorescence was broken by the fall of the plant, and the flowers were growing limp and brown at the edges of the petals. The doctor stooped towards it, then saw that one of the aërial rootlets still stirred feebly, and hesitated.

The next morning the strange orchid still lay there, black now and putrescent. The door banged intermittingly in the morning breeze, and all the array of Wedderburn's orchids was shrivelled and prostrate. But Wedderburn himself was bright and garrulous upstairs in the glory of his strange adventure.

# THE NEW ACCELERATOR

Certainly, if ever a man found a guinea when he was looking for a pin it is my good friend Professor Gibberne. I have heard before of investigators overshooting the mark, but never quite to the extent that he has done. He has really, this time at any rate, without any touch of exaggeration in the phrase, found something to revolutionise human life. And that when he was simply seeking an all-round nervous stimulant to bring languid people up to the stresses of these pushful days. I have tasted the stuff now several times, and I cannot do better than describe the effect the thing had on me. That there are astonishing experiences in store for all in search of new sensations will become apparent enough.

Professor Gibberne, as many people know, is my neighbour in Folkestone. Unless my memory plays me a trick, his portrait at various ages has already appeared in *The Strand Magazine*—I think late in 1899; but I am unable to look it up because I have lent that volume to some one who has never sent it back. The reader may, perhaps, recall the high forehead and the singularly long black eyebrows that give such a Mephistophelian touch to his face. He occupies one of those pleasant little detached houses in the mixed style that make the western end of the Upper Sandgate Road so interesting. His is the one with the Flemish gables and the Moorish portico, and it is in the little room with the mullioned bay window that he works when he is down here, and in which of an evening we have so often smoked and talked together. He is a mighty jester, but, besides, he likes to talk to me about his work; he is one of those men who find a help and stimulus in talking, and so I have been able to follow the conception of the New Accelerator right up from a very early stage. Of course, the greater portion of his experimental work is not done in Folkestone, but in Gower Street, in the fine new laboratory next to the hospital that he has been the first to use.

As every one knows, or at least as all intelligent people know, the special department in which Gibberne has gained so great and deserved a reputation among physiologists is the action of drugs upon the nervous system. Upon soporifics, sedatives, and anæsthetics he is, I am told, unequalled. He is also a chemist of considerable eminence, and I suppose in the subtle and complex jungle of riddles that centres about the ganglion cell and the axis fibre there are little cleared places of his making, little glades of illumination, that, until he sees fit to publish his results, are still inaccessible to every other living man. And in the last few years he has been particularly assiduous upon this question of nervous stimulants, and already, before the discovery of the New Accelerator, very successful with them. Medical science has to thank him for at least three distinct and absolutely safe invigorators of unrivalled value to practising men. In cases of exhaustion the preparation known as Gibberne's B Syrup has, I suppose, saved more lives already than any lifeboat round the coast.

"But none of these little things begin to satisfy me yet," he told me nearly a year ago. "Either they increase the central energy without affecting the nerves or they simply increase the available energy by lowering the nervous conductivity; and all of them are unequal and local in their operation. One wakes up the heart and viscera and leaves the brain stupefied, one gets at the brain champagne fashion and does nothing good for the solar plexus, and what I want—and what, if it's an earthly possibility, I mean to have—is a stimulant that stimulates all round, that wakes you up for a time from the crown of your head to the tip of your great toe, and makes you go two—or even three to everybody else's one. Eh? That's the thing I'm after."

"It would tire a man," I said.

"Not a doubt of it. And you'd eat double or treble—and all that. But just think what the thing would mean. Imagine yourself with a little phial like this"—he held up a little bottle of green glass and marked his points with it—"and in this precious phial is the power to think twice as fast, move twice as quickly, do twice as much work in a given time as you could otherwise do."

"But is such a thing possible?"

"I believe so. If it isn't, I've wasted my time for a year. These various preparations of the hypophosphites, for example, seem to show that something of the sort . . . Even if it was only one and a half times as fast it would do."

"It *would* do," I said.

"If you were a statesman in a corner, for example, time rushing up against you, something urgent to be done, eh?"

"He could dose his private secretary," I said.

"And gain—double time. And think if *you,* for example, wanted to finish a book."

"Usually," I said, "I wish I'd never begun 'em."

"Or a doctor, driven to death, wants to sit down and think out a case. Or a barrister—or a man cramming for an examination."

"Worth a guinea a drop," said I, "and more—to men like that."

"And in a duel, again," said Gibberne, "where it all depends on your quickness in pulling the trigger."

"Or in fencing," I echoed.

"You see," said Gibberne, "if I get it as an all-round thing it will really do you no harm at all—except perhaps to an infinitesimal degree it brings you nearer old age. You will just have lived twice to other people's once——"

"I suppose," I meditated, "in a duel—it would be fair?"

"That's a question for the seconds," said Gibberne.

I harked back further. "And you really think such a thing *is* possible?" I said.

"As possible," said Gibberne, and glanced at something that went throbbing by the window, "as a motor-bus. As a matter of fact——"

He paused and smiled at me deeply, and tapped slowly on the edge of his desk with the green phial. "I think I know the stuff. . . . Already I've got something coming." The nervous smile upon his face betrayed the gravity of his revelation. He rarely talked of his actual experimental work unless things were very near the end. "And it may be, it may be—I shouldn't be surprised—it may even do the thing at a greater rate than twice."

"It will be rather a big thing," I hazarded.

"It will be, I think, rather a big thing."

But I don't think he quite knew what a big thing it was to be, for all that.

I remember we had several talks about the stuff after that. "The New Accelerator" he called it, and his tone about it grew more confident on each occasion. Sometimes he talked nervously of unexpected physiological results its use might have, and then he would get a little unhappy; at others he was frankly mercenary, and we debated long and anxiously how the preparation might be turned to commercial account. "It's a good thing," said Gibberne, "a tremendous thing. I know I'm giving the world something, and I think it only reasonable we should expect the world to pay. The dignity of science is all very well, but I think somehow I must have the monopoly of the stuff for, say, ten years. I don't see why *all* the fun in life should go to the dealers in ham."

My own interest in the coming drug certainly did not wane in the time. I have always had a queer little twist towards metaphysics in my mind. I have always been given to paradoxes about space and time, and it seemed to me that Gibberne was really preparing no less than the absolute acceleration of life. Suppose a man repeatedly dosed with such a preparation: he would live an active and record life indeed, but he would be an adult at eleven, middle-aged at twenty-five, and by thirty well on the road to senile decay. It seemed to me that so far Gibberne was only going to do for any one who took his drug exactly what Nature has done for the Jews and Orientals, who are men in their teens and aged by fifty, and quicker in thought and act than we are all the time. The marvel of drugs has always been great to my mind; you can madden a man, calm a man, make him incredibly strong and alert or a helpless log, quicken this passion and allay that, all by means of drugs, and here was a new miracle to be added to this strange armoury of phials the doctors use! But Gibberne was far too eager upon his technical points to enter very keenly into my aspect of the question.

It was the 7th or 8th of August when he told me the distillation that decide his failure or success for a time was going forward as we talked, and it was on the 10th that he told me the thing was done and the New Accelerator a tangible reality in the world. I met him as I was going up the Sandgate Hill towards Folkestone—I think I was going to get my hair cut, and he came hurrying down to meet me—I suppose he was coming to my house to tell me at once of his success. I remember that his eyes were unusually bright and his face flushed, and I noted even the swift alacrity of his step.

"It's done," he cried, and gripped my hand, speaking very fast; "it's more than done. Come up to my house and see."

"Really?"

"Really!" he shouted. "Incredibly! Come up and see."

"And it does—twice?"

"It does more, much more. It scares me. Come up and see the stuff. Taste it! Try it! It's the most amazing stuff on earth." He gripped my arm and, walking at such a pace that he forced me into a trot, went shouting with me up the hill. A whole *char-à-banc*-ful of people turned and stared at us in unison after the manner of people in *chars-à-banc*. It was one of those hot, clear days that Folkestone sees so much of, every colour incredibly bright and every outline hard. There was a breeze, of course, but not so much breeze as sufficed under these conditions to keep me cool and dry. I panted for mercy.

"I'm not walking fast, am I?" cried Gibberne, and slackened his pace to a quick march.

"You've been taking some of this stuff," I puffed.

"No," he said. "At the utmost a drop of water that stood in a beaker from which I had washed out the last traces of the stuff. I took some last night, you know. But that is ancient history, now."

"And it goes twice?" I said, nearing his doorway in a grateful perspiration.

"It goes a thousand times, many thousand times!" cried Gibberne, with a dramatic gesture, flinging open his Early English carved oak gate.

"Phew!" said I, and followed him to the door.

"I don't know how many times it goes," he said, with his latch-key in his hand.

"And you——"

"It throws all sorts of light on nervous physiology, it kicks the theory of vision into a perfectly new shape! . . . Heaven knows how many thousand times. We'll try all that after——The thing is to try the stuff now."

"Try the stuff?" I said, as we went along the passage.

"Rather," said Gibberne, turning on me in his study. "There it is in that little green phial there! Unless you happen to be afraid?"

I am a careful man by nature, and only theoretically adventurous. I *was* afraid. But on the other hand there is pride.

"Well," I haggled. "You say you've tried it?"

"I've tried it," he said, "and I don't look hurt by it, do I? I don't even look livery and I *feel*——"

I sat down. "Give me the potion," I said. "If the worst comes to the worst it will save having my hair cut, and that I think is one of the most hateful duties of a civilised man. How do you take the mixture?"

"With water," said Gibberne, whacking down a carafe.

He stood up in front of his desk and regarded me in his easy chair; his manner was suddenly affected by a touch of the Harley Street specialist. "It's rum stuff, you know," he said.

I made a gesture with my hand.

"I must warn you in the first place as soon as you've got it down to shut your eyes, and open them very cautiously in a minute or so's time. One still sees. The sense of vision is a question of length of vibration, and not of multitude of impacts; but there's a kind of shock to the retina, a nasty giddy confusion just at the time, if the eyes are open. Keep 'em shut."

"Shut," I said. "Good!"

"And the next thing is, keep still. Don't begin to whack about. You may fetch something a nasty rap if you do. Remember you will be going several thousand times faster than you ever did before, heart, lungs, muscles, brain—everything—and you will hit hard without knowing it. You won't know it, you know. You'll feel just as you do now. Only everything in the world will seem to be going ever so many thousand times slower that it ever went before. That's what makes it so deuced queer."

"Lor'," I said. "And you mean——"

"You'll see," said he, and took up a little measure. He glanced at the material on his desk. "Glasses," he said, "water. All here. Mustn't take too much for the first attempt."

The little phial glucked out its precious contents. "Don't forget what I told you," he said, turning the contents of the measure into a glass in the manner of an Italian waiter measuring whisky. "Sit with the eyes tightly shut and in absolute stillness for two minutes," he said. "Then you will hear me speak."

He added an inch or so of water to the little dose in each glass.

"By-the-by," he said, "don't put your glass down. Keep it in your hand and rest your hand on your knee. Yes—so. And now——"

He raised his glass.

"The New Accelerator," I said.

"The New Accelerator," he answered, and we touched glasses and drank, and instantly I closed my eyes.

You know that blank non-existence into which one drops when one has taken "gas." For an indefinite interval it was like that. Then I heard Gibberne telling me to wake up, and I stirred and opened my eyes. There he stood as he had been standing, glass still in hand. It was empty, that was all the difference.

"Well?" said I.

"Nothing out of the way?"

"Nothing. A slight feeling of exhilaration, perhaps. Nothing more."

"Sounds?"

"Things are still," I said. "By Jove! yes! They *are* still. Except the sort of faint pat, patter, like rain falling on different things. What is it?"

"Analysed sounds," I think he said, but I am not sure. He glanced at the window. "Have you ever seen a curtain before a window fixed in that way before?"

I followed his eyes, and there was the end of the curtain, frozen, as it were, corner high, in the act of flapping briskly in the breeze.

"No," said I; "that's odd."

"And here," he said, and opened the hand that held the glass. Naturally I winced, expecting the glass to smash. But so far from smashing it did not even seem to stir; it hung in mid-air—motionless. "Roughly speaking," said Gibberne, "an object in these latitudes falls 16 feet in the first second. This glass is falling 16 feet in a second now. Only, you see, it hasn't been falling yet for the hundredth part of a second. That gives you some idea of the pace of my Accelerator." And he waved his hand round and round, over and under the slowly sinking glass. Finally he took it by the bottom, pulled it down, and placed it very carefully on the table. "Eh?" he said to me, and laughed.

"That seems all right," I said, and began very gingerly to raise myself from my chair. I felt perfectly well, very light and comfortable, and quite confident in my mind. I was going fast all over. My heart, for example, was beating a thousand times a second, but that caused me no discomfort at all. I looked out of the window. An immovable cyclist, head down and with a frozen puff of dust behind his driving-wheel, scorched to overtake a galloping *char-à-banc* that did not stir. I gaped in amazement at this incredible spectacle. "Gibberne," I cried, "how long will this confounded stuff last?"

"Heaven knows!" he answered. "Last time I took it I went to bed and slept it off. I tell you, I was frightened. It must have lasted some minutes, I think—it seemed like hours. But after a bit it slows down rather suddenly, I believe."

I was proud to observe that I did not feel frightened—I suppose because there were two of us. "Why shouldn't we go out?" I asked.

"Why not?"

"They'll see us."

"Not they. Goodness, no! Why, we shall be going a thousand times faster than the quickest conjuring trick that was ever done. Come along! Which way shall we go? Window, or door?"

And out by the window we went.

Assuredly of all the strange experiences that I have ever had, or imagined, or read of other people having or imagining, that little raid I made with Gibberne on the Folkestone Leas, under the influence of the New Accelerator, was the strangest and maddest of all. We went out by his gate into the road, and there we made a minute examination of the statuesque passing traffic. The tops of the wheels and some of the legs of the horses of this *char-à-banc,* the end of the whip-lash and the lower jaw of the conductor—who was just beginning to yawn—were perceptibly in motion, but all the rest of the lumbering conveyance seemed still. And quite noiseless except for a faint rattling that came from one man's throat! And as parts of this frozen edifice there were a driver, you know, and a conductor, and eleven people! The effect as we walked about the thing began by being madly queer, and ended by being—disagreeable. There they were, people like ourselves and yet not like ourselves, frozen in careless attitudes, caught in mid-gesture. A girl and a man smiled at one another, a leering smile that threatened to last for evermore; a woman in a floppy capelline rested her arm on the rail and stared at Gibberne's house with the unwinking stare of eternity; a man stroked his moustache like a figure of wax, and another stretched a tiresome stiff hand with extended fingers towards his loosened hat. We stared at them, we laughed at them, we made faces at them, and then a sort of disgust of them came upon us, and we turned away and walked round in front of the cyclist towards the Leas.

"Goodness!" cried Gibberne, suddenly; "look there!"

He pointed, and there at the tip of his finger and sliding down the air with wings flapping slowly and at the speed of an exceptionally languid snail—was a bee.

And so we came out upon the Leas. There the thing seemed madder than ever. The band was playing in the upper stand, though all the sound it made for us was a low-pitched, wheezy rattle, a sort of prolonged last sigh that passed at times into a sound like the slow, muffled ticking of some monstrous clock. Frozen people stood erect, strange, silent, self-conscious-looking dummies hung unstably in mid-stride, promenading upon the grass. I passed close to a little poodle dog suspended in the act of leaping, and watched the slow movement of his legs as he sank to the earth. "Lord, look *here!*" cried Gibberne, and we halted for a moment before a magnificent person in white faint-striped flannels, white shoes, and a Panama hat, who turned back to wink at two gaily dressed ladies he had passed. A wink, studied with such leisurely deliberation as we could afford, is an unattractive thing. It loses any quality of alert gaiety, and one remarks that the winking eye does not completely close, that under its drooping lid appears the lower edge of an eyeball and a little line of white. "Heaven give me memory," said I, "and I will never wink again."

"Or smile," said Gibberne, with his eye on the lady's answering teeth.

"It's infernally hot, somehow," said I. "Let's go slower."

"Oh, come along!" said Gibberne.

We picked our way among the bath-chairs in the path. Many of the people sitting in the chairs seemed almost natural in their passive poses, but the contorted scarlet of the bandsmen was not a restful thing to see. A purple-faced little gentleman was frozen in the midst of a violent struggle to refold his newspaper against the wind; there were many evidences that all these people in their sluggish way were exposed to a considerable breeze, a breeze that had no existence so far as our sensations went. We came out and walked a little way from the crowd, and turned and regarded it. To see all that multitude changed to a picture, smitten rigid, as it were, into the semblance of realistic wax, was impossibly wonderful. It was absurd, of course; but it filled me with an irrational, an exultant sense of superior advantage. Consider the wonder of it! All that I had said, and thought, and done since the stuff had begun to work in my veins had happened, so far as those people, so far as the world in general went, in the twinkling of an eye. "The New Accelerator——" I began, but Gibberne interrupted me.

"There's that infernal old woman!" he said.

"What old woman?"

"Lives next door to me," said Gibberne. "Has a lapdog that yaps. Gods! The temptation is strong!"

There is something very boyish and impulsive about Gibberne at times. Before I could expostulate with him he had dashed forward, snatched the unfortunate animal out of visible existence, and was running violently with it towards the cliff of the Leas. It was most extraordinary. The little brute, you know, didn't bark or wriggle or make the slightest sign of vitality. It kept quite stiffly in an attitude of somnolent repose, and Gibberne held it by the neck. It was like running about with a dog of wood. "Gibberne," I cried, "put it down!" Then I said something else. "If you run like that, Gibberne," I cried, "you'll set your clothes on fire. Your linen trousers are going brown as it is!"

He clapped his hand on his thigh and stood hesitating on the verge. "Gibberne," I cried, coming up, "put it down. This heat is too much! It's our running so! Two or three miles a second! Friction of the air!"

"What?" he said, glancing at the dog.

"Friction of the air," I shouted. "Friction of the air. Going too fast. Like meteorites and things. Too hot. And, Gibberne! Gibberne! I'm all over pricking and a sort of perspiration. You can see people stirring slightly. I believe the stuff's working off! Put that dog down."

"Eh?" he said.

"It's working off," I repeated. "We're too hot and the stuff's working off! I'm wet through."

He stared at me. Then at the band, the wheezy rattle of whose performance was certainly going faster. Then with a tremendous sweep of the arm he hurled the dog away from him and it went spinning upward, still inanimate, and hung at last over the grouped parasols of a knot of chattering people. Gibberne was gripping my elbow. "By Jove!" he cried. "I believe it is! A sort of hot pricking and—yes. That man's moving his pocket-handkerchief! Perceptibly. We must get out of this sharp."

But we could not get out of it sharply enough. Luckily, perhaps! For we might have run, and if we had run we should, I believe, have burst into flames. Almost certainly we should have burst into flames! You know we had neither of us thought of that. . . . But before we could even begin to run the action of the drug had ceased. It was the business of a minute fraction of a second. The effect of the New Accelerator passed like the drawing of a curtain, vanished in the movement of a hand. I heard Gibberne's voice in infinite alarm. "Sit down," he said, and flop, down upon the turf at the edge of the Leas I sat—scorching as I sat. There is a patch of burnt grass there still where I sat down. The whole stagnation seemed to wake up as I did so, the disarticulated vibration of the band rushed together into a blast of music, the promenaders put their feet down and walked their ways, the papers and flags began flapping, smiles passed into words, the winker finished his wink and went on his way complacently, and all the seated people moved and spoke.

The whole world had come alive again, was going as fast as we were, or rather we were going no faster than the rest of the world. It was like slowing down as one comes into a railway station. Everything seemed to spin round for a second or two, I had the most transient feeling of nausea, and that was all. And the little dog which had seemed to hang for a moment when the force of Gibberne's arm was expended fell with a swift acceleration clean through a lady's parasol!

That was the saving of us. Unless it was for one corpulent old gentleman in a bath-chair, who certainly did start at the sight of us and afterwards regarded us at intervals with a darkly suspicious eye, and, finally, I believe, said something to his nurse about us, I doubt if a solitary person remarked our sudden appearance among them. Plop! We must have appeared abruptly. We ceased to smoulder almost at once, though the turf beneath me was uncomfortably hot. The attention of every one—including even the Amusements' Association band, which on this occasion, for the only time in its history, got out of tune—was arrested by the amazing fact, and the still more amazing yapping and uproar caused by the fact that a respectable, over-fed lap-dog sleeping quietly to the east of the bandstand should suddenly fall through the parasol of a lady on the west—in a slightly singed condition due to the extreme velocity of its movements through the air. In these absurd days, too, when we are all trying to be as psychic, and silly, and superstitious as possible! People got up and trod on other people, chairs were overturned, the Leas policeman ran. How the matter settled itself I do not know—we were much too anxious to disentangle ourselves from the affair and get out of range of the eye of the old gentleman in the bath-chair to make minute inquiries. As soon as we were sufficiently cool and sufficiently recovered from our giddiness and nausea and confusion of mind to do so we stood up and, skirting the crowd, directed our steps back along the road below the Metropole towards Gibberne's house. But amidst the din I heard very distinctly the gentleman who had been sitting beside the lady of the ruptured sunshade using quite unjustifiable threats and language to one of those chair-attendants who have "Inspector" written on their caps. "If you didn't throw the dog," he said, "who *did?*"

The sudden return of movement and familiar noises, and our natural anxiety about ourselves (our clothes were still dreadfully hot, and the fronts of the thighs of Gibberne's white trousers were scorched a drabbish brown), prevented the minute observations I should have liked to make on all these things. Indeed, I really made no observations of any scientific value on that return. The bee, of course, had gone. I looked for that cyclist, but he was already out of sight as we came into the Upper Sandgate Road or hidden from us by traffic; the *char-à-banc,* however, with its people now all alive and stirring, was clattering along at a spanking pace almost abreast of the nearer church.

We noted, however, that the window-sill on which we had stepped in getting out of the house was slightly singed, and that the impressions of our feet on the gravel of the path were unusually deep.

So it was I had my first experience of the New Accelerator. Practically we had been running about and saying and doing all sorts of things in the space of a second or so of time. We had lived half an hour while the band had played, perhaps, two bars. But the effect it had upon us was that the whole world had stopped for our convenient inspection. Considering all things, and particularly considering our rashness in venturing out of the house, the experience might certainly have been much more disagreeable than it was. It showed, no doubt, that Gibberne has still much to learn before his preparation is a manageable convenience, but its practicability it certainly demonstrated beyond all cavil.

Since that adventure he has been steadily bringing its use under control, and I have several times, and without the slightest bad result, taken measured doses under his direction; though I must confess I have not yet ventured abroad again while under its influence. I may mention, for example, that this story has been written at one sitting and without interruption, except for the nibbling of some chocolate, by its means. I began at 6:25, and my watch is now very nearly at the minute past the half-hour. The convenience of securing a long, uninterrupted spell of work in the midst of a day full of engagements cannot be exaggerated. Gibberne is now working at the quantitative handling of his preparation, with especial reference to its distinctive effects upon different types of constitution. He then hopes to find a Retarder with which to dilute its present rather excessive potency. The Retarder will, of course, have the reverse effect to the Accelerator; used alone it should enable the patient to spread a few seconds over many hours of ordinary time, and so to maintain an apathetic inaction, a glacier-like absence of alacrity, amidst the most animated or irritating surroundings. The two things together must necessarily work an entire revolution in civilised existence. It is the beginning of our escape from that Time Garment of which Carlyle speaks. While this Accelerator will enable us to concentrate ourselves with tremendous impact upon any moment or occasion that demands our utmost sense and vigour, the Retarder will enable us to pass in passive tranquillity through infinite hardship and tedium. Perhaps I am a little optimistic about the Retarder, which has indeed still to be discovered, but about the Accelerator there is no possible sort of doubt whatever. Its appearance upon the market in a convenient, controllable, and assimilable form is a matter of the next few months. It will be obtainable of all chemists and druggists, in small green bottles, at a high but, considering its extraordinary qualities, by no means excessive price. Gibberne's Nervous Accelerator it will be called, and he hopes to be able to supply it in three strengths: one in 200, one in 900, and one in 2000, distinguished by yellow, pink, and white labels respectively.

No doubt its use renders a great number of very extraordinary things possible; for, of course, the most remarkable and, possibly, even criminal proceedings may be effected with impunity by thus dodging, as it were, into the interstices of time. Like all potent preparations it will be liable to abuse. We have, however, discussed this aspect of the question very thoroughly, and we have decided that this is purely a matter of medical jurisprudence and altogether outside our province. We shall manufacture and sell the Accelerator, and, as for the consequences—we shall see.

# THE DIAMOND MAKER

Some business had detained me in Chancery Lane until nine in the evening, and thereafter, having some inkling of a headache, I was disinclined either for entertainment or further work. So much of the sky as the high cliffs of that narrow canyon of traffic left visible spoke of a serene night, and I determined to make my way down to the Embankment, and rest my eyes and cool my head by watching the variegated lights upon the river. Beyond comparison the night is the best time for this place; a merciful darkness hides the dirt of the waters, and the lights of this transition age, red, glaring orange, gas-yellow, and electric white, are set in shadowy outlines of every possible shade between grey and deep purple. Through the arches of Waterloo Bridge a hundred points of light mark the sweep of the Embankment, and above its parapet rise the towers of Westminster, warm grey against the starlight. The black river goes by with only a rare ripple breaking its silence, and disturbing the reflections of the lights that swim upon its surface.

"A warm night," said a voice at my side.

I turned my head, and saw the profile of a man who was leaning over the parapet beside me. It was a refined face, not unhandsome, though pinched and pale enough, and the coat collar turned up and pinned round the throat marked his status in life as sharply as a uniform. I felt I was committed to the price of a bed and breakfast if I answered him.

I looked at him curiously. Would he have anything to tell me worth the money, or was he the common incapable—incapable even of telling his own story? There was a quality of intelligence in his forehead and eyes, and a certain tremulousness in his nether lip that decided me.

"Very warm," said I; "but not too warm for us here."

"No," he said, still looking across the water, "it is pleasant enough here . . . just now.

"It is good," he continued after a pause, "to find anything so restful as this in London. After one has been fretting about business all day, about getting on, meeting obligations, and parrying dangers, I do not know what one would do if it were not for such pacific corners." He spoke with long pauses between the sentences. "You must know a little of the irksome labour of the world, or you would not be here. But I doubt if you can be so brain-weary and footsore as I am . . . Bah! Sometimes I doubt if the game is worth the candle. I feel inclined to throw the whole thing over—name, wealth, and position—and take to some modest trade. But I know if I abandoned my ambition—hardly as she uses me—I should have nothing but remorse left for the rest of my days."

He became silent. I looked at him in astonishment. If ever I saw a man hopelessly hard-up it was the man in front of me. He was ragged and he was dirty, unshaven and unkempt; he looked as though he had been left in a dust-bin for a week. And he was talking to *me* of the irksome worries of a large business. I almost laughed outright. Either he was mad or playing a sorry jest on his own poverty.

"If high aims and high positions," said I, "have their drawbacks of hard work and anxiety, they have their compensations. Influence, the power of doing good, of assisting those weaker and poorer than ourselves; and there is even a certain gratification in display. . . ."

My banter under the circumstances was in very vile taste. I spoke on the spur of the contrast of his appearance and speech. I was sorry even while I was speaking.

He turned a haggard but very composed face upon me. Said he: "I forget myself. Of course you would not understand."

He measured me for a moment. "No doubt it is very absurd. You will not believe me even when I tell you, so that it is fairly safe to tell you. And it will be a comfort to tell someone. I really have a big business in hand, a very big business. But there are troubles just now. The fact is . . . I make diamonds."

"I suppose," said I, "you are out of work just at present?"

"I am sick of being disbelieved," he said impatiently, and suddenly unbuttoning his wretched coat he pulled out a little canvas bag that was hanging by a cord round his neck. From this he produced a brown pebble. "I wonder if you know enough to know what that is?" He handed it to me.

Now, a year or so ago, I had occupied my leisure in taking a London science degree, so that I have a smattering of physics and mineralogy. The thing was not unlike an uncut diamond of the darker sort, though far too large, being almost as big as the top of my thumb. I took it, and saw it had the form of a regular octahedron, with the curved faces peculiar to the most precious of minerals. I took out my penknife and tried to scratch it—vainly. Leaning forward towards the gas-lamp, I tried the thing on my watch-glass, and scored a white line across that with the greatest ease.

I looked at my interlocutor with rising curiosity. "It certainly is rather like a diamond. But, if so, it is a Behemoth of diamonds. Where did you get it?"

"I tell you I made it," he said. "Give it back to me."

He replaced it hastily and buttoned his jacket. "I will sell it you for one hundred pounds," he suddenly whispered eagerly. With that my suspicions returned. The thing might, after all, be merely a lump of that almost equally hard substance, corundum, with an accidental resemblance in shape to the diamond. Or if it was a diamond, how came he by it, and why should he offer it at a hundred pounds?

We looked into one another's eye. He seemed eager, but honestly eager. At that moment I believed it was a diamond he was trying to sell. Yet I am a poor man, a hundred pounds would leave a visible gap in my fortunes and no sane man would buy a diamond by gas-light from a ragged tramp on his personal warranty only. Still, a diamond that size conjured up a vision of many thousands of pounds. Then, thought I, such a stone could scarcely exist without being mentioned in every book on gems, and again I called to mind the stories of contraband and lightfingered Kaffirs at the Cape. I put the question of purchase on one side.

"How did you get it?" said I.

"I made it."

I had heard something of Moissan, but I knew his artificial diamonds were very small. I shook my head.

"You seem to know something of this kind of thing. I will tell you a little about myself. Perhaps then you may think better of the purchase." He turned round with his back to the river, and put his hands in his pockets. He sighed. "I know you will not believe me.

"Diamonds," he began—and as he spoke his voice lost its faint flavour of the tramp and assumed something of the easy tone of an educated man—"are to be made by throwing carbon out of combination in a suitable flux and under a suitable pressure; the carbon crystallises out, not as black-lead or charcoal-powder, but as small diamonds. So much has been known to chemists for years, but no one yet has hit upon exactly the right flux in which to melt up the carbon, or exactly the right pressure for the best results. Consequently the diamonds made by chemists are small and dark, and worthless as jewels. Now I, you know, have given up my life to this problem—given my life to it.

"I began to work at the conditions of diamond making when I was seventeen, and now I am thirty-two. It seemed to me that it might take all the thought and energies of a man for ten years, or twenty years, but even if it did, the game was still worth the candle. Suppose one to have at last just hit the right trick, before the secret got out and diamonds became as common as coal, one might realise millions. Millions!"

He paused and looked for my sympathy. His eyes shone hungrily. "To think," said he, "that I am on the verge of it all, and here!

"I had," he proceeded, "about a thousand pounds when I was twenty-one, and this, I thought, eked out by a little teaching, would keep my researches going. A year or two was spent in study, at Berlin chiefly, and then I continued on my own account. The trouble was the secrecy. You see, if once I had let out what I was doing, other men might have been spurred on by my belief in the practicability of the idea; and I do not pretend to be such a genius as to have been sure of coming in first, in the case of a race for the discovery. And you see it was important that if I really meant to make a pile, people should not know it was an artificial process and capable of turning out diamonds by the ton. So I had to work all alone. At first I had a little laboratory, but as my resources began to run out I had to conduct my experiments in a wretched unfurnished room in Kentish Town, where I slept at last on a straw mattress on the floor among all my apparatus. The money simply flowed away. I grudged myself everything except scientific appliances. I tried to keep things going by a little teaching, but I am not a very good teacher, and I have no university degree, nor very much education except in chemistry, and I found I had to give a lot of time and labour for precious little money. But I got nearer and nearer the thing. Three years ago I settled the problem of the composition of the flux, and got near the pressure by putting this flux of mine and a certain carbon composition into a closed-up gun-barrel, filling up with water, sealing tightly, and heating."

He paused.

"Rather risky," said I.

"Yes. It burst, and smashed all my windows and a lot of my apparatus; but I got a kind of diamond powder nevertheless. Following out the problem of getting a big pressure upon the molten mixture from which the things were to crystallise, I hit upon some researches of Daubrée's at the Paris *Laboràtorie des Poudres et Salpêtres.* He exploded dynamite in a tightly screwed steel cylinder, too strong to burst, and I found he could crush rocks into a muck not unlike the South African bed in which diamonds are found. It was a tremendous strain on my resources, but I got a steel cylinder made for my purpose after his pattern. I put in all my stuff and my explosives, built up a fire in my furnace, put the whole concern in, and—went out for a walk."

I could not help laughing at his matter-of-fact manner. "Did you not think it would blow up the house? Were there other people in the place?"

"It was in the interest of science," he said, ultimately. "There was a coster-monger family on the floor below, a begging-letter writer in the room behind mine, and two flower-women were upstairs. Perhaps it was a bit thoughtless. But possibly some of them were out.

"When I came back the thing was just where I left it, among the white-hot coals. The explosive hadn't burst the case. And then I had a problem to face. You know time is an important element in crystallisation. If you hurry the process the crystals are small—it is only by prolonged standing that they grow to any size. I resolved to let this apparatus cool for two years, letting the temperature go down slowly during that time. And I was now quite out of money; and with a big fire and the rent of my room, as well as my hunger to satisfy, I had scarcely a penny in the world.

"I can hardly tell you all the shifts I was put to while I was making the diamonds. I have sold newspapers, held horses, opened cab-doors. For many weeks I addressed envelopes. I had a place as assistant to a man who owned a barrow, and used to call down one side of the road while he called down the other. Once for a week I had absolutely nothing to do, and I begged. What a week that was! One day the fire was going out and I had eaten nothing all day, and a little chap taking his girl out gave me sixpence—to show-off. Thank heaven for vanity! How the fish-shops smelt! But I went and spent it all on coals, and had the furnace bright red again, and then——Well, hunger makes a fool of a man.

"At last, three weeks ago, I let the fire out. I took my cylinder and unscrewed it while it was still so hot that it punished my hands, and I scraped out the crumbling lava-like mass with a chisel, and hammered it into a powder upon an iron plate. And I found three big diamonds and five small ones. As I sat on the floor hammering, my door opened, and my neighbour, the begging-letter writer, came in. He was drunk—as he usually is. 'Nerchist,' said he. 'You're drunk,' said I. "Structive scoundrel,' said he. 'Go to your father,' said I, meaning the Father of Lies. 'Never you mind,' said he, and gave me a cunning wink, and hiccuped, and leaning up against the door, with his other eye against the door-post, began to babble of how he had been prying in my room, and how he had gone to the police that morning, and how they had taken down everything he had to say—"siffiwas a ge'm,' said he. Then I suddenly realised I was in a hole. Either I should have to tell these police my little secret, and get the whole thing blown upon, or be lagged as an Anarchist. So I went up to my neighbour and took him by the collar, and rolled him about a bit, and then I gathered up my diamonds and cleared out. The evening newspapers called my den the Kentish-Town Bomb Factory. And now I cannot part with the things for love or money.

"If I go in to respectable jewellers they ask me to wait, and go and whisper to a clerk to fetch a policeman, and then I say I cannot wait. And I found out a receiver of stolen goods, and he simply stuck to the one I gave him and told me to prosecute if I wanted it back. I am going about now with several hundred thousand pounds' worth of diamonds round my neck, and without either food or shelter. You are the first person I have taken into my confidence. But I like your face and I am hard-driven."

He looked into my eyes.

"It would be madness," said I, "for me to buy a diamond under the circumstances. Besides, I do not carry hundreds of pounds about in my pocket. Yet I more than half believe your story. I will, if you like, do this: come to my office to-morrow. . . ."

"You think I am a thief!" said he keenly. "You will tell the police. I am not coming into a trap."

"Somehow I am assured you are no thief. Here is my card. Take that, anyhow. You need not come to any appointment. Come when you will."

He took the card, and an earnest of my good will.

"Think better of it and come," said I.

He shook his head doubtfully. "I will pay back your half-crown with interest some day— such interest as will amaze you," said he. "Anyhow, you will keep the secret? . . . Don't follow me."

He crossed the road and went into the darkness towards the little steps under the archway leading into Essex Street, and I let him go. And that was the last I ever saw of him.

Afterwards I had two letters from him asking me to send bank-notes—not cheques—to certain addresses. I weighed the matter over, and took what I conceived to be the wisest course. Once he called upon me when I was out. My urchin described him as a very thin, dirty, and ragged man, with a dreadful cough. He left no message. That was the finish of him so far as my story goes. I wonder sometimes what has become of him. Was he an ingenious monomaniac, or a fraudulent dealer in pebbles, or has he really made diamonds as he asserted? The latter is just sufficiently credible to make me think at times that I have missed the most brilliant opportunity of my life. He may of course be dead, and his diamonds carelessly thrown aside—one, I repeat, was almost as big as my thumb. Or he may be still wandering about trying to sell the things. It is just possible he may yet emerge upon society, and, passing athwart my heavens in the serene altitude sacred to the wealthy and the well-advertised, reproach me silently for my want of enterprise. I sometimes think I might at least have risked five pounds.

# THE APPLE

"I must get rid of it," said the man in the corner of the carriage, abruptly breaking the silence.

Mr. Hinchcliff looked up, hearing imperfectly. He had been lost in the rapt contemplation of the college cap tied by a string to his portmanteau handles—the outward and visible sign of his newly-gained pedagogic position—in the rapt appreciation of the college cap and the pleasant anticipations it excited. For Mr. Hinchcliff had just matriculated at London University, and was going to be junior assistant at the Holmwood Grammar School—a very enviable position. He stared across the carriage at his fellow-traveller.

"Why not give it away?" said this person. "Give it away! Why not?"

He was a tall, dark, sunburnt man with a pale face. His arms were folded tightly, and his feet were on the seat in front of him. He was pulling at a lank, black moustache. He stared hard at his toes.

"Why not?" he said.

Mr. Hinchcliff coughed.

The stranger lifted his eyes—they were curious, dark-grey eyes—and stared blankly at Mr. Hinchcliff for the best part of a minute, perhaps. His expression grew to interest.

"Yes," he said slowly. "Why not? And end it."

"I don't quite follow you, I'm afraid," said Mr. Hinchcliff, with another cough.

"You don't quite follow me?" said the stranger, quite mechanically, his singular eyes wandering from Mr. Hinchcliff to the bag with its ostentatiously displayed cap, and back to Mr. Hinchcliff's downy face.

"You're so abrupt, you know," apologised Mr. Hinchcliff.

"Why shouldn't I?" said the stranger, following his thoughts. "You are a student?" he said, addressing Mr. Hinchcliff.

"I am—by Correspondence—of the London University," said Mr. Hinchcliff, with irrepressible pride, and feeling nervously at his tie.

"In pursuit of knowledge," said the stranger, and suddenly took his feet off the seat, put his fist on his knees, and stared at Mr. Hinchcliff as though he had never seen a student before. "Yes," he said, and flung out an index finger. Then he rose, took a bag from the hat-rack, and unlocked it. Quite silently, he drew out something round and wrapped in a quantity of silver-paper, and unfolded this carefully. He held it out towards Mr. Hinchcliff,—a small, very smooth, golden-yellow fruit.

Mr. Hinchcliff's eyes and mouth were open. He did not offer to take this object—if he was intended to take it.

"That," said this fantastic stranger, speaking very slowly, "is the Apple of the Tree of Knowledge. Look at it—small, and bright, and wonderful—Knowledge—and I am going to give it to you."

Mr. Hinchcliff's mind worked painfully for a minute, and then the sufficient explanation, "Mad!" flashed across his brain, and illuminated the whole situation. One humoured madmen. He put his head a little on one side.

"The Apple of the Tree of Knowledge, eigh!" said Mr. Hinchcliff, regarding it with a finely assumed air of interest, and then looking at the interlocutor. "But don't you want to eat it yourself? And besides—how did you come by it?"

"It never fades. I have had it now three months. And it is ever bright and smooth and ripe and desirable, as you see it." He laid his hand on his knee and regarded the fruit musingly. Then he began to wrap it again in the papers, as though he had abandoned his intention of giving it away.

"But how did you come by it?" said Mr. Hinchcliff, who had his argumentative side. "And how do you know that it *is* the Fruit of the Tree?"

"I bought this fruit," said the stranger, "three months ago—for a drink of water and a crust of bread. The man who gave it to me—because I kept the life in him—was an Armenian. Armenia! that wonderful country, the first of all countries, where the ark of the Flood remains to this day, buried in the glaciers of Mount Ararat. This man, I say, fleeing with others from the Kurds who had come upon them, went up into desolate places among the mountains—places beyond the common knowledge of men. And fleeing from imminent pursuit, they came to a slope high among the mountain-peaks, green with a grass like knife-blades, that cut and slashed most pitilessly at any one who went into it. The Kurds were close behind, and there was nothing for it but to plunge in, and the worst of it was that the paths they made through it at the price of their blood served for the Kurds to follow. Every one of the fugitives was killed save this Armenian and another. He heard the screams and cries of his friends, and the swish of the grass about those who were pursuing them—it was tall grass rising overhead. And then a shouting and answers, and when presently he paused, everything was still. He pushed out again, not understanding, cut and bleeding, until he came out on a steep slope of rocks below a precipice, and then he saw the grass was all on fire, and the smoke of it rose like a veil between him and his enemies."

The stranger paused. "Yes?" said Mr. Hinchcliff. "Yes?"

"There he was, all torn and bloody from the knife-blades of the grass, the rocks blazing under the afternoon sun,—the sky molten brass, —and the smoke of the fire driving towards him. He dared not stay there. Death he did not mind, but torture! Far away beyond the smoke he heard shouts and cries. Women screaming. So he went clambering up a gorge in the rocks—everywhere were bushes with dry branches that stuck out like thorns among the leaves—until he clambered over the brow of a ridge that hid him. And then he met his companion, a shepherd, who had also escaped. And, counting cold and famine and thirst as nothing against the Kurds, they went on into the heights, and among the snow and ice. They wandered three whole days.

"The third day came the vision. I suppose hungry men often do see visions, but then there is this fruit." He lifted the wrapped globe in his hand. "And I have heard it, too, from other mountaineers who have known something of the legend. It was in the evening time, when the stars were increasing, that they came down a slope of polished rock into a huge, dark valley all set about with strange, contorted trees, and in these trees hung little globes like glow-worm spheres, strange, round, yellow lights.

"Suddenly this valley was lit far away, many miles away, far down it, with a golden flame marching slowly athwart it, that made the stunted trees against it black as night, and turned the slopes all about them and their figures to the likeness of fiery gold. And at the vision they, knowing the legends of the mountains, instantly knew that it was Eden they saw, or the sentinel of Eden, and they fell upon their faces like men struck dead.

"When they dared to look again, the valley was dark for a space, and then the light came again—returning, a burning amber.

"At that the shepherd sprang to his feet, and with a shout began to run down towards the light; but the other man was too fearful to follow him. He stood stunned, amazed, and terrified, watching his companion recede towards the marching glare. And hardly had the shepherd set out when there came a noise like thunder, the beating of invisible wings hurrying up the valley, and a great and terrible fear; and at that the man who gave me the fruit turned—if he might still escape. And hurrying headlong up the slope again, with that tumult sweeping after him, he stumbled against one of these stunted bushes, and a ripe fruit came off it into his hand. This fruit. Forthwith, the wings and the thunder rolled all about him. He fell and fainted, and when he came to his senses, he was back among the blackened ruins of his own village, and I and the others were attending to the wounded. A vision? But the golden fruit of the tree was still clutched in his hand. There were others there who knew the legend, knew what that strange fruit might be." He paused. "And this is it," he said.

It was a most extraordinary story to be told in a third-class carriage on a Sussex railway. It was as if the real was a mere veil to the fantastic, and here was the fantastic poking through. "Is it?" was all Mr. Hinchcliff could say.

"The legend," said the stranger, "tells that those thickets of dwarfed trees growing about the garden sprang from the apple that Adam carried in his hand when he and Eve were driven forth. He felt something in his hand, saw the half-eaten apple, and flung it petulantly aside. And there they grow, in that desolate valley, girdled round with the everlasting snows; and there the fiery swords keep ward against the Judgment Day."

"But I thought these things were—" Mr. Hinchcliff paused—"fables —parables rather. Do you mean to tell me that there in Armenia—"

The stranger answered the unfinished question with the fruit in his open hand.

"But you don't know," said Mr. Hinchcliff, "that that *is* the fruit of the Tree of Knowledge. The man may have had—a sort of mirage, say. Suppose—"

"Look at it," said the stranger.

It was certainly a strange-looking globe, not really an apple, Mr. Hinchcliff saw, and a curious glowing golden colour, almost as though light itself was wrought into its substance. As he looked at it, he began to see more vividly the desolate valley among the mountains, the guarding swords of fire, the strange antiquities of the story he had just heard. He rubbed a knuckle into his eye. "But—" said he.

"It has kept like that, smooth and full, three months. Longer than that it is now by some days. No drying, no withering, no decay."

"And you yourself," said Mr. Hinchcliff, "really believe that—"

"Is the Forbidden Fruit."

There was no mistaking the earnestness of the man's manner and his perfect sanity. "The Fruit of Knowledge," he said.

"Suppose it was?" said Mr. Hinchcliff, after a pause, still staring at it. "But after all," said Mr. Hinchcliff, "it's not my kind of knowledge—not the sort of knowledge. I mean, Adam and Eve have eaten it already."

"We inherit their sins—not their knowledge," said the stranger. "That would make it all clear and bright again. We should see into everything, through everything, into the deepest meaning of everything—"

"Why don't you eat it, then?" said Mr. Hinchcliff, with an inspiration.

"I took it intending to eat it," said the stranger. "Man has fallen. Merely to eat again could scarcely—"

"Knowledge is power," said Mr. Hinchcliff.

"But is it happiness? I am older than you—more than twice as old. Time after time I have held this in my hand, and my heart has failed me at the thought of all that one might know, that terrible lucidity—Suppose suddenly all the world became pitilessly clear?"

"That, I think, would be a great advantage," said Mr. Hinchcliff, "on the whole."

Suppose you saw into the hearts and minds of every one about you, into their most secret recesses—people you loved, whose love you valued?"

"You'd soon find out the humbugs," said Mr. Hinchcliff, greatly struck by the idea.

"And worse—to know yourself, bare of your most intimate illusions. To see yourself in your place. All that your lusts and weaknesses prevented your doing. No merciful perspective."

"That might be an excellent thing too. 'Know thyself,' you know."

"You are young," said the stranger.

"If you don't care to eat it, and it bothers you, why don't you throw it away?"

"There again, perhaps, you will not understand me. To me, how could one throw away a thing like that, glowing, wonderful? Once one has it, one is bound. But, on the other hand, to *give* it away! To give it away to some one who thirsted after knowledge, who found no terror in the thought of that clear perception—"

"Of course," said Mr. Hinchcliff, thoughtfully, "it might be some sort of poisonous fruit."

And then his eye caught something motionless, the end of a white board black-lettered outside the carriage-window. "–MWOOD," he saw. He started convulsively. "Gracious!" said Mr. Hinchcliff. "Holmwood!"–and the practical present blotted out the mystic realisations that had been stealing upon him.

In another moment he was opening the carriage-door, portmanteau in hand. The guard was already fluttering his green flag. Mr. Hinchcliff jumped out. "Here!" said a voice behind him, and he saw the dark eyes of the stranger shining and the golden fruit, bright and bare, held out of the open carriage-door. He took it instinctively, the train was already moving.

*"No!"* shouted the stranger, and made a snatch at it as if to take it back.

"Stand away," cried a country porter, thrusting forward to close the door. The stranger shouted something Mr. Hinchcliff did not catch, head and arm thrust excitedly out of the window, and then the shadow of the bridge fell on him, and in a trice he was hidden. Mr. Hinchcliff stood astonished, staring at the end of the last waggon receding round the bend, and with the wonderful fruit in his hand. For the fraction of a minute his mind was confused, and then he became aware that two or three people on the platform were regarding him with interest. Was he not the new Grammar School master making his début? It occurred to him that, so far as they could tell, the fruit might very well be the naïve refreshment of an orange. He flushed at the thought, and thrust the fruit into his side pocket, where it bulged undesirably. But there was no help for it, so he went towards them, awkwardly concealing his sense of awkwardness, to ask the way to the Grammar School, and the means of getting his portmanteau and the two tin boxes which lay up the platform thither. Of all the odd and fantastic yarns to tell a fellow!

His luggage could be taken on a truck for sixpence, he found, and he could precede it on foot. He fancied an ironical note in the voices. He was painfully aware of his contour.

The curious earnestness of the man in the train, and the glamour of the story he told, had, for a time, diverted the current of Mr. Hinchcliff's thoughts. It drove like a mist before his immediate concerns. Fires that went to and fro! But the preoccupation of his new position, and the impression he was to produce upon Holmwood generally, and the school people in particular, returned upon him with reinvigorating power before he left the station and cleared his mental atmosphere. But it is extraordinary what an inconvenient thing the addition of a soft and rather brightly-golden fruit, not three inches in diameter, may prove to a sensitive youth on his best appearance. In the pocket of his black jacket it bulged dreadfully, spoilt the lines altogether. He passed a little old lady in black, and he felt her eye drop upon the excrescence at once. He was wearing one glove and carrying the other, together with his stick, so that to bear the fruit openly was impossible. In one place, where the road into the town seemed suitably secluded, he took his encumbrance out of his pocket and tried it in his hat. It was just too large, the hat wobbled ludicrously, and just as he was taking it out again, a butcher's boy came driving round the corner.

"Confound it!" said Mr. Hinchcliff.

He would have eaten the thing, and attained omniscience there and then, but it would seem so silly to go into the town sucking a juicy fruit—and it certainly felt juicy. If one of the boys should come by, it might do him a serious injury with his discipline so to be seen. And the juice might make his face sticky and get upon his cuffs—or it might be an acid juice as potent as lemon, and take all the colour out of his clothes.

Then round a bend in the lane came two pleasant, sunlit, girlish figures. They were walking slowly towards the town and chattering —at any moment they might look round and see a hot-faced young man behind them carrying a kind of phosphorescent yellow tomato! They would be sure to laugh.

*"Hang!"* said Mr. Hinchcliff, and with a swift jerk sent the encumbrance flying over the stone wall of an orchard that there abutted on the road. As it vanished, he felt a faint twinge of loss that lasted scarcely a moment. He adjusted the stick and glove in his hand, and walked on, erect and self-conscious, to pass the girls.

But in the darkness of the night Mr. Hinchcliff had a dream, and saw the valley, and the flaming swords, and the contorted trees, and knew that it really was the Apple of the Tree of Knowledge that he had thrown regardlessly away. And he awoke very unhappy.

In the morning his regret had passed, but afterwards it returned and troubled him; never, however, when he was happy or busily occupied. At last, one moonlight night about eleven, when all Holmwood was quiet, his regrets returned with redoubled force, and therewith an impulse to adventure. He slipped out of the house and over the playground wall, went through the silent town to Station Lane, and climbed into the orchard where he had thrown the fruit. But nothing was to be found of it there among the dewy grass and the faint intangible globes of dandelion down.

# THE PURPLE PILEUS

Mr. Coombes was sick of life. He walked away from his unhappy home, and, sick not only of his own existence, but of everybody else's, turned aside down Gaswork Lane to avoid the town, and, crossing the wooden bridge that goes over the canal to Starling's Cottages, was presently alone in the damp pinewoods and out of sight and sound of human habitation. He would stand it no longer. He repeated aloud with blasphemies unusual to him that he would stand it no longer.

He was a pale-faced little man, with dark eyes and a fine and very black moustache. He had a very stiff, upright collar slightly frayed, that gave him an illusory double chin, and his overcoat (albeit shabby) was trimmed with astrachan. His gloves were a bright brown with black stripes over the knuckles, and split at the finger-ends. His appearance, his wife had said once in the dear, dead days beyond recall, —before he married her, that is,—was military. But now she called him— It seems a dreadful thing to tell of between husband and wife, but she called him "a little grub." It wasn't the only thing she had called him, either.

The row had arisen about that beastly Jennie again. Jennie was his wife's friend, and, by no invitation of Mr. Coombes, she came in every blessed Sunday to dinner, and made a shindy all the afternoon. She was a big, noisy girl, with a taste for loud colours and a strident laugh; and this Sunday she had outdone all her previous intrusions by bringing in a fellow with her, a chap as showy as herself. And Mr. Coombes, in a starchy, clean collar and his Sunday frock-coat, had sat dumb and wrathful at his own table, while his wife and her guests talked foolishly and undesirably, and laughed aloud. Well, he stood that, and after dinner (which, "as usual," was late), what must Miss Jennie do but go to the piano and play banjo tunes, for all the world as if it were a week-day! Flesh and blood could not endure such goings-on. They would hear next door; they would hear in the road; it was a public announcement of their disrepute. He had to speak.

He had felt himself go pale, and a kind of rigour had affected his respiration as he delivered himself. He had been sitting on one of the chairs by the window—the new guest had taken possession of the arm-chair. He turned his head. "Sun Day!" he said over the collar, in the voice of one who warns. "Sun Day!" What people call a "nasty" tone it was.

Jennie had kept on playing; but his wife, who was looking through some music that was piled on the top of the piano, had stared at him. "What's wrong now?" she said; "can't people enjoy themselves?"

"I don't mind rational 'njoyment, at all," said little Coombes; "but I ain't a-going to have week-day tunes playing on a Sunday in this house."

"What's wrong with my playing now?" said Jennie, stopping and twirling round on the music-stool with a monstrous rustle of flounces.

Coombes saw it was going to be a row, and opened too vigorously, as is common with your timid, nervous men all the world over. "Steady on with that music-stool!" said he; "it ain't made for 'eavy weights."

"Never you mind about weights," said Jennie, incensed. "What was you saying behind my back about my playing?"

"Surely you don't 'old with not having a bit of music on a Sunday, Mr. Coombes?" said the new guest, leaning back in the arm-chair, blowing a cloud of cigarette smoke and smiling in a kind of pitying way. And simultaneously his wife said something to Jennie about "Never mind 'im. You go on, Jinny."

"I do," said Mr. Coombes, addressing the new guest.

"May I arst why?" said the new guest, evidently enjoying both his cigarette and the prospect of an argument. He was, by-the-by, a lank young man, very stylishly dressed in bright drab, and a white cravat and a pearl and silver pin. It had been better taste to come in a black coat, Mr. Coombes thought.

"Because," began Mr. Coombes, "it don't suit me. I'm a business man. I 'ave to study my connection. Rational 'njoyment—"

"His connection!" said Mrs. Coombes, scornfully. "That's what he's always a-saying. We got to do this, and we got to do that—"

"If you don't mean to study my connection," said Mr. Coombes, "what did you marry me for?"

"I wonder," said Jennie, and turned back to the piano.

"I never saw such a man as you," said Mrs. Coombes. "You've altered all round since we were married. Before—"

Then Jennie began at the tum, tum, tum again.

"Look here!" said Mr. Coombes, driven at last to revolt, standing up and raising his voice. "I tell you I won't have that." The frock-coat heaved with his indignation.

"No vi'lence, now," said the long young man in drab, sitting up.

"Who the juice are you?" said Mr. Coombes, fiercely.

Whereupon they all began talking at once. The new guest said he was Jennie's "intended," and meant to protect her, and Mr. Coombes said he was welcome to do so anywhere but in his (Mr. Coombes') house; and Mrs. Coombes said he ought to be ashamed of insulting his guests, and (as I have already mentioned) that he was getting a regular little grub; and the end was, that Mr. Coombes ordered his visitors out of the house, and they wouldn't go, and so he said he would go himself. With his face burning and tears of excitement in his eyes, he went into the passage, and as he struggled with his overcoat—his frock-coat sleeves got concertinaed up his arm—and gave a brush at his silk hat, Jennie began again at the piano, and strummed him insultingly out of the house. Tum, tum, tum. He slammed the shop-door so that the house quivered. That, briefly, was the immediate making of his mood. You will perhaps begin to understand his disgust with existence.

As he walked along the muddy path under the firs,—it was late October, and the ditches and heaps of fir-needles were gorgeous with clumps of fungi,—he recapitulated the melancholy history of his marriage. It was brief and commonplace enough. He now perceived with sufficient clearness that his wife had married him out of a natural curiosity and in order to escape from her worrying, laborious, and uncertain life in the workroom; and, like the majority of her class, she was far too stupid to realise that it was her duty to co-operate with him in his business. She was greedy of enjoyment, loquacious, and socially-minded, and evidently disappointed to find the restraints of poverty still hanging about her. His worries exasperated her, and the slightest attempt to control her proceedings resulted in a charge of "grumbling." Why couldn't he be nice—as he used to be? And Coombes was such a harmless little man, too, nourished mentally on "Self-Help," and with a meagre ambition of self-denial and competition, that was to end in a "sufficiency." Then Jennie came in as a female Mephistopheles, a gabbling chronicle of "fellers," and was always wanting his wife to go to theatres, and "all that." And in addition were aunts of his wife, and cousins (male and female), to eat up capital, insult him personally, upset business arrangements, annoy good customers, and generally blight his life. It was not the first occasion by many that Mr. Coombes had fled his home in wrath and indignation, and something like fear, vowing furiously and even aloud that he wouldn't stand it, and so frothing away his energy along the line of least resistance. But never before had he been quite so sick of life as on this particular Sunday afternoon. The Sunday dinner may have had its share in his despair—and the greyness of the sky. Perhaps, too, he was beginning to realise his unendurable frustration as a business man as the consequence of his marriage. Presently bankruptcy, and after that— Perhaps she might have reason to repent when it was too late. And destiny, as I have already intimated, had planted the path through the wood with evil-smelling fungi, thickly and variously planted it, not only on the right side, but on the left.

A small shopman is in such a melancholy position, if his wife turns out a disloyal partner. His capital is all tied up in his business, and to leave her, means to join the unemployed in some strange part of the earth. The luxuries of divorce are beyond him altogether. So that the good old tradition of marriage for better or worse holds inexorably for him, and things work up to tragic culminations. Bricklayers kick their wives to death, and dukes betray theirs; but it is among the small clerks and shopkeepers nowadays that it comes most often to a cutting of throats. Under the circumstances it is not so very remarkable—and you must take it as charitably as you can—that the mind of Mr. Coombes ran for awhile on some such glorious close to his disappointed hopes, and that he thought of razors, pistols, bread-knives, and touching letters to the coroner denouncing his enemies by name, and praying piously for forgiveness. After a time his fierceness gave way to melancholia. He had been married in this very overcoat, in his first and only frockcoat that was buttoned up beneath it. He began to recall their courting along this very walk, his years of penurious saving to get capital, and the bright hopefulness of his marrying days. For it all to work out like this! Was there no sympathetic ruler anywhere in the world? He reverted to death as a topic.

He thought of the canal he had just crossed, and doubted whether he shouldn't stand with his head out, even in the middle, and it was while drowning was in his mind that the purple pileus caught his eye. He looked at it mechanically for a moment, and stopped and stooped towards it to pick it up, under the impression that it was some such small leather object as a purse. Then he saw that it was the purple top of a fungus, a peculiarly poisonous-looking purple: slimy, shiny, and emitting a sour odour. He hesitated with his hand an inch or so from it, and the thought of poison crossed his mind.

With that he picked the thing, and stood up again with it in his hand.

The odour was certainly strong—acrid, but by no means disgusting. He broke off a piece, and the fresh surface was a creamy white, that changed like magic in the space of ten seconds to a yellowish-green colour. It was even an inviting-looking change. He broke off two other pieces to see it repeated. They were wonderful things, these fungi, thought Mr. Coombes, and all of them the deadliest poisons, as his father had often told him. Deadly poisons!

There is no time like the present for a rash resolve. Why not here and now? thought Mr. Coombes. He tasted a little piece, a very little piece indeed—a mere crumb. It was so pungent that he almost spat it out again, then merely hot and full-flavoured,—a kind of German mustard with a touch of horse-radish and—well, mushroom. He swallowed it in the excitement of the moment. Did he like it or did he not? His mind was curiously careless. He would try another bit. It really wasn't bad—it was good. He forgot his troubles in the interest of the immediate moment. Playing with death it was. He took another bite, and then deliberately finished a mouthful. A curious tingling sensation began in his finger-tips and toes. His pulse began to move faster. The blood in his ears sounded like a millrace. "Try bi' more," said Mr. Coombes. He turned and looked about him, and found his feet unsteady. He saw and struggled towards a little patch of purple a dozen yards away. "Jol' goo' stuff," said Mr. Coombes. "E—lomore ye' " He pitched forward and fell on his face, his hands outstretched towards the cluster of pilei. But he did not eat any more of them. He forgot forthwith.

He rolled over and sat up with a look of astonishment on his face. His carefully brushed silk hat had rolled away towards the ditch. He pressed his hand to his brow. Something had happened, but he could not rightly determine what it was. Anyhow, he was no longer dull—he felt bright, cheerful. And his throat was afire. He laughed in the sudden gaiety of his heart. Had he been dull? He did not know; but at any rate he would be dull no longer. He got up and stood unsteadily, regarding the universe with an agreeable smile. He began to remember. He could not remember very well, because of a steam roundabout that was beginning in his head. And he knew he had been disagreeable at home, just because they wanted to be happy. They were quite right; life should be as gay as possible. He would go home and make it up, and reassure them. And why not take some of this delightful toadstool with him, for them to eat? A hatful, no less. Some of those red ones with white spots as well, and a few yellow. He had been a dull dog, an enemy to merriment; he would make up for it. It would be gay to turn his coat-sleeves inside out, and stick some yellow gorse into his waist-coat pockets. Then home—singing—for a jolly evening.

After the departure of Mr. Coombes, Jennie discontinued playing, and turned round on the music-stool again. "What a fuss about nothing," said Jennie.

"You see, Mr. Clarence, what I've got to put up with," said Mrs. Coombes.

"He is a bit hasty," said Mr. Clarence, judicially.

"He ain't got the slightest sense of our position," said Mrs. Coombes; "that's what I complain of. He cares for nothing but his old shop; and if I have a bit of company, or buy anything to keep myself decent, or get any little thing I want out of the housekeeping money, there's disagreeables. 'Economy,' he says; 'struggle for life,' and all that. He lies awake of nights about it, worrying how he can screw me out of a shilling. He wanted us to eat Dorset butter once. If once I was to give in to him—there!"

"Of course," said Jennie.

"If a man values a woman," said Mr. Clarence, lounging back in the arm-chair, "he must be prepared to make sacrifices for her. For my own part," said Mr. Clarence, with his eye on Jennie, "I shouldn't think of marrying till I was in a position to do the thing in style. It's downright selfishness. A man ought to go through the rough-and-tumble by himself, and not drag her—"

"I don't agree altogether with that," said Jennie. "I don't see why a man shouldn't have a woman's help, provided he doesn't treat her meanly, you know. It's meanness—"

"You wouldn't believe," said Mrs. Coombes. "But I was a fool to 'ave 'im. I might 'ave known. If it 'adn't been for my father, we shouldn't have had not a carriage to our wedding."

"Lord! he didn't stick out at that?" said Mr. Clarence, quite shocked.

"Said he wanted the money for his stock, or some such rubbish. Why, he wouldn't have a woman in to help me once a week if it wasn't for my standing out plucky. And the fusses he makes about money—comes to me, well pretty near crying, with sheets of paper and figgers. 'If only we can tide over this year,' he says, 'the business is bound to go.' 'If only we can tide over this year,' I says; 'then it'll be, if only we can tide over next year. I know you,' I says. 'And you don't catch me screwing myself lean and ugly. Why didn't you marry a slavey,' I says, 'if you wanted one—instead of a respectable girl?' I says."

So Mrs. Coombes. But we will not follow this unedifying conversation further. Suffice it that Mr. Coombes was very satisfactorily disposed of, and they had a snug little time round the fire. Then Mrs. Coombes went to get the tea, and Jennie sat coquettishly on the arm of Mr. Clarence's chair until the tea-things clattered outside. "What was that I heard?" asked Mrs. Coombes, playfully, as she entered, and there was badinage about kissing. They were just sitting down to the little circular table when the first intimation of Mr. Coombes' return was heard.

This was a fumbling at the latch of the front door.

"'Ere's my lord," said Mrs. Coombes. "Went out like a lion and comes back like a lamb, I'll lay."

Something fell over in the shop: a chair, it sounded like. Then there was a sound as of some complicated step exercise in the passage. Then the door opened and Coombes appeared. But it was Coombes transfigured. The immaculate collar had been torn carelessly from his throat. His carefully-brushed silk hat, half-full of a crush of fungi, was under one arm; his coat was inside out, and his waistcoat adorned with bunches of yellow-blossomed furze. These little eccentricities of Sunday costume, however, were quite overshadowed by the change in his face; it was livid white, his eyes were unnaturally large and bright, and his pale blue lips were drawn back in a cheerless grin. "Merry!" he said. He had stopped dancing to open the door. "Rational 'njoyment. Dance." He made three fantastic steps into the room, and stood bowing.

"Jim!" shrieked Mrs. Coombes, and Mr. Clarence sat petrified, with a dropping lower jaw.

"Tea," said Mr. Coombes. "Jol' thing, tea. Tose-stools, too. Brosher."

"He's drunk," said Jennie, in a weak voice. Never before had she seen this intense pallor in a drunken man, or such shining, dilated eyes.

Mr. Coombes held out a handful of scarlet agario to Mr. Clarence. "Jo' stuff," said he; "ta' some."

At that moment he was genial. Then at the sight of their startled faces he charged, with the swift transition of insanity, into overbearing fury. And it seemed as if he had suddenly recalled the quarrel of his departure. In such a huge voice as Mrs. Coombes had never heard before, he shouted, "My house. I'm master 'ere. Eat what I give yer!" He bawled this, as it seemed, without an effort, without a violent gesture, standing there as motionless as one who whispers, holding out a handful of fungus.

Clarence approved himself a coward. He could not meet the mad fury in Coombes' eyes; he rose to his feet, pushing back his chair, and turned, stooping. At that Coombes rushed at him. Jennie saw her opportunity, and, with the ghost of a shriek, made for the door. Mrs. Coombes followed her. Clarence tried to dodge. Over went the tea-table with a smash as Coombes clutched him by the collar and tried to thrust the fungus into his mouth. Clarence was content to leave his collar behind him, and shot out into the passage with red patches of fly agaric still adherent to his face. "Shut 'im in!" cried Mrs. Coombes, and would have closed the door, but her supports deserted her; Jennie saw the shop-door open and vanished thereby, locking it behind her, while Clarence went on hastily into the kitchen. Mr. Coombes came heavily against the door, and Mrs. Coombes, finding the key was inside, fled upstairs and locked herself in the spare bedroom.

So the new convert to *joie de vivre* emerged upon the passage, his decorations a little scattered, but that respectable hatful of fungi still under his arm. He hesitated at the three ways, and decided on the kitchen. Whereupon Clarence, who was fumbling with the key, gave up the attempt to imprison his host, and fled into the scullery, only to be captured before he could open the door into the yard. Mr. Clarence is singularly reticent of the details of what occurred. It seems that Mr. Coombes' transitory irritation had vanished again, and he was once more a genial playfellow. And as there were knives and meat-choppers about, Clarence very generously resolved to humour him and so avoid anything tragic. It is beyond dispute that Mr. Coombes played with Mr. Clarence to his heart's content; they could not have been more playful and familiar if they had known each other for years. He insisted gaily on Clarence trying the fungi, and after a friendly tussle, was smitten with remorse at the mess he was making of his guest's face. It also appears that Clarence was dragged under the sink and his face scrubbed with the blacking-brush,—he being still resolved to humour the lunatic at any cost,—and that finally, in a somewhat dishevelled, chipped, and discoloured condition, he was assisted to his coat and shown out by the back door, the shopway being barred by Jennie. Mr. Coombes' wandering thoughts then turned to Jennie. Jennie had been unable to unfasten the shop-door, but she shot the bolts against Mr. Coombes' latch-key, and remained in possession of the shop for the rest of the evening.

It would appear that Mr. Coombes then returned to the kitchen, still in pursuit of gaiety, and, albeit a strict Good Templar, drank (or spilt down the front of the first and only frock-coat) no less than five bottles of the stout Mrs. Coombes insisted upon having for her health's sake. He made cheerful noises by breaking off the necks of the bottle with several of his wife's wedding-present dinner-plates, and during the earlier part of this great drunk he sang divers merry ballads. He cut his finger rather badly with one of the bottles,—the only bloodshed in this story,—and what with that, and the systematic convulsion of his inexperienced physiology by the liquorish brand of Mrs. Coombes' stout, it may be the evil of the fungus poison was somehow allayed. But we prefer to draw a veil over the concluding incidents of this Sunday afternoon. They ended in the coal cellar, in a deep and healing sleep.

An interval of five years elapsed. Again it was a Sunday afternoon in October, and again Mr. Coombes walked through the pinewood beyond the canal. He was still the same dark-eyed, black-moustached little man that he was at the outset of the story, but his double chin was now scarcely so illusory as it had been. His overcoat was new, with a velvet lapel, and a stylish collar with turndown corners, free of any coarse starchiness, had replaced the original all-round article. His hat was glossy, his gloves newish—though one finger had split and been carefully mended. And a casual observer would have noticed about him a certain rectitude of bearing, a certain erectness of head that marks the man who thinks well of himself. He was a master now, with three assistants. Beside him walked a larger sunburnt parody of himself, his brother Tom, just back from Australia. They were recapitulating their early struggles, and Mr. Coombes had just been making a financial statement.

"It's a very nice little business, Jim," said brother Tom. "In these days of competition you're jolly lucky to have worked it up so. And you're jolly lucky, too, to have a wife who's willing to help like yours does."

"Between ourselves," said Mr. Coombes, "it wasn't always so. It wasn't always like this. To begin with, the missus was a bit giddy. Girls are funny creatures."

"Dear me!"

"Yes. You'd hardly think it, but she was downright extravagant, and always having slaps at me. I was a bit too easy and loving, and all that, and she thought the whole blessed show was run for her. Turned the 'ouse into a regular caravansary, always having her relations and girls from business in, and their chaps. Comic songs a' Sunday, it was getting to, and driving trade away. And she was making eyes at the chaps, too! I tell you, Tom, the place wasn't my own."

"Shouldn't 'a' thought it."

"It was so. Well—I reasoned with her. I said, 'I ain't a duke, to keep a wife like a pet animal. I married you for 'elp and company.' I said, 'You got to 'elp and pull the business through.' She wouldn't 'ear of it. 'Very well,' I says; 'I'm a mild man till I'm roused,' I says, 'and it's getting to that.' But she wouldn't 'ear of no warnings."

"Well?"

"It's the way with women. She didn't think I 'ad it in me to be roused. Women of her sort (between ourselves, Tom) don't respect a man until they're a bit afraid of him. So I just broke out to show her. In comes a girl named Jennie, that used to work with her, and her chap. We 'ad a bit of a row, and I came out 'ere—it was just such another day as this—and I thought it all out. Then I went back and pitched into them."

"You did?"

"I did. I was mad, I can tell you. I wasn't going to 'it 'er, if I could 'elp it, so I went back and licked into this chap, just to show 'er what I could do. 'E was a big chap, too. Well, I chucked him, and smashed things about, and gave 'er a scaring, and she ran up and locked 'erself into the spare room."

"Well?"

"That's all. I says to 'er the next morning, "Now you know,' I says, "what I'm like when I'm roused.' And I didn't 'ave to say anything more."

"And you've been happy ever after, eh?"

"So to speak. There's nothing like putting your foot down with them. If it 'adn't been for that afternoon I should 'a' been tramping the roads now, and she'd 'a' been grumbling at me, and all her family grumbling for bringing her to poverty—I know their little ways. But we're all right now. And it's a very decent little business, as you say."

They proceed on their way meditatively. "Women are funny creatures," said brother Tom.

"They want a firm hand," says Coombes.

"What a lot of these funguses there are about here!" remarked brother Tom, presently. "I can't see what use they are in the world."

Mr. Coombes looked. "I dessay they're sent for some wise purpose," said Mr. Coombes.

And that was as much thanks as the purple pileus ever got for maddening this absurd little man to the pitch of decisive action, and so altering the whole course of his life.

# A DREAM OF ARMAGEDDON

The man with the white face entered the carriage at Rugby. He moved slowly in spite of the urgency of his porter, and even while he was still on the platform I noted how ill he seemed. He dropped into the corner over against me with a sigh, made an incomplete attempt to arrange his travelling shawl, and became motionless, with his eyes staring vacantly. Presently he was moved by a sense of my observation, looked up at me, and put out a spiritless hand for his newspaper. Then he glanced again in my direction.

I feigned to read. I feared I had unwittingly embarrassed him, and in a moment I was surprised to find him speaking.

"I beg your pardon?" said I.

"That book," he repeated, pointing a lean finger, "is about dreams."

"Obviously," I answered, for it was Fortnum-Roscoe's *Dream States,* and the title was on the cover.

He hung silent for a space as if he sought words. "Yes," he said at last, "but they tell you nothing."

I did not catch his meaning for a second.

"They don't know," he added.

I looked a little more attentively at his face.

"There are dreams," he said, "and dreams."

That sort of proposition I never dispute.

"I suppose——" he hesitated. "Do you ever dream? I mean vividly."

"I dream very little," I answered. "I doubt if I have three vivid dreams in a year."

"Ah!" he said, and seemed for a moment to collect his thoughts.

"Your dreams don't mix with your memories?" he asked abruptly.

"You don't find yourself in doubt; did this happen or did it not?"

"Hardly ever. Except just for a momentary hesitation now and then. I suppose few people do."

"Does *he* say——" he indicated the book.

"Says it happens at times and gives the usual explanation about intensity of impression and the like to account for its not happening as a rule. I suppose you know something of these theories——"

"Very little—except that they are wrong."

His emaciated hand played with the strap of the window for a time. I prepared to resume reading, and that seemed to precipitate his next remark. He leant forward almost as though he would touch me.

"Isn't there something called consecutive dreaming—that goes on night after night?"

"I believe there is. There are cases given in most books on mental trouble."

"Mental trouble! Yes. I dare say there are. It's the right place for them. But what I mean——" He looked at his bony knuckles. "Is that sort of thing always dreaming? *Is* it dreaming? Or is it something else? Mightn't it be something else?"

I should have snubbed his persistent conversation but for the drawn anxiety of his face. I remember now the look of his faded eyes and the lids red-stained—perhaps you know that look.

"I'm not just arguing about a matter of opinion," he said. "The thing's killing me."

"Dreams?"

"If you call them dreams. Night after night. Vivid!—so vivid . . . this——" (he indicated the landscape that went streaming by the window) "seems unreal in comparison! I can scarcely remember who I am, what business I am on. . . ."

He paused. "Even now——"

"The dream is always the same—do you mean?" I asked.

"It's over."

"You mean?"

"I died."

"Died?"

"Smashed and killed, and now, so much of me as that dream was, is dead. Dead for ever. I dreamt I was another man, you know, living in a different part of the world and in a different time. I dreamt that night after night. Night after night I woke into that other life. Fresh scenes and fresh happenings—until I came upon the last——"

"When you died?"

"When I died."

"And since then——"

"No," he said. "Thank God! That was the end of the dream. . . ."

It was clear I was in for this dream. And after all, I had an hour before me, the light was fading fast, and Fortnum-Roscoe has a dreary way with him. "Living in a different time," I said: "do you mean in some different age?"

"Yes."

"Past?"

"No, to come—to come."

"The year three thousand, for example?"

"I don't know what year it was. I did when I was asleep, when I was dreaming, that is, but not now—not now that I am awake. There's a lot of things I have forgotten since I woke out of these dreams, though I knew them at the time when I was—I suppose it was dreaming. They called the year differently from our way of calling the year. . . . What *did* they call it?" He put his hand to his forehead. "No," said he, "I forget."

He sat smiling weakly. For a moment I feared he did not mean to tell me his dream. As a rule I hate people who tell their dreams, but this struck me differently. I proffered assistance even. "It began ——" I suggested.

"It was vivid from the first. I seemed to wake up in it suddenly. And it's curious that in these dreams I am speaking of I never remembered this life I am living now. It seemed as if the dream life was enough while it lasted. Perhaps—— But I will tell you how I find myself when I do my best to recall it all. I don't remember anything clearly until I found myself sitting in a sort of loggia looking out over the sea. I had been dozing, and suddenly I woke up—fresh and vivid—not a bit dream-like—because the girl had stopped fanning me."

"The girl?"

"Yes, the girl. You must not interrupt or you will put me out."

He stopped abruptly. "You don't think I'm mad?" he said.

"No," I answered; "you've been dreaming. Tell me your dream."

"I woke up, I say, because the girl had stopped fanning me. I was not surprised to find myself there or anything of that sort, you understand. I did not feel I had fallen into it suddenly. I simply took it up at that point. Whatever memory I had of *this* life, this nineteenth century life, faded as I woke, vanished like a dream. I knew all about myself, knew that my name was no longer Cooper but Hedon, and all about my position in the world. I've forgotten a lot since I woke—there's a want of connection—but it was all quite clear and matter of fact then."

He hesitated again, gripping the window strap, putting his face forward and looking up at me appealingly.

"This seems bosh to you?"

"No, no!" I cried. "Go on. Tell me what this loggia was like."

"It was not really a loggia—I don't know what to call it. It faced south. It was small. It was all in shadow except the semicircle above the balcony that showed the sky and sea and the corner where the girl stood. I was on a couch—it was a metal couch with light striped cushions—and the girl was leaning over the balcony with her back to me. The light of the sunrise fell on her ear and cheek. Her pretty white neck and the little curls that nestled there, and her white shoulder were in the sun, and all the grace of her body was in the cool blue shadow. She was dressed—how can I describe it? It was easy and flowing. And altogether there she stood, so that it came to me how beautiful and desirable she was, as though I had never seen her before. And when at last I sighed and raised myself upon my arm she turned her face to me——"

He stopped.

"I have lived three-and-fifty years in this world. I have had mother, sisters, friends, wife, and daughters—all their faces, the play of their faces, I know. But the face of this girl—it is much more real to me. I can bring it back into memory so that I see it again—I could draw it or paint it. And after all——"

He stopped—but I said nothing.

"The face of a dream—the face of a dream. She was beautiful. Not that beauty which is terrible, cold, and worshipful, like the beauty of a saint; nor that beauty that stirs fierce passions; but a sort of radiation, sweet lips that softened into smiles, and grave grey eyes. And she moved gracefully, she seemed to have part with all pleasant and gracious things——"

He stopped, and his face was downcast and hidden. Then he looked up at me and went on, making no further attempt to disguise his absolute belief in the reality of his story.

"You see, I had thrown up my plans and ambitions, thrown up all I had ever worked for or desired for her sake. I had been a master man away there in the north, with influence and property and a great reputation, but none of it had seemed worth having beside her. I had come to the place, this city of sunny pleasures, with her, and left all those things to wreck and ruin just to save a remnant at least of my life. While I had been in love with her before I knew that she had any care for me, before I had imagined that she would dare—that we should dare, all my life had seemed vain and hollow, dust and ashes. It *was* dust and ashes. Night after night and through the long days I had longed and desired—my soul had beaten against the thing forbidden!

"But it is impossible for one man to tell another just these things. It's emotion, it's a tint, a light that comes and goes. Only while it's there, everything changes, everything. The thing is I came away and left them in their Crisis to do what they could."

"Left whom?" I asked, puzzled.

"The people up in the north there. You see—in this dream, anyhow—I had been a big man, the sort of man men come to trust in, to group themselves about. Millions of men who had never seen me were ready to do things and risk things because of their confidence in me. I had been playing that game for years, that big laborious game, that vague, monstrous political game amidst intrigues and betrayals, speech and agitation. It was a vast weltering world, and at last I had a sort of leadership against the Gang—you know it was called the Gang—a sort of compromise of scoundrelly projects and base ambitions and vast public emotional stupidities and catchwords—the Gang that kept the world noisy and blind year by year, and all the while that it was drifting, drifting towards infinite disaster. But I can't expect you to understand the shades and complications of the year—the year something or other ahead. I had it all—down to the smallest details—in my dream. I suppose I had been dreaming of it before I awoke, and the fading outline of some queer new development I had imagined still hung about me as I rubbed my eyes. It was some grubby affair that made me thank God for the sunlight. I sat up on the couch and remained looking at the woman and rejoicing—rejoicing that I had come away out of all that tumult and folly and violence before it was too late. After all, I thought, this is life—love and beauty, desire and delight, are they not worth all those dismal struggles for vague, gigantic ends? And I blamed myself for having ever sought to be a leader when I might have given my days to love. But then, thought I, if I had not spent my early days sternly and austerely, I might have wasted myself upon vain and worthless women, and at the thought all my being went out in love and tenderness to my dear mistress, my dear lady, who had come at last and compelled me—compelled me by her invincible charm for me—to lay that life aside.

"'You are worth it,' I said, speaking without intending her to hear; 'you are worth it, my dearest one; worth pride and praise and all things. Love! to have *you* is worth them all together.' And at the murmur of my voice she turned about.

"'Come and see,' she cried—I can hear her now—'come and see the sunrise upon Monte Solaro.'

"I remember how I sprang to my feet and joined her at the balcony. She put a white hand upon my shoulder and pointed towards great masses of limestone, flushing, as it were, into life. I looked. But first I noted the sunlight on her face caressing the lines of her cheeks and neck. How can I describe to you the scene we had before us? We were at Capri——"

"I have been there," I said. "I have clambered up Monte Solaro and drunk *vero Capri*—muddy stuff like cider—at the summit."

"Ah!" said the man with the white face; "then perhaps you can tell me—you will know if this was indeed Capri. For in this life I have never been there. Let me describe it. We were in a little room, one of a vast multitude of little rooms, very cool and sunny, hollowed out of the limestone of a sort of cape, very high above the sea. The whole island, you know, was one enormous hotel, complex beyond explaining, and on the other side there were miles of floating hotels, and huge floating stages to which the flying machines came. They called it a pleasure city. Of course, there was none of that in your time—rather, I should say, *is* none of that *now*. Of course. Now!—yes.

"Well, this room of ours was at the extremity of the cape, so that one could see east and west. Eastward was a great cliff—a thousand feet high perhaps—coldly grey except for one bright edge of gold, and beyond it the Isle of the Sirens, and a falling coast that faded and passed into the hot sunrise. And when one turned to the west, distinct and near was a little bay, a little beach still in shadow. And out of that shadow rose Solaro straight and tall, flushed and golden crested, like a beauty throned, and the white moon was floating behind her in the sky. And before us from east to west stretched the many-tinted sea all dotted with little sailing boats.

"To the eastward, of course, these little boats were grey and very minute and clear, but to the westward they were little boats of gold—shining gold—almost like little flames. And just below us was a rock with an arch worn through it. The blue sea-water broke to green and foam all round the rock, and a galley came gliding out of the arch."

"I know that rock," I said. "I was nearly drowned there. It is called the Faraglioni."

"*I Faraglioni?* Yes, *she* called it that," answered the man with the white face. "There was some story—but that——"

He put his hand to his forehead again. "No," he said, "I forget that story."

"Well, that is the first thing I remember, the first dream I had, that little shaded room and the beautiful air and sky and that dear lady of mine, with her shining arms and her graceful robe, and how we sat and talked in half whispers to one another. We talked in whispers not because there was any one to hear, but because there was still such a freshness of mind between us that our thoughts were a little frightened, I think, to find themselves at last in words. And so they went softly.

"Presently we were hungry and we went from our apartment, going by a strange passage with a moving floor, until we came to the great breakfast room—there was a fountain and music. A pleasant and joyful place it was, with its sunlight and splashing, and the murmur of plucked strings. And we sat and ate and smiled at one another, and I would not heed a man who was watching me from a table near by.

"And afterwards we went on to the dancing-hall. But I cannot describe that hall. The place was enormous—larger than any building you have ever seen—and in one place there was the old gate of Capri, caught into the wall of a gallery high overhead. Light girders, stems and threads of gold, burst from the pillars like fountains, streamed like an Aurora across the roof and interlaced, like—like conjuring tricks. All about the great circle for the dancers there were beautiful figures, strange dragons, and intricate and wonderful grotesques bearing lights. The place was inundated with artificial light that shamed the newborn day. And as we went through the throng the people turned about and looked at us, for all through the world my name and face were known, and how I had suddenly thrown up pride and struggle to come to this place. And they looked also at the lady beside me, though half the story of how at last she had come to me was unknown or mistold. And few of the men who were there, I know, but judged me a happy man, in spite of all the shame and dishonour that had come upon my name.

"The air was full of music, full of harmonious scents, full of the rhythm of beautiful motions. Thousands of beautiful people swarmed about the hall, crowded the galleries, sat in a myriad recesses; they were dressed in splendid colours and crowned with flowers; thousands danced about the great circle beneath the white images of the ancient gods, and glorious processions of youths and maidens came and went. We two danced, not the dreary monotonies of your days—of this time, I mean—but dances that were beautiful, intoxicating. And even now I can see my lady dancing—dancing joyously. She danced, you know, with a serious face; she danced with a serious dignity, and yet she was smiling at me and caressing me—smiling and caressing with her eyes.

"The music was different," he murmured. "It went—I cannot describe it; but it was infinitely richer and more varied than any music that has ever come to me awake.

"And then—it was when we had done dancing—a man came to speak to me. He was a lean, resolute man, very soberly clad for that place, and already I had marked his face watching me in the breakfasting hall, and afterwards as we went along the passage I had avoided his eye. But now, as we sat in a little alcove, smiling at the pleasure of all the people who went to and fro across the shining floor, he came and touched me, and spoke to me so that I was forced to listen. And he asked that he might speak to me for a little time apart.

" 'No,' I said. 'I have no secrets from this lady. What do you want to tell me?'

"He said it was a trivial matter, or at least a dry matter, for a lady to hear.

" 'Perhaps for me to hear,' said I.

"He glanced at her, as though almost he would appeal to her. Then he asked me suddenly if I had heard of a great and avenging declaration that Evesham had made. Now, Evesham had always before been the man next to myself in the leadership of that great party in the north. He was a forcible, hard and tactless man, and only I had been able to control and soften him. It was on his account even more than my own, I think, that the others had been so dismayed at my retreat. So this question about what he had done reawakened my old interest in the life I had put aside just for a moment.

" 'I have taken no heed of any news for many days,' I said. 'What has Evesham been saying?'

"And with that the man began, nothing loath, and I must confess even I was struck by Evesham's reckless folly in the wild and threatening words he had used. And this messenger they had sent to me not only told me of Evesham's speech, but went on to ask counsel and to point out what need they had of me. While he talked, my lady sat a little forward and watched his face and mine.

"My old habits of scheming and organising reasserted themselves. I could even see myself suddenly returning to the north, and all the dramatic effect of it. All that this man said witnessed to the disorder of the party indeed, but not to its damage. I should go back stronger than I had come. And then I thought of my lady. You see—how can I tell you? There were certain peculiarities of our relationship—as things are I need not tell you about that—which would render her presence with me impossible. I should have had to leave her; indeed, I should have had to renounce her clearly and openly, if I was to do all that I could do in the north. And the man knew *that,* even as he talked to her and me, knew it as well as she did, that my steps to duty were—first separation, then abandonment. At the touch of that thought my dream of a return was shattered. I turned on the man suddenly, as he was imagining his eloquence was gaining ground with me.

" 'What have I to do with these things now?' I said. 'I have done with them. Do you think I am coquetting with your people in coming here?'

" 'No,' he said; 'but——'

" 'Why cannot you leave me alone? I have done with these things. I have ceased to be anything but a private man.'

" 'Yes,' he answered. 'But have you thought?—this talk of war, these reckless challenges, these wild aggressions—'

"I stood up.

" 'No,' I cried. 'I won't hear you. I took count of all those things, I weighed them—and I have come away.'

"He seemed to consider the possibility of persistence. He looked from me to where the lady sat regarding us.

" 'War,' he said, as if he were speaking to himself, and then turned slowly from me and walked away.

"I stood, caught in the whirl of thoughts his appeal had set going.

"I heard my lady's voice.

" 'Dear,' she said; 'but if they have need of you——'

"She did not finish her sentence, she let it rest there. I turned to her sweet face, and the balance of my mood swayed and reeled.

" 'They want me only to do the thing they dare not do themselves,' I said. 'If they distrust Evesham they must settle with him themselves.'

"She looked at me doubtfully.

" 'But war——' she said.

"I saw a doubt on her face that I had seen before, a doubt of herself and me, the first shadow of the discovery that, seen strongly and completely, must drive us apart for ever.

"Now, I was an older mind than hers, and I could sway her to this belief or that.

" 'My dear one,' I said, 'you must not trouble over these things. There will be no war. Certainly there will be no war. The age of wars is past. Trust me to know the justice of this case. They have no right upon me, dearest, and no one has a right upon me. I have been free to choose my life, and I have chosen this.'

" 'But *war*——,' she said.

"I sat down beside her. I put an arm behind her and took her hand in mine. I set myself to drive that doubt away—I set myself to fill her mind with pleasant things again. I lied to her, and in lying to her I lied also to myself. And she was only too ready to believe me, only too ready to forget.

"Very soon the shadow had gone again, and we were hastening to our bathing-place in the Grotto del Bove Marino, where it was our custom to bathe every day. We swam and splashed one another, and in that buoyant water I seemed to become something lighter and stronger than a man. And at last we came out dripping and rejoicing and raced among the rocks. And then I put on a dry bathing-dress, and we sat to bask in the sun, and presently I nodded, resting my head against her knee, and she put her hand upon my hair and stroked it softly and I dozed. And behold! as it were with the snapping of the string of a violin, I was awakening, and I was in my own bed in Liverpool, in the life of to-day.

"Only for a time I could not believe that all these vivid moments had been no more than the substance of a dream.

"In truth, I could not believe it a dream for all the sobering reality of things about me. I bathed and dressed as it were by habit, and as I shaved I argued why I of all men should leave the woman I loved to go back to fantastic politics in the hard and strenuous north. Even if Evesham did force the world back to war, what was that to me? I was a man, with the heart of a man, and why should I feel the responsibility of a deity for the way the world might go?

"You know that is not quite the way I think about affairs, about my real affairs. I am a solicitor, you know, with a point of view.

"The vision was so real, you must understand, so utterly unlike a dream that I kept perpetually recalling little irrelevant details; even the ornament of a book-cover that lay on my wife's sewing-machine in the breakfast-room recalled with the utmost vividness the gilt line that ran about the seat in the alcove where I had talked with the messenger from my deserted party. Have you ever heard of a dream that had a quality like that?"

"Like——?"

"So that afterwards you remembered little details you had forgotten."

I thought. I had never noticed the point before, but he was right.

"Never," I said. "That is what you never seem to do with dreams."

"No," he answered. "But that is just what I did. I am a solicitor, you must understand, in Liverpool, and I could not help wondering what the clients and business people I found myself talking to in my office would think if I told them suddenly I was in love with a girl who would be born a couple of hundred years or so hence, and worried about the politics of my great-great-great-grandchildren. I was chiefly busy that day negotiating a ninety-nine-year building lease. It was a private builder in a hurry, and we wanted to tie him in every possible way. I had an interview with him, and he showed a certain want of temper that sent me to bed still irritated. That night I had no dream. Nor did I dream the next night, at least, to remember.

"Something of that intense reality of conviction vanished. I began to feel sure it *was* a dream. And then it came again.

"When the dream came again, nearly four days later, it was very different. I think it certain that four days had also elapsed in the dream. Many things had happened in the north, and the shadow of them was back again between us, and this time it was not so easily dispelled. I began, I know, with moody musings. Why, in spite of all, should I go back, go back for all the rest of my days to toil and stress, insults and perpetual dissatisfaction, simply to save hundreds of millions of common people, whom I did not love, whom too often I could do no other than despise, from the stress and anguish of war and infinite misrule? And after all I might fail. *They* all sought their own narrow ends, and why should not I—why should not I also live as a man? And out of such thoughts her voice summoned me, and I lifted my eyes.

"I found myself awake and walking. We had come out above the Pleasure City, we were near the summit of Monte Solaro and looking towards the bay. It was the late afternoon and very clear. Far away to the left Ischia hung in a golden haze between sea and sky, and Naples was coldly white against the hills, and before us was Vesuvius with a tall and slender streamer feathering at last towards the south, and the ruins of Torre dell'Annunziata and Castellamare glittering and near."

I interrupted suddenly: "You have been to Capri, of course?"

"Only in this dream," he said, "only in this dream. All across the bay beyond Sorrento were the floating palaces of the Pleasure City moored and chained. And northward were the broad floating stages that received the aeroplanes. Aeroplanes fell out of the sky every afternoon, each bringing its thousands of pleasure-seekers from the uttermost parts of the earth to Capri and its delights. All these things, I say, stretched below.

"But we noticed them only incidentally because of an unusual sight that evening had to show. Five war aeroplanes that had long slumbered useless in the distant arsenals of the Rhinemouth were manœuvring now in the eastward sky. Evesham had astonished the world by producing them and others, and sending them to circle here and there. It was the threat material in the great game of bluff he was playing, and it had taken even me by surprise. He was one of those incredibly stupid energetic people who seem sent by Heaven to create disasters. His energy to the first glance seemed so wonderfully like capacity! But he had no imagination, no invention, only a stupid, vast, driving force of will, and a mad faith in his stupid idiot 'luck' to pull him through. I remember how we stood out upon the headland watching the squadron circling far away, and how I weighed the full meaning of the sight, seeing clearly the way things must go. And then even it was not too late. I might have gone back, I think, and saved the world. The people of the north would follow me, I knew, granted only that in one thing I respected their moral standards. The east and south would trust me as they would trust no other northern man. And I knew I had only to put it to her and she would have let me go. . . . Not because she did not love me!

"Only I did not want to go; my will was all the other way about. I had so newly thrown off the incubus of responsibility: I was still so fresh a renegade from duty that the daylight clearness of what I *ought* to do had no power at all to touch my will. My will was to live, to gather pleasures and make my dear lady happy. But though this sense of vast neglected duties had no power to draw me, it could make me silent and preoccupied, it robbed the days I had spent of half their brightness and roused me into dark meditations in the silence of the night. And as I stood and watched Evesham's aeroplanes sweep to and fro—those birds of infinite ill omen—she stood beside me watching me, perceiving the trouble indeed, but not perceiving it clearly—her eyes questioning my face, her expression shaded with perplexity. Her face was grey because the sunset was fading out of the sky. It was no fault of hers that she held me. She had asked me to go from her, and again in the night time and with tears she had asked me to go.

"At last it was the sense of her that roused me from my mood. I turned upon her suddenly and challenged her to race down the mountain slopes. 'No,' she said, as if I jarred with her gravity, but I was resolved to end that gravity, and made her run—no one can be very grey and sad who is out of breath—and when she stumbled I ran with my hand beneath her arm. We ran down past a couple of men, who turned back staring in astonishment at my behaviour—they must have recognised my face. And halfway down the slope came a tumult in the air, clang-clank, clang-clank, and we stopped, and presently over the hill-crest those war things came flying one behind the other."

The man seemed hesitating on the verge of a description.

"What were they like?" I asked.

"They had never fought," he said. "They were just like our ironclads are nowadays; they had never fought. No one knew what they might do, with excited men inside them; few even cared to speculate. They were great driving things shaped like spearheads without a shaft, with a propeller in the place of the shaft."

"Steel?"

"Not steel."

"Aluminum?"

"No, no, nothing of that sort. An alloy that was very common—as common as brass, for example. It was called—let me see——." He squeezed his forehead with the fingers of one hand. "I am forgetting everything," he said.

"And they carried guns?"

"Little guns, firing high explosive shells. They fired the guns backwards, out of the base of the leaf, so to speak, and rammed with the beak. That was the theory, you know, but they had never been fought. No one could tell exactly what was going to happen. And meanwhile I suppose it was very fine to go whirling through the air like a flight of young swallows, swift and easy. I guess the captains tried not to think too clearly what the real thing would be like. And these flying war machines, you know, were only one sort of the endless war contrivances that had been invented and had fallen into abeyance during the long peace. There were all sorts of these things that people were routing out and furbishing up; infernal things, silly things; things that had never been tried; big engines, terrible explosives, great guns. You know the silly way of these ingenious sort of men who make these things; they turn 'em out as beavers build dams, and with no more sense of the rivers they're going to divert and the lands they're going to flood!

"As we went down the winding stepway to our hotel again, in the twilight, I foresaw it all: I saw how clearly and inevitably things were driving for war in Evesham's silly, violent hands, and I had some inkling of what war was bound to be under these new conditions. And even then, though I knew it was drawing near the limit of my opportunity, I could find no will to go back."

He sighed.

"That was my last chance.

"We didn't go into the city until the sky was full of stars, so we walked out upon the high terrace, to and fro, and—she counselled me to go back.

" 'My dearest,' she said, and her sweet face looked up to me, 'this is Death. This life you lead is Death. Go back to them, go back to your duty——.'

"She began to weep, saying, between her sobs, and clinging to my arm as she said it, 'Go back—Go back.'

"Then suddenly she fell mute, and, glancing down at her face, I read in an instant the thing she had thought to do. It was one of those moments when one *sees*.

" 'No!' I said.

" 'No?' she asked, in surprise, and I think a little fearful at the answer to her thought.

" 'Nothing,' I said, 'shall send me back. Nothing! I have chosen. Love, I have chosen, and the world must go. Whatever happens I will live this life—I will live for *you!* It—nothing shall turn me aside; nothing, my dear one. Even if you died—even if you died——'

" 'Yes,' she murmured, softly.

" 'Then—I also would die.'

"And before she could speak again I began to talk, talking eloquently—as I *could* do in that life—talking to exalt love, to make the life we were living seem heroic and glorious; and the thing I was deserting something hard and enormously ignoble that it was a fine thing to set aside. I bent all my mind to throw that glamour upon it, seeking not only to convert her but myself to that. We talked, and she clung to me, torn too between all that she deemed noble and all that she knew was sweet. And at last I did make it heroic, made all the thickening disaster of the world only a sort of glorious setting to our unparalleled love, and we two poor foolish souls strutted there at last, clad in that splendid delusion, drunken rather with that glorious delusion, under the still stars.

"And so my moment passed.

"It was my last chance. Even as we went to and fro there, the leaders of the south and east were gathering their resolve, and the hot answer that shattered Evesham's bluffing for ever, took shape and waited. And all over Asia, and the ocean, and the south, the air and the wires were throbbing with their warnings to prepare—prepare.

"No one living, you know, knew what war was; no one could imagine, with all these new inventions, what horror war might bring. I believe most people still believed it would be a matter of bright uniforms and shouting charges and triumphs and flags and bands—in a time when half the world drew its food supply from regions ten thousand miles away——."

The man with the white face paused. I glanced at him, and his face was intent on the floor of the carriage. A little railway station, a string of loaded trucks, a signal-box, and the back of a cottage, shot by the carriage window, and a bridge passed with a clap of noise, echoing the tumult of the train.

"After that," he said, "I dreamt often. For three weeks of nights that dream was my life. And the worst of it was there were nights when I could not dream, when I lay tossing on a bed in *this* accursed life; and *there*—somewhere lost to me—things were happening momentous, terrible things. . . . I lived at nights—my days, my waking days, this life I am living now, became a faded, far-away dream, a drab setting, the cover of the book."

He thought.

"I could tell you all, tell you every little thing in the dream, but as to what I did in the daytime—no. I could not tell—I do not remember. My memory—my memory has gone. The business of life slips from me——"

He leant forward, and pressed his hands upon his eyes. For a long time he said nothing.

"And then?" said I.

"The war burst like a hurricane."

He stared before him at unspeakable things.

"And then?" I urged again.

"One touch of unreality," he said, in the low tone of a man who speaks to himself, "and they would have been nightmares. But they were not nightmares—they were not nightmares. *No!*"

He was silent for so long that it dawned upon me that there was a danger of losing the rest of the story. But he went on talking again in the same tone of questioning self-communion.

"What was there to do but flight? I had not thought the war would touch Capri—I had seemed to see Capri as being out of it all, as the contrast to it all; but two nights after the whole place was shouting and bawling, every woman almost and every other man wore a badge—Evesham's badge—and there was no music but a jangling war-song over and over again, and everywhere men enlisting, and in the dancing halls they were drilling. The whole island was awhirl with rumours; it was said, again and again, that fighting had begun. I had not expected this. I had seen so little of the life of pleasure that I had failed to reckon with this violence of the amateurs. And as for me, I was out of it. I was like a man who might have prevented the firing of a magazine. The time had gone. I was no one; the vainest stripling with a badge counted for more than I. The crowd jostled us and bawled in our ears; that accursed song deafened us; a woman shrieked at my lady because no badge was on her, and we two went back to our own place again, ruffled and insulted—my lady white and silent, and I aquiver with rage. So furious was I, I could have quarrelled with her if I could have found one shade of accusation in her eyes.

"All my magnificence had gone from me. I walked up and down our rock cell, and outside was the darkling sea and a light to the southward that flared and passed and came again.

" 'We must get out of this place,' I said over and over. 'I have made my choice, and I will have no hand in these troubles. I will have nothing of this war. We have taken our lives out of all these things. This is no refuge for us. Let us go.'

"And the next day we were already in flight from the war that covered the world.

"And all the rest was Flight—all the rest was Flight."

He mused darkly.

"How much was there of it?"

He made no answer.

"How many days?"

His face was white and drawn and his hands were clenched. He took no heed of my curiosity.

I tried to draw him back to his story with questions.

"Where did you go?" I said.

"When?"

"When you left Capri."

"Southwest," he said, and glanced at me for a second. "We went in a boat."

"But I should have thought an aeroplane?"

"They had been seized."

I questioned him no more. Presently I thought he was beginning again. He broke out in an argumentative monotone:

"But why should it be? If, indeed, this battle, this slaughter and stress *is* life, why have we this craving for pleasure and beauty? If there *is* no refuge, if there is no place of peace, and if all our dreams of quiet places are a folly and a snare, why have we such dreams? Surely it was no ignoble cravings, no base intentions, had brought us to this; it was Love had isolated us. Love had come to me with her eyes and robed in her beauty, more glorious than all else in life, in the very shape and colour of life, and summoned me away. I had silenced all the voices, I had answered all the questions—I had come to her. And suddenly there was nothing but War and Death!"

I had an inspiration. "After all," I said, "it could have been only a dream."

"A dream!" he cried, flaming upon me, "a dream—when even now——."

For the first time he became animated. A faint flush crept into his cheek. He raised his open hand and clenched it, and dropped it to his knee. He spoke, looking away from me, and for all the rest of the time he looked away. "We are but phantoms," he said, "and the phantoms of phantoms, desires like cloud shadows and wills of straw that eddy in the wind; the days pass, use and wont carry us through as a train carries the shadow of its lights—so be it! But one thing is real and certain, one thing is no dreamstuff, but eternal and enduring. It is the centre of my life, and all other things about it are subordinate or altogether vain. I loved her, that woman of a dream. And she and I are dead together!

"A dream! How can it be a dream, when it drenched a living life with unappeasable sorrow, when it makes all that I have lived for and cared for, worthless and unmeaning?

"Until that very moment when she was killed I believed we had still a chance of getting away," he said. "All through the night and morning that we sailed across the sea from Capri to Salerno, we talked of escape. We were full of hope, and it clung about us to the end, hope for the life together we should lead, out of it all, out of the battle and struggle, the wild and empty passions, the empty arbitrary 'thou shalt' and 'thou shalt not' of the world. We were uplifted, as though our quest was a holy thing, as though love for one another was a mission. . . .

"Even when from our boat we saw the fair face of that great rock Capri—already scarred and gashed by the gun emplacements and hiding-places that were to make it a fastness—we reckoned nothing of the imminent slaughter, though the fury of preparation hung about in puffs and clouds of dust at a hundred points amidst the grey; but, indeed, I made a text of that and talked. There, you know, was the rock, still beautiful, for all its scars, with its countless windows and arches and ways, tier upon tier, for a thousand feet, a vast carving of grey, broken by vine-clad terraces, and lemon and orange groves, and masses of agave and prickly pear, and puffs of almond blossom. And out under the archway that is built over the Piccola Marina other boats were coming; and as we came round the cape and within sight of the mainland, another little string of boats came into view, driving before the wind towards the southwest. In a little while a multitude had come out, the remoter just little specks of ultramarine in the shadow of the eastward cliff.

" 'It is love and reason," I said, 'fleeing from all this madness of war.'

"And though we presently saw a squadron of aeroplanes flying across the southern sky we did not heed it. There it was—a line of little dots in the sky—and then more, dotting the southeastern horizon, and then still more, until all that quarter of the sky was stippled with blue specks. Now they were all thin little strokes of blue, and now one and now a multitude would heel and catch the sun and become short flashes of light. They came rising and falling and growing larger, like some huge flight of gulls or rooks or such-like birds moving with a marvellous uniformity, and ever as they drew nearer they spread over a greater width of sky. The southward wing flung itself in an arrow-headed cloud athwart the sun. And then suddenly they swept round to the eastward and streamed eastward, growing smaller and smaller and clearer and clearer again until they vanished from the sky. And after that we noted to the northward and very high Evesham's fighting machines hanging high over Naples like an evening swarm of gnats.

"It seemed to have no more to do with us than a flight of birds.

"Even the mutter of guns far away in the southeast seemed to us to signify nothing. . . .

"Each day, each dream after that, we were still exalted, still seeking that refuge where we might live and love. Fatigue had come upon us, pain and many distresses. For though we were dusty and stained by our toilsome tramping, and half starved and with the horror of the dead men we had seen and the flight of the peasants—for very soon a gust of fighting swept up the peninsula—with these things haunting our minds it still resulted only in a deepening resolution to escape. O, but she was brave and patient! She who had never faced hardship and exposure had courage for herself—and me. We went to and fro seeking an outlet, over a country all commandeered and ransacked by the gathering hosts of war. Always we went on foot. At first there were other fugitives, but we did not mingle with them. Some escaped northward, some were caught in the torrent of peasantry that swept along the main roads; many gave themselves into the hands of the soldiery and were sent northward. Many of the men were impressed. But we kept away from these things; we had brought no money to bribe a passage north, and I feared for my lady at the hands of these conscript crowds. We had landed at Salerno, and we had been turned back from Cava, and we had tried to cross towards Taranto by a pass over Mount Alburno, but we had been driven back for want of food, and so we had come down among the marshes by Pæstum, where those great temples stand alone. I had some vague idea that by Pæstum it might be possible to find a boat or something, and take once more to sea. And there it was the battle overtook us.

"A sort of soul-blindness had me. Plainly I could see that we were being hemmed in; that the great net of that giant Warfare had us in its toils. Many times we had seen the levies that had come down from the north going to and fro, and had come upon them in the distance amidst the mountains making ways for the ammunition and preparing the mounting of the guns. Once we fancied they had fired at us, taking us for spies—at any rate a shot had gone shuddering over us. Several times we had hidden in woods from hovering aeroplanes.

"But all these things do not matter now, these nights of flight and pain. . . . We were in an open place near those great temples at

Pæstum, at last, on a blank stony place dotted with spiky bushes, empty and desolate and so flat that a grove of eucalyptus far away showed to the feet of its stems. How I can see it! My lady was sitting down under a bush, resting a little, for she was very weak and weary, and I was standing up watching to see if I could tell the distance of the firing that came and went. They were still, you know, fighting far from each other, with those terrible new weapons that had never before been used: guns that would carry beyond sight, and aeroplanes that would do——What *they* would do no man could foretell.

"I knew that we were between the two armies, and that they drew together. I knew we were in danger, and that we could not stop there and rest!

"Though all these things were in my mind, they were in the background. They seemed to be affairs beyond our concern. Chiefly, I was thinking of my lady. An aching distress filled me. For the first time she had owned herself beaten and had fallen a-weeping. Behind me I could hear her sobbing, but I would not turn round to her because I knew she had need of weeping, and had held herself so far and so long for me. It was well, I thought, that she would weep and rest and then we would toil on again, for I had no inkling of the thing that hung so near. Even now I can see her as she sat there, her lovely hair upon her shoulder, can mark again the deepening hollow of her cheek.

" 'If we had parted,' she said, 'if I had let you go.'

" 'No,' said I. 'Even now, I do not repent. I will not repent; I made my choice, and I will hold on to the end.'

"And then——

"Overhead in the sky flashed something and burst, and all about us I heard the bullets making a noise like a handful of peas suddenly thrown. They chipped the stones about us, and whirled fragments from the bricks and passed. . . ."

He put his hand to his mouth, and then moistened his lips.

"At the flash I had turned about. . . .

"You know—she stood up——

"She stood up, you know, and moved a step towards me——

"As though she wanted to reach me——

"And she had been shot through the heart."

He stopped and stared at me. I felt all that foolish incapacity an Englishman feels on such occasions. I met his eyes for a moment, and then stared out of the window. For a long space we kept silence. When at last I looked at him he was sitting back in his corner, his arms folded, and his teeth gnawing at his knuckles.

He bit his nail suddenly, and stared at it.

"I carried her," he said, "towards the temples, in my arms—as though it mattered. I don't know why. They seemed a sort of sanctuary, you know, they had lasted so long, I suppose.

"She must have died almost instantly. Only—I talked to her—all the way."

Silence again.

"I have seen those temples," I said abruptly, and indeed he had brought those still, sunlit arcades of worn sandstone very vividly before me.

"It was the brown one, the big brown one. I sat down on a fallen pillar and held her in my arms. . . . Silent after the first babble was over. And after a little while the lizards came out and ran about again, as though nothing unusual was going on, as though nothing had changed. . . . It was tremendously still there, the sun high, and the shadows still; even the shadows of the weeds upon the entablature were still—in spite of the thudding and banging that went all about the sky.

"I seem to remember that the aeroplanes came up out of the south, and that the battle went away to the west. One aeroplane was struck, and overset and fell. I remember that—though it didn't interest me in the least. It didn't seem to signify. It was like a wounded gull, you know—flapping for a time in the water. I could see it down the aisle of the temple—a black thing in the bright blue water.

"Three or four times shells burst about the beach, and then that ceased. Each time that happened all the lizards scuttled in and hid for a space. That was all the mischief done, except that once a stray bullet gashed the stone hard by—made just a fresh bright surface.

"As the shadows grew longer, the stillness seemed greater.

"The curious thing," he remarked, with the manner of a man who makes a trivial conversation, "is that I didn't *think*—I didn't think at all. I sat with her in my arms amidst the stones—in a sort of lethargy—stagnant.

"And I don't remember waking up. I don't remember dressing that day. I know I found myself in my office, with my letters all slit open in front of me, and how I was struck by the absurdity of being there, seeing that in reality I was sitting, stunned, in that Pæstum temple with a dead woman in my arms. I read my letters like a machine. I have forgotten what they were about."

He stopped, and there was a long silence.

Suddenly I perceived that we were running down the incline from Chalk Farm to Euston. I started at this passing of time. I turned on him with a brutal question, with the tone of "Now or never."

"And did you dream again?"

"Yes."

He seemed to force himself to finish. His voice was very low.

"Once more, and as it were only for a few instants. I seemed to have suddenly awakened out of a great apathy, to have risen into a sitting position, and the body lay there on the stones beside me. A gaunt body. Not her, you know. So soon—it was not her. . . .

"I may have heard voices. I do not know. Only I knew clearly that men were coming into the solitude and that that was a last outrage.

"I stood up and walked through the temple, and then there came into sight—first one man with a yellow face, dressed in a uniform of dirty white, trimmed with blue, and then several, climbing to the crest of the old wall of the vanished city, and crouching there. They were little bright figures in the sunlight, and there they hung, weapon in hand, peering cautiously before them.

"And further away I saw others and then more at another point in the wall. It was a long lax line of men in open order.

"Presently the man I had first seen stood up and shouted a command, and his men came tumbling down the wall and into the high weeds towards the temple. He scrambled down with them and led them. He came facing towards me, and when he saw me he stopped.

"At first I had watched these men with a mere curiosity, but when I had seen they meant to come to the temple I was moved to forbid them. I shouted to the officer.

" 'You must not come here,' I cried, '*I* am here. I am here with my dead.'

"He stared, and then shouted a question back to me in some unknown tongue.

"I repeated what I had said.

"He shouted again, and I folded my arms and stood still. Presently he spoke to his men and came forward. He carried a drawn sword.

"I signed to him to keep away, but he continued to advance. I told him again very patiently and clearly: 'You must not come here. These are old temples and I am here with my dead.'

"Presently he was so close I could see his face clearly. It was a narrow face, with dull grey eyes, and a black moustache. He had a scar on his upper lip, and he was dirty and unshaven. He kept shouting unintelligible things, questions perhaps, at me.

"I know now that he was afraid of me, but at the time that did not occur to me. As I tried to explain to him he interrupted me in imperious tones, bidding me, I suppose, stand aside.

"He made to go past me, and I caught hold of him.

"I saw his face change at my grip.

" 'You fool,' I cried. 'Don't you know? She is dead!'

"He started back. He looked at me with cruel eyes. I saw a sort of exultant resolve leap into them—delight. Then, suddenly, with a scowl, he swept his sword back—*so*—and thrust."

He stopped abruptly. I became aware of a change in the rhythm of the train. The brakes lifted their voices and the carriage jarred and jerked. This present world insisted upon itself, became clamorous. I saw through the steamy window huge electric lights glaring down from tall masts upon a fog, saw rows of stationary empty carriages passing by, and then a signal-box, hoisting its constellation of green and red into the murky London twilight, marched after them. I looked again at his drawn features.

"He ran me through the heart. It was with a sort of astonishment—no fear, no pain—but just amazement, that I felt it pierce me, felt the sword drive home into my body. It didn't hurt, you know. It didn't hurt at all."

The yellow platform lights came into the field of view, passing first rapidly, then slowly, and at last stopping with a jerk. Dim shapes of men passed to and fro without.

"Euston!" cried a voice.

"Do you mean——?"

"There was no pain, no sting or smart. Amazement and then darkness sweeping over everything. The hot, brutal face before me, the face of the man who had killed me, seemed to recede. It swept out of existence——"

"Euston!" clamoured the voices outside; "Euston!"

The carriage door opened, admitting a flood of sound, and a porter stood regarding us. The sounds of doors slamming, and the hoof-clatter of cab-horses, and behind these things the featureless remote roar of the London cobble-stones, came to my ears. A truckload of lighted lamps blazed along the platform.

"A darkness, a flood of darkness that opened and spread and blotted out all things."

"Any luggage, sir?" said the porter.

"And that was the end?" I asked.

He seemed to hesitate. Then, almost inaudibly, he answered, *"No."*

"You mean?"

"I couldn't get to her. She was there on the other side of the temple—— And then——"

"Yes," I insisted. "Yes?"

"Nightmares," he cried; "nightmares indeed! My God! Great birds that fought and tore."

# AEPYORNIS ISLAND

The man with the scarred face leant over the table and looked at my bundle.

"Orchids?" he asked.

"A few," I said.

"Cypripediums?" he said.

"Chiefly," said I.

"Anything new?—I thought not. *I* did these islands twenty-five—twenty-seven years ago. If you find anything new here—well, it's brand new. I didn't leave much."

"I'm not a collector," said I.

"I was young then," he went on. "Lord! how I used to fly round." He seemed to take my measure. "I was in the East Indies two years, and in Brazil seven. Then I went to Madagascar."

"I know a few explorers by name," I said anticipating a yarn. "Who did you collect for?"

"Dawsons. I wonder if you've heard the name of Butcher ever?"

"Butcher—Butcher?" The name seemed vaguely present in my memory; then I recalled *Butcher* v. *Dawson*. "Why!" said I, "you are the man who sued them for four years' salary—got cast away on a desert island—"

"Your servant," said the man with the scar, bowing. "Funny case, wasn't it? Here was me, making a little fortune on that island, doing nothing for it neither, and them quite unable to give me notice. It often used to amuse me thinking over it while I was there. I did calculations of it—big—all over the blessed atoll in ornamental figuring."

"How did it happen?" said I. "I don't rightly remember the case."

"Well—you've heard of the Æpyornis?"

"Rather. Andrews was telling me of a new species he was working on only a month or so ago. Just before I sailed. They've got a thigh bone, it seems, nearly a yard long. Monster the thing must have been!"

"I believe you," said the man with the scar. "It *was* a monster. Sinbad's roc was just a legend of 'em. But when did they find these bones?"

"Three or four years ago—'91 I fancy. Why?"

"Why?—Because *I* found 'em—Lord!—it's nearly twenty years ago. If Dawsons hadn't been silly about that salary they might have made a perfect ring in 'em.—*I* couldn't help the infernal boat going adrift."

He paused. "I suppose it's the same place. A kind of swamp about ninety miles north of Antananarivo. Do you happen to know? You have to go to it along the coast by boats. You don't happen to remember, perhaps?"

"I don't. I fancy Andrews said something about a swamp."

"It must be the same. It's on the east coast. And somehow there's something in the water that keeps things from decaying. Like creosote it smells. It reminded me of Trinidad. Did they get any more eggs? Some of the eggs I found were a foot and a half long. The swamp goes circling round, you know, and cuts off this bit. It's mostly salt, too. Well— What a time I had of it! I found the things quite by accident. We went for eggs, me and two native chaps, in one of those rum canoes all tied together, and found the bones at the same time. We had a tent and provisions for four days, and we pitched on one of the firmer places. To think of it brings that odd tarry smell back even now. It's funny work. You go probing into the mud with iron rods, you know. Usually the egg gets smashed. I wonder how long it is since these Æpyornises really lived. The missionaries say the natives have legends about when they were alive, but I never hard any such stories myself.[1] But certainly those eggs we got were as fresh as if they had been new-laid. Fresh! Carrying them down to the boat one of my negro chaps dropped one on a rock and it smashed. How I lammed into the beggar! But sweet it was as if it was new-laid, not even smelly, and its mother dead these four hundred years perhaps. Said a centipede had bit him. However, I'm getting off the straight with the story. It had taken us all day to dig into the slush and get these eggs out unbroken, and we were all covered

[1] No European is known to have seen a live Æpyornis, with the doubtful exception of MacAndrew, who visited Madagascar in 1745. H. G. W.

with beastly black mud, and naturally I was cross. So far as I knew they were the only eggs that had ever been got out not even cracked. I went afterwards to see the ones they have at the Natural History Museum in London: all of them were cracked and just stuck together like a mosaic, and bits missing. Mine were perfect, and I meant to blow them when I got back. Naturally I was annoyed at the silly devil dropping three hours' work just on account of a centipede. I hit him about rather."

The man with the scar took out a clay pipe. I placed my pouch before him. He filled up absent-mindedly.

"How about the others? Did you get those home? I don't remember—"

"That's the queer part of the story. I had three others. Perfectly fresh eggs. Well, we put 'em in the boat, and then I went up to the tent to make some coffee, leaving my two heathens down by the beach—the one fooling about with his sting and the other helping him. It never occurred to me that the beggars would take advantage of the peculiar position I was in to pick a quarrel. But I suppose the centipede poison and the kicking I'd given him had upset the one—he was always a cantankerous sort—and he persuaded the other.

"I remember I was sitting and smoking and boiling up the water over a spirit-lamp business I used to take on these expeditions. Incidentally I was admiring the swamp under the sunset. All black and blood red it was, in streaks—a beautiful sight. And up beyond, the land rose grey and hazy to the hills, and the sky behind them red, like a furnace mouth. And fifty yards behind the back of me was these blessed heathen—quite regardless of the tranquil air of things—plotting to cut off with the boat and leave me all alone with three days provisions and a canvas tent, and nothing to drink whatsoever, beyond a little keg of water. I heard a kind of yelp behind me, and there they were in this canoe affair—it wasn't properly a boat—and perhaps twenty yards from land. I realised what was up in a moment. My gun was in the tent, and besides I had no bullets—only duck shot. They knew that. But I had a little revolver in my pocket and I pulled that out as I ran down to the beach.

" 'Come back!' says I, flourishing it.

"They jabbered something at me, and the man that broke the egg jeered. I aimed at the other—because he was unwounded and had the paddle, and I missed. They laughed. However, I wasn't beat. I knew I had to keep cool, and I tried him again and made him jump with the whang of it. The third time I got his head, and over he went, and the paddle with him. It was a precious lucky shot for a revolver. I reckon it was fifty yards. He went right under. I don't know if he was shot, or simply stunned and drowned. Then I began to shout to the other chap to come back, but he huddled up in the canoe and refused to answer. So I fired out my revolver at him and never got near him.

"I felt a precious fool, I can tell you. There I was on this rotten, black beach, flat swamp all behind me, and the flat sea, cold after the sunset, and just this black canoe drifting steadily out to sea. I tell you I damned Dawsons and Jamrachs and Museums and all the rest of it just to rights. I bawled to this Negro to come back, until my voice went up into a scream.

"There was nothing for it but to swim after him and take my luck with the sharks. So I opened my clasp-knife and put it in my mouth and took off my clothes and waded in. As soon as I was in the water I lost sight of the canoe, but I aimed, as I judged, to head it off. I hoped the man in it was too bad to navigate it, and that it would keep on drifting in the same direction. Presently it came up over the horizon again to the south-westward about. The afterglow of sunset was well over now and the dim of night creeping up. The stars were coming through the blue. I swam like a champion, though my legs and arms were soon aching.

"However, I came up to him by the time the stars were fairly out. As it got darker I began to see all manner of glowing things in the water—phosphorescence, you know. At times it made me giddy. I hardly knew which was stars and which was phosphorescence, and whether I was swimming on my head or my heels. The canoe was as black as sin, and the ripple under the bows like liquid fire. I was naturally chary of clambering up into it. I was anxious to see what he was up to first. He seemed to be lying cuddled up in a lump in the bows, and the stern was all out of water. The thing kept turning round slowly as it drifted—kind of waltzing, don't you know. I went to the stern and pulled it down, expecting him to wake up. Then I began to clamber in with my knife in my hand, and ready for a rush. But he never stirred. So there I sat in the stern of the little canoe, drifting away over the calm phosphorescent sea, and with all the host of the stars above me, waiting for something to happen.

"After a long time I called him by name, but he never answered. I was too tired to take any risks by going along to him. So we sat there. I fancy I dozed once or twice. When the dawn came I saw he was as dead as a doornail and all puffed up and purple. My three eggs and the bones were lying in the middle of the canoe, and the keg of water and some coffee and biscuits wrapped in a Cape 'Argus' by his feet, and a tin of methylated spirit underneath him. There was no paddle, nor in fact anything except the spirit tin that one could use as one, so I settled to drift until I was picked up. I held an inquest on him, brought in a verdict against some snake, scorpion, or centipede unknown, and sent him overboard.

"After that I had a drink of water and a few biscuits, and took a look round. I suppose a man low down as I was don't see very far; leastways, Madagascar was clean out of sight, and any trace of land at all. I saw a sail going south-westward—looked like a schooner, but her hull never came up. Presently the sun got high in the sky and began to beat down upon me. Lord!—it pretty near made my brains boil. I tried dipping my head in the sea, but after a while my eye fell on the Cape 'Argus,' and I lay down flat in the canoe and spread this over me. Wonderful things these newspapers. I never read one through thoroughly before, but it's odd what you get up to when you're alone, as I was. I suppose I read that blessed old Cape 'Argus' twenty times. The pitch in the canoe simply reeked with the heat and rose up into big blisters.

"I drifted ten days," said the man with the scar. "It's a little thing in the telling, isn't it? Every day was like the last. Except in the morning and the evening I never kept a look-out even—the blaze was so infernal. I didn't see a sail after the first three days, and those I saw took no notice of me. About the sixth night a ship went by scarcely half a mile away from me, with all its lights ablaze and its ports open, looking like a big firefly. There was music aboard. I stood up and shouted and screamed at it. The second day I broached one of the Æpyornis eggs, scraped the shell away at the end bit by bit, and tried it, and I was glad to find it was good enough to eat. A bit flavoury—not bad, I mean, but with something of the taste of a duck's egg. There was a kind of circular patch about six inches across on one side of the yolk, and with streaks of blood and a white mark like a ladder in it that I thought queer, but I didn't understand what this meant at the time, and I wasn't inclined to be particular. The egg lasted me three days, with biscuits and a drink of water. I chewed coffee berries too—invigorating stuff. The second egg I opened about the eighth day. And it scared me."

The man with the scar paused. "Yes," he said—"developing.

"I daresay you find it hard to believe. *I* did, with the thing before me. There the egg had been, sunk in that cold black mud, perhaps three hundred years. But there was no mistaking it. There was the—what is it?—embryo, with its big head and curved back and its heart beating under its throat, and the yolk shrivelled up and great membranes spreading inside of the shell and all over the yolk. Here was I hatching out the eggs of the biggest of all extinct birds, in a little canoe in the midst of the Indian Ocean. If old Dawson had known that! It was worth four years' salary. What do *you* think?

"However, I had to eat that precious thing up, every bit of it, before I sighted the reef, and some of the mouthfuls were beastly unpleasant. I left the third one alone. I held it up to the light, but the shell was too thick for me to get any notion of what might be happening inside; and though I fancied I heard blood pulsing, it might have been the rustle in my own ears, like what you listen to in a seashell.

"Then came the atoll. Came out of the sunrise, as it were, suddenly, close up to me. I drifted straight towards it until I was about half a mile from shore—not more, and then the current took a turn, and I had to paddle as hard as I could with my hands and bits of the Æpyornis shell to make the place. However, I got there. It was just a common atoll about four miles round, with a few trees growing and a spring in one place and the lagoon full of parrot fish. I took the egg ashore and put it in a good place well above the tide lines and in the sun, to give it all the chance I could, and pulled the canoe up safe, and loafed about prospecting. It's rum how dull an atoll is. When I was a kid I thought nothing could be finer or more adventurous than the Robinson Crusoe business, but that place was as monotonous as a book of sermons. I went round finding eatable things and generally thinking; but I tell you I was bored to death before the first day was out. It shows my luck—the very day I landed the weather changed. A thunderstorm went by to the north and flicked its wing over the island, and in the night there came a drencher and a howling wind slap over us. It wouldn't have taken much, you know, to upset that canoe.

"I was sleeping under the canoe, and the egg was luckily among the sand higher up the beach, and the first thing I remember was a sound like a hundred pebbles hitting the boat at once and a rush of water over my body. I'd been dreaming of Antananarivo, and I sat up and holloaed to Intoshi to ask her what the devil was up, and clawed out at the chair where the matches used to be. Then I remembered where I was. There were phosphorescent waves rolling up as if they meant to eat me, and all the rest of the night as black as pitch. The air was simply yelling. The clouds seemed down on your head almost, and the rain fell as if heaven was sinking and they were baling out the waters above the firmament. One great roller came writhing at me, like a fiery serpent, and I bolted. Then I thought of the canoe, and ran down to it as the water went hissing back again, but the thing had gone. I wondered about the egg then, and felt my way to it. It was all right and well out of reach of the maddest waves, so I sat down beside it and cuddled it for company. Lord! What a night that was!

"The storm was over before the morning. There wasn't a rag of cloud left in the sky when the dawn came, and all along the beach there were bits of plank scattered—which was the disarticulated skeleton, so to speak, of my canoe. However, that gave me something to do, for, taking advantage of two of the trees being together, I rigged up a kind of storm shelter with these vestiges. And that day the egg hatched.

"Hatched, sir, when my head was pillowed on it and I was asleep I heard a whack and felt a jar and sat up, and there was the end of the egg pecked out and a rum little brown head looking out at me. 'Lord!' I said, 'you're welcome,' and with a little difficulty he came out.

"He was a nice friendly little chap, at first, about the size of a small hen—very much like most other young birds, only bigger. His plumage was a dirty brown to begin with, with a sort of grey scab that fell off it very soon, and scarcely feathers—a kind of downy hair. I can hardly express how pleased I was to see him. I tell you, Robinson Crusoe don't make near enough of his loneliness. But here was interesting company. He looked at me and winked his eye from the front backwards like a hen, and gave a chirp and began to peck about at once, as though being hatched three hundred years too late was just nothing. 'Glad to see you, Man Friday!' says I, for I had naturally settled he was to be called Man Friday if ever he was hatched, as soon as ever I found the egg in the canoe had developed. I was a bit anxious about his feed, so I gave him a lump of raw parrot fish at once. He took it and opened his beak for more. I was glad of that, for, under the circumstances, if he'd been fanciful, I should have had to eat him after all.

"You'd be surprised what an interesting bird that Æpyornis chick was. He followed me about from the very beginning. He used to stand by me and watch while I fished in the lagoon and go shares in anything I caught. And he was sensible, too. There were nasty green warty things, like pickled gherkins, used to lie about on the beach, and he tried one of these and it upset him. He never even looked at any of them again.

"And he grew. You could almost see him grow. And as I was never much of a society man, his quiet, friendly ways suited me to a T. For nearly two years we were as happy as we could be on that island. I had no business worries, for I knew my salary was mounting up at Dawsons'. We would see a sail now and then, but nothing ever came near us. I amused myself too by decorating the island with designs worked in sea-urchins and fancy shells of various kinds. I put

ÆPYORNIS ISLAND all round the place very nearly, in big letters, like what you see done with coloured stones at railway stations in the old country. And I used to lie watching the blessed bird stalking round and growing, growing, and think how I could make a living out of him by showing him about if ever I got taken off. After his first moult he began to get handsome, with a crest and a blue wattle, and a lot of green feathers at the behind of him. And then I used to puzzle whether Dawsons had any right to claim him or not. Stormy weather and in the rainy season we lay snug under the shelter I had made out of the old canoe, and I used to tell him lies about my friends at home. It was a kind of idyll, you might say. If only I had had some tobacco it would have been simply just like Heaven.

"It was about the end of the second year our little Paradise went wrong. Friday was then about fourteen feet high to the bill of him, with a big broad head like the end of a pickaxe, and two huge brown eyes with yellow rims set together like a man's—not out of sight of each other like a hen's. His plumage was fine—none of the half mourning style of your ostrich—more like a cassowary as far as colour and texture go. And then it was he began to cock his comb at me and give himself airs and show signs of a nasty temper.

"At last came a time when my fishing had been rather unlucky and he began to hang about me in a queer, meditative way. I thought he might have been eating sea-cucumbers or something, but it was really just discontent on his part. I was hungry too, and when at last I landed a fish I wanted it for myself. Tempers were short that morning on both sides. He pecked at it and grabbed it, and I gave him a whack on the head to make him leave go. And at that he went for me. Lord!

"He gave me this in the face." The man indicated his scar. "Then he kicked me. It was like a cart horse. I got up, and seeing he hadn't finished I started off full tilt with my arms doubled up over my face. But he ran on those gawky legs of his faster than a race horse, and kept landing out at me with sledge-hammer kicks, and bringing his pickaxe down on the back of my head. I made for the lagoon, and went in up to my neck. He stopped at the water, for he hated getting his feet wet, and began to make a shindy, something like a peacock's, only hoarser. He started strutting up and down the beach. I'll admit I felt small to see this blessed fossil lording it there. And my head and face were all bleeding, and—well, my body just one jelly of bruises.

"I decided to swim across the lagoon and leave him alone for a bit, until the affair blew over. I shinned up the tallest palm-tree and sat there thinking of it all. I don't suppose I ever felt so hurt by anything before or since. It was the brutal ingratitude of the creature. I'd been more than a brother to him. I'd hatched him. Educated him. A great, gawky, out-of-date bird! And me a human being—heir of the ages and all that.

"I thought after a time he'd begin to see things in that light himself, and feel a little sorry for his behaviour. I thought if I was to catch some nice little bits of fish, perhaps, and go to him presently in a casual kind of way, and offer them to him, he might do the sensible thing. It took me some time to learn how unforgiving and cantankerous an extinct bird can be. Malice!

"I won't tell you all the little devices I tried to get that bird round again. I simply can't. It makes my cheek burn with shame even now to think of the snubs and buffets I had from this infernal curiosity. I tried violence. I chucked lumps of coral at him from a safe distance, but he only swallowed them. I shied my open knife at him and almost lost it, though it was too big for him to swallow. I tried starving him out and struck fishing, but he took to picking along the beach at low water after worms and rubbed along on that. Half my time I spent up to my neck in the lagoon, and the rest up the palm-trees. One of them was scarcely high enough, and when he caught me up it he had a regular Bank Holiday with the calves of my legs. It got unbearable. I don't know if you have ever tried sleeping up a palm-tree. It gave me the most horrible nightmares. Think of the shame of it too! Here was this extinct animal mooning about my island like a sulky duke, and me not allowed to rest the sole of my foot on the place. I used to cry with weariness and vexation. I told him straight that I didn't mean to be chased about a desert island by any damned anachronisms. I told him to go and peck a navigator of his own age. But he only snapped his beak at me. Great ugly bird—all legs and neck!

"I shouldn't like to say how long that went on altogether. I'd have killed him sooner if I'd known how. However, I hit on a way of settling him at last. It's a South American dodge. I joined all my fishing lines together with stems of seaweed and things, and made a stoutish string, perhaps twelve yards in length or more, and I fastened two lumps of coral rock to the ends of this. It took me some time to do, because every now and then I had to go into the lagoon or up a tree as the fancy took me. This I whirled rapidly round my head and then let it go at him. The first time I missed, but the next time the string caught his legs beautifully and wrapped round them again and again. Over he went. I threw it standing waist-deep in the lagoon, and as soon as he went down I was out of the water and sawing at his neck with my knife—

"I don't like to think of that even now. I felt like a murderer while I did it, though my anger was hot against him. When I stood over him and saw him bleeding on the white sand and his beautiful great legs and neck writhing in his last agony—Pah!

"With that tragedy, Loneliness came upon me like a curse. Good Lord! you can't imagine how I missed that bird. I sat by his corpse and sorrowed over him, and shivered as I looked round the desolate, silent reef. I thought of what a jolly little bird he had been when he was hatched, and of a thousand pleasant tricks he had played before he went wrong. I thought if I'd only wounded him I might have nursed him round into a better understanding. If I'd had any means of digging into the coral rock I'd have buried him. I felt exactly as if he was human. As it was I couldn't think of eating him, so I put him in the lagoon and the little fishes picked him clean. Then one day a chap cruising about in a yacht had a fancy to see if my atoll still existed.

"He didn't come a moment too soon, for I was about sick enough of the desolation of it, and only hesitating whether I should walk out into the sea and finish up the business that way, or fall back on the green things.

"I sold the bones to a man named Winslow—a dealer near the British Museum, and he says he sold them to old Havers. It seems Havers didn't understand they were extra large, and it was only after his death they attracted attention. They called 'em Æpyornis—what was it?"

*"Æpyornis vastus,"* said I. "It's funny, the very thing was mentioned to me by a friend of mine. When they found an Æpyornis with a thigh a yard long they thought they had reached the top of the scale and called him *Æpyornis maximus.* Then some one turned up another thigh bone four feet six or more, and that they called *Æpyornis Titan.* Then your *vastus* was found after old Havers died, in his collection, and then a *vastissimus* turned up."

"Winslow was telling me as much," said the man with the scar. "If they get any more Æpyornises, he reckons some scientific swell will go and burst a blood-vessel. But it was a queer thing to happen to a man; wasn't it—altogether?"

# IN THE ABYSS

The lieutenant stood in front of the steel sphere and gnawed a piece of pine splinter. "What do you think of it, Steevens?" he asked.

"It's an idea," said Steevens, in the tone of one who keeps an open mind.

"I believe it will smash—flat," said the lieutenant.

"He seems to have calculated it all out pretty well," said Steevens, still impartial.

"But think of the pressure," said the lieutenant. "At the surface of the water it's fourteen pounds to the inch, thirty feet down it's double that; sixty, treble; ninety, four times; nine hundred, forty times; five thousand three hundred—that's a mile—it's two hundred and forty times fourteen pounds; that's—let's see—thirty hundred-weight—a ton and a half, Steevens; *a ton and a half* to the square inch. And the ocean where he's going is five miles deep. That's seven and a half—"

"Sounds a lot," said Steevens, "but it's jolly thick steel."

The lieutenant made no answer, but resumed his pine splinter. The object of their conversation was a huge globe of steel, having an exterior diameter of perhaps eight feet. It looked like the shot for some Titanic piece of artillery. It was elaborately nested in a monstrous scaffolding built into the framework of the vessel, and the gigantic spars that were presently to sling it overboard gave the stern of the ship an appearance that had raised the curiosity of every decent sailor who had sighted it, from the pool of London to the Tropic of Capricorn. In two places, one above the other, the steel gave place to a couple of circular windows of enormously thick glass, and one of these, set in a steel frame of great solidity, was now partially unscrewed. Both the men had seen the interior of this globe for the first time that morning. It was elaborately padded with air cushions, with little studs sunk between bulging pillows to work the simple mechanism of the affair. Everything was elaborately padded, even the Myer's apparatus which was to absorb carbonic acid and replace the oxygen inspired by its tenant, when he had crept in by the glass manhole, and had been screwed in. It was so elaborately padded that a man might have been fired from a gun in it with perfect safety. And it had need to be, for presently a man was to crawl in through that glass manhole, to be screwed up tightly, and to be flung overboard, and to sink down—down—down, for five miles, even as the lieutenant said. It had taken the strongest hold of his imagination; it made him a bore at mess; and he found Steevens, the new arrival aboard, a godsend to talk to about it, over and over again.

"It's my opinion," said the lieutenant, "that that glass will simply bend in and bulge and smash, under a pressure of that sort. Daubrée has made rocks run like water under big pressures—and, you mark my words—"

"If the glass did break in," said Steevens, "what then?"

"The water would shoot in like a jet of iron. Have you ever felt a straight jet of high pressure water? It would hit as hard as a bullet. It would simply smash and flatten him. It would tear down his throat, and into his lungs; it would blow in his ears—"

"What a detailed imagination you have," protested Steevens, who saw things vividly.

"It's a simple statement of the inevitable," said the lieutenant.

"And the globe?"

"Would just give out a few little bubbles, and it would settle down comfortably against the day of judgment, among the oozes and the bottom clay—with poor Elstead spread over his own smashed cushions like butter over bread."

He repeated this sentence as though he liked it very much. "Like butter over bread," he said.

"Having a look at the jigger?" said a voice behind them, and Elstead stood behind them, spick and span in white, with a cigarette between his teeth, and his eyes smiling out of the shadow of his ample hat-brim. "What's this about bread and butter, Weybridge? Grumbling as usual about the insufficient pay of naval officers? It won't be more than a day now before I start. We are to get the slings ready to-day. This clean sky and gentle swell is just the kind of thing for swinging off twenty tons of lead and iron; isn't it?"

"It won't affect you much," said Weybridge.

"No. Seventy or eighty feet down, and I shall be there in a dozen seconds, there's not a particle moving, though the wind shriek itself hoarse up above, and the water lifts halfway to the clouds. No. Down there—" He moved to the side of the ship and the other two followed him. All three leant forward on their elbows and stared down into the yellow-green water.

"*Peace*," said Elstead, finishing his thought aloud.

"Are you dead certain that clockwork will act?" asked Weybridge, presently.

"It has worked thirty-five times," said Elstead. "It's bound to work."

"But if it doesn't?"

"Why shouldn't it?"

"I wouldn't go down in that confounded thing," said Weybridge, "for twenty thousand pounds."

"Cheerful chap you are," said Elstead, and spat sociably at a bubble below.

"I don't understand yet how you mean to work the thing," said Steevens.

"In the first place I'm screwed into the sphere," said Elstead, "and when I've turned the electric light off and on three times to show I'm cheerful, I'm swung out over the stern by that crane, with all those big lead sinkers slung below me. The top lead weight has a roller carrying a hundred fathoms of strong cord rolled up, and that's all that joins the sinkers to the sphere, except the slings that will be cut when the affair is dropped. We use cord rather than wire rope because it's easier to cut and more buoyant—necessary points as you will see.

"Through each of these lead weights you notice there is a hole, and an iron rod will be run through that and will project six feet on the lower side. If that rod is rammed up from below it knocks up a lever and sets the clockwork in motion at the side of the cylinder on which the cord winds.

"Very well. The whole affair is lowered gently into the water, and the slings are cut. The sphere floats—with the air in it, it's lighter than water; but the lead weights go down straight and the cord runs out. When the cord is all paid out, the sphere will go down too, pulled down by the cord."

"But why the cord?" asked Steevens. "Why not fasten the weights directly to the sphere?"

"Because of the smash down below. The whole affair will go rushing down, mile after mile, at a headlong pace at last. It would be knocked to pieces on the bottom if it wasn't for that cord. But the weights will hit the bottom, and directly they do the buoyancy of the sphere will come into play. It will go on sinking slower and slower; come to a stop at last and then begin to float upward again.

"That's where the clockwork comes in. Directly the weights smash against the sea bottom, the rod will be knocked through and will kick up the clockwork, and the cord will be rewound on the reel. I shall be lugged down to the sea bottom. There I shall stay for half an hour, with the electric light on, looking about me. Then the clockwork will release a spring knife, the cord will be cut, and up I shall rush again, like a soda-water bubble. The cord itself will help the flotation."

"And if you should chance to hit a ship?" said Weybridge.

"I should come up at such a pace, I should go clean through it," said Elstead, "like a cannon ball. You needn't worry about that."

"And suppose some nimble crustacean should wriggle into your clockwork—"

"It would be a pressing sort of invitation for me to stop," said Elstead, turning his back on the water and staring at the sphere.

. . . . . . .

They had swung Elstead overboard by eleven o'clock. The day was serenely bright and calm, with the horizon lost in haze. The electric glare in the little upper compartment beamed cheerfully three times. Then they let him down slowly to the surface of the water, and a sailor in the stern chains hung ready to cut the tackle that held the lead weights and the sphere together. The globe, which had looked so large on deck, looked the smallest thing conceivable under the stern of the ship. It rolled a little, and its two dark windows, which floated uppermost, seemed like eyes turned up in round wonderment at the people who crowded the rail. A voice wondered how Elstead liked the rolling. "Are you ready?" sang out the Commander. "Aye, aye, sir!" "Then let her go!"

The rope of the tackle tightened against the blade and was cut, and an eddy rolled over the globe in a grotesquely helpless fashion. Some one waved a handkerchief, some one else tried an ineffectual cheer, a middy was counting slowly: "Eight, nine, ten!" Another roll, then with a jerk and a splash the thing righted itself.

It seemed to be stationary for a moment, to grow rapidly smaller, and then the water closed over it, and it became visible, enlarged by refraction and dimmer, below the surface. Before one could count three it had disappeared. There was a flicker of white light far down in the water, that diminished to a speck and vanished. Then there was nothing but a depth of water going down into blackness, through which a shark was swimming.

Then suddenly the screw of the cruiser began to rotate, the water was crickled, the shark disappeared in a wrinkled confusion, and a torrent of foam rushed across the crystalline clearness that had swallowed up Elstead. "What's the idee?" said one A.B. to another.

"We're going to lay off about a couple of miles, 'fear he should hit us when he comes up," said his mate.

The ship steamed slowly to her new position. Aboard her almost every one who was unoccupied remained watching the breathing swell into which the sphere had sunk. For the next half hour it is doubtful if a word was spoken that did not bear directly or indirectly on Elstead. The December sun was now high in the sky, and the heat very considerable.

"He'll be cold enough down there," said Weybridge. "They say that below a certain depth sea-water's always just about freezing."

"Where'll he come up?" asked Steevens. "I've lost my bearings."

"That's the spot," said the Commander, who prided himself on his omniscience. He extended a precise finger south-eastward. "And this, I reckon, is pretty nearly the moment," he said. "He's been thirty-five minutes."

"How long does it take to reach the bottom of the ocean?" asked Steevens.

"For a depth of five miles, and reckoning—as we did—an acceleration of two foot per second, both ways, is just about three-quarters of a minute."

"Then he's overdue," said Weybridge.

"Pretty nearly," said the Commander. "I suppose it takes a few minutes for that cord of his to wind in."

"I forgot that," said Weybridge, evidently relieved.

And then began the suspense. A minute slowly dragged itself out, and no sphere shot out of the water. Another followed, and nothing broke the low oily swell. The sailors explained to one another that little point about the winding-in of the cord. The rigging was dotted with expectant faces. "Come up, Elstead!" called one hairy-chested salt, impatiently, and the others caught it up, and shouted as though they were waiting for the curtain of a theatre to rise.

The Commander glanced irritably at them.

"Of course, if the acceleration's less than two," he said, "he'll be all the longer. We aren't absolutely certain that was the proper figure. I'm no slavish believer in calculations."

Steevens agreed concisely. No one on the quarter-deck spoke for a couple of minutes. Then Steeven's watch-case clicked.

When, twenty-one minutes after, the sun reached the zenith, they were still waiting for the globe to re-appear, and not a man aboard had dared to whisper that hope was dead. It was Weybridge who first gave expression to that realisation. He spoke while the sound of eight bells still hung in the air. "I always distrusted that window," he said quite suddenly to Steevens.

"Good God!" said Steevens, "you don't think—"

"Well!" said Weybridge, and left the rest to his imagination.

"I'm no great believer in calculations myself," said the Commander, dubiously, "so that I'm not altogether hopeless yet." And at midnight the gunboat was steaming slowly in a spiral round the spot where the globe had sunk, and the white beam of the electric light fled and halted and swept discontentedly onward again over the waste of phosphorescent waters under the little stars.

"If his window hasn't burst and smashed him," said Weybridge, "then it's a cursed sight worse, for his clockwork has gone wrong and he's alive now, five miles under our feet, down there in the cold and dark, anchored in that little bubble of his, where never a ray of light has shone or a human being lived, since the waters were gathered together. He's there without food, feeling hungry and thirsty and scared, wondering whether he'll starve or stifle. Which will it be? The Myer's apparatus is running out, I suppose. How long do they last?

"Good Heavens!" he exclaimed, "what little things we are! What daring little devils! Down there, miles and miles of water—all water, and all this empty water about us and this sky. Gulfs!" He threw his hands out, and as he did so a little white streak swept noiselessly up the sky, travelling more slowly, stopped, became a motionless dot as though a new star had fallen up into the sky. Then it went sliding back again and lost itself amidst the reflections of the stars, and the white haze of the sea's phosphorescence.

At the sight he stopped, arm extended and mouth open. He shut his mouth, opened it again and waved his arms with an impatient gesture. Then he turned, shouted, "El-stead ahoy," to the first watch, and went at a run to Lindley and the search light. "I saw him," he said. "Starboard there! His light's on and he's just shot out of the water. Bring the light round. We ought to see him drifting, when he lifts on the swell."

But they never picked up the explorer until dawn. Then they almost ran him down. The crane was swung out and a boat's crew hooked the chain to the sphere. When they had shipped the sphere they unscrewed the manhole and peered into the darkness of the interior (for the electric light chamber was intended to illuminate the water about the sphere, and was shut off entirely from its general cavity).

The air was very hot within the cavity, and the india-rubber at the lip of the manhole was soft. There was no answer to their eager questions and no sound of movement within. Elstead seemed to be lying motionless, crumpled up in the bottom of the globe. The ship's doctor crawled in and lifted him out to the men outside. For a moment or so they did not know whether Elstead was alive or dead. His face, in the yellow glow of the ship's lamps, glistened with perspiration. They carried him down to his own cabin.

He was not dead, they found, but in a state of absolute nervous collapse, and besides cruelly bruised. For some days he had to lie perfectly still. It was a week before he could tell his experiences.

Almost his first words were that he was going down again. The sphere would have to be altered, he said, in order to allow him to throw off the cord if need be, and that was all. He had had the most marvellous experience. "You thought I should find nothing but ooze," he said. "You laughed at my explorations, and I've discovered a new world!" He told his story in disconnected fragments, and chiefly from the wrong end, so that it is impossible to re-tell it in his words. But what follows is the narrative of his experience.

It began atrociously, he said. Before the cord ran out the thing kept rolling over. He felt like a frog in a football. He could see nothing but the crane and the sky overhead, with an occasional glimpse of the people on the ship's rail. He couldn't tell a bit which way the thing would roll next. Suddenly he would find his feet going up and try to step, and over he went rolling, head over heels and just anyhow on the padding. Any other shape would have been more comfortable, but no other shape was to be relied upon under the huge pressure of the nethermost abyss.

Suddenly the swaying ceased; the globe righted, and when he had picked himself up, he saw the water all about him greeny-blue with an attenuated light filtering down from above, and a shoal of little floating things went rushing up past him, as it seemed to him, towards the light. And even as he looked it grew darker and darker, until the water above was as dark as the midnight sky, albeit of a greener shade, and the water below black. And little transparent things in the water developed a faint glint of luminosity, and shot past him in faint greenish streaks.

And the feeling of falling! It was just like the start of a lift, he said, only it kept on. One has to imagine what that means, that keeping on. It was then of all times that Elstead repented of his adventure. He saw the chances against him in an altogether new light. He thought of the big cuttle-fish people knew to exist in the middle waters, the kind of things they find half-digested in whales at times, or floating dead and rotten and half eaten by fish. Suppose one caught hold and wouldn't leave go. And had the clockwork really been sufficiently tested? But whether he wanted to go on or go back mattered not the slightest now.

In fifty seconds everything was as black as night outside, except where the beam from his light struck through the waters, and picked out every now and then some fish or scrap of sinking matter. They flashed by too fast for him to see what they were. Once he thought he passed a shark. And then the sphere began to get hot by friction against the water. They had under-estimated this, it seems.

The first thing he noticed was that he was perspiring, and then he heard a hissing, growing louder, under his feet, and saw a lot of little bubbles—very little bubbles they were—rushing upward like a fan through the water outside. Steam! He felt the window and it was hot. He turned on the minute glow lamp that lit his own cavity, looked at the padded watch by the studs, and saw he had been travelling now for two minutes. It came into his head that the window would crack through the conflict of temperatures, for he knew the bottom water was very near freezing.

Then suddenly the floor of the sphere seemed to press against his feet, the rush of bubbles outside grew slower and slower and the hissing diminished. The sphere rolled a little. The window had not cracked, nothing had given, and he knew that the dangers of sinking, at any rate, were over.

In another minute or so, he would be on the floor of the abyss. He thought, he said, of Steevens and Weybridge and the rest of them five miles overhead, higher to him than the very highest clouds that ever floated over land are to us, steaming slowly and staring down and wondering what had happened to him.

He peered out of the window. There were no more bubbles now, and the hissing had stopped. Outside there was a heavy blackness—as black as black velvet—except where the electric light pierced the empty water and showed the colour of it—a yellow green. Then three things like shapes of fire swam into sight, following each other through the water. Whether they were little and near, or big and far off, he could not tell.

Each was outlined in a bluish light almost as bright as the lights of a fishing-smack, a light which seemed to be smoking greatly, and all along the sides of them were specks of this, like the lighted portholes of a ship. Their phosphorescence seemed to go out as they came into the radiance of his lamp, and he saw then that they were indeed fish of some strange sort, with huge heads, vast eyes, and dwindling bodies and tails. Their eyes were turned towards him, and he judged they were following him down. He supposed they were attracted by his glare.

Presently others of the same sort joined them. As he went on down he noticed that the water became of a pallid colour, and that little specks twinkled in his ray like motes in a sunbeam. This was probably due to the clouds of ooze and mud that the impact of his leaden sinkers had disturbed.

By the time he was drawn down to the lead weights he was in a dense fog of white that his electric light failed altogether to pierce for more than a few yards, and many minutes elapsed before the hanging sheets of sediment subsided to any extent. Then, lit by his light and by the transient phosphorescence of a distant shoal of fishes, he was able to see under the huge blackness of the super-incumbent water an undulating expanse of greyish-white ooze, broken here and there by tangled thickets of a growth of sea lilies, waving hungry tentacles in the air.

Farther away were the graceful translucent outlines of a group of gigantic sponges. About this floor there were scattered a number of bristling flattish tufts of rich purple and black, which he decided must be some sort of sea-urchin, and small, large-eyed or blind things, having a curious resemblance, some to woodlice, and others to lobsters, crawled sluggishly across the track of the light and vanished into the obscurity again, leaving furrowed trails behind them.

Then suddenly the hovering swarm of little fishes veered about and came towards him as a flight of starlings might do. They passed over him like a phosphorescent snow, and then he saw behind them some larger creature advancing towards the sphere.

At first he could see it only dimly, a faintly moving figure remotely suggestive of a walking man, and then it came into the spray of light that the lamp shot out. As the glare struck it, it shut its eyes, dazzled. He stared in rigid astonishment.

It was a strange, vertebrated animal. Its dark purple head was dimly suggestive of a chameleon, but it had such a high forehead and such a braincase as no reptile ever displayed before; the vertical pitch of its face gave it a most extraordinary resemblance to a human being.

Two large and protruding eyes projected from sockets in chameleon fashion, and it had a broad reptilian mouth with horny lips beneath its little nostrils. In the position of the ears were two huge gill covers, and out of these floated a branching tree of coralline filaments, almost like the tree-like gills that very young rays and sharks possess.

But the humanity of the face was not the most extraordinary thing about the creature. It was a biped, its almost globular body was poised on a tripod of two frog-like legs and a long thick tail, and its fore limbs, which grotesquely caricatured the human hand much as a frog's do, carried a long shaft of bone, tipped with copper. The colour of the creature was variegated: its head, hands, and legs were purple; but its skin, which hung loosely upon it, even as clothes might do, was a phosphorescent grey. And it stood there, blinded by the light.

At last this unknown creature of the abyss blinked its eyes open, and, shading them with its disengaged hand, opened its mouth and gave vent to a shouting noise, articulate almost as speech might be, that penetrated even the steel case and padded jacket of the sphere. How a shouting may be accomplished without lungs Elstead does not profess to explain. It then moved sideways out of the glare into the mystery of shadow that bordered it on either side, and Elstead felt rather than saw that it was coming towards him. Fancying the light had attracted it, he turned the switch that cut off the current. In another moment something soft dabbed upon the steel, and the globe swayed.

Then the shouting was repeated, and it seemed to him that a distant echo answered it. The dabbing recurred, and the globe swayed and ground against the spindle over which the wire was rolled. He stood in the blackness, and peered out into the everlasting night of the abyss. And presently he saw, very faint and remote, other phosphorescent quasi-human forms hurrying towards him.

Hardly knowing what he did, he felt about in his swaying prison for the stud of the exterior electric light, and came by accident against his own small glow lamp in its padded recess. The sphere twisted, and then threw him down; he heard shouts like shouts of surprise, and when he rose to his feet he saw two pairs of stalked eyes peering into the lower window and reflecting his light.

In another moment hands were dabbing vigorously at his steel casing, and there was a sound, horrible enough in his position, of the metal protection of the clockwork being vigorously hammered. That indeed, sent his heart into his mouth, for if these strange creatures succeeded in stopping that his release would never occur. Scarcely had he thought as much when he felt the sphere sway violently, and the floor of it press hard against his feet. He turned off the small glow lamp that lit the interior, and sent the ray of the large light in the separate compartment out into the water. The sea floor and the man-like creatures had disappeared, and a couple of fish chasing each other dropped suddenly by the window.

He thought at once that these strange denizens of the deep sea had broken the wire rope, and that he had escaped. He drove up faster and faster, and then stopped with a jerk that sent him flying against the padded roof of his prison. For half a minute perhaps he was too astonished to think.

Then he felt that the sphere was spinning slowly, and rocking, and it seemed to him that it was also being drawn through the water. By crouching close to the window he managed to make his weight effective and roll that part of the sphere downward, but he could see nothing save the pale ray of his light striking down ineffectively into the darkness. It occurred to him that he would see more if he turned the lamp off and allowed his eyes to grow accustomed to the profound obscurity.

In this he was wise. After some minutes the velvety blackness became a translucent blackness, and then far away, and as faint as the zodiacal light of an English summer evening, he saw shapes moving below. He judged these creatures had detached his cable and were towing him along the sea bottom.

And then he saw something faint and remote across the undulations of the submarine plain, a broad horizon of pale luminosity that extended this way and that way as far as the range of his little window permitted him to see. To this he was being towed, as a balloon might be towed by men out of the open country into a town. He approached it very slowly, and very slowly the dim irradiation was gathered together into more definite shapes.

It was nearly five o'clock before he came over this luminous area, and by that time he could make out an arrangement suggestive of streets and houses grouped about a vast roofless erection that was grotesquely suggestive of a ruined abbey. It was spread out like a map below him. The houses were all roofless inclosures of walls, and their substance being, as he afterwards saw, of phosphorescent bones, gave the place an appearance as if it were built of drowned moonshine.

Among the inner caves of the place waving trees of crinoid stretched their tentacles, and tall, slender, glassy sponges shot like shining minarets and lilies of filmy light out of the general glow of the city. In the open spaces of the place he could see a stirring movement as of crowds of people, but he was too many fathoms above them to distinguish the individuals in those crowds.

Then slowly they pulled him down, and as they did so the details of the place crept slowly upon his apprehension. He saw that the courses of the cloudy buildings were marked out with beaded lines of round objects, and then he perceived that at several points below him in broad open spaces were forms like the encrusted shapes of ships.

Slowly and surely he was drawn down, and the forms below him became brighter, clearer, were more distinct. He was being pulled down, he perceived, towards the large building in the centre of the town, and he could catch a glimpse ever and again of the multitudinous forms that were lugging at his cord. He was astonished to see that the rigging of one of the ships, which formed such a prominent feature of the place, was crowded with a host of gesticulating figures regarding him, and then the walls of the great building rose about him silently, and hid the city from his eyes.

And such walls they were, of water-logged wood, and twisted wire rope and iron spars, and copper, and the bones and skulls of dead men.

The skulls ran in curious zigzag lines and spirals and fantastic curves over the building; and in and out of their eye-sockets, and over the whole surface of the place, lurked and played a multitude of silvery little fishes.

And now he was at such a level that he could see these strange people of the abyss plainly once more. To his astonishment, he perceived that they were prostrating themselves before him, all save one, dressed as it seemed in a robe of placoid scales, and crowned with a luminous diadem, who stood with his reptilian mouth opening and shutting as though he led the chanting of the worshippers.

They continued worshipping him, without rest or intermission, for the space of three hours.

Most circumstantial was Elstead's account of this astounding city and its people, these people of perpetual night, who have never seen sun or moon or stars, green vegetation, nor any living air-breathing creatures, who know nothing of fire, nor any light but the phosphorescent light of living things.

Startling as is his story, it is yet more startling to find that scientific men, of such eminence as Adams and Jenkins, find nothing incredible in it. They tell me they see no reason why intelligent, water-breathing, vertebrated creatures inured to a low temperature and enormous pressure, and of such a heavy structure, that neither alive nor dead would they float, might not live upon the bottom of the deep sea, and quite unsuspected by us, descendants like ourselves of the great Theriomorpha of the New Red Sandstone age.

We should be known to them, however, as strange meteoric creatures wont to fall catastrophically dead out of the mysterious blackness of their watery sky. And not only we ourselves, but our ships, our metals, our appliances, would come raining down out of the night. Sometimes sinking things would smite down and crush them, as if it were the judgment of some unseen power above, and sometimes would come things of the utmost rarity or utility or shapes of inspiring suggestion. One can understand, perhaps, something of their behaviour at the descent of a living man, if one thinks what a bar-

baric people might do, to whom an enhaloed shining creature came suddenly out of the sky.

At one time or another Elstead probably told the officers of the *Ptarmigan* every detail of his strange twelve hours in the abyss. That he also intended to write them down is certain, but he never did, and so unhappily we have to piece together the discrepant fragments of his story from the reminiscences of Commander Simmons, Weybridge, Steevens, Lindley, and the others.

We see the thing darkly in fragmentary glimpses—the huge ghostly building, the bowing, chanting people, with their dark, chameleon-like heads and faintly luminous forms, and Elstead, with his light turned on again, vainly trying to convey to their minds that the cord by which the sphere was held was to be severed. Minute after minute slipped away, and Elstead, looking at his watch, was horrified to find that he had oxygen only for four hours more. But the chant in his honour kept on as remorselessly as if it was the marching song of his approaching death.

The manner of his release he does not understand, but to judge by the end of cord that hung from the sphere, it had been cut through by rubbing against the edge of the altar. Abruptly the sphere rolled over, and he swept up, out of their world, as an ethereal creature clothed in a vacuum would sweep through our own atmosphere back to its native ether again. He must have torn out of their sight as a hydrogen bubble hastens upwards from our air. A strange ascension it must have seemed to them.

The sphere rushed up with even greater velocity than, when weighed with the lead sinkers, it had rushed down. It became exceedingly hot. It drove up with the windows uppermost, and he remembers the torrent of bubbles frothing against the glass. Every moment he expected this to fly. Then suddenly something like a huge wheel seemed to be released in his head, the padded compartment began spinning about him, and he fainted. His next recollection was of his cabin, and of the doctor's voice.

But that is the substance of the extraordinary story that Elstead related in fragments to the officers of the *Ptarmigan*. He promised to write it all down at a later date. His mind was chiefly occupied with the improvement of his apparatus, which was effected at Rio.

It remains only to tell that on February 2d, 1896, he made his second descent into the ocean abyss, with the improvements his first experience suggested. What happened we shall probably never know. He never returned. The *Ptarmigan* beat about over the point of his submersion, seeking him in vain for thirteen days. Then she returned to Rio, and the news was telegraphed to his friends. So the matter remains for the present. But it is hardly probable that any further attempt will be made to verify his strange story of these hitherto unsuspected cities of the deep sea.

# THE STAR

It was on the first day of the new year that the announcement was made, almost simultaneously from three observatories, that the motion of the planet Neptune, the outermost of all the planets that wheel about the sun, had become very erratic. Ogilvy had already called attention to a suspected retardation in its velocity in December. Such a piece of news was scarcely calculated to interest a world the greater portion of whose inhabitants were unaware of the existence of the planet Neptune, nor outside the astronomical profession did the subsequent discovery of a faint remote speck of light in the region of the perturbed planet cause any very great excitement. Scientific people, however, found the intelligence remarkable enough, even before it became known that the new body was rapidly growing larger and brighter, that its motion was quite different from the orderly progress of the planets, and that the deflection of Neptune and its satellite was becoming now of an unprecedented kind.

Few people without a training in science can realise the huge isolation of the solar system. The sun with its specks of planets, its dust of planetoids, and its impalpable comets, swims in a vacant immensity that almost defeats the imagination. Beyond the orbit of Neptune there is space, vacant so far as human observation has penetrated, without warmth or light or sound, blank emptiness, for twenty million times a million miles. That is the smallest estimate of the distance to be traversed before the very nearest of the stars is attained. And, saving a few comets more unsubstantial than the thinnest flame, no matter had ever to human knowledge crossed this gulf of space, until early in the twentieth century this strange wanderer appeared. A vast mass of matter it was, bulky, heavy, rushing without warning out of the black mystery of the sky into the radiance of the sun. By the second day it was clearly visible to any decent instrument, as a speck with a barely sensible diameter, in the constellation Leo near Regulus. In a little while an opera glass could attain it.

On the third day of the new year the newspaper readers of two hemispheres were made aware for the first time of the real importance of this unusual apparition in the heavens. "A Planetary Collision," one London paper headed the news, and proclaimed Duchaine's opinion that this strange new planet would probably collide with Neptune. The leader writers enlarged upon the topic. So that in most of the capitals of the world, on January 3rd, there was an expectation, however vague, of some imminent phenomenon in the sky; and as the night followed the sunset round the globe, thousands of men turned their eyes skyward to see—the old familiar stars just as they had always been.

Until it was dawn in London and Pollux setting and the stars overhead grown pale. The Winter's dawn it was, a sickly filtering accumulation of daylight, and the light of gas and candles shone yellow in the windows to show where people were astir. But the yawning policeman saw the thing, the busy crowds in the markets stopped agape, workmen going to their work betimes, milkmen, the drivers of newscarts, dissipation going home jaded and pale, homeless wanderers, sentinels on their beats, and in the country, labourers trudging afield, poachers slinking home, all over the dusky quickening country it could be seen—and out at sea by seamen watching for the day—a great white star, come suddenly into the westward sky!

Brighter it was than any star in our skies; brighter than the evening star at its brightest. It still glowed out white and large, no mere twinkling spot of light, but a small round clear shining disc, an hour after the day had come. And where science has not reached, men stared and feared, telling one another of the wars and pestilences that are foreshadowed by these fiery signs in the Heavens. Sturdy Boers, dusky Hottentots, Gold Coast Negroes, Frenchmen, Spaniards, Portuguese, stood in the warmth of the sunrise watching the setting of this strange new star.

And in a hundred observatories there had been suppressed excitement, rising almost to shouting pitch, as the two remote bodies had rushed together, and a hurrying to and fro, to gather photographic apparatus and spectroscope, and this appliance and that, to record this novel astonishing sight, the destruction of a world. For it was a world, a sister planet of our earth, far greater than our earth indeed, that had so suddenly flashed into flaming death. Neptune it was, had been struck, fairly and squarely, by the strange planet from outer space and the heat of the concussion had incontinently turned two solid globes into one vast mass of incandescence. Round the world that day, two hours before the dawn, went the pallid great white star, fading only as it sank westward and the sun mounted above it. Everywhere men marvelled at it, but of all those who saw it none could have marvelled more than those sailors, habitual watchers of the stars, who far away at sea had heard nothing of its advent and saw it now rise like a pigmy moon and climb zenithward and hang overhead and sink westward with the passing of the night.

And when next it rose over Europe everywhere were crowds of watchers on hilly slopes, on house-roofs, in open spaces, staring eastward for the rising of the great new star. It rose with a white glow in front of it, like the glare of a white fire, and those who had seen it come into existence the night before cried out at the sight of it. "It is larger," they cried. "It is brighter!" And, indeed the moon a quarter full and sinking in the west was in its apparent size beyond comparison, but scarcely in all its breadth had it as much brightness now as the little circle of the strange new star.

"It is brighter!" cried the people clustering in the streets. But in the dim observatories the watchers held their breath and peered at one another. *"It is nearer,"* they said. *"Nearer!"*

And voice after voice repeated, "It is nearer," and the clicking telegraph took that up, and it trembled along telephone wires, and in a thousand cities grimy compositors fingered the type. "It is nearer." Men writing in offices, struck with a strange realisation, flung down their pens, men talking in a thousand places suddenly came upon a grotesque possibility in those words, "It is nearer." It hurried along awakening streets, it was shouted down the frost-stilled ways of quiet villages; men who had read these things from the throbbing tape stood in yellow-lit doorways shouting the news to the passers-by. "It is nearer." Pretty women, flushed and glittering, heard the news told jestingly between the dances, and feigned an intelligent interest they did not feel. "Nearer! Indeed. How curious! How very, very clever people must be to find out things like that!"

Lonely tramps faring through the wintry night murmured those words to comfort themselves—looking skyward. "It has need to be nearer, for the night's as cold as charity. Don't seem much warmth from it if it *is* nearer, all the same."

"What is a new star to me?" cried the weeping woman kneeling beside her dead.

The schoolboy, rising early for his examination work, puzzled it out for himself—with the great white star, shining broad and bright through the frost-flowers of his window. "Centrifugal, centripetal," he said, with his chin on his fist. "Stop a planet in its flight, rob it of its centrifugal force, what then? Centripetal has it, and down it falls into the sun! And this—!"

"Do *we* come in the way? I wonder—"

The light of that day went the way of its brethren, and with the later watches of the frosty darkness rose the strange star again. And it was now so bright that the waxing moon seemed but a pale yellow ghost of itself, hanging huge in the sunset. In a South African city a great man had married, and the streets were alight to welcome his return with his bride. "Even the skies have illuminated," said the flatterer. Under Capricorn, two Negro lovers, daring the wild beasts and evil spirits, for love of one another, crouched together in a cane brake where the fire-flies hovered. "That is our star," they whispered, and felt strangely comforted by the sweet brilliance of its light.

The master mathematician sat in his private room and pushed the papers from him. His calculations were already finished. In a small white phial there still remained a little of the drug that had kept him awake and active for four long nights. Each day, serene, explicit, patient as ever, he had given his lecture to his students, and then had come back at once to this momentous calculation. His face was grave, a little drawn and hectic from his drugged activity. For some time he seemed lost in thought. Then he went to the window, and the blind went up with a click. Half way up the sky, over the clustering roofs, chimneys and steeples of the city, hung the star.

He looked at it as one might look into the eyes of a brave enemy. "You may kill me," he said after a silence. "But I can hold you—and all the universe for that matter—in the grip of this little brain. I would not change. Even now."

He looked at the little phial. "There will be no need of sleep again," he said. The next day at noon, punctual to the minute, he entered his lecture theatre, put his hat on the end of the table as his habit was, and carefully selected a large piece of chalk. It was a joke among his students that he could not lecture without that piece of chalk to fumble in his fingers, and once he had been stricken to impotence by their hiding his supply. He came and looked under his grey eyebrows at the rising tiers of young fresh faces, and spoke with his accustomed studied commonness of phrasing. "Circumstances have arisen—circumstances beyond my control," he said and paused, "which will debar me from completing the course I had designed. It would seem, gentlemen, if I may put the thing clearly and briefly, that—Man has lived in vain."

The students glanced at one another. Had they heard aright? Mad?

Raised eyebrows and grinning lips there were, but one or two faces remained intent upon his calm grey-fringed face. "It will be interesting," he was saying, "to devote this morning to an exposition, so far as I can make it clear to you, of the calculations that have led me to this conclusion. Let us assume—"

He turned towards the blackboard, meditating a diagram in the way that was usual to him. "What was that about 'lived in vain?' " whispered one student to another. "Listen,'" said the other, nodding towards the lecturer.

And presently they began to understand.

That night the star rose later, for its proper eastward motion had carried it some way across Leo towards Virgo, and its brightness was so great that the sky became a luminous blue as it rose, and every star was hidden in its turn, save only Jupiter near the zenith, Capella, Aldebaran, Sirius and the pointers of the Bear. It was very white and beautiful. In many parts of the world that night a pallid halo encircled it about. It was perceptibly larger; in the clear refractive sky of the tropics it seemed as if it were nearly a quarter the size of the moon. The frost was still on the ground in England, but the world was as brightly lit as if it were midsummer moonlight. One could see to read quite ordinary print by that cold clear light, and in the cities the lamps burnt yellow and wan.

And everywhere the world was awake that night, and throughout Christendom a sombre murmur hung in the keen air over the country side like the belling of bees in the heather, and this murmurous tumult grew to a clangour in the cities. It was the tolling of the bells in a million belfry towers and steeples, summoning the people to sleep no more, to sin no more, but to gather in their churches and pray. And overhead, growing larger and brighter, as the earth rolled on its way and the night passed, rose the dazzling star.

And the streets and houses were alight in all the cities, the shipyards glared, and whatever roads led to high country were lit and crowded all night long. And in all the seas about the civilised lands, ships with throbbing engines, and ships with bellying sails, crowded with men and living creatures, were standing out to ocean and the north. For already the warning of the master mathematician had been telegraphed all over the world, and translated into a hundred tongues. The new planet and Neptune, locked in a fiery embrace, were whirling headlong, ever faster and faster towards the sun. Already every second this blazing mass flew a hundred miles, and every second its terrific velocity increased. As it flew now, indeed, it must pass a hundred million of miles wide of the earth and scarcely affect it. But near its destined path, as yet only slightly perturbed, spun the mighty planet

Jupiter and his moons sweeping splendid round the sun. Every moment now the attraction between the fiery star and the greatest of the planets grew stronger. And the result of that attraction? Inevitably Jupiter would be deflected from its orbit into an elliptical path, and the burning star, swung by his attraction wide of its sunward rush, would "describe a curved path" and perhaps collide with, and certainly pass very close to, our earth. "Earthquakes, volcanic outbreaks, cyclones, sea waves, floods, and a steady rise in temperature to I know not what limit"—so prophesied the master mathematician.

And overhead, to carry out his words, lonely and cold and livid, blazed the star of the coming doom.

To many who stared at it that night until their eyes ached, it seemed that it was visibly approaching. And that night, too, the weather changed, and the frost that had gripped all Central Europe and France and England softened towards a thaw.

But you must not imagine because I have spoken of people praying through the night and people going aboard ships and people fleeing towards mountainous country that the whole world was already in a terror because of the star. As a matter of fact, use and wont still ruled the world, and save for the talk of idle moments and the splendour of the night, nine human beings out of ten were still busy at their common occupations. In all the cities the shops, save one here and there, opened and closed at their proper hours, the doctor and the undertaker plied their trades, the workers gathered in the factories, soldiers drilled, scholars studied, lovers sought one another, thieves lurked and fled, politicians planned their schemes. The presses of the newspapers roared through the nights, and many a priest of this church and that would not open his holy building to further what he considered a foolish panic. The newspapers insisted on the lesson of the year 1000—for then, too, people had anticipated the end. The star was no star—mere gas—a comet; and were it a star it could not possibly strike the earth. There was no precedent for such a thing. Common sense was sturdy everywhere, scornful, jesting, a little inclined to persecute the obdurate fearful. That night, at seven-fifteen by Greenwich time, the star would be at its nearest to Jupiter. Then the world would see the turn things would take. The master mathematician's grim warnings were treated by many as so much mere elaborate self-advertisement. Common sense at last, a little heated by argument, signified its unalterable convictions by going to bed. So, too, barbarism and savagery, already tired of the novelty, went about their nightly business, and save for a howling dog here and there, the beast world left the star unheeded.

And yet, when at last the watchers in the European States saw the star rise, an hour later it is true, but no larger than it had been the night before, there were still plenty awake to laugh at the master mathematician—to take the danger as if it had passed.

But hereafter the laughter ceased. The star grew–it grew with a terrible steadiness hour after hour, a little larger each hour, a little nearer the midnight zenith, and brighter and brighter, until it had turned night into a second day. Had it come straight to the earth instead of in a curved path, had it lost no velocity to Jupiter, it must have leapt the intervening gulf in a day, but as it was it took five days altogether to come by our planet. The next night it had become a third the size of the moon before it set to English eyes, and the thaw was assured. It rose over America near the size of the moon, but blinding white to look at, and *hot;* and a breath of hot wind blew now with its rising and gathering strength, and in Virginia, and Brazil, and down the St. Lawrence valley, it shone intermittently through a driving reek of thunder-clouds, flickering violet lightning, and hail unprecedented. In Manitoba was a thaw and devastating floods. And upon all the mountains of the earth the snow and ice began to melt that night, and all the rivers coming out of high country flowed thick and turbid, and soon—in their upper reaches—with swirling trees and the bodies of beasts and men. They rose steadily, steadily in the ghostly brilliance, and came trickling over their banks at last, behind the flying population of their valleys.

And along the coast of Argentina and up the South Atlantic the tides were higher than had ever been in the memory of man, and the storms drove the waters in many cases scores of miles inland, drowning whole cities. And so great grew the heat during the night that the rising of the sun was like the coming of a shadow. The earthquakes began and grew until all down America, from the Arctic Circle to Cape Horn, hillsides were sliding, fissures were openings, and houses and walls crumbling to destruction. The whole side of Cotopaxi slipped out in one vast convulsion, and a tumult of lava poured out so high and broad and swift and liquid that in one day it reached the sea.

So the star, with the wan moon in its wake, marched across the Pacific, trailed the thunderstorms like the hem of a robe, and the growing tidal wave that toiled behind it, frothing and eager, poured over island and island and swept them clear of men. Until that wave came at last–in a blinding light and with the breath of a furnace, swift and terrible it came–a wall of water, fifty feet high, roaring hungrily, upon the long coasts of Asia, and swept inland across the plains of China. For a space the star, hotter now and larger and brighter than the sun in its strength, showed with pitiless brillance the wide and populous country; towns and villages with their pagodas and trees, roads, wide cultivated fields, millions of sleepless people staring in helpless terror at the incandescent sky; and then, low and growing, came the murmur of the flood. And thus it was with millions of men that night—a flight nowhither, with limbs heavy with heat and breath fierce and scant, and the flood like a wall swift and white behind. And then death.

China was lit glowing white, but over Japan and Java and all the islands of Eastern Asia the great star was a ball of dull red fire because of the steam and smoke and ashes the volcanoes were spouting forth to salute its coming. Above was the lava, hot gases and ash, and below the seething floods, and the whole earth swayed and rumbled with the earthquake shocks. Soon the immemorial snows of Tibet and the Himalaya were melting and pouring down by ten million deepening converging channels upon the plains of Burmah and Hindostan. The tangled summits of the Indian jungles were aflame in a thousand places, and below the hurrying waters around the stems were dark objects that still struggled feebly and reflected the blood-red tongues of fire. And in a rudderless confusion a multitude of men and women fled down the broad river-ways to that one last hope of men—the open sea.

Larger grew the star, and larger, hotter, and brighter with a terrible swiftness now. The tropical ocean had lost its phosphorescence, and the whirling steam rose in ghostly wreaths from the black waves that plunged incessantly, speckled with storm-tossed ships.

And then came a wonder. It seemed to those who in Europe watched for the rising of the star that the world must have ceased its rotation. In a thousand open spaces of down and upland the people who had fled thither from the floods and the falling houses and sliding slopes of hill watched for that rising in vain. Hour followed hour through a terrible suspense, and the star rose not. Once again men set their eyes upon the old constellations they had counted lost to them forever. In England it was hot and clear overhead, though the ground quivered perpetually, but in the tropics, Sirius and Capella and Aldebaran showed through a veil of steam. And when at last the great star rose near ten hours late, the sun rose close upon it, and in the centre of its white heart was a disc of black.

Over Asia it was the star had begun to fall behind the movement of the sky, and then suddenly, as it hung over India, its light had been veiled. All the plain of India from the mouth of the Indus to the mouths of the Ganges was a shallow waste of shining water that night, out of which rose temples and palaces, mounds and hills, black with people. Every minaret was a clustering mass of people, who fell one by one into the turbid waters, as heat and terror overcame them. The whole land seemed a-wailing, and suddenly there swept a shadow across that furnace of despair, and a breath of cold wind, and a gathering of clouds, out of the cooling air. Men looking up, near blinded, at the star, saw that a black disc was creeping across the light. It was the moon, coming between the star and the earth. And even as men cried to God at this respite, out of the East with a strange inexplicable swiftness sprang the sun. And then star, sun and moon rushed together across the heavens.

So it was that presently, to the European watchers, star and sun rose close upon each other, drove headlong for a space and then slower, and at last came to rest, star and sun merged into one glare of flame at the zenith of the sky. The moon no longer eclipsed the star but was lost to sight in the brilliance of the sky. And though those who were still alive regarded it for the most part with that dull stupidity that hunger, fatigue, heat and despair engender, there were still men who could perceive the meaning of these signs. Star and earth had been at their nearest, had swung about one another, and the star had passed. Already it was receding, swifter and swifter, in the last stage of its headlong journey downward into the sun.

And then the clouds gathered, blotting out the vision of the sky, the thunder and lightning wove a garment round the world; all over the earth was such a downpour of rain as men had never before seen, and where the volcanoes flared red against the cloud canopy there descended torrents of mud. Everywhere the waters were pouring off the land, leaving mud-silted ruins, and the earth littered like a storm-worn beach with all that had floated, and the dead bodies of the men and brutes, its children. For days the water streamed off the land, sweeping away soil and trees and houses in the way, and piling huge dykes and scooping out Titanic gullies over the country side. Those were the days of darkness that followed the star and the heat. All through them, and for many weeks and months, the earthquakes continued.

But the star had passed, and men, hunger-driven and gathering courage only slowly, might creep back to their ruined cities, buried granaries, and sodden fields. Such few ships as had escaped the storms of that time came stunned and shattered and sounding their way cautiously through the new marks and shoals of once familiar ports. And as the storms subsided men perceived that everywhere the days were hotter than of yore, and the sun larger, and the moon, shrunk to a third of its former size, took now fourscore days between its new and new.

But of the new brotherhood that grew presently among men, of the saving of laws and books and machines, of the strange change that had come over Iceland and Greenland and the shores of Baffin's Bay, so that the sailors coming there presently found them green and gracious, and could scarce believe their eyes, this story does not tell. Nor of the movement of mankind now that the earth was hotter, northward and southward towards the poles of the earth. It concerns itself only with the coming and the passing of the Star.

The Martian astronomers—for there are astronomers on Mars, although they are very different beings from men—were naturally profoundly interested by these things. They saw them from their own standpoint of course. "Considering the mass and temperature of the missile that was flung through our solar system into the sun," one wrote, "it is astonishing what a little damage the earth, which it missed so narrowly, has sustained. All the familiar continental markings and the masses of the seas remain intact, and indeed the only difference seems to be a shrinkage of the white discoloration (supposed to be frozen water) round either pole." Which only shows how small the vastest of human catastrophes may seem, at a distance of a few million miles.

# THE LORD OF THE DYNAMOS

The chief attendant of the three dynamos that buzzed and rattled at Camberwell, and kept the electric railway going, came out of Yorkshire, and his name was James Holroyd. He was a practical electrician, but fond of whiskey, a heavy red-haired brute with irregular teeth. He doubted the existence of the deity, but accepted Carnot's cycle, and he had read Shakespeare and found him weak in chemistry. His helper came out of the mysterious East, and his name was Azuma-zi. But Holroyd called him Pooh-bah. Holroyd liked Negro help because he would stand kicking—a habit with Holroyd—and did not pry into the machinery and try to learn the ways of it. Certain odd possibilities of the Negro mind brought into abrupt contact with the crown of our civilisation Holroyd never fully realised, though just at the end he got some inkling of them.

To define Azuma-zi was beyond ethnology. He was, perhaps, more Negroid than anything else, though his hair was curly rather than frizzy, and his nose had a bridge. Moreover, his skin was brown rather than black, and the whites of his eyes were yellow. His broad cheekbones and narrow chin gave his face something of the viperine V. His head, too, was broad behind, and low and narrow at the forehead, as if his brain had been twisted round in the reverse way to a European's. He was short of stature and still shorter of English. In conversation he made numerous odd noises of no known marketable value, and his infrequent words were carved and wrought into heraldic grotesqueness. Holroyd tried to elucidate his religious beliefs, and—especially after whiskey—lectured to him against superstition and missionaries. Azuma-zi, however, shirked the discussion of his gods, even though he was kicked for it.

Azuma-zi had come, clad in white but insufficient raiment, out of the stoke-hole of the *Lord Clive,* from the Straits Settlements, and beyond, into London. He had heard even in his youth of the greatness and riches of London, where all the women are white and fair, and even the beggars in the streets are white; and he had arrived, with newly earned gold coins in his pocket, to worship at the shrine of civilisation. The day of his landing was a dismal one; the sky was dun, and a wind-worried drizzle filtered down to the greasy streets, but he plunged boldly into the delights of Shadwell, and was presently cast up, shattered in health, civilised in costume, penniless, and, except in matters of the direst necessity, practically a dumb animal, to toil for James Holroyd and to be bullied by him in the dynamo shed at Camberwell. And to James Holroyd bullying was a labour of love.

There were three dynamos with their engines at Camberwell. The two that have been there since the beginning are small machines; the larger one was new. The smaller machines made a reasonable noise; their straps hummed over the drums, every now and then the brushes buzzed and fizzled, and the air churned steadily, whoo! whoo! whoo! between their poles. One was loose in its foundations and kept the shed vibrating. But the big dynamo drowned these little noises altogether with the sustained drone of its iron core, which somehow set part of the ironwork humming. The place made the visitor's head reel with the throb, throb, throb of the engines, the rotation of the big wheels, the spinning ball-valves, the occasional spittings of the steam, and over all the deep, unceasing, surging note of the big dynamo. This last noise was from an engineering point of view a defect; but Azuma-zi accounted it unto the monster for mightiness and pride.

If it were possible we would have the noises of that shed always about the reader as he reads, we would tell all our story to such an accompaniment. It was a steady stream of din, from which the ear picked out first one thread and then another; there was the intermittent snorting, panting, and seething of the steam-engines, the suck and thud of their pistons, the dull beat on the air as the spokes of the great driving-wheels came round, a note the leather straps made as they ran tighter and looser, and a fretful tumult from the dynamos; and, over all, sometimes inaudible, as the ear tired of it, and then creeping back upon the senses again, was this trombone note of the big machine. The floor never felt steady and quiet beneath one's feet, but quivered and jarred. It was a confusing, unsteady place, and enough to send any one's thoughts jerking into odd zigzags. And for three months, while the big strike of the engineers was in progress,

Holroyd, who was a blackleg, and Azuma-zi, who was a mere black, were never out of the stir and eddy of it, but slept and fed in the little wooden shanty between the shed and the gates.

Holroyd delivered a theological lecture on the text of his big machine soon after Azuma-zi came. He had to shout to be heard in the din. "Look at that," said Holroyd, "where's your 'eathen idol to match 'im?" And Azuma-zi looked. For a moment Holroyd was inaudible, and then Azuma-zi heard: "Kill a hundred men. Twelve per cent on the ordinary shares," said Holroyd, "and that's something like a Gord!"

Holroyd was proud of his big dynamo, and expatiated upon its size and power to Azuma-zi until heaven knows what odd currents of thought that, and the incessant whirling and shindy, set up within the curly, black cranium. He would explain in the most graphic manner the dozen or so ways in which a man might be killed by it, and once he gave Azuma-zi a shock as a sample of its quality. After that, in the breathing-times of his labour—it was heavy labour, being not only his own but most of Holroyd's—Azuma-zi would sit and watch the big machine. Now and then the brushes would sparkle and spit blue flashes, at which Holroyd would swear, but all the rest was as smooth and rhythmic as breathing. The band ran shouting over the shaft, and ever behind one as one watched was the complacent thud of the piston. So it lived all day in this big airy shed, with him and Holroyd to wait upon it; not prisoned up and slaving to drive a ship as the other engines he knew—mere captive devils of the British Solomon—had been, but a machine enthroned. Those two smaller dynamos, Azuma-zi by force of contrast despised; the large one he privately christened the Lord of the Dynamos. They were fretful and irregular, but the big dynamo was steady. How great it was! How serene and easy in its working! Greater and calmer even than the Buddahs he had seen at Rangoon, and yet not motionless, but living! The great black coils spun, spun, spun, the rings ran round under the brushes, and the deep note of its coil steadied the whole. It affected Azuma-zi queerly.

Azuma-zi was not fond of labour. He would sit about and watch the Lord of the Dynamos while Holroyd went away to persuade the yard porter to get whiskey, although his proper place was not in the dynamo shed but behind the engines, and, moreover, if Holroyd caught him skulking he got hit for it with a rod of stout copper wire. He would go and stand close to the colossus and look up at the great leather band running overhead. There was a black patch on the band that came round, and it pleased him somehow among all the clatter to watch this return again and again. Odd thoughts spun with the whirl of it. Scientific people tell us that savages give souls to rocks and trees—and a machine is a thousand times more alive than a rock or a tree. And Azuma-zi was practically a savage still; the veneer of civilisation lay no deeper than his slop suit, his bruises and the coal grime on his face and hands. His father before him had worshipped a meteoric stone, kindred blood, it may be, had splashed the broad wheels of Juggernaut.

He took every opportunity Holroyd gave him of touching and handling the great dynamo that was fascinating him. He polished and cleaned it until the metal parts were blinding in the sun. He felt a mysterious sense of service in doing this. He would go up to it and touch its spinning coils gently. The gods he had worshipped were all far away. The people in London hid their gods.

At last his dim feelings grew more distinct, and took shape in thoughts and acts. When he came into the roaring shed one morning he salaamed to the Lord of the Dynamos; and then, when Holroyd was away, he went and whispered to the thundering machine that he was its servant, and prayed it to have pity on him and save him from Holroyd. As he did so a rare gleam of light came in through the open archway of the throbbing machine-shed, and the Lord of the Dynamos, as he whirled and roared, was radiant with pale gold. Then Azuma-zi knew that his service was acceptable to his Lord. After that he did not feel so lonely as he had done, and he had indeed been very much alone in London. And even when his work time was over, which was rare, he loitered about the shed.

Then, the next time Holroyd maltreated him, Azuma-zi went presently to the Lord of the Dynamos and whispered, "Thou seest, O my Lord!" and the angry whirr of the machinery seemed to answer him. Thereafter it appeared to him that whenever Holroyd came into the shed a different note came into the sounds of the great dynamo. "My Lord bides his time," said Azuma-zi to himself. "The iniquity of the fool is not yet ripe." And he waited and watched for the day of reckoning. One day there was evidence of short circuiting, and Holroyd, making an unwary examination—it was in the afternoon—got a rather severe shock. Azuma-zi from behind the engine saw him jump off and curse at the peccant coil.

"He is warned," said Azuma-zi to himself. "Surely my Lord is very patient."

Holroyd had at first initiated his Negro into such elementary conceptions of the dynamo's working as would enable him to take temporary charge of the shed in his absence. But when he noticed the manner in which Azuma-zi hung about the monster, he became suspicious. He dimly perceived his assistant was "up to something," and connecting him with the anointing of the coils with oil that had rotted the varnish in one place, he issued an edict, shouted above the confusion of the machinery, "Don't 'ee go nigh that big dynamo any more, Pooh-bah, or a'll take thy skin off!" Besides, if it pleased Azuma-zi to be near the big machine, it was plain sense and decency to keep him away from it.

Azuma-zi obeyed at the time, but later he was caught bowing before the Lord of the Dynamos. At which Holroyd twisted his arm and kicked him as he turned to go away. As Azuma-zi presently stood behind the engine and glared at the back of the hated Holroyd, the noises of the machinery took a new rhythm, and sounded like four words in his native tongue.

It is hard to say exactly what madness is. I fancy Azuma-zi was mad. The incessant din and whirl of the dynamo shed may have churned up his little store of knowledge and big store of superstitious fancy, at last, into something akin to frenzy. At any rate, when the idea of making Holroyd a sacrifice to the Dynamo Fetich was thus suggested to him, it filled him with a strange tumult of exultant emotion.

That night the two men and their black shadows were alone in the shed together. The shed was lit with one big arc light that winked and flickered purple. The shadows lay black behind the dynamos, the ball governors of the engines whirled from light to darkness, and their pistons beat loud and steady. The world outside seen through the open end of the shed seemed incredibly dim and remote. It seemed absolutely silent, too, since the riot of the machinery drowned every external sound. Far away was the black fence of the yard with grey, shadowy houses behind, and above was the deep blue sky and the pale little stars. Azuma-zi suddenly walked across the centre of the shed above which the leather bands were running, and went into the shadow by the big dynamo. Holroyd heard a click, and the spin of the armature changed.

"What are you dewin' with that switch?" he bawled in surprise. "Ha'n't I told you—"

Then he saw the set expression of Azuma-zi's eyes as the Asiatic came out of the shadow towards him.

In another moment the two men were grappling fiercely in front of the great dynamo.

"You coffee-headed fool!" gasped Holroyd, with a brown hand at his throat. "Keep off those contact rings." In another moment he was tripped and reeling back upon the Lord of the Dynamos. He instinctively loosened his grip upon his antagonist to save himself from from the machine.

The messenger, sent in furious haste from the station to find out what had happened in the dynamo shed, met Azuma-zi at the porter's lodge by the gate. Azuma-zi tried to explain something, but the messenger could make nothing of the black's incoherent English, and hurried on to the shed. The machines were all noisily at work, and nothing seemed to be disarranged. There was, however, a queer smell of singed hair. Then he saw an odd-looking, crumpled mass clinging to the front of the big dynamo, and, approaching, recognised the distorted remains of Holroyd.

The man stared and hesitated a moment. Then he saw the face and shut his eyes convulsively. He turned on his heel before he opened them, so that he should not see Holroyd again, and went out of the shed to get advice and help.

When Azuma-zi saw Holroyd die in the grip of the Great Dynamo he had been a little scared about the consequences of his act. Yet he felt strangely elated, and knew that the favour of the Lord Dynamo was upon him. His plan was already settled when he met the man coming from the station, and the scientific manager who speedily arrived on the scene jumped at the obvious conclusion of suicide. This expert scarcely noticed Azuma-zi except to ask a few questions. Did he see Holroyd kill himself? Azuma-zi explained he had been out of sight at the engine furnace until he heard a difference in the noise from the dynamo. It was not a difficult examination, being untinctured by suspicion.

The distorted remains of Holroyd, which the electrician removed from the machine, were hastily covered by the porter with a coffee-stained tablecloth. Somebody, by a happy inspiration, fetched a medical man. The expert was chiefly anxious to get the machine at work again, for seven or eight trains had stopped midway in the stuffy tunnels of the electric railway. Azuma-zi, answering or misunderstanding the questions of the people who had by authority or impudence come into the shed, was presently sent back to the stoke-hole by the scientific manager. Of course a crowd collected outside the gates of the yard,—a crowd, for no known reason, always hovers for a day or two near the scene of a sudden death in London; two or three reporters percolated somehow into the engine-shed, and one even got to Azuma-zi; but the scientific expert cleared them out again, being himself an amateur journalist.

Presently the body was carried away, and public interest departed with it. Azuma-zi remained very quietly at his furnace, seeing over and over again in the coals a figure that wriggled violently and became still. An hour after the murder, to any one coming into the shed it would have looked exactly as if nothing remarkable had ever happened there. Peeping presently from his engine-room the black saw the Lord Dynamo spin and whirl beside his little brothers, the driving wheels were beating round, and the steam in the pistons went thud, thud, exactly as it had been earlier in the evening. After all, from the mechanical point of view, it had been a most insignificant incident—the mere temporary deflection of a current. But now the slender form and slender shadow of the scientific manager replaced the sturdy outline of Holroyd travelling up and down the lane of light upon the vibrating floor under the straps between the engines and the dynamos.

"Have I not served my Lord?" said Azuma-zi, inaudibly, from his shadow, and the note of the great dynamo rang out full and clear. As he looked at the big, whirling mechanism the strange fascination of it that had been a little in abeyance since Holroyd's death resumed its sway.

Never had Azuma-zi seen a man killed so swiftly and pitilessly. The big, humming machine had slain its victim without wavering for a second from its steady beating. It was indeed a mighty god.

The unconscious scientific manager stood with his back to him, scribbling on a piece of paper. His shadow lay at the foot of the monster.

"Was the Lord Dynamo still hungry? His servant was ready."

Azuma-zi made a stealthy step forward, then stopped. The scientific manager suddenly stopped writing, and walked down the shed to the endmost of the dynamos, and began to examine the brushes.

Azuma-zi hesitated, and then slipped across noiselessly into the shadow by the switch. There he waited. Presently the manager's footsteps could be heard returning. He stopped in his old position, unconscious of the stoker crouching ten feet away from him. Then the big dynamo suddenly fizzled, and in another moment Azuma-zi had sprung out of the darkness upon him.

First, the scientific manager was gripped round the body and swung towards the big dynamo, then, kicking with his knee and forcing his antagonist's head down with his hands, he loosened the grip on his waist and swung round away from the machine. Then the black grasped him again, putting a curly head against his chest, and they swayed and panted as it seemed for an age or so. Then the scientific manager was impelled to catch a black ear in his teeth and bite furiously. The black yelled hideously.

They rolled over on the floor, and the black, who had apparently slipped from the vice of the teeth or parted with some ear—the scientific manager wondered which at the time—tried to throttle him. The scientific manager was making some ineffectual efforts to claw something with his hands and to kick, when the welcome sound of quick footsteps sounded on the floor. The next moment Azuma-zi had left him and darted towards the big dynamo. There was a splutter amid the roar.

The officer of the company, who had entered, stood staring as Azuma-zi caught the naked terminals in his hands, gave one horrible convulsion, and then hung motionless from the machine, his face violently distorted.

"I'm jolly glad you came in when you did," said the scientific manager, still sitting on the floor.

He looked at the still quivering figure. "It is not a nice death to die, apparently,—but it is quick."

The official was still staring at the body. He was a man of slow apprehension.

There was a pause.

The scientific manager got up on his feet rather awkwardly. He ran his fingers along his collar thoughtfully, and moved his head to and fro several times.

"Poor Holroyd! I see now." Then almost mechanically he went towards the switch in the shadow and turned the current into the railway circuit again. As he did so the singed body loosened its grip upon the machine and fell forward on its face. The cone of the dynamo roared out loud and clear, and the armature beat the air.

So ended prematurely the Worship of the Dynamo Deity, perhaps the most short-lived of all religions. Yet withal it could boast a Martyrdom and a Human Sacrifice.

# THE STORY OF DAVIDSON'S EYES

## I

The transitory mental aberration of Sidney Davidson, remarkable enough in itself, is still more remarkable if Wade's explanation is to be credited. It sets one dreaming of the oddest possibilities of intercommunication in the future, of spending an intercalary five minutes on the other side of the world, or being watched in our most secret operations by unsuspected eyes. It happened that I was the immediate witness of Davidson's seizure, and so it falls naturally to me to put the story upon paper.

When I say that I was the immediate witness of his seizure, I mean that I was the first on the scene. The thing happened at the Harlow Technical College just beyond the Highgate Archway. He was alone in the larger laboratory when the thing happened. I was in the smaller room, where the balances are, writing up some notes. The thunderstorm had completely upset my work, of course. It was just after one of the louder peals that I thought I heard some glass smash in the other room. I stopped writing, and turned round to listen. For a moment I heard nothing; the hail was playing the devil's tattoo on the corrugated zinc of the roof. Then came another sound, a smash—no doubt of it this time. Something heavy had been knocked off the bench. I jumped up at once and went and opened the door leading into the big laboratory.

I was surprised to hear a queer sort of laugh, and saw Davidson standing unsteadily in the middle of the room, with a dazzled look on his face. My first impression was that he was drunk. He did not notice me. He was clawing out at something invisible a yard in front of his face. He put out his hand, slowly, rather hesitatingly, and then clutched nothing. "What's come to it?" he said. He held up his hands to his face, fingers spread out. "Great Scott!" he said. The thing happened three or four years ago, when every one swore by that personage. Then he began raising his feet clumsily, as though he had expected to find them glued to the floor.

"Davidson!" cried I. "What's the matter with you?" He turned round in my direction and looked about for me. He looked over me and at me and on either side of me, without the slightest sign of seeing me. "Waves," he said; "and a remarkably neat schooner. I'd swear that was Bellows's voice. *Hullo!*" He shouted suddenly at the top of his voice.

I thought he was up to some foolery. Then I saw littered about his feet the shattered remains of the best of our electrometers. "What's up, man?" said I. "You've smashed the electrometer!"

"Bellows again!" said he. "Friends left, if my hands are gone. Something about electrometers. Which way *are* you, Bellows?" He suddenly came staggering towards me. "The damned stuff cuts like butter," he said. He walked straight into the bench and recoiled. "'None so buttery, that!" he said, and stood swaying.

I felt scared. "Davidson," said I, "what on earth's come over you?"

He looked round him in every direction. "I could swear that was Bellows. Why don't you show yourself like a man, Bellows?"

It occurred to me that he must be suddenly struck blind. I walked round the table and laid my hand upon his arm. I never saw a man more startled in my life. He jumped away from me, and came round into an attitude of self-defence, his face fairly distorted with terror. "Good God!" he cried. "What was that?"

"It's I—Bellows. Confound it, Davidson!"

He jumped when I answered him and stared—how can I express it?—right through me. He began talking, not to me, but to himself. "Here in broad daylight on a clear beach. Not a place to hide in." He looked about him wildly. "Here! I'm *off*." He suddenly turned and ran headlong into the big electro-magnet—so violently that, as we found afterwards, he bruised his shoulder and jawbone cruelly. At that he stepped back a pace, and cried out with almost a whimper, "What, in Heaven's name, has come over me?" He stood, blanched with terror and trembling violently, with his right arm clutching his left, where that had collided with the magnet.

By that time I was excited, and fairly excited. "Davidson," said I, "don't be afraid."

He was startled at my voice, but not so excessively as before. I repeated my words in as clear and firm a tone as I could asume. "Bellows," he said, "is that you?"

"Can't you see it's me?"

He laughed. "I can't even see it's myself. Where the devil are we?"

"Here," said I, "in the laboratory."

"The laboratory!" he answered, in a puzzled tone, and put his hand to his forehead. "I *was* in the laboratory—till that flash came, but I'm hanged if I'm there now. What ship is that?"

"There's no ship," said I. "Do be sensible, old chap."

"No ship!" he repeated, and seemed to forget my denial forthwith. "I suppose," said he, slowly, "we're both dead. But the rummy part is I feel just as though I still had a body. Don't get used to it all at once, I suppose. The old shop was struck by lightning, I suppose. Jolly quick thing, Bellows—eigh?"

"Don't talk nonsense. You're very much alive. You are in the laboratory, blundering about. You've just smashed a new electrometer. I don't envy you when Boyce arrives."

He stared away from me towards the diagrams of cryohydrates. "I must be deaf," said he. "They've fired a gun, for there goes the puff of smoke, and I never heard a sound."

I put my hand on his arm again, and this time he was less alarmed. "We seem to have a sort of invisible bodies," said he. "By Jove! there's a boat coming round the headland! It's very much like the old life after all—in a different climate."

I shook his arm. "Davidson," I cried, "wake up!"

## II

It was just then that Boyce came in. So soon as he spoke Davidson exclaimed: "Old Boyce! Dead too! What a lark!" I hastened to explain that Davidson was in a kind of somnambulistic trance. Boyce was interested at once. We both did all we could to rouse the fellow out of his extraordinary state. He answered our questions, and asked us some of his own, but his attention seemed distracted by his hallucination about a beach and a ship. He kept interpolating observations concerning some boat and the davits and sails filling with the wind. It made one feel queer, in the dusky laboratory, to hear him saying such things.

He was blind and helpless. We had to walk him down the passage, one at each elbow, to Boyce's private room, and while Boyce talked to him there, and humoured him about this ship idea, I went along the corridor and asked old Wade to come and look at him. The voice of our Dean sobered him a little, but not very much. He asked where his hands were, and why he had to walk about up to his waist in the ground. Wade thought over him a long time—you know how he knits his brows—and then made him feel the couch, guiding his hands to it. "That's a couch," said Wade. "The couch in the private room of Professor Boyce. Horsehair stuffing."

Davidson felt about, and puzzled over it, and answered presently that he could feel it all right, but he couldn't see it.

"What *do* you see?" asked Wade. Davidson said he could see nothing but a lot of sand and broken-up shells. Wade gave him some other things to feel, telling him what they were, and watching him keenly.

"The ship is almost hull down," said Davidson, presently, *apropos* of nothing.

"Never mind the ship," said Wade. "Listen to me, Davidson. Do you know what hallucination means?"

"Rather," said Davidson.

"Well, everything you see is hallucinatory."

"Bishop Berkeley," said Davidson.

"Don't mistake me," said Wade. "You are alive, and in this room of Boyce's. But something has happened to your eyes. You cannot see; you can feel and hear, but not see. Do you follow me?"

"It seems to me that I see too much." Davidson rubbed his knuckles into his eyes. "Well?" he said.

"That's all. Don't let it perplex you. Bellows, here, and I will take you home in a cab."

"Wait a bit." Davidson thought. "Help me to sit down," said he, presently; "and now—I'm sorry to trouble you—but will you tell me all that over again?"

Wade repeated it very patiently. Davidson shut his eyes, and pressed his hands upon his forehead. "Yes," said he. "It's quite right. Now my eyes are shut I know you're right. That's you, Bellows, sitting by me on the couch. I'm in England again. And we're in the dark."

Then he opened his eyes. "And there," said he, "is the sun just rising, and the yards of the ship, and a tumbled sea, and a couple of birds flying. I never saw anything so real. And I'm sitting up to my neck in a bank of sand."

He bent forward and covered his face with his hands. Then he opened his eyes again. "Dark sea and sunrise! And yet I'm sitting on a sofa in old Boyce's room!—God help me!"

## III

That was the beginning. For three weeks this strange affection of Davidson's eyes continued unabated. It was far worse than being blind. He was absolutely helpless, and had to be fed like a newly-hatched bird, and led about and undressed. If he attempted to move he fell over things or struck himself against walls or doors. After a day or so he got used to hearing our voices without seeing us, and willingly admitted he was at home, and that Wade was right in what he told him. My sister, to whom he was engaged, insisted on coming to see him, and would sit for hours every day while he talked about this beach of his. Holding her hand seemed to comfort him immensely. He explained that when we left the College and drove home,—he lived in Hampstead Village,—it appeared to him as if we drove right through a sandhill—it was perfectly black until he emerged again—and through rocks and trees and solid obstacles, and when he was taken to his own room it made him giddy and almost frantic with the fear of falling, because going upstairs seemed to lift him thirty or forty feet above the rocks of his imaginary island. He kept saying he should smash all the eggs. The end was that he had to be taken down into his father's consulting room and laid upon a couch that stood there.

He described the island as being a bleak kind of place on the whole, with very little vegetation, except some peaty stuff, and a lot of bare rock. There were multitudes of penguins, and they made the rocks white and disagreeable to see. The sea was often rough, and once there was a thunderstorm, and he lay and shouted at the silent flashes. Once or twice seals pulled up on the beach, but only on the first two or three days. He said it was very funny the way in which the penguins used to waddle right through him, and how he seemed to lie among them without disturbing them.

I remember one odd thing, and that was when he wanted very badly to smoke. We put a pipe in his hands—he almost poked his eye out with it—and lit it. But he couldn't taste anything. I've since found it's the same with me—I don't know if it's the usual case—that I cannot enjoy tobacco at all unless I can see the smoke.

But the queerest part of his vision came when Wade sent him out in a bath-chair to get fresh air. The Davidsons hired a chair, and got that deaf and obstinate dependent of theirs, Widgery, to attend to it. Widgery's ideas of healthy expeditions were peculiar. My sister, who had been to the Dog's Home, met them in Camden Town, towards King's Cross. Widgery trotting along complacently, and Davidson evidently most distressed, trying in his feeble, blind way to attract Widgery's attention.

He positively wept when my sister spoke to him. "Oh, get me out of this horrible darkness!" he said, feeling for her hand. "I must get out of it, or I shall die." He was quite incapable of explaining what was the matter, but my sister decided he must go home, and presently, as they went up the hill towards Hampstead, the horror seemed to drop from him. He said it was good to see the stars again, though it was then about noon and a blazing day.

"It seemed," he told me afterwards, "as if I was being carried irresistibly towards the water. I was not very much alarmed at first. Of course it was night there—a lovely night."

"Of course?" I asked, for that struck me as odd.

"Of course," said he. "It's always night there when it is day here—Well, we went right into the water, which was calm and shining under the moonlight—just a broad swell that seemed to grow broader and flatter as I came down into it. The surface glistened just like a skin—it might have been empty space underneath for all I could tell to the contrary. Very slowly, for I rode slanting into it, the water crept up to my eyes. Then I went under, and the skin seemed to break and heal again about my eyes. The moon gave a jump up in the sky and grew green and dim, and fish, faintly glowing, came darting round me—and things that seemed made of luminous glass, and I passed through a tangle of seaweeds that shone with an oily lustre. And so I drove down into the sea, and the stars went out one by one, and the moon grew greener and darker, and the seaweed became a luminous purple-red. It was all very faint and mysterious, and everything seemed to quiver. And all the while I could hear the wheels of the bath-chair creeking, and the footsteps of people going by, and a man with a bell crying coals.

"I kept sinking down deeper and deeper into the water. It became inky black about me, not a ray from above came down into that darkness, and the phosphorescent things grew brighter and brighter. The snaky branches of the deeper weeds flickered like the flames of spirit lamps; but, after a time, there were no more weeds. The fishes came staring and gaping towards me, and into me and through me. I never imagined such fishes before. They had lines of fire along the sides of them as though they had been outlined with a luminous pencil. And there was a ghastly thing swimming backwards with a lot of twining arms. And then I saw, coming very slowly towards me through the gloom, a hazy mass of light that resolved itself as it drew nearer into multitudes of fishes, struggling and darting round something that drifted. I drove on straight towards it, and presently I saw in the midst of the tumult, and by the light of the fish, a bit of splintered spar looming over me, and a dark hull tilting over, and some glowing phosphorescent forms that were shaken and writhed as the fish bit at them. Then it was I began to try to attract Widgery's attention. A horror came upon me. Ugh! I should have driven right into those half-eaten—things. If your sister had not come! They had great holes in them. Bellows, and—Never mind. But it was ghastly!"

## IV

For three weeks Davidson remained in this singular state, seeing what at the time we imagined was an altogether phantasmal world, and stone blind to the world around him. Then, one Tuesday, when I called, I met old Davidson in the passage. "He can see his thumb!" the old gentleman said, in a perfect transport. He was struggling into his overcoat. "He can see his thumb, Bellows!" he said, with the tears in his eyes. "The lad will be all right yet."

I rushed in to Davidson. He was holding up a little book before his face, and looking at it and laughing in a weak kind of way.

"It's amazing," said he. "There's a kind of patch come there." He pointed with his finger. "I'm on the rocks as usual, and the penguins are staggering and flapping about as usual, and there's been a whale showing every now and then, but it's got too dark now to make him out. But put something *there,* and I see it—I do see it. It's very dim and broken in places, but I see it all the same, like a faint spectre of itself. I found it out this morning while they were dressing me. It's like a hole in this infernal phantom world. Just put your hand by mine. No—not there. Ah! Yes! I see it. The base of your thumb and a bit of cuff! It looks like the ghost of a bit of your hand sticking out of the darkening sky. Just by it there's a group of stars like a cross coming out."

From that time Davidson began to mend. His account of the change, like his account of the vision, was oddly convincing. Over patches of his field of vision the phantom world grew fainter, grew transparent, as it were, and through these translucent gaps he began to see dimly the real world about him. The patches grew in size and number, ran together and spread until only here and there were blind spots left upon his eyes. He was able to get up and steer himself about, feed himself once more, read, smoke, and behave like an ordinary citizen again. At first it was very confusing to him to have these two pictures overlapping each other like the changing views of a lantern, but in a little while he began to distinguish the real from the illusory.

At first he was unfeignedly glad, and seemed only too anxious to complete his cure by taking exercise and tonics. But as that odd island of his began to fade away from him, he became queerly interested in it. He wanted particularly to go down into the deep sea again, and would spend half his time wandering about the low-lying parts of London, trying to find the water-logged wreck he had seen drifting. The glare of real daylight very soon impressed him so vividly as to blot out everything of his shadowy world, but of a night-time, in a darkened room, he could still see the white-splashed rocks of the island, and the clumsy penguins staggering to and fro. But even these grew fainter and fainter, and, at last, soon after he married my sister, he saw them for the last time.

## V

And now to tell of the queerest thing of all. About two years after his cure, I dined with the Davidsons, and after dinner a man named Atkins called in. He is a lieutenant in the Royal Navy, and a pleasant, talkative man. He was on friendly terms with my brother-in-law, and was soon on friendly terms with me. It came out that he was engaged to Davidson's cousin, and incidentally he took out a kind of pocket photograph case to show us a new rendering of his *fiancée*. "And, by-the-by," said he, "here's the old *Fulmar*."

Davidson looked at it casually. Then suddenly his face lit up. "Good heavens!" said he. "I could almost swear—"

"What?" said Atkins.

"That I had seen that ship before."

"Don't see how you can have. She hasn't been out of the South Seas for six years, and before then—"

"But," began Davidson, and then, "Yes—that's the ship I dreamt of. I'm sure that's the ship I dreamt of. She was standing off and island that swarmed with penguins, and she fired a gun."

"Good Lord!" said Atkins, who had never heard the particulars of the seizure. "How the deuce could you dream that?"

And then, bit by bit, it came out that on the very day Davidson was seized, H.M.S. *Fulmar* had actually been off a little rock to the south of Antipodes Island. A boat had landed overnight to get penguins' eggs, had been delayed, and a thunderstorm drifting up, the boat's crew had waited until the morning before rejoining the ship. Atkins had been one of them, and he corroborated, word for word, the descriptions Davidson had given of the island and the boat. There is not the slightest doubt in any of our minds that Davidson has really seen the place. In some unaccountable way, while he moved hither and thither in London, his sight moved hither and thither in a manner that corresponded, about this distant island. *How* is absolutely a mystery.

That completes the remarkable story of Davidson's eyes. It is perhaps the best authenticated case in existence of a real vision at a distance. Explanation there is none forthcoming, except what Professor Wade has thrown out. But his explanation invokes the Fourth Dimension, and a dissertation on theoretical kinds of space. To talk of there being "a kink in space" seems mere nonsense to me; it may be because I am no mathematician. When I said that nothing would alter the fact that the place is eight thousand miles away, he answered that two points might be a yard away on a sheet of paper and yet be brought together by bending the paper round. The reader may grasp his argument, but I certainly do not. His idea seems to be that Davidson, stooping between the poles of the big electro-magnet, had some extraordinary twist given to his retinal elements through the sudden change in the field of force due to the lightning.

He thinks, as a consequence of this, that it may be possible to live visually in one part of the world, while one lives bodily in another. He has even made some experiments in support of his views; but, so far, he has simply succeeded in blinding a few dogs. I believe that is the net result of his work, though I have not seen him for some weeks. Latterly, I have been so busy with my work in connection with the Saint Pancras installation that I have had little opportunity of calling to see him. But the whole of his theory seems fantastic to me. The facts concerning Davidson stand on an altogether different footing, and I can testify personally to the accuracy of every detail I have given.

# IN THE AVU OBSERVATORY

The observatory at Avu, in Borneo, stands on the spur of the mountain. To the north rises the old crater, black against the unfathomable blue of the sky. From the little circular building, with its mushroom dome, the slopes plunge steeply downward into the black mysteries of the tropical forest beneath. The little house in which the observer and his assistant live is about fifty yards from the observatory, and beyond this are the huts of their native attendants.

Thaddy, the chief observer, was down with a slight fever. His assistant, Woodhouse, paused for a moment in silent contemplation of the tropical night before commencing his solitary vigil. The night was very silent. Now and then voices and laughter came from the native huts, or the cry of some strange animal was heard from the midst of the mystery of the forest. Nocturnal insects appeared in ghostly fashion out of the darkness, and fluttered round his light. He thought, perhaps, of all the possibilities of discovery that still lay in the black tangle beneath him; for to the naturalist the virgin forests of Borneo are still a wonderland, full of strange questions and half-suspected discoveries. Woodhouse carried a small lantern in his hand, and its yellow glow contrasted vividly with the infinite series of tints between lavender-blue and black in which the landscape was painted. His hands and face were smeared with ointment against the attacks of the mosquitoes.

Even in these days of celestial photography, work done in a purely temporary erection, and with only the most primitive appliances in addition to the telescope, still involves a very large amount of cramped and motionless watching. He sighed as he thought of the physical fatigues before him, stretched himself, and entered the observatory.

The reader is probably familiar with the structure of an ordinary astronomical observatory. The building is usually cylindrical in shape, with a very light hemispherical roof capable of being turned round from the interior. The telescope is supported upon a stone pillar in the centre, and a clockwork arrangement compensates for the earth's rotation, and allows a star once found to be continuously observed. Besides this, there is a compact tracery of wheels and screws about its point of support, by which the astronomer adjusts it. There is, of course, a slit in the movable roof which follows the eye of the telescope in its survey of the heavens. The observer sits or lies on a sloping wooden arrangement, which he can wheel to any part of the observatory as the position of the telescope may require. Within it is advisable to have things as dark as possible, in order to enhance the brilliance of the stars observed.

The lantern flared as Woodhouse entered his circular den, and the general darkness fled into black shadows behind the big machine, from which it presently seemed to creep back over the whole place again as the light waned. The slit was a profound transparent blue, in which six stars shone with tropical brilliance, and their light lay, a pallid gleam, along the black tube of the instrument. Woodhouse shifted the roof, and then proceeding to the telescope, turned first one wheel and then another, the great cylinder slowly swinging into a new position. Then he glanced through the finder, the little companion telescope, moved the roof a little more, made some further adjustments, and set the clockwork in motion. He took off his jacket, for the night was very hot, and pushed into position the uncomfortable seat to which he was condemned for the next four hours. Then with a sigh he resigned himself to his watch upon the mysteries of space.

There was no sound now in the observatory, and the lantern waned steadily. Outside there was the occasional cry of some animal in alarm or pain, or calling to its mate, and the intermittent sounds of the Malay and Dyak servants. Presently one of the men began a queer chanting song, in which the others jointed at intervals. After this it would seem that they turned in for the night, for no further sound came from their direction, and the whispering stillness became more and more profound.

The clockwork ticked steadily. The shrill hum of a mosquito explored the place and grew shriller in indignation at Woodhouse's ointment. Then the lantern went out and all the observatory was black.

Woodhouse shifted his position presently, when the slow movement of the telescope had carried it beyond the limits of his comfort.

He was watching a little group of stars in the Milky Way, in one of which his chief had seen or fancied a remarkable colour variability. It was not a part of the regular work for which the establishment existed, and for that reason perhaps Woodhouse was deeply interested. He must have forgotten things terrestrial. All his attention was concentrated upon the great blue circle of the telescope field—a circle powdered, so it seemed, with an innumerable multitude of stars, and all luminous against the blackness of its setting. As he watched, he seemed to himself to become incorporeal, as if he too were floating in the ether of space. Infinitely remote was the faint red spot he was observing.

Suddenly the stars were blotted out. A flash of blackness passed, and they were visible again.

"Queer," said Woodhouse. "Must have been a bird."

The thing happened again, and immediately after the great tube shivered as though it had been struck. Then the dome of the observatory resounded with a series of thundering blows. The stars seemed to sweep aside as the telescope swung round and away from the slit in the roof.

"Great Scott!" cried Woodhouse. "What's this?"

Some huge, vague, black shape, with a flapping something like a wing, seemed to be struggling in the aperture of the roof. In another moment the slit was clear again, and the luminous haze of the Milky Way shone warm and bright.

The interior of the roof was perfectly black, and only a scraping sound marked the whereabouts of the unknown creature.

Woodhouse had scrambled from the seat to his feet. He was trembling violently and in a perspiration with the suddenness of the occurrence. Was the thing, whatever it was, inside or out? It was big, whatever else it might be. Something shot across the skylight, and the telescope swayed. He started violently and put his arm up. It was in the observatory, then, with him. It was clinging to the roof, apparently. What the devil was it? Could it see him?

He stood for perhaps a minute in a state of stupefaction. The beast, whatever it was, clawed at the interior of the dome, and then something flapped almost into his face, and he saw the momentary gleam of starlight on a skin like oiled leather. His water-bottle was knocked off his little table with a smash.

The sense of some strange bird-creature hovering a few yards from his face in the darkness was indescribably unpleasant to Woodhouse. As his thought returned he concluded that it must be some night-bird or large bat. At any risk he would see what it was, and pulling a match from his pocket, he tried to strike it on the telescope seat. There was a smoking streak of phosphorescent light, the match flared for a moment, and he saw a vast wing sweeping towards him, a gleam of grey-brown fur, and then he was struck in the face and the match knocked out of his hand. The blow was aimed at his temple, and a claw tore sideways down to his cheek. He reeled and fell, and he heard the extinguished lantern smash. Another blow followed as he fell. He was partly stunned, he felt his own warm blood stream out upon his face. Instinctively he felt his eyes had been struck at, and, turning over on his face to protect them, tried to crawl under the protection of the telescope.

He was struck again upon the back, and he heard his jacket rip, and then the thing hit the roof of the observatory. He edged as far as he could between the wooden seat and the eyepiece of the instrument, and turned his body round so that it was chiefly his feet that were exposed. With these he could at least kick. He was still in a mystified state. The strange beast banged about in the darkness, and presently clung to the telescope, making it sway and the gear rattle. Once it flapped near him, and he kicked out madly and felt a soft body with his feet. He was horribly scared now. It must be a big thing to swing the telescope like that. He saw for a moment the outline of a head black against the starlight, with sharply-pointed upstanding ears and a crest between them. It seemed to him to be as big as a mastiff's. Then he began to bawl out as loudly as he could for help.

At that the thing came down upon him again. As it did so his hand touched something beside him on the floor. He kicked out, and the next moment his ankle was gripped and held by a row of keen teeth. He yelled again, and tried to free his leg by kicking with the other. Then he realised he had the broken water-bottle at his hand, and, snatching it, he struggled into a sitting posture, and feeling in the darkness towards his foot, gripped a velvety ear, like the ear of a big cat. He had seized the water-bottle by its neck and brought it down with a shivering crash upon the head of the strange beast. He repeated the blow, and then stabbed and jobbed with the jagged end of it, in the darkness, where he judged the face might be.

The small teeth relaxed their hold, and at once Woodhouse pulled his leg free and kicked hard. He felt the sickening feel of fur and bone giving under his boot. There was a tearing bite at his arm, and he struck over it at the face, as he judged, and hit damp fur.

There was a pause; then he heard the sound of claws and the dragging of a heavy body away from him over the observatory floor. Then there was silence, broken only by his own sobbing breathing, and a sound like licking. Everything was black except the parallelogram of the blue skylight with the luminous dust of stars, against which the end of telescope now appeared in silhouette. He waited, as it seemed, an interminable time.

Was the thing coming on again? He felt in his trouser-pocket for some matches, and found one remaining. He tried to strike this, but the floor was wet, and it spat and went out. He cursed. He could not see where the door was situated. In his struggle he had quite lost his bearings. The strange beast, disturbed by the splutter of the match, began to move again. "Time!" called Woodhouse, with a sudden gleam of mirth, but the thing was not coming at him again. He must have hurt it, he thought, with the broken bottle. He felt a dull pain in his ankle. Probably he was bleeding there. He wondered if it would support him if he tried to stand up. The night outside was very still. There was no sound of any one moving. The sleepy fools had not heard those wings battering upon the dome, nor his shouts. It was no good wasting strength in shouting. The monster flapped its wings and startled him into a defensive attitude. He hit his elbow against the seat, and it fell over with a crash. He cursed this, and then he cursed the darkness.

Suddenly the oblong patch of starlight seemed to sway to and fro. Was he going to faint? It would never do to faint. He clenched his fists and set his teeth to hold himself together. Where had the door got to? It occurred to him he could get his bearings by the stars visible through the skylight. The patch of stars he saw was in Sagittarius and south-eastward; the door was north—or was it north by west? He tried to think. If he could get the door open he might retreat. It might be the thing was wounded. The suspense was beastly. "Look here!" he said, "if you don't come on, I shall come at you."

Then the thing began clambering up the side of the observatory, and he saw its black outline gradually blot out the skylight. Was it in retreat? He forgot about the door, and watched as the dome shifted and creaked. Somehow he did not feel very frightened or excited now. He felt a curious sinking sensation inside him. The sharply-defined patch of light, with the black form moving across it, seemed to be growing smaller and smaller. That was curious. He began to feel very thirsty, and yet he did not feel inclined to get anything to drink. He seemed to be sliding down a long funnel.

He felt a burning sensation in his throat, and then he perceived it was broad daylight, and that one of the Dyak servants was looking at him with a curious expression. Then there was the top of Thaddy's face upside down. Funny fellow Thaddy, to go about like that! Then he grasped the situation better, and perceived that his head was on Thaddy's knee, and Thaddy was giving him brandy. And then he saw the eyepiece of the telescope with a lot of red smears on it. He began to remember.

"You've made this observatory in a pretty mess," said Thaddy.

The Dyak boy was beating up an egg in brandy. Woodhouse took this and sat up. He felt a sharp twinge of pain. His ankle was tied up, so were his arm and the side of his face. The smashed glass, red-stained, lay upon the floor, the telescope seat was overturned, and by the opposite wall was a dark pool. The door was open, and he saw the grey summit of the mountain against a brilliant background of blue sky.

"Pah!" said Woodhouse. "Who's been killing calves here? Take me out of it."

Then he remembered the Thing, and the fight he had had with it.

"What *was* it?" he said to Thaddy—"the Thing I fought with?"

"*You* know that best," said Thaddy. "But anyhow, don't worry yourself now about it. Have some more to drink."

Thaddy, however, was curious enough, and it was a hard struggle between duty and inclination to keep Woodhouse quiet until he was decently put away in bed, and had slept upon the copious dose of meat-extract Thaddy considered advisable. They then talked it over together.

"It was," said Woodhouse, "more like a big bat than anything else in the world. It had sharp, short ears, and soft fur, and its wings were leathery. Its teeth were little, but devilish sharp, and its jaw could not have been very strong or else it would have bitten through my ankle."

"It has pretty nearly," said Thaddy.

"It seemed to me to hit out with its claws pretty freely. That is about as much as I know about the beast. Our conversation was intimate, so to speak, and yet not confidential."

"The Dyak chaps talk about a Big Colugo, a Klang-utang—whatever that may be. It does not often attack man, but I suppose you made it nervous. They say there is a Big Colugo and a Little Colugo, and a something else that sounds like gobble. They all fly about at night. For my own part I know there are flying foxes and flying lemurs about here; but they are none of them very big beasts."

"There are more things in heaven and earth," said Woodhouse,—and Thaddy groaned at the quotation,—"and more particularly in the forests of Borneo, than are dreamt of in our philosophies. On the whole, if the Borneo fauna is going to disgorge any more of its novelties upon me, I should prefer that it did so when I was not occupied in the observatory at night and alone."

# THE SEA RAIDERS

## I

Until the extraordinary affair at Sidmouth, the peculiar species *Haploteuthis ferox* was known to science only generically, on the strength of a half-digested tentacle obtained near the Azores, and a decaying body pecked by birds and nibbled by fish, found early in 1896 by Mr. Jennings, near Land's End.

In no department of zoölogical science, indeed, are we quite so much in the dark as with regard to the deep-sea cephalopods. A mere accident, for instance, it was that led to the Prince of Monaco's discovery of nearly a dozen new forms in the summer of 1895, a discovery in which the before-mentioned tentacle was included. It chanced that a cachalot was killed off Terceira by some sperm-whalers, and in its last struggles charged almost to the Prince's yacht, missed it, rolled under, and died within twenty yards of his rudder. And in its agony it threw up a number of large objects, which the Prince, dimly perceiving they were strange and important, was, by a happy expedient, able to secure before they sank. He set his screws in motion, and kept them circling in the vortices thus created until a boat could be lowered. And these specimens were whole cephalopods and fragments of cephalopods, some of gigantic proportions, and almost all of them unknown to science!

It would seem, indeed, that these large and agile creatures, living in the middle depths of the sea, must, to a large extent, for ever remain unknown to us, since under water they are too nimble for nets, and it is only by such rare unlooked-for accidents that specimens can be obtained. In the case of *Haploteuthis ferox*, for instance, we are still altogether ignorant of its habitat, as ignorant as we are of the breeding-ground of the herring or the sea-ways of the salmon. And zoölogists are altogether at a loss to account for its sudden appearance on our coast. Possibly it was the stress of a hunger migration that drove it hither out of the deep. But it will be, perhaps, better to avoid necessarily inconclusive discussion, and to proceed at once with our narrative.

The first human being to set eyes upon a living *Haploteuthis*—the first human being to survive, that is, for there can be little doubt now that the wave of bathing fatalities and boating accidents that travelled along the coast of Cornwall and Devon in early May was due to this cause—was a retired tea-dealer of the name of Fison, who was stopping at a Sidmouth boarding-house. It was in the afternoon, and he was walking along the cliff path between Sidmouth and Ladram Bay. The cliffs in this direction are very high, but down the red face of them in one place a kind of ladder staircase has been made. He was near this when his attention was attracted by what at first he thought to be a cluster of birds struggling over a fragment of food that caught the sunlight, and glistened pinkish-white. The tide was right out, and this object was not only far below him, but remote across a broad waste of rock reefs covered with dark seaweed and interspersed with silvery, shining, tidal pools. And he was, moreover, dazzled by the brightness of the further water.

In a minute, regarding this again, he perceived that his judgment was in fault, for over this struggle circled a number of birds, jackdaws and gulls for the most part, the latter gleaming blindingly when the sunlight smote their wings, and they seemed minute in comparison with it. And his curiosity was, perhaps, aroused all the more strongly because of his first insufficient explanations.

As he had nothing better to do than amuse himself, he decided to make this object, whatever it was, the goal of his afternoon walk, instead of Ladram Bay, conceiving it might perhaps be a great fish of some sort, stranded by some chance, and flapping about in its distress. And so he hurried down the long steep ladder, stopping at intervals of thirty feet or so to take breath and scan the mysterious movement.

At the foot of the cliff he was, of course, nearer his object than he had been; but, on the other hand, it now came up against the incandescent sky, beneath the sun, so as to seem dark and indistinct. Whatever was pinkish of it was now hidden by a skerry of weedy boulders. But he perceived that it was made up of seven rounded bodies, distinct or connected, and that the birds kept up a constant croaking and screaming, but seemed afraid to approach it too closely.

Mr. Fison, torn by curiosity, began picking his way across the wave-worn rocks, and finding the wet seaweed that covered them thickly rendered them extremely slippery, he stopped, removed his shoes and socks, and coiled his trousers above his knees. His object was, of course, merely to avoid stumbling into the rocky pools about him, and perhaps he was rather glad, as all men are, of an excuse to resume, even for a moment, the sensations of his boyhood. At any rate, it is to this, no doubt, that he owes his life.

He approached his mark with all the assurance which the absolute security of the country against all forms of animal life gives its inhabitants. The round bodies moved to and fro, but it was only when he surmounted the skerry of boulders I have mentioned that he realised the horrible nature of the discovery. It came upon him with some suddenness.

The rounded bodies fell apart as he came into sight over the ridge, and displayed the pinkish object to be the partially devoured body of a human being, but whether of a man or woman he was unable to say. And the rounded bodies were new and ghastly-looking creatures, in shape somewhat resembling an octopus, and with huge and very long and flexible tentacles, coiled copiously on the ground. The skin had a glistening texture, unpleasant to see, like shiny leather. The downward bend of the tentacle-surrounded mouth, the curious excrescence at the bend, the tentacles, and the large, intelligent eyes, gave the creatures a grotesque suggestion of a face. They were the size of a fair-sized swine about the body, and the tentacles seemed to him to be many feet in length. There were, he thinks, seven or eight at least of the creatures. Twenty yards beyond them, amid the surf of the now returning tide, two others were emerging from the sea.

Their bodies lay flatly on the rocks, and their eyes regarded him with evil interest; but it does not appear that Mr. Fison was afraid, or that he realised that he was in any danger. Possibly his confidence is to be ascribed to the limpness of their attitudes. But he was horrified, of course, and intensely excited and indignant at such revolting creatures preying upon human flesh. He thought they had chanced upon a drowned body. He shouted to them, with the idea of driving them off, and, finding they did not budge, cast about him, picked up a big rounded lump of rock, and flung it at one.

And then, slowly uncoiling their tentacles, they all began moving towards him—creeping at first deliberately, and making a soft, purring sound to each other.

In a moment Mr. Fison realised that he was in danger. He shouted again, threw both his boots, and started off, with a leap, forthwith. Twenty yards off he stopped and faced about, judging them slow, and, behold! the tentacles of their leader were already pouring over the rocky ridge on which he had just been standing!

At that he shouted again, but this time not threatening, but a cry of dismay, and began jumping, striding, slipping, wading across the uneven expanse between him the beach. The tall red cliffs seemed suddenly at a vast distance, and he saw, as though they were creatures in another world, two minute workmen engaged in the repair of the ladder-way, and little suspecting the race for life that was beginning below them. At one time he could hear the creatures splashing in the pools not a dozen feet behind him, and once he slipped and almost fell.

They chased him to the very foot of the cliffs, and desisted only when he had been joined by the workmen at the foot of the ladder-way up the cliff. All three of the men pelted them with stones for a time, and then hurried to the cliff top and along the path towards Sidmouth, to secure assistance and a boat, and to rescue the desecrated body from the clutches of these abominable creatures.

## II

And, as if he had not already been in sufficient peril that day, Mr. Fison went with the boat to point out the exact spot of his adventure.

As the tide was down, it required a considerable detour to reach the spot, and when at last they came off the ladder-way, the mangled body had disappeared. The water was now running in, submerging first one slab of slimy rock and then another, and the four men in the boat—the workmen, that is, the boatman, and Mr. Fison—now turned their attention from the bearings off shore to the water beneath the keel.

At first they could see little below them, save a dark jungle of laminaria, with an occasional darting fish. Their minds were set on adventure, and they expressed their disappointment freely. But presently they saw one of the monsters swimming through the water seaward, with a curious rolling motion that suggested to Mr. Fison the spinning roll of a captive balloon. Almost immediately after, the waving streamers of laminaria were extraordinarily perturbed, parted for a moment, and three of these beasts became darkly visible, struggling for what was probably some fragment of the drowned man. In a moment the copious olive-green ribbons had poured again over this writhing group.

At that all four men, greatly excited, began beating the water with oars and shouting, and immediately they saw a tumultuous movement among the weeds. They desisted, to see more clearly, and as soon as the water was smooth, they saw, as it seemed to them, the whole sea bottom among the weeds set with eyes.

"Ugly swine!" cried one of the men. "Why there's dozens!"

And forthwith the things began to rise through the water about them. Mr. Fison has since described to the writer this startling eruption out of the waving laminaria meadows. To him it seemed to occupy a considerable time, but it is probable that really it was an affair of a few seconds only. For a time nothing but eyes, and then he speaks of tentacles streaming out and parting the weed fronds this way and that. Then these things, growing larger, until at last the bottom was hidden by their intercoiling forms, and the tips of tentacles rose darkly here and there into the air above the swell of the waters.

One came up boldly to the side of the boat, and, clinging to this with three of its sucker-set tentacles, threw four others over the gunwale, as if with an intention either of oversetting the boat or of clambering into it. Mr. Fison at once caught up the boathook, and, jabbing furiously at the soft tentacles, forced it to desist. He was struck in the back and almost pitched overboard by the boatman, who was using his oar to resist a similar attack on the other side of the boat. But the tentacles on either side at once relaxed their hold at this, slid out of sight, and splashed into the water.

"We'd better get out of this," said Mr. Fison, who was trembling violently. He went to the tiller, while the boatman and one of the workmen seated themselves and began rowing. The other workman stood up in the fore part of the boat, with the boathook, ready to strike any more tentacles that might appear. Nothing else seems to have been said. Mr. Fison had expressed the common feeling beyond amendment. In a hushed, scared mood, with faces white and drawn, they set about escaping from the position into which they had so recklessly blundered.

But the oars had scarcely dropped into the water before dark, tapering, serpentine ropes had bound them, and were about the rudder; and creeping up the sides of the boat with a looping motion came the suckers again. The men gripped their oars and pulled, but it was like trying to move a boat in a floating raft of weeds. "Help here!" cried the boatman, and Mr. Fison and the second workman rushed to help lug at the oar.

Then the man with the boathook—his name was Ewan, or Ewen—sprang up with a curse, and began striking downward over the side, as far as he could reach, at the bank of tentacles that now clustered along the boat's bottom. And, at the same time, the two rowers stood up to get a better purchase for the recovery of their oars. The boatman handed his to Mr. Fison, who lugged desperately, and, meanwhile, the boatman opened a big clasp-knife, and, leaning over the side of the boat, began hacking at the spiring arms upon the oar shaft.

Mr. Fison, staggering with the quivering rocking of the boat, his teeth set, his breath coming short, and the veins starting on his hands as he pulled at his oar, suddenly cast his eyes seaward. And there, not fifty yards off, across the long rollers of the incoming tide, was a large boat standing in towards them, with three women and a little child in it. A boatman was rowing, and a little man in a pink-ribboned straw hat and whites stood in the stern, hailing them. For a moment, of course, Mr. Fison thought of help, and then he thought of the child. He abandoned his oar forthwith, threw up his arms in a frantic gesture, and screamed to the party in the boat to keep away "for God's sake!" It says much for the modesty and courage of Mr. Fison that he does not seem to be aware that there was any quality of heroism in his action at this juncture. The oar he had abandoned was at once drawn under, and presently reappeared floating about twenty yards away.

At the same moment Mr. Fison felt the boat under him lurch violently, and a hoarse scream, a prolonged cry of terror from Hill, the boatman, caused him to forget the party of excursionists altogether. He turned, and saw Hill crouching by the forward rowlock, his face convulsed with terror, and his right arm over the side drawn tightly down. He gave now a succession of short, sharp cries, "Oh! oh! oh!—oh!" Mr. Fison believes that he must have been hacking at the tentacles below the water-line, and have been grasped by them, but, of course, it is quite impossible to say now certainly what had happened. The boat was heeling over, so that the gunwale was within ten inches of the water, and both Ewan and the other labourer were striking down into the water, with oar and boathook, on either side of Hill's arm. Mr. Fison instinctively placed himself to counterpoise them.

Then Hill, who was a burly, powerful man, made a strenuous effort, and rose almost to a standing position. He lifted his arm, indeed, clean out of the water. Hanging to it was a complicated tangle of brown ropes; and the eyes of one of the brutes that had hold of him, glaring straight and resolute, showed momentarily above the surface. The boat heeled more and more, and the green-brown water came pouring in a cascade over the side. Then Hill slipped and fell with his ribs across the side, and his arm and the mass of tentacles about it splashed back into the water. He rolled over; his boot kicked Mr.

Fison's knee as that gentleman rushed forward to seize him, and in another moment fresh tentacles had whipped about his waist and neck, and after a brief, convulsive struggle, in which the boat was nearly capsized, Hill was lugged overboard. The boat righted with a violent jerk that all but sent Mr. Fison over the other side, and hid the struggle in the water from his eyes.

He stood staggering to recover his balance for a moment, and as he did so, he became aware that the struggle and the inflowing tide had carried them close upon the weedy rocks again. Not four yards off a table of rock still rose in rhythmic movements above the in-wash of the tide. In a moment Mr. Fison seized the oar from Ewan, gave one vigorous stroke, then, dropping it, ran to the bow and leapt. He felt his feet slide over the rock, and, by a frantic effort, leapt again towards a further mass. He stumbled over this, came to his knees, and rose again.

"Look out!" cried some one, and a large drab body struck him. He was knocked flat into a tidal pool by one of the workmen, and as he went down he heard smothered, choking cries, that he believed at the time came from Hill. Then he found himself marvelling at the shrillness and variety of Hill's voice. Some one jumped over him, and a curving rush of foamy water poured over him, and passed. He scrambled to his feet, dripping, and, without looking seaward, ran as fast as his terror would let him shoreward. Before him, over the flat space of scattered rocks, stumbled the two workmen—one a dozen yards in front of the other.

He looked over his shoulder at last, and, seeing that he was not pursued, faced about. He was astonished. From the moment of the rising of the cephalopods out of the water, he had been acting too swiftly to fully comprehend his actions. Now it seemed to him as if he had suddenly jumped out of an evil dream.

For there were the sky, cloudless and blazing with the afternoon sun, the sea, weltering under its pitiless brightness, the soft creamy foam of the breaking water, and the low, long, dark ridges of rock. The righted boat floated, rising and falling gently on the swell about a dozen yards from shore. Hill and the monsters, all the stress and tumult of that fierce fight for life, had vanished as though they had never been.

Mr. Fison's heart was beating violently; he was throbbing to the finger-tips, and his breath came deep.

There was something missing. For some seconds he could not think clearly enough what this might be. Sun, sky, sea, rocks—what was it? Then he remembered the boatload of excursionists. It had vanished. He wondered whether he had imagined it. He turned, and saw the two workmen standing side by side under the projecting masses of the tall pink cliffs. He hesitated whether he should make one last attempt to save the man Hill. His physical excitement seemed to desert him suddenly, and leave him aimless and helpless. He turned shoreward, stumbling and wading towards his two companions.

He looked back again, and there were now two boats floating, and the one farthest out at sea pitched clumsily, bottom upward.

## III

So it was *Haploteuthis ferox* made its appearance upon the Devonshire coast. So far, this has been its most serious aggression. Mr. Fison's account, taken together with the wave of boating and bathing casualties to which I have already alluded, and the absence of fish from the Cornish coasts that year, points clearly to a shoal of these voracious deep-sea monsters prowling slowly along the sub-tidal coastline. Hunger migration has, I know, been suggested as the force that drove them hither; but, for my own part, I prefer to believe the alternative theory of Hemsley. Hemsley holds that a pack or shoal of these creatures may have become enamoured of human flesh by the accident of a foundered ship sinking among them, and have wandered in search of it out of their accustomed zone; first waylaying and following ships, and so coming to our shores in the wake of the Atlantic traffic. But to discuss Hemsley's cogent and admirably-stated arguments would be out of place here.

It would seem that the appetites of the shoal were satisfied by the catch of eleven people—for so far as can be ascertained, there were ten people in the second boat, and certainly these creatures gave no further signs of their presence off Sidmouth that day. The coast between Seaton and Budleigh Salterton was patrolled all that evening and night by four Preventive Service boats, the men in which were armed with harpoons and cutlasses, and as the evening advanced, a number of more or less similarly equipped expeditions, organised by private individuals, joined them. Mr. Fison took no part in any of these expeditions.

About midnight excited hails were heard from a boat about a couple of miles out at sea to the south-east of Sidmouth, and a lantern was seen waving in a strange manner to and fro and up and down. The nearer boats at once hurried towards the alarm. The venturesome occupants of the boat, a seaman, a curate, and two schoolboys, had actually seen the monsters passing under their boat. The creatures, it seems, like most deep-sea organisms, were phosphorescent, and they had been floating, five fathoms deep or so, like creatures of moonshine through the blackness of the water, their tentacles retracted and as if asleep, rolling over and over, and moving slowly in a wedge-like formation towards the south-east.

These people told their story in gesticulated fragments, as first one boat drew alongside and then another. At last there was a little fleet of eight or nine boats collected together, and from them a tumult, like the chatter of a marketplace, rose into the stillness of the night. There was little or no disposition to pursue the shoal, the people had neither weapons nor experience for such a dubious chase, and presently—even with a certain relief, it may be—the boats turned shoreward.

And now to tell what is perhaps the most astonishing fact in this whole astonishing raid. We have not the slightest knowledge of the subsequent movements of the shoal, although the whole southwest coast was now alert for it. But it may, perhaps, be significant that a cachalot was stranded off Sark on June 3. Two weeks and three days after this Sidmouth affair, a living *Haploteuthis* came ashore on Calais sands. It was alive, because several witnesses saw its tentacles moving in a convulsive way. But it is probable that it was dying. A gentleman named Pouchet obtained a rifle and shot it.

That was the last appearance of a living *Haploteuthis*. No others were seen on the French coast. On the 15th of June a dead body, almost complete, was washed ashore near Torquay, and a few days later a boat from the Marine Biological station, engaged in dredging off Plymouth, picked up a rotting specimen, slashed deeply with a cutlass wound. How the former specimen had come by its death it is impossible to say. And on the last day of June, Mr. Egbert Caine, an artist, bathing near Newlyn, threw up his arms, shrieked, and was drawn under. A friend bathing with him made no attempt to save him, but swam at once for the shore. This is the last fact to tell of this extraordinary raid from the deeper sea. Whether it is really the last of these horrible creatures it is, as yet, premature to say. But it is believed, and certainly it is to be hoped, that they have returned now, and returned for good, to the sunless depths of the middle seas, out of which they have so strangely and so mysteriously arisen.

# FILMER

In truth the mastery of flying was the work of thousands of men—this man a suggestion and that an experiment, until at last only one vigorous intellectual effort was needed to finish the work. But the inexorable injustice of the popular mind has decided that of all these thousands, one man, and that a man who never flew, should be chosen as the discoverer, just as it has chosen to honour Watt as the discoverer of steam and Stephenson of the steam-engine. And surely of all honoured names none is so grotesquely and tragically honoured as poor Filmer's, the timid, intellectual creature who solved the problem over which the world had hung perplexed and a little fearful for so many generations, the man who pressed the button that has changed peace and warfare and well-nigh every condition of human life and happiness. Never has that recurring wonder of the littleness of the scientific man in the face of the greatness of his science found such an amazing exemplification. Much concerning Filmer is, and must remain, profoundly obscure—Filmers attract no Boswells—but the essential facts and the concluding scene are clear enough, and there are letters, and notes, and casual allusions to piece the whole together. And this is the story one makes, putting this thing with that, of Filmer's life and death.

The first authentic trace of Filmer on the page of history is a document in which he applies for admission as a paid student in physics to the Government laboratories at South Kensington, and therein he describes himself as the son of a "military bootmaker" ("cobbler" in the vulgar tongue) of Dover, and lists his various examination proofs of a high proficiency in chemistry and mathematics.

With a certain want of dignity he seeks to enhance these attainments by a profession of poverty and disadvantages, and he writes of the laboratory as the "gaol" of his ambitions, a slip which reinforces his claim to have devoted himself exclusively to the exact sciences. The document is endorsed in a manner that shows Filmer was admitted to this coveted opportunity; but until quite recently no traces of his success in the Government institution could be found.

It has now, however, been shown that in spite of his professed zeal for research, Filmer, before he had held this scholarship a year, was tempted, by the possibility of a small increase in his immediate income, to abandon it in order to become one of the nine-pence-an-hour computers employed by a well-known Professor in his vicarious conduct of those extensive researches of his in solar physics—researches which are still a matter of perplexity to astronomers. Afterwards, for the space of seven years, save for the pass lists of the London University, in which he is seen to climb slowly to a double first class B.Sc., in mathematics and chemistry, there is no evidence of how Filmer passed his life. No one knows how or where he lived, though it seems highly probable that he continued to support himself by teaching while he prosecuted the studies necessary for this distinction. And then, oddly enough, one finds him mentioned in the correspondence of Arthur Hicks, the poet.

"You remember Filmer," Hicks writes to his friend Vance; "well, *he* hasn't altered a bit, the same hostile mumble and the nasty chin—how *can* a man contrive to be always three days from shaving?—and a sort of furtive air of being engaged in sneaking in front of one; even his coat and that frayed collar of his show no further signs of the passing years. He was writing in the library and I sat down beside him in the name of God's charity, whereupon he deliberately insulted me by covering up his memoranda. It seems he has some brilliant research on hand that he suspects me of all people—with a Bodley Booklet a-printing!—of stealing. He has taken remarkable honours at the University—he went through them with a sort of hasty slobber, as though he feared I might interrupt him before he had told me all—and he spoke of taking his D.Sc. as one might speak of taking a cab. And he asked what I was doing—with a sort of comparative accent, and his arm was spread nervously, positively a protecting arm, over the paper that hid the precious idea—his one hopeful idea.

"'Poetry,' he said, 'poetry. And what do you profess to teach in it, Hicks?'

"The thing's a provincial professorling in the very act of budding, and I thank the Lord devoutly that but for the precious gift of indolence I also might have gone this way to D.Sc. and destruction . . ."

A curious little vignette that I am inclined to think caught Filmer in or near the very birth of his discovery.

Hicks was wrong in anticipating a provincial professorship for Filmer. Our next glimpse of him is lecturing on "rubber and rubber substitutes," to the Society of Arts—he had become manager to a great plastic-substance manufactory—and at that time, it is now known, he was a member of the Aeronautical Society, albeit he contributed nothing to the discussions of that body, preferring no doubt to mature his great conception without external assistance. And within two years of that paper before the Society of Arts he was hastily taking out a number of patents and proclaiming in various undignified ways the completion of the divergent inquiries which made his flying machine possible. The first definite statement to that effect appeared in a halfpenny evening paper through the agency of a man who lodged in the same house with Filmer. His final haste after his long laborious secret patience seems to have been due to a needless panic, Bootle, the notorious American scientific quack, having made an announcement that Filmer interpreted wrongly as an anticipation of his idea.

Now what precisely was Filmer's idea? Really a very simple one. Before his time the pursuit of aeronautics had taken two divergent lines, and had developed on the one hand balloons—large apparatus lighter than air, easy in ascent, and comparatively safe in descent, but floating helplessly before any breeze that took them; and on the other, flying machines that flew only in theory—vast flat structures heavier than air, propelled and kept up by heavy engines and for the most part smashing at the first descent. But, neglecting the fact that the inevitable final collapse rendered them impossible, the weight of the flying machines gave them this theoretical advantage, that they could go through the air against a wind, a necessary condition if aerial navigation was to have any practical value. It is Filmer's particular merit that he perceived the way in which the contrasted and hitherto incompatible merits of balloon and heavy flying machine might be combined in one apparatus, which should be at choice either heavier or lighter than air. He took hints from the contractile bladders of fish and the pneumatic cavities of birds. He devised an arrangement of contractile and absolutely closed balloons which when expanded could lift the actual flying apparatus with ease, and when retracted by the complicated "musculature" he wove about them, were withdrawn almost completely into the frame; and he built the large framework which these balloons sustained, of hollow, rigid tubes, the air in which, by an ingenious contrivance, was automatically pumped out as the apparatus fell, and which then remained exhausted so long as the aeronaut desired. There were no wings or propellers to his machine, such as there had been to all previous aeroplanes, and the only engine required was the compact and powerful little appliance needed to contract the balloons. He perceived that such an apparatus as he had devised might rise with frame exhausted and balloons expanded to a considerable height, might then contract its balloons and let the air into its frame, and by an adjustment of its weights slide down the air in any desired direction. As it fell it would accumulate velocity and at the same time lose weight, and the momentum accumulated by its down-rush could be utilised by means of a shifting of its weights to drive it up in the air again as the balloons expanded. This conception, which is still the structural conception of all successful flying machines, needed, however, a vast amount of toil upon its details before it could actually be realised, and such toil Filmer—as he was accustomed to tell the numerous interviewers who crowded upon him in the heyday of his fame—"ungrudgingly and unsparingly gave." His particular difficulty was the elastic lining of the contractile balloon. He found he needed a new substance, and in the discovery and manufacture of that new substance he had, as he never failed to impress upon the interviewers, "performed a far more arduous work than even in the actual achievement of my seemingly greater discovery."

But it must not be imagined that these interviews followed hard upon Filmer's proclamation of his invention. An interval of nearly five years elapsed during which he timidly remained at his rubber factory—he seems to have been entirely dependent on his small income from this source—making misdirected attempts to assure a quite indifferent public that he really *had* invented what he had invented. He occupied the greater part of his leisure in the composition of letters to the scientific and daily press, and so forth, stating precisely the net result of his contrivances, and demanding financial aid. That alone would have sufficed for the suppression of his letters. He spent such holidays as he could arrange in unsatisfactory interviews with the doorkeepers of leading London papers—he was singularly not adapted for inspiring hall-porters with confidence—and he positively attempted to induce the War Office to take up his work with him. There remains a confidential letter from Major-General Volleyfire to the Earl of Frogs. "The man's a crank and a bounder to boot," says the Major-General in his bluff, sensible, army way, and so left it open for the Japanese to secure, as they subsequently did, the priority in this side of warfare—a priority they still to our great discomfort retain.

And then by a stroke of luck the membrane Filmer had invented for his contractile balloon was discovered to be useful for the valves of a new oil-engine, and he obtained the means for making a trial model of his invention. He threw up his rubber factory appointment, desisted from all further writing, and, with a certain secrecy that seems to have been an inseparable characteristic of all his proceedings, set to work upon the apparatus. He seems to have directed the making of its parts and collected most of it in a room in Shoreditch, but its final putting together was done at Dymchurch, in Kent. He did not make the affair large enough to carry a man, but he made an extremely ingenious use of what were then called the Marconi rays to control its flight. The first flight of this first practicable flying machine took place over some fields near Burford Bridge, near Hythe, in Kent, and Filmer followed and controlled its flight upon a specially constructed motor tricycle.

The flight was, considering all things, an amazing success. The apparatus was brought in a cart from Dymchurch to Burford Bridge, ascended there to a height of nearly three hundred feet, swooped thence very nearly back to Dymchurch, came about in its sweep, rose again, circled, and finally sank uninjured in a field behind the Burford Bridge Inn. At its descent a curious thing happened. Filmer got off his tricycle, scrambled over the intervening dyke, advanced perhaps twenty yards towards his triumph, threw out his arms in a strange gesticulation, and fell down in a dead faint. Every one could then recall the ghastliness of his features and all the evidences of extreme excitement they had observed throughout the trial, things they might otherwise have forgotten. Afterwards in the inn he had an unaccountable gust of hysterical weeping.

Altogether there were not twenty witnesses of this affair, and those for the most part uneducated men. The New Romney doctor saw the ascent but not the descent, his horse being frightened by the electrical apparatus on Filmer's tricycle and giving him a nasty spill. Two members of the Kent constabulary watched the affair from a cart in an unofficial spirit, and a grocer calling round the Marsh for orders and two lady cyclists seem almost to complete the list of educated people. There were two reporters present, one representing a Folkstone paper and the other being a fourth-class interviewer and "symposium" journalist, whose expenses down, Filmer, anxious as ever for adequate advertisement—and now quite realising the way in which adequate advertisement may be obtained—had paid. The latter was one of those writers who can throw a convincing air of unreality over the most credible events, and his half-facetious account of the affair appeared in the magazine page of a popular journal. But, happily for Filmer, this person's colloquial methods were more convincing. He went to offer some further screed upon the subject to Banghurst, the proprietor of the *New Paper,* and one of the ablest and most unscrupulous men in London journalism, and Banghurst instantly seized upon the situation. The interviewer vanishes from the narrative, no doubt very doubtfully remunerated, and Banghurst, Banghurst himself, double chin, grey twill suit, abdomen, voice, gestures and all, appears at Dymchurch, following his large, unrivalled journalistic nose. He had seen the whole thing at a glance, just what it was and what it might be.

At his touch, as it were, Filmer's long-pent investigations exploded into fame. He instantly and most magnificently was a Boom. One turns over the files of the journals of the year 1907 with a quite incredulous recognition of how swift and flaming the boom of those days could be. The July papers know nothing of flying, see nothing in flying, state by a most effective silence that men never would, could or should fly. In August flying and Filmer and flying and parachutes and aerial tactics and the Japanese Government and Filmer and again flying, shouldered the war in Yunnan and the gold mines of Upper Greenland off the leading page. And Banghurst had given ten thousand pounds, and, further, Banghurst was giving five thousand pounds, and Banghurst had devoted his well-known, magnificent (but hitherto sterile) private laboratories and several acres of land near his private residence on the Surrey hills to the strenuous and violent completion—Banghurst fashion—of the life-size practicable flying machine. Meanwhile, in the sight of privileged multitudes in the walled-garden of the Banghurst town residence in Fulham, Filmer was exhibited at weekly garden parties putting the working model through its paces. At enormous initial cost, but with a final profit, the *New Paper* presented its readers with a beautiful photographic souvenir of the first of these occasions.

Here again the correspondence of Arthur Hicks and his friend Vance comes to our aid.

"I saw Filmer in his glory," he writes, with just the touch of envy natural to his position as a poet *passé*. "The man is brushed and shaved, dressed in the fashion of a Royal-Institution-Afternoon Lecturer, the very newest shape in frock-coats and long patent shoes, and altogether in a state of extraordinary streakiness between an owlish great man and a scared abashed self-conscious bounder cruelly exposed. He hasn't a touch of colour in the skin of his face, his head juts forward, and those queer little dark amber eyes of his watch furtively round him for his fame. His clothes fit perfectly and yet sit upon him as though he had bought them ready-made. He speaks in a mumble still, but he says, you perceive indistinctly, enormous self-assertive things, he backs into the rear of groups by instinct if Banghurst drops the line for a minute, and when he walks across Banghurst's lawn one perceives him a little out of breath and going jerky, and that his weak white hands are clenched. His is a state of tension—horrible tension. And he is the Greatest Discoverer of This or Any Age—the Greatest Discoverer of This or Any Age! What strikes one so forcibly about him is that he didn't somehow quite expect it ever, at any rate, not at all like this. Banghurst is about everywhere, the energetic M.C. of his great little catch, and I swear he will have every one down on his lawn there before he has finished with the engine; he had bagged the prime minister yesterday, and he, bless his heart! didn't look particularly outsize, on the very first occasion. Conceive it! Filmer! Our obscure unwashed Filmer, the Glory of British science! Duchesses crowd upon him, beautiful, bold peeresses say in their beautiful, clear loud voices—have you noticed how penetrating the great lady is becoming nowadays?—'Oh, Mr. Filmer, how *did* you do it?'

"Common men on the edge of things are too remote for the answer. One imagines something in the way of that interview, 'toil ungrudgingly and unsparingly given, Madam, and, perhaps—I don't know—but perhaps a little special aptitude.'"

So far Hicks and the photographic supplement to the *New Paper* are in sufficient harmony with the description. In one picture the machine swings down towards the river, and the tower of Fulham church appears below it through a gap in the elms, and in another, Filmer sits at his guiding batteries, and the great and beautiful of the earth stand around him, with Banghurst massed modestly but resolutely in the rear. The grouping is oddly apposite. Occluding much of Banghurst, and looking with a pensive, speculative expression at Filmer, stands the Lady Mary Elkinghorn, still beautiful, in spite of the breath of scandal and her eight-and-thirty years, the only person whose face does not admit a perception of the camera that was in the act of snapping them all.

So much for the exterior facts of the story, but, after all, they are very exterior facts. About the real interest of the business one is necessarily very much in the dark. How was Filmer feeling at the time? How much was a certain unpleasant anticipation present inside that very new and fashionable frock-coat? He was in the half-penny, penny, six-penny, and more expensive papers alike, and acknowledged by the whole world as "the Greatest Discoverer of This or Any Age." He had invented a practicable flying machine, and every day down among the Surrey hills the life-sized model was getting ready. And when it was ready, it followed as a clear inevitable consequence of his having invented and made it—everybody in the world, indeed, seemed to take it for granted; there wasn't a gap anywhere in that serried front of anticipation—that he would proudly and cheerfully get aboard it, ascend with it, and fly.

But we know now pretty clearly that simple pride and cheerfulness in such an act were singularly out of harmony with Filmer's private constitution. It occurred to no one at the time, but there the fact is. We can guess with some confidence now that it must have been drifting about in his mind a great deal during the day, and, from a little note to his physician complaining of persistent insomnia, we have the soundest reason for supposing it dominated his nights—the idea that it would be after all, in spite of his theoretical security, an abominably sickening, uncomfortable, and dangerous thing for him to flap about in nothingness a thousand feet or so in the air. It must have dawned upon him quite early in the period of being the Greatest Discoverer of This or Any Age, the vision of doing this and that with an extensive void below. Perhaps somewhen in his youth he had looked down a great height or fallen down in some excessively uncomfortable way; perhaps some habit of sleeping on the wrong side had resulted in that disagreeable falling nightmare one knows, and given him his horror; of the strength of that horror there remains now not a particle of doubt.

Apparently he had never weighed this duty of flying in his earlier days of research; the machine had been his end, but now things were opening out beyond his end, and particularly this giddy whirl up above there. He was a Discoverer and he had Discovered. But he was not a Flying Man, and it was only now that he was beginning to perceive clearly that he was expected to fly. Yet, however much the thing was present in his mind he gave no expression to it until the very end, and meanwhile he went to and fro from Banghurst's magnificent laboratories, and was interviewed and lionised, and wore good clothes, and ate good food, and lived in an elegant flat, enjoying a very abundant feast of such good, coarse, wholesome Fame and Success as a man, starved for all his years as he had been starved, might be reasonably expected to enjoy.

After a time, the weekly gatherings in Fulham ceased. The model had failed one day just for a moment to respond to Filmer's guidance, or he had been distracted by the compliments of an archbishop. At any rate, it suddenly dug its nose into the air just a little too steeply as the archbishop was sailing through a Latin quotation for all the world like an archbishop in a book, and it came down in the Fulham Road within three yards of a 'bus horse. It stood for a second perhaps, astonishing and in its attitude astonished, then it crumpled, shivered into pieces, and the 'bus horse was incidentally killed.

Filmer lost the end of the archiepiscopal compliment. He stood up and stared as his invention swooped out of sight and reach of him. His long, white hands still gripped his useless apparatus. The archbishop followed his skyward stare with an apprehension unbecoming in an archbishop.

Then came the crash and the shouts and uproar from the road to relieve Filmer's tension. "My God!" he whispered, and sat down.

Every one else almost was staring to see where the machine had vanished, or rushing into the house.

The making of the big machine progressed all the more rapidly for this. Over its making presided Filmer, always a little slow and very careful in his manner, always with a growing preoccupation in his mind. His care over the strength and soundness of the apparatus was prodigious. The slightest doubt, and he delayed everything until the doubtful part could be replaced. Wilkinson, his senior assistant, fumed at some of these delays, which, he insisted, were for the most part unnecessary. Banghurst magnified the patient certitude of Filmer in the *New Paper,* and reviled it bitterly to his wife, and MacAndrew, the second assistant, approved Filmer's wisdom. "We're not wanting a *fiasco,* man," said MacAndrew. "He's perfectly well advised."

And whenever an opportunity arose Filmer would expound to Wilkinson and MacAndrew just exactly how every part of the flying machine was to be controlled and worked, so that in effect they would be just as capable, and even more capable, when at last the time came, of guiding it through the skies.

Now I should imagine that if Filmer had seen fit at this stage to define just what he was feeling, and to take a definite line in the matter of his ascent, he might have escaped that painful ordeal quite easily. If he had had it clearly in his mind he could have done endless things. He would surely have found no difficulty with a specialist to demonstrate a weak heart, or something gastric or pulmonary, to stand in his way—that is the line I am astonished he did not take,—or he might, had he been man enough, have declared simply and finally that he did not intend to do the thing. But the fact is, though the dread was hugely present in his mind, the thing was by no means sharp and clear. I fancy that all through this period he kept telling himself that when the occasion came he would find himself equal to it. He was like a man just gripped by a great illness, who says he feels a little out of sorts, and expects to be better presently. Meanwhile he delayed the completion of the machine, and let the assumption that he was going to fly it take root and flourish exceedingly about him. He even accepted anticipatory compliments on his courage. And, barring this secret squeamishness, there can be no doubt he found all the praise and distinction and fuss he got a delightful and even intoxicating draught.

The Lady Mary Elkinghorn made things a little more complicated for him.

How *that* began was a subject of inexhaustible speculation to Hicks. Probably in the beginning she was just a little "nice" to him with that impartial partiality of hers, and it may be that to her eyes, standing out conspicuously as he did ruling his monster in the upper air, he had a distinction that Hicks was not disposed to find. And somehow they must have had a moment of sufficient isolation, and the great Discoverer a moment of sufficient courage for something just a little personal to be mumbled or blurted. However it began, there is no doubt that it did begin, and presently became quite perceptible to a world accustomed to find in the proceedings of the Lady Mary Elkinghorn a matter of entertainment. It complicated things, because the state of love in such a virgin mind as Filmer's would brace his resolution, if not sufficiently, at any rate considerably, towards facing a danger he feared, and hampered him in such attempts at evasion as would otherwise be natural and congenial.

It remains a matter for speculation just how the Lady Mary felt for Filmer and just what she thought of him. At thirty-eight one may have gathered much wisdom and still be not altogether wise, and the imagination still functions actively enough in creating glamours and effecting the impossible. He came before her eyes as a very central man, and that always counts, and he had powers, unique powers as it seemed, at any rate in the air. The performance with the model had just a touch of the quality of a potent incantation, and women have ever displayed an unreasonable disposition to imagine that when a man has powers he must necessarily have Power. Given so much, and what was not good in Filmer's manner and appearance became an added merit. He was modest, he hated display, but given an occasion where *true* qualities are needed, then—then one would see!

The late Mrs. Bampton thought it wise to convey to Lady Mary her opinion that Filmer, all things considered, was rather a "grub." "He's certainly not a sort of man I have ever met before," said the Lady Mary, with a quite unruffled serenity. And Mrs. Bampton, after a swift, imperceptible glance at that serenity, decided that so far as saying anything to Lady Mary went, she had done as much as could be expected of her. But she said a great deal to other people.

And at last, without any undue haste or unseemliness, the day dawned, the great day, when Banghurst had promised his public—the world in fact—that flying should be finally attained and overcome. Filmer saw it dawn, watched even in the darkness before it dawned, watched its stars fade and the grey and pearly pinks give place at last to the clear blue sky of a sunny, cloudless day. He watched it from the window of his bedroom in the new-built wing of Banghurst's Tudor house. And as the stars were overwhelmed and the shapes and substances of things grew into being out of the amorphous dark, he must have seen more and more distinctly the festive preparations beyond the beech clumps near the green pavilion in the outer park, the three stands for the privileged spectators, the raw new fencing of the enclosure, the sheds and workshops, the Venetian masts and fluttering flags that Banghurst had considered essential, black and limp in the breezeless dawn, and amidst all these things a great shape covered with tarpaulin. A strange and terrible portent for humanity was that shape, a beginning that must surely spread and widen and change and dominate all the affairs of men, but to Filmer it is very doubtful whether it appeared in anything but a narrow and personal light. Several people heard him pacing in the small hours—for the vast place was packed with guests by a proprietor editor who, before all things, understood compression. And about five o'clock, if not before, Filmer left his room and wandered out of the sleeping house into the park, alive by that time with sunlight and birds and squirrels and the fallow deer. MacAndrew, who was also an early riser, met him near the machine, and they went and had a look at it together.

It is doubtful if Filmer took any breakfast, in spite of the urgency of Banghurst. So soon as the guests began to be about in some number he seems to have retreated to his room. Thence about ten he went into the shrubbery, very probably because he had seen the Lady Mary Elkinghorn there. She was walking up and down, engaged in conversation with her old school friend, Mrs. Brewis-Craven, and although Filmer had never met the latter lady before, he joined them and walked beside them for some time. There were several silences in spite of the Lady Mary's brilliance. The situation was a difficult one, and Mrs. Brewis-Craven did not master its difficulty. "He struck me," she said afterwards with a luminous self-contradiction, "as a very unhappy person who had something to say, and wanted before all things to be helped to say it. But how was one to help him when one didn't know what it was?"

At half-past eleven the enclosures for the public in the outer park were crammed, there was an intermittent stream of equipages along the belt which circles the outer park, and the house party was dotted over the lawn and shrubbery and the corner of the inner park, in a series of brilliantly attired knots, all making for the flying machine. Filmer walked in a group of three with Banghurst, who was supremely and conspicuously happy, and Sir Theodore Hickle, the president of the Aeronautical Society. Mrs. Banghurst was close behind with the Lady Mary Elkinghorn, Georgina Hickle, and the Dean of Stays. Banghurst was large and copious in speech, and such interstices as he left were filled in by Hickle with complimentary remarks to Filmer. And Filmer walked between them saying not a word except by way of unavoidable reply. Behind, Mrs. Banghurst listened to the admirably suitable and shapely conversation of the Dean with that fluttered attention to the ampler clergy ten years of social ascent and ascendency had not cured in her; and the Lady Mary watched, no doubt with an entire confidence in the world's disillusionment, the drooping shoulders of the sort of man she had never met before.

There was some cheering as the central party came into view of the enclosures, but it was not very unanimous nor invigorating cheering. They were within fifty yards of the apparatus when Filmer took a hasty glance over his shoulder to measure the distance of the ladies behind them, and decided to make the first remark he had initiated since the house had been left. His voice was just a little hoarse, and he cut in on Banghurst in mid-sentence on Progress.

"I say, Banghurst," he said, and stopped.

"Yes," said Banghurst.

"I wish——" He moistened his lips. "I'm not feeling well."

Banghurst stopped dead. "Eh?" he shouted.

"A queer feeling." Filmer made to move on, but Banghurst was immovable. "I don't know. I may be better in a minute. If not—perhaps . . . MacAndrew——"

"You're not feeling *well?*" said Banghurst, and stared at his white face.

"My dear!" he said, as Mrs. Banghurst came up with them, "Filmer says he isn't feeling *well.*"

"A little queer," exclaimed Filmer, avoiding the Lady Mary's eyes. "It may pass off——"

There was a pause.

It came to Filmer that he was the most isolated person in the world.

"In any case," said Banghurst, "the ascent must be made. Perhaps if you were to sit down somewhere for a moment——"

"It's the crowd, I think," said Filmer.

There was a second pause. Banghurst's eye rested in scrutiny on Filmer, and then swept the sample of public in the enclosure.

"It's unfortunate," said Sir Theodore Hickle; "but still—I suppose ——Your assistants——Of course, if you feel out of condition and disinclined——"

"I don't think Mr. Filmer would permit *that* for a moment," said the Lady Mary.

"But, if Mr. Filmer's nerve is run——It might even be dangerous for him to attempt——" Hickle coughed.

"It's just because it's dangerous," began the Lady Mary, and felt she had made her point of view and Filmer's plain enough.

Conflicting motives struggled for Filmer.

"I feel I ought to go up," he said, regarding the ground. He looked up and met the Lady Mary's eyes. "I want to go up," he said, and smiled whitely at her. He turned towards Banghurst. "If I could just sit down somewhere for a moment out of the crowd and sun——"

Banghurst, at least, was beginning to understand the case. "Come into my little room in the green pavilion," he said. "It's quite cool there." He took Filmer by the arm.

Filmer turned his face to the Lady Mary Elkinghorn again. "I shall be all right in five minutes," he said. "I'm tremendously sorry——"

The Lady Mary Elkinghorn smiled at him. "I couldn't think——" he said to Hickle, and obeyed the compulsion of Banghurst's pull.

The rest remained watching the two recede.

"He is so fragile," said the Lady Mary.

"He's certainly a highly nervous type," said the Dean, whose weakness it was to regard the whole world, except married clergymen with enormous families, as "neurotic."

"Of course," said Hickle, "it isn't absolutely necessary for him to go up because he has invented——"

"How *could* he avoid it?" asked the Lady Mary, with the faintest shadow of scorn.

"It's certainly most unfortunate if he's going to be ill now," said Mrs. Banghurst a little severely.

"He's not going to be ill," said the Lady Mary, and certainly she had met Filmer's eye.

"*You'll* be all right," said Banghurst, as they went towards the pavilion. "All you want is a nip of brandy. It ought to be you, you know. You'll be–you'd get it rough, you know, if you let another man——"

"Oh, I want to go," said Filmer. "I shall be all right. As a matter of fact I'm almost inclined *now*——. No! I think I'll have that nip of brandy first."

Banghurst took him into the little room and routed out an empty decanter. He departed in search of a supply. He was gone perhaps five minutes.

The history of those five minutes cannot be written. At intervals Filmer's face could be seen by the people on the easternmost of the stands erected for spectators, against the window pane peering out, and then it would recede and fade. Banghurst vanished shouting behind the grand stand, and presently the butler appeared going pavilionward with a tray.

The apartment in which Filmer came to his last solution was a pleasant little room very simply furnished with green furniture and an old bureau—for Banghurst was simple in all his private ways. It was hung with little engravings after Morland and it had a shelf of books. But as it happened, Banghurst had left a rook rifle he sometimes played with on the top of the desk, and on the corner of the mantleshelf was a tin with three or four cartridges remaining in it. As Filmer went up and down that room wrestling with his intolerable dilemma he went first towards the neat little rifle athwart the blotting-pad and then towards the neat little red label

".22 LONG."

The thing must have jumped into his mind in a moment.

Nobody seems to have connected the report with him, though the gun, being fired in a confined space, must have sounded loud, and there were several people in the billiard-room, separated from him only by a lath-and-plaster partition. But directly Banghurst's butler opened the door and smelt the sour smell of the smoke, he knew, he says, what had happened. For the servants at least of Banghurst's household had guessed something of what was going on in Filmer's mind.

All through that trying afternoon Banghurst behaved as he held a man should behave in the presence of hopeless disaster, and his guests for the most part succeeded in not insisting upon the fact—though to conceal their perception of it altogether was impossible—that Banghurst had been pretty elaborately and completely swindled by the deceased. The public in the enclosure, Hicks told me, dispersed "like a party that has been ducking a welsher," and there wasn't a soul in the train to London, it seems, who hadn't known all along that flying was a quite impossible thing for man. "But he might have tried it," said many, "after carrying the thing so far."

In the evening, when he was comparatively alone, Banghurst broke down and went on like a man of clay. I have been told he wept, which must have made an imposing scene, and he certainly said Filmer had ruined his life, and offered and sold the whole apparatus to MacAndrew for half-a-crown. "I've been thinking——" said MacAndrew at the conclusion of the bargain, and stopped.

The next morning the name of Filmer was, for the first time, less conspicuous in the *New Paper* than in any other daily paper in the world. The rest of the world's instructors, with varying emphasis, according to their dignity and the degree of competition between themselves and the *New Paper,* proclaimed the "Entire Failure of the New Flying Machine," and "Suicide of the Impostor." But in the district of North Surrey the reception of the news was tempered by a perception of unusual aerial phenomena.

Overnight Wilkinson and MacAndrew had fallen into violent argument on the exact motives of their principal's rash act.

"The man was certainly a poor, cowardly body, but so far as his science went he was *no* impostor," said MacAndrew, "and I'm prepared to give that proposition a very practical demonstration, Mr. Wilkinson, so soon as we've got the place a little more to ourselves. For I've no faith in all this publicity for experimental trials."

And to that end, while all the world was reading of the certain failure of the new flying machine, MacAndrew was soaring and curvetting with great amplitude and dignity over the Epsom and Wimbledon divisions; and Banghurst, restored once more to hope and energy, and regardless of public security and the Board of Trade, was pursuing his gyrations and trying to attract his attention, on a motor car and in his pyjamas—he had caught sight of the ascent when pulling up the blind of his bedroom window—equipped, among other things, with a film camera that was subsequently discovered to be jammed.

And Filmer was lying on the billiard table in the green pavilion with a sheet about his body.

A CATALOG OF SELECTED

# DOVER BOOKS

IN ALL FIELDS OF INTEREST

# A CATALOG OF SELECTED DOVER BOOKS IN ALL FIELDS OF INTEREST

FRANK LLOYD WRIGHT'S DANA HOUSE, Donald Hoffmann. Pictorial essay of residential masterpiece with over 160 interior and exterior photos, plans, elevations, sketches and studies. 128pp. $9^1/_4$ x $10^3/_4$. 29120-0

THE MALE AND FEMALE FIGURE IN MOTION: 60 Classic Photographic Sequences, Eadweard Muybridge. 60 true-action photographs of men and women walking, running, climbing, bending, turning, etc., reproduced from rare 19th-century masterpiece. vi + 121pp. 9 x 12. 24745-7

1001 QUESTIONS ANSWERED ABOUT THE SEASHORE, N. J. Berrill and Jacquelyn Berrill. Queries answered about dolphins, sea snails, sponges, starfish, fishes, shore birds, many others. Covers appearance, breeding, growth, feeding, much more. 305pp. $5^1/_4$ x $8^1/_4$. 23366-9

ATTRACTING BIRDS TO YOUR YARD, William J. Weber. Easy-to-follow guide offers advice on how to attract the greatest diversity of birds: birdhouses, feeders, water and waterers, much more. 96pp. $5^3/_{16}$ x $8^1/_4$. 28927-3

MEDICINAL AND OTHER USES OF NORTH AMERICAN PLANTS: A Historical Survey with Special Reference to the Eastern Indian Tribes, Charlotte Erichsen-Brown. Chronological historical citations document 500 years of usage of plants, trees, shrubs native to eastern Canada, northeastern U.S. Also complete identifying information. 343 illustrations. 544pp. $6^1/_2$ x $9^1/_4$. 25951-X

STORYBOOK MAZES, Dave Phillips. 23 stories and mazes on two-page spreads: Wizard of Oz, Treasure Island, Robin Hood, etc. Solutions. 64pp. $8^1/_4$ x 11. 23628-5

AMERICAN NEGRO SONGS: 230 Folk Songs and Spirituals, Religious and Secular, John W. Work. This authoritative study traces the African influences of songs sung and played by black Americans at work, in church, and as entertainment. The author discusses the lyric significance of such songs as "Swing Low, Sweet Chariot," "John Henry," and others and offers the words and music for 230 songs. Bibliography. Index of Song Titles. 272pp. $6^1/_2$ x $9^1/_4$. 40271-1

MOVIE-STAR PORTRAITS OF THE FORTIES, John Kobal (ed.). 163 glamor, studio photos of 106 stars of the 1940s: Rita Hayworth, Ava Gardner, Marlon Brando, Clark Gable, many more. 176pp. $8^3/_8$ x $11^1/_4$. 23546-7

BENCHLEY LOST AND FOUND, Robert Benchley. Finest humor from early 30s, about pet peeves, child psychologists, post office and others. Mostly unavailable elsewhere. 73 illustrations by Peter Arno and others. 183pp. $5^3/_8$ x $8^1/_2$. 22410-4

YEKL and THE IMPORTED BRIDEGROOM AND OTHER STORIES OF YIDDISH NEW YORK, Abraham Cahan. Film Hester Street based on *Yekl* (1896). Novel, other stories among first about Jewish immigrants on N.Y.'s East Side. 240pp. $5^3/_8$ x $8^1/_2$. 22427-9

SELECTED POEMS, Walt Whitman. Generous sampling from *Leaves of Grass*. Twenty-four poems include "I Hear America Singing," "Song of the Open Road," "I Sing the Body Electric," "When Lilacs Last in the Dooryard Bloom'd," "O Captain! My Captain!"–all reprinted from an authoritative edition. Lists of titles and first lines. 128pp. $5^3/_{16}$ x $8^1/_4$. 26878-0

THE BEST TALES OF HOFFMANN, E. T. A. Hoffmann. 10 of Hoffmann's most important stories: "Nutcracker and the King of Mice," "The Golden Flowerpot," etc. 458pp. 5⅜ x 8½. 21793-0

FROM FETISH TO GOD IN ANCIENT EGYPT, E. A. Wallis Budge. Rich detailed survey of Egyptian conception of "God" and gods, magic, cult of animals, Osiris, more. Also, superb English translations of hymns and legends. 240 illustrations. 545pp. 5⅜ x 8½. 25803-3

FRENCH STORIES/CONTES FRANÇAIS: A Dual-Language Book, Wallace Fowlie. Ten stories by French masters, Voltaire to Camus: "Micromegas" by Voltaire; "The Atheist's Mass" by Balzac; "Minuet" by de Maupassant; "The Guest" by Camus, six more. Excellent English translations on facing pages. Also French-English vocabulary list, exercises, more. 352pp. 5⅜ x 8½. 26443-2

CHICAGO AT THE TURN OF THE CENTURY IN PHOTOGRAPHS: 122 Historic Views from the Collections of the Chicago Historical Society, Larry A. Viskochil. Rare large-format prints offer detailed views of City Hall, State Street, the Loop, Hull House, Union Station, many other landmarks, circa 1904-1913. Introduction. Captions. Maps. 144pp. 9⅜ x 12¼. 24656-6

OLD BROOKLYN IN EARLY PHOTOGRAPHS, 1865-1929, William Lee Younger. Luna Park, Gravesend race track, construction of Grand Army Plaza, moving of Hotel Brighton, etc. 157 previously unpublished photographs. 165pp. 8⅞ x 11¾. 23587-4

THE MYTHS OF THE NORTH AMERICAN INDIANS, Lewis Spence. Rich anthology of the myths and legends of the Algonquins, Iroquois, Pawnees and Sioux, prefaced by an extensive historical and ethnological commentary. 36 illustrations. 480pp. 5⅜ x 8½. 25967-6

AN ENCYCLOPEDIA OF BATTLES: Accounts of Over 1,560 Battles from 1479 B.C. to the Present, David Eggenberger. Essential details of every major battle in recorded history from the first battle of Megiddo in 1479 B.C. to Grenada in 1984. List of Battle Maps. New Appendix covering the years 1967-1984. Index. 99 illustrations. 544pp. 6½ x 9¼. 24913-1

SAILING ALONE AROUND THE WORLD, Captain Joshua Slocum. First man to sail around the world, alone, in small boat. One of great feats of seamanship told in delightful manner. 67 illustrations. 294pp. 5⅜ x 8½. 20326-3

ANARCHISM AND OTHER ESSAYS, Emma Goldman. Powerful, penetrating, prophetic essays on direct action, role of minorities, prison reform, puritan hypocrisy, violence, etc. 271pp. 5⅜ x 8½. 22484-8

MYTHS OF THE HINDUS AND BUDDHISTS, Ananda K. Coomaraswamy and Sister Nivedita. Great stories of the epics; deeds of Krishna, Shiva, taken from puranas, Vedas, folk tales; etc. 32 illustrations. 400pp. 5⅜ x 8½. 21759-0

THE TRAUMA OF BIRTH, Otto Rank. Rank's controversial thesis that anxiety neurosis is caused by profound psychological trauma which occurs at birth. 256pp. 5⅜ x 8½. 27974-X

A THEOLOGICO-POLITICAL TREATISE, Benedict Spinoza. Also contains unfinished Political Treatise. Great classic on religious liberty, theory of government on common consent. R. Elwes translation. Total of 421pp. 5⅜ x 8½. 20249-6

PIANO TUNING, J. Cree Fischer. Clearest, best book for beginner, amateur. Simple repairs, raising dropped notes, tuning by easy method of flattened fifths. No previous skills needed. 4 illustrations. 201pp. 5⅜ x 8½. 23267-0

HINTS TO SINGERS, Lillian Nordica. Selecting the right teacher, developing confidence, overcoming stage fright, and many other important skills receive thoughtful discussion in this indispensible guide, written by a world-famous diva of four decades' experience. 96pp. 5⅜ x 8½. 40094-8

THE COMPLETE NONSENSE OF EDWARD LEAR, Edward Lear. All nonsense limericks, zany alphabets, Owl and Pussycat, songs, nonsense botany, etc., illustrated by Lear. Total of 320pp. 5⅜ x 8½. (Available in U.S. only.) 20167-8

VICTORIAN PARLOUR POETRY: An Annotated Anthology, Michael R. Turner. 117 gems by Longfellow, Tennyson, Browning, many lesser-known poets. "The Village Blacksmith," "Curfew Must Not Ring Tonight," "Only a Baby Small," dozens more, often difficult to find elsewhere. Index of poets, titles, first lines. xxiii + 325pp. 5⅜ x 8¼. 27044-0

DUBLINERS, James Joyce. Fifteen stories offer vivid, tightly focused observations of the lives of Dublin's poorer classes. At least one, "The Dead," is considered a masterpiece. Reprinted complete and unabridged from standard edition. 160pp. 5$\frac{3}{16}$ x 8¼. 26870-5

GREAT WEIRD TALES: 14 Stories by Lovecraft, Blackwood, Machen and Others, S. T. Joshi (ed.). 14 spellbinding tales, including "The Sin Eater," by Fiona McLeod, "The Eye Above the Mantel," by Frank Belknap Long, as well as renowned works by R. H. Barlow, Lord Dunsany, Arthur Machen, W. C. Morrow and eight other masters of the genre. 256pp. 5⅜ x 8½. (Available in U.S. only.) 40436-6

THE BOOK OF THE SACRED MAGIC OF ABRAMELIN THE MAGE, translated by S. MacGregor Mathers. Medieval manuscript of ceremonial magic. Basic document in Aleister Crowley, Golden Dawn groups. 268pp. 5⅜ x 8½. 23211-5

NEW RUSSIAN-ENGLISH AND ENGLISH-RUSSIAN DICTIONARY, M. A. O'Brien. This is a remarkably handy Russian dictionary, containing a surprising amount of information, including over 70,000 entries. 366pp. 4½ x 6⅛. 20208-9

HISTORIC HOMES OF THE AMERICAN PRESIDENTS, Second, Revised Edition, Irvin Haas. A traveler's guide to American Presidential homes, most open to the public, depicting and describing homes occupied by every American President from George Washington to George Bush. With visiting hours, admission charges, travel routes. 175 photographs. Index. 160pp. 8¼ x 11. 26751-2

NEW YORK IN THE FORTIES, Andreas Feininger. 162 brilliant photographs by the well-known photographer, formerly with *Life* magazine. Commuters, shoppers, Times Square at night, much else from city at its peak. Captions by John von Hartz. 181pp. 9¼ x 10¾. 23585-8

INDIAN SIGN LANGUAGE, William Tomkins. Over 525 signs developed by Sioux and other tribes. Written instructions and diagrams. Also 290 pictographs. 111pp. 6⅛ x 9¼. 22029-X

THE WIT AND HUMOR OF OSCAR WILDE, Alvin Redman (ed.). More than 1,000 ripostes, paradoxes, wisecracks: Work is the curse of the drinking classes; I can resist everything except temptation; etc. 258pp. 5⅜ x 8½. 20602-5

SHAKESPEARE LEXICON AND QUOTATION DICTIONARY, Alexander Schmidt. Full definitions, locations, shades of meaning in every word in plays and poems. More than 50,000 exact quotations. 1,485pp. 6½ x 9¼. 2-vol. set.
Vol. 1: 22726-X
Vol. 2: 22727-8

SELECTED POEMS, Emily Dickinson. Over 100 best-known, best-loved poems by one of America's foremost poets, reprinted from authoritative early editions. No comparable edition at this price. Index of first lines. 64pp. 5³⁄₁₆ x 8¼. 26466-1

THE INSIDIOUS DR. FU-MANCHU, Sax Rohmer. The first of the popular mystery series introduces a pair of English detectives to their archnemesis, the diabolical Dr. Fu-Manchu. Flavorful atmosphere, fast-paced action, and colorful characters enliven this classic of the genre. 208pp. 5³⁄₁₆ x 8¼. 29898-1

THE MALLEUS MALEFICARUM OF KRAMER AND SPRENGER, translated by Montague Summers. Full text of most important witchhunter's "bible," used by both Catholics and Protestants. 278pp. 6⅝ x 10. 22802-9

SPANISH STORIES/CUENTOS ESPAÑOLES: A Dual-Language Book, Angel Flores (ed.). Unique format offers 13 great stories in Spanish by Cervantes, Borges, others. Faithful English translations on facing pages. 352pp. 5⅜ x 8½. 25399-6

GARDEN CITY, LONG ISLAND, IN EARLY PHOTOGRAPHS, 1869–1919, Mildred H. Smith. Handsome treasury of 118 vintage pictures, accompanied by carefully researched captions, document the Garden City Hotel fire (1899), the Vanderbilt Cup Race (1908), the first airmail flight departing from the Nassau Boulevard Aerodrome (1911), and much more. 96pp. 8⅞ x 11¾. 40669-5

OLD QUEENS, N.Y., IN EARLY PHOTOGRAPHS, Vincent F. Seyfried and William Asadorian. Over 160 rare photographs of Maspeth, Jamaica, Jackson Heights, and other areas. Vintage views of DeWitt Clinton mansion, 1939 World's Fair and more. Captions. 192pp. 8⅞ x 11. 26358-4

CAPTURED BY THE INDIANS: 15 Firsthand Accounts, 1750-1870, Frederick Drimmer. Astounding true historical accounts of grisly torture, bloody conflicts, relentless pursuits, miraculous escapes and more, by people who lived to tell the tale. 384pp. 5⅜ x 8½. 24901-8

THE WORLD'S GREAT SPEECHES (Fourth Enlarged Edition), Lewis Copeland, Lawrence W. Lamm, and Stephen J. McKenna. Nearly 300 speeches provide public speakers with a wealth of updated quotes and inspiration–from Pericles' funeral oration and William Jennings Bryan's "Cross of Gold Speech" to Malcolm X's powerful words on the Black Revolution and Earl of Spenser's tribute to his sister, Diana, Princess of Wales. 944pp. 5⅜ x 8⅜. 40903-1

THE BOOK OF THE SWORD, Sir Richard F. Burton. Great Victorian scholar/adventurer's eloquent, erudite history of the "queen of weapons"–from prehistory to early Roman Empire. Evolution and development of early swords, variations (sabre, broadsword, cutlass, scimitar, etc.), much more. 336pp. 6⅛ x 9¼.
25434-8